PATHS ALONG THE WAY

By Paul Kenney

KINVARA
PRODUCTIONS

CHAPTER 1

He knew it was dangerous. He knew it was forbidden. Maybe that's why it was so exciting, that and the way she looked. He had talked to Michael about it. He talked to Michael about almost everything personal. The sarcasm that flashed across Michael's face was amplified in his words.

"You're not really gonna take her out?"

"I'm gonna meet her tonight after she gets outta work. She's a beautiful girl, I . . ."

"Are you shitting me," Michael interrupted, "She's a spade!"

Chris didn't care about the color of her skin; he just wanted to see her. He couldn't wait until 9:30 when she would meet him outside of Jordan Marsh, one of Boston's classier department stores. It had taken him three months of seeing her every school day at Egleston Square Station to summon the courage to speak to her.

"You go to Jeremiah Burke?" he had asked tentatively, glancing at the purple and white covers surrounding the books that she held curled between her right elbow and breast. He hoped she wouldn't ignore him, he couldn't bear that. She didn't.

"Yes, I go to the Burke. Where do you go to school?"

"I go to CM, Catholic Memorial."

"Where's that?" she inquired, looking directly into his face. Her manner was polite, inquisitive and cautiously receptive.

1

"In West Roxbury," Chris answered, doing his best to overcome the sudden dryness in his throat.

"What are you, rich or somethin'?"

"No, my mother wanted me to go there." What a stupid thing to say, he thought immediately afterwards. He was afraid that she would think he was a mama's boy. It was tough enough for her to talk to him. He figured if he was tough and cool enough, she would feel comfortable, maybe reassured, and take a chance with him. She seemed to like him. He really liked her.

Her face was the color of caramel cream candy. She was a head shorter than Chris, who at the time was an awkward six feet or so, locked into the battle with his body called adolescence. He was seventeen.

Her name was Lorna. At sixteen she possessed an athletic sleekness to her body. Her legs were what he noticed first. They actually seemed to glisten when the morning sun was filtered through the skylights of the bus station and embraced them in its glow. Her skirt was above the knee, but not too short to make her appear cheap. There was a character about her, a class; the way she stood. The way she carried herself; the way she smiled. Chris had studied her inconspicuously since the first day he saw her.

She was like one of those beautiful statues he had seen in the art museum. And her hair, it was golden brown, worn in a natural way, like the saints in the stain glass windows wore a halo. Now he was to meet her alone. Maybe they could go for a walk and then he would take her home to Parker Hill Avenue.

"You goin' to Parker Hill with her? Michael had asked in disbelief.

"That's where she lives."

"You gonna take some protection?" The tone in Michael's voice and the way he twisted the corners of his mouth when he asked the question told his best friend that he was being stupid, careless. Michael was a lot of things, but stupid wasn't one.

"What do ya mean?"

"Just wait there a minute, I gotta get something for you," Michael demanded, as he sauntered down the stairs into the tunnel. They had been standing on the platform of the concrete stairway leading to the tunnel that crossed under the Transit Authority tracks in the rear of the projects, where Chris and Michael lived.

Chris had known Michael McLean since his family had moved into the Bromley Court Housing Projects. At their first encounter, Michael had punched Chris under his left eye for not according him the respect he felt he deserved during a game of stickball in the lot behind the incinerator. Chris remembered his rage as he pulled Michael's jacket over his head and delivered three punches and one kick before Chris's older brothers intervened, forcing the two eleven year olds to forget their injured feelings and to accompany them to Mariva's for a large American sub with everything. The boys had been running buddies since then.

Michael's father was a drunk. At one time he had been a longshoreman until he supposedly hurt his back. Since then he had been miserable. Once, Christopher remembered crossing the concrete expanse where the women of the projects hung the family clothes on green metal clotheslines and smoked Lucky Strikes, when he heard Michael's old man unleashing a relentless torrent of profane insults at Michael and his mother from within the confines of the tiny McLean apartment. Blows would always accompany such a tirade. Chris felt sorry for Michael, having to put up with that shit. Chris's father was dead and he felt that the world would be a better place if old man McLean would die and leave Michael, his mother and little brother in peace.

Michael was a good looking kid with short, orange-blonde hair and piercing blue eyes that the girls loved. During the winter months he would wear a black leather car coat. He told Chris that he stole it from a car near English High School. During the warm weather he would wear a black V neck sweater with no shirt underneath. When summer rolled around, he would wear no shirt, just his thin gold neck chain with the shamrock. These were his trademarks; these and the expressions he made up. His favorite was, "Learn the fuckin' score and want more." If you did, you could survive, if you didn't you were fucked, pure and simple.

Suddenly, he reappeared from the tunnel into the twilight of that June night. After looking around, he removed a black 45 caliber pistol from under his sweater, thrusting it in Christopher's direction.

"Take this fuckin' thing with you, man."

"Are you shitting me?! I'll blow my leg off." Chris protested. He had seen guns before but had never held one.

"Not if you know what you're doing," Michael said reassuringly.

"Where did you get it?"

"Jimmy D got it in a housebreak in Brighton. I got it for twelve bucks."

"You gotta be crazy buying a gun from that junkie. What's a matter with you, Mike?" Chris momentarily reflected on the dark side of Michael McLean. There was a point where he would take risks and do things that other kids, even project kids, wouldn't do. Yet he still managed to coax Christopher down the stairs into the confines of the tunnel. There were three indented ceiling lights protected by metal grates that provided a dim incandescence within. Under the light located in the center, Michael offered Chris a private class in handling a deadly weapon.

"Just keep the safety on, see, and tuck it in your little school bag with all of those fuckin' books you lug around. If you get mixed up in somethin' up there, just click the safety off and squeeze." The discharge of the weapon was deafening. It reverberated throughout the tunnel like a howitzer, causing Michael and Chris to race up the stairs and across the basketball court to the back of the incinerator.

"You're crazy, man, you coulda killed somebody," Chris gasped, bending over to catch his breath.

"I'm crazy? What the fuck, you're goin' out with the nigger chick."

"Just shut up, will ya!" Chris snapped, resenting not the words; he had grown up hearing worse. It was the tone of Michael's voice that offended him. He didn't know Lorna. He didn't have a clue about someone like her. She was just a piece of inferior meat to him. Chris had never really thought much about the black and white thing, but the "times they were a changin'." All you were hearing on the radio or seeing on the television was somebody marching, somebody protesting, somebody pissed off about something. It was 1967.

Jamaica Plain where Chris and Mike lived was a unique part of Boston, where different cultures coexisted like weeds through concrete. In the summer, the streets would beat to Motown and Wilson Pickett outside the Jewish-owned stores surrounded by the sons and daughters of the Irish, the Italian and the Black. It was an urban salad mixed together by circumstance and need, yet it all seemed to work. People got along in the neighborhood. But other parts of the city were no venture zones, silently off limits, enclosed by invisible walls of hate and fear.

Michael slapped the cold black iron of the pistol into Chris's reluctant hand, pressing the safety on. His words focused on his best friend's survival.

"It ain't like JP up there, man. You gotta take this piece with you, promise me. Don't think 'cause you ain't out to hurt them that they don't hate your white ass. Just take it and know the fuckin' score."

"All right, all right," Chris relented, "But if I blow my leg off, I'm gonna use this on you," he joked, concealing the pistol behind his back under his shirt. The cold black iron against his back made Christopher feel a strange exhilaration as he and Michael parted company, agreeing to catch up with each other later that night.

As Chris approached the trash-strewn entrance to his building and climbed the stairs to the fourth floor apartment where he and his family had survived since they moved from the South End, he thought about how much he hated the projects. He hated to think of his mother coming home from working in a laundry all day to spend her nights there.

As his nostrils filled with the stench of urine that dwelled in the hallways along with the roaches and rats, his eyes focused on the vandalized mail boxes that made life even more difficult for the building's inhabitants. He promised himself he would escape from there. At that moment, the cold bulge beneath his shirt made him feel that he had the power to do just that.

CHAPTER 2

As the train passed over the elevated tracks, rattling and groaning as it made its way through the right angle that signaled the approach of Dudley Station, Christopher Conley was looking at his reflection in its window. That night he had vigorously brushed his unruly brown hair straight back and admired its highlights in the bathroom mirror. He had saved his black Ban-Lon shirt, gold iridescent pants and black suede shoes for the occasion.

Pride in his appearance injected his walk with the trace of a swagger. He had succeeded in removing the last vestige of a pimple from under his left cheekbone and stared approvingly at the reflection of the dark blue eyes that never seemed to tell anyone what was going on in the brain behind them. He liked it that way.

He was certain that this would be a special night. He could feel it. The thrill of meeting Lorna, at being able to enjoy her company without a crowd around made him almost forget the contents of his green school bag—a notebook, a religion textbook with the title "The Way, The Truth and The Life," and a .45 caliber automatic pistol with the safety on. The books provided a perfect cover for the lethal cargo encompassed within.

Across from him, standing in the corner of the train, was a blind, black man supporting himself against one of the train's metal poles. He was accompanied by an oversized, yet docile, German shepherd. The dog allowed him to navigate the train, selling newspapers.

Chris had seen this man on the subway a lot. Once when Chris was coming home from Fenway Park where he worked selling unwanted souvenirs to annually disappointed Red Sox fans, he had spoken with this man. Christopher remembered that the man seemed very smart and good natured. Chris admired people that were smart. He also remembered the tone of his singing voice, which you could barely detect beneath the blare of his transistor.

The flickering of the train lights signaled the approach of Washington Street Station. At that time, the blind man's transistor was rocking with the Isley Brothers' song, "This Old Heart of Mine." Chris hesitated a moment to hear his favorite part of the song before he departed from the train, "But if you leave me a hundred times, a hundred times I'll take you back." Chris thought to himself that it was good to be seventeen and alive on a warm June night. Hearing this song locked the moment in the chest of his memory. It was a special night all right. He was ecstatic. His heart was wrapped and throbbing in the joy of undefeated youth.

Outside Jordan Marsh, Lorna approached him displaying a shy but unmistakably happy smile. She was wearing a pink dress that fit snugly to the contours of her body. Chris hadn't seen Lorna dressed up for work before that night. His eyes admired the way in which she moved so effortlessly. The heels that she wore made her legs appear even longer.

"You look great, Lorna," Chris said, as he offered to carry the shopping bag that she clutched in her right hand.

"No, you're already carrying something. Did you come from school or something?" Lorna asked inquisitively, focusing on the incongruity of the bag Chris held in his hand.

"No, I had to pick up some books that a friend borrowed." Chris stammered, hoping that he could divert her from any further inquiry of the school bag and its contents.

"Is that a hard school you go to?" Lorna questioned, as they walked together down Chauncy Street beside Jordan Marsh.

"Yeah, the Christian Brothers run it and they make it hard on you, if you don't do your work."

"Like what?" Lorna asked, while she glanced amiably at the clothes Christopher was wearing.

"Well, if you fool around too much, they give you a beatin'."

"You're kidding me," she said disapprovingly.

"No, the Christian Brothers come from Ireland and that's the way they do things." Christopher felt strange attempting to excuse the Christian Brothers' methods, methods with which he had become all too familiar in his four years at Catholic Memorial. "Anyway, let's forget about school. I'm gonna graduate next week and summer is here. I'm gonna have a blast. Where do you want to go?"

"How about if we take a walk through the Public Gardens? I love to go there when it's nice out. It's just so beautiful."

Christopher agreed with Lorna's suggestion, observing in her face the look he had seen in other young girls attempting to make the best of growing up in the city; a city changing for the worse.

As they stood on the foot bridge overlooking the pond created years before for the swan boats, the lights of the office buildings downtown gave the Public Gardens an amber glow in the June darkness. The moon and the stars seemed perfectly in place. The lilac trees enveloped them in their sweet fragrance, like expensive perfume in a hotel lobby. They walked together feeling close, feeling alive. He felt different with Lorna. Not because she was black and he was white; it was something else. She was refined and he was self-conscious, almost awkward.

"How do you like your job?" he asked, wanting to forget his insecurity.

"Oh, it's fun sometimes and boring sometimes, like most jobs I guess. I'm not going to stay at Jordan's forever; I'm going to become somebody."

Chris stared at Lorna, momentarily reflecting on her confidence and her desire to escape, to succeed. Christopher knew these feelings well. Michael wouldn't understand her; he knew that. Michael didn't know the score about everything, he thought. Michael couldn't feel the strength and warmth of this girl; he wouldn't want to.

Their young faces were inches apart. Their kiss was spontaneous and perfect. For an instant the world seemed to stop, leaving them standing there suspended in time and space. They were as one in a beautiful garden, in the city of Boston. Suddenly, Christopher remembered the pistol concealed between the books in his school bag and felt ashamed.

As they meandered across the foot bridge, an older couple approached in the opposite direction. When they drew near, Chris followed the man's eyes as they perused Lorna's torso and then focused upon him. The contempt of his stare was like a slap to a day dreaming child. Chris hated the look of this middle aged business type. He shot a surly stare back at the man, hoping for a confrontation.

"Don't waste your time, Chris," Lorna cautioned, holding his elbow and directing him away from the couple. "I don't pay attention to that and you shouldn't either." Lorna's words were soothing. The tone of her voice seemed to calm his turbulence.

"We ought to start heading to my house. My mamma gets worried if I'm not home by 10:30."

The two of them emerged from the gates of the Public Garden onto Arlington Street. Christopher's left arm was curled around Lorna's elbow, while the cords of the school bag were wrapped tightly around his right hand.

CHAPTER 3

From the top of Parker Hill Avenue there is a majestic, panoramic view of the City of Boston. At one time, this section of the city had been the home of the genteel and the established. Over the years it had deteriorated into a patchwork of decaying brown stones and neglected cobblestone streets. It was part of Roxbury, once the aorta of the city, before the diseases of ignorance and prejudice made it a jungle.

In 1967 Roxbury's residents were mostly black and poor. They referred to their portion of the city as "Bury", betraying a tone of despair. Behind closed doors at Boston City Hall, the mayor and his confidantes referred to it as the ghetto. In the heat of the summer fast approaching, it was ebony and blood red, an angry, exposed organ in Boston's body.

"That's my house down there," Lorna said, pointing to a brown brick three story near the base of the hill, obscured in the shadow of a broken street light. Christopher could barely make out the 12 cement stairs leading to a set of double doors that led to Lorna's home.

He wondered whether Lorna would invite him in to meet her mother. He became anxious as the thought flashed in his brain. He was also becoming increasingly uneasy about the area. He had heard voices coming from behind and between alley walls as he and Lorna descended the hill toward her house, voices that seemed to grow louder and angrier. Suddenly he heard footsteps behind them. Footsteps of more than one person that became faster as they approached.

As he began to turn, Christopher felt the shock of a blow to the base of his skull. The impact caused a flash of white, then bluish purple to shoot across his brain. He fell forward, smashing his face on the cobblestone street. He could feel the warm liquidity of his blood curling under the hair on the back of his head. Momentarily his face was numb, then it began to pulsate with pain.

The screams that Lorna attempted were choked off and muffled by the incredibly large hands of a black male in his late twenties. In the shadows of the hill, he was accompanied by two other black males, one of whom had struck Chris on the back of the head with a half empty bottle of wine, shattering the bottle on impact. Chris knelt helplessly on the street, attempting to clear the blurred images racing through his brain and focus his energies on getting to his feet. He heard Lorna's voice pleading to be left alone. The pleas were in vain.

Chris became sick when he saw that Lorna was being held by two of these men. The bigger man enveloped nearly all of Lorna's face and neck with his hands, while his smaller accomplice ran his long bony fingers across Lorna's breasts and down between her legs.

Chris managed to get almost to his feet when the third man, very tall and pencil thin, wearing a brimmed white hat, turned and kicked him in the throat. He tumbled onto his side, sliding on the wetness of the pavement, the wetness of his own blood moistening the cobblestones, the smell of cheap wine in his nostrils.

As he lay there motionless, he thought about dying. He wasn't afraid really. He was drifting in and out of consciousness. He was watching a film of his death on Parker Hill. Suddenly the film snapped. The taste of his own blood brought him to his senses. He could hear the pain in Lorna's muffled moans, as the three predators encircled her, clutching and groaning. Incredibly, they were laughing.

Michael's face flashed across Chris's mind. Next to the face was the image of his school bag with the pistol. He gathered the strength he had left, the strength of liberating desperation; like a combat soldier who sees death coming over the hill and reacts instinctively. There was no choice but to strike. Could he find the school bag in time, he wondered. Oh, please God, it was there on the street within his grasp. He reached inside.

He reached and felt hatred. He reached and felt rage. He reached and felt that he could kill the animals brutalizing Lorna.

"Mother fuckers!" Chris screamed, rising to his feet, interrupting the fiendish pleasure of their attack. His voice was that of the jungle, the voice of a primitive animal. He was pointing the pistol at the face of the one with beast-like hands. He could almost touch him.

"Let her fuckin' go or I'll blow your fuckin' heads off!"

The faces confronting him were a blur. There was the white hat and a profane challenge, then movement in his direction. Trigger squeezed—stunned silence. Safety on—certain death. Click, it was off. Flash to his right, the pencil thin attacker clutching a knife in his black fist slashing toward his neck. Two explosions — the pavement drenched with free flowing spurting blood — a white hat on the cobblestones turning red. Chris standing over a terror-filled black face with hands immersed in wounds to his belly and leg. Screams of rage, screams of horror. Two men fleeing; one left to bleed.

Lorna was staring at him, trembling. Chris was staring back, crying, then running down the hill past her house, tucking the gun under his shirt at first and then returning it to the school bag he had remembered to retrieve from the gutter on Parker Hill.

CHAPTER 4

Her name at baptism was Mary. She was the oldest of seven children in a house supported by an angry Irish bootlegger known as "Black Mike". Her mother feared him and appeased him. The girl that came to be called May, despised him.

At the age of twelve, her father used her like a mule to transport prohibition whiskey in suitcases on the trolleys that ran from the South End into Roxbury. The police, he told her, would never suspect such a pretty Irish girl with such beautiful green eyes. It was his way, first the sweet talk and then the dark endeavor. She hated alcohol. She had seen the devils it awakened in her father. The devils that brought on the violent rage and the beatings she endured by his hands and by the thick black buckled belt he kept in the drawer in the kitchen.

"Keep screaming and he will stop," her younger sister had begged repeatedly during the beatings. She never screamed. She wouldn't give him the satisfaction. It would have been weak to scream. Her sullen silence was stronger than his drunken rage. His death came as a blessing.

She was a child of the Depression who waited because of "hard times" until she was twenty eight, before marrying. Her husband was the only man she loved. He was handsome like the Hollywood stars and he made her laugh. Most of all, he made her laugh. Through her support, he became a Boston police officer. They had four children. He died suddenly, without being sick, when her youngest child was two. Her happiness died with him, but not her dignity and not her pride. Her youngest child was Christopher Conley.

She was seated on a plastic covered red sofa in a spotless parlor behind the thick green metal door of the apartment. A Crosley television beamed the 11 o'clock news in her direction, barely receiving a response from her fatigued and drowsy brain. It was almost bedtime, the close of another tiring day. She heard the lock being penetrated by the key and the thud of the door shutting behind her youngest son.

"Christopher, I left you some tuna fish, make yourself a sandwich," she called as she heard the key drop into the tea cup adjacent to the front door. There was no response.

"Christopher," she called again.

At that moment, he entered the parlor. He had a towel draped over the back of his neck. The expression on his battered face propelled his mother toward him.

"What has happened to you, Christopher?" she said, as she rose from the couch and reached to comfort her disconsolate son.

"Oh, Ma, I just shot a black guy on Parker Hill," Christopher sobbed. His words shattered his mother's world like a hammer crashing down on a porcelain vase.

"Oh, my Jesus, Mary and Joseph!" she cried. "How did it happen? How could you shoot anybody?"

Christopher cried repeatedly as he described to her the attack upon Lorna and his use of the gun. He refused to tell her where he had gotten the weapon. It was a nightmare. He felt the sickening realization that this terrible, violent occurrence had befallen him and not somebody else. He couldn't tell himself that it would be all right. He could only think of escaping from Boston.

"Do you think Jack will let me stay with him for a while?" speaking of his older brother who had been living in Los Angeles since his discharge from the Air Force.

"What are you talking about? We have to tell the police about this. I'll call Tom Dow. He was a friend of your father's."

"No, Ma," Chris interrupted, "I had a gun, I have a record. Maybe they won't know who did it. I'm supposed to graduate next week. If I get arrested for this, I'm screwed. Please, Ma, I'll come back when it's all right. Oh, Ma, I'm so sorry." The tears gripped Christopher's throat, as he collapsed next to the plastic covered sofa. His mother knelt beside him on the floor. She hadn't caressed her youngest son since he was a little boy. As they huddled together, May Conley resorted to prayer.

"Oh, Mother of God, protect us. Please Mary, Mother of God, protect my son. Help us to do the right thing, help us Mary."

The sobbing and praying of Christopher and his mother blended together like a requiem at a funeral. From the television in the corner of the apartment a voice informed Boston as other voices across the country informed America that six Americans and 63 Viet Cong were killed in fighting in Vietnam.

CHAPTER 5

He had never experienced a sleepless night before. His body was beyond exhaustion and he couldn't control it. His bowels groaned with nervous mutterings as his mind raced recklessly through blood drenched cobblestoned nightmares. Thoughts of imprisonment, insanity and annihilation gripped him. He prayed that the morning would rush into his room. He had to speak to Michael about what had taken place.

At seven o'clock, Chris dressed quickly and left his mother in the bathroom behind a closed door. She had cried and prayed all night. She was crying still. He ran through the playground and basketball court and hurtled the backstairs to Michael's building. As he approached the door of the McLean apartment, Christopher tried to compose himself. He didn't want to appear too agitated, too scared. Of course, it would have been easier to call Michael on the phone, but Michael's phone was always disconnected.

Christopher wanted to be rid of the weapon that had saved him, but could destroy him. He had concealed the pistol back in the school bag by wrapping newspapers around its cold metal form. He couldn't recall just exactly how he had retrieved the bag in the mayhem of the previous night. He was glad that he hadn't left it on the street to hound his mind. He felt the fear of the felon who hides in the darkness, wondering if his crime has been discovered.

The door to the McLean apartment opened cautiously. The metal chain affixed to the lock prevented intrusion. A voice behind the door inquired angrily, "What do you want?"

"Can I speak to Michael, Mrs. McLean? It's Chris."

"He's sleepin', it's Saturday. Come back later."

"I can't, Mrs. McLean. Would you please wake him up?"

"What's the matter? Are you two in trouble again?" She asked, as she unfastened the chain and confronted Christopher in the hallway.

"No, we were supposed to look at a car I wanna buy. He told me to wake him up." He had become pretty good at making up believable explanations that didn't sound like lies without really thinking too much. He was uncertain as to whether Michael's mother had been fooled. She was wearing a ragged bathrobe and her red hair was a mess. She stared at him for an instant and then disappeared behind the door.

It seemed a lifetime before Michael opened the door, revealing a glimpse of his father's drunken body, sleeping it off on the linoleum of the apartment's kitchen.

"What the fuck happened to you?" Michael whispered.

Christopher gestured to Michael not to speak until they had left the building. They walked quickly and without a word down the three flights of stairs and out the back door into the cloudy June morning. They crossed the project yard and climbed the wall that led to Havilland Street. At the end of Havilland Street, they sat down on a faded green, wooden and concrete bench.

"I shot a fuckin' guy last night, Mike," Chris whispered anxiously. His throat ached from all the crying.

"You're shittin' me? Is he dead?" Michael demanded, staring at his friend's anguished face.

"Jesus, I don't think so. He was screaming like a bastard when I screwed." Once again Chris recited the circumstances of the previous night's pain. Chris was shocked to see that Michael was smiling, as he described shooting the man coming at him with a knife.

"You're a bad bastard, Conley," Michael remarked, tilting his head back and shaking it from side to side. "Aren't you glad you brought my little friend with you? Your mother would be crying right now, if you went up there without protection. How did it feel when you shot the prick?"

Michael's reaction and his expression made Christopher uneasy. That was the difference between him and Michael. Could it be that if Michael had fired the gun into the body of the man spraying his blood on the street, it wouldn't have bothered him? Was he that crazy? Chris wondered, becoming angry.

"Hey, I don't feel good about this, man," Chris protested. "It wasn't like fuckin' TV when the guy just drops. This guy was howling — you remember when Gulsky's dog got hit by the car and the cop shot it. That was what it was like. It scared the shit outta me."

Michael looked at Chris and shook his head disapprovingly. Chris resented the look, yet somehow Michael's reaction lifted a burden from him. Michael reminded his friend that he had no choice; that the guy was trying to kill him. It was the first time in twelve hours that the turbine of his mind had stopped whirring. After a while, he spoke of the future.

"Hey Mike, I'm gonna go live with my brother, Jack, in California, until this dies down." His words provoked a look of immediate disappointment on Michael's face. Michael looked away across the project yard toward downtown. He seemed distant at first and then resigned to the turn that fate had engineered in their lives.

Chris continued to speak anxiously, "I didn't see anythin' in the paper and nothin' was on the radio. My mother said if he had died, it woulda been in the news, don't you think?"

Michael glanced back at his friend, this time with a softer look of care and disapproval. "They don't give a shit, man. It's just another nigger gettin' shot in Roxbury. That ain't news. It happens every fuckin' day. What about the chick? Will she keep her mouth shut?"

Michael's inquiry triggered a torrent of thoughts about Lorna. Sweet Lorna, what would happen to her? Would she tell the cops? Would the pricks come back for her? Christopher felt selfish that he hadn't thought about her that much. He had only thought about his own skin, not hers. He resolved that he would call her and tell her his plans. He mentioned it to Michael.

"You don't wanna have anythin' to do with her, man. You better split and I'll talk to her. Remember, she can put your ass in jail if she says the wrong shit. She works at Jordan's right? You tell me where she works and I'll go by and see if it's cool. You just go."

Christopher thought about what Mike had said and decided once again that his friend's instincts were right. He could trust Mike to check it out. He knew he had $400 bucks saved for college. He would clean that out and jump on a plane as soon as he could. That was the only way to do it. His mother would make the arrangements with his brother. It might just work out all right. After all, the prick really did deserve it. He deserved it for trying to stab him, for trying to hurt Lorna. He felt better after talking with Michael. He felt almost grateful.

The two friends were facing each other, as Christopher placed his arm on Michael's shoulder and looked directly into his eyes. Those Irish eyes weren't smiling. Those crazy Irish eyes had tears in their corners. Then Chris pulled him close and hugged him.

"I love you like I love my brothers," Chris whispered. The tears had returned. Michael said nothing. His embrace was enough of a sign that the feelings were mutual and the feelings were deep. After a while, Michael broke the silence, seeming to clear the tears from his own throat.

"You don't think you'll be shootin' anybody else for a while, do you?"

"No, I don't think so, Mike."

"Good," Michael responded, "cause I don't want people thinking you're crazier than me."

As he spoke, he took the school bag from Chris' hand and hugged him again forcefully. Christopher realized that this was the place where the two boys would go their separate ways. Two boys who would become men, before they saw each other again.

CHAPTER 6

American Airlines Flight 106 descended into the humid, gray vapor that enveloped Los Angeles. Christopher stared at the Boston newspaper wedged into the pocket of the airplane seat in front of him. His thoughts flew from Lorna, to Michael, to his mother, then to the Boston he was leaving. He felt no remorse now for the shooting, only anxiety that his life could be ruined by it.

He hadn't seen any mention of the incident in the paper. Maybe Michael was right and nobody did give a shit. What about Lorna? What would happen to her? he wondered, feeling an emptiness, a longing to speak and be with her. He must forget her. He had to get on with his changed life.

"Please God, help it to be all right," he prayed in a whisper, as the plane landed and taxied to the terminal. He was supposed to meet his older brother out in front of the Olympic Hotel in Los Angeles. Why couldn't his brother meet him at the airport? he thought, as he stared from the window of the cab with nerves like tangled electrical wires shooting errant charges through various parts of his body. Every face that glanced his way was a cause for alarm; every police uniform brought a throb of apprehension. He was alone; he felt like he was being hunted, a fugitive in his mind, seeking asylum from a brother he hadn't seen in two years.

The car tail lights on the freeway undulated like a giant red snake toward Los Angeles, as Christopher's mind flickered like a projector over the memories of his brother. Jack Conley was a loner, who had been on his own since he brought the Air Force enlistment papers to his mother on the day he graduated from Jamaica Plain High School. She couldn't sign them fast enough, telling her second son that the service was the only way he could avoid the life of a loser.

He was never a student. To a mother who preached the value of an education, he was a disappointment. Christopher remembered endless mornings of his mother haranguing him to get out of bed and get to school. He remembered when his brother was expelled from Cathedral High School for threatening a nun who struck him from behind in the lunch room. He remembered the girls that his brother would bring home while his mother was at work, the willing girls, the ones with the wild spark in their eyes, who seemed mesmerized by his older brother.

Like his father, Jack Conley had black hair and an angular face with eyes the color of violets. He was nearly six feet tall and lean like a distance runner. His smile made you smile and it warmed the hearts of the lady teachers who seemed to pass him for showing up most of the time.

Chris recalled coming home from St. Timothy's School in the fourth grade to find his fifteen year old brother making love to Janice Nutoni in his mother's bed. Other than fleeting glimpses of his sister, that was the first time that Christopher had seen a young girl naked. A half smile wedged its way into the edges of his mouth, as his memory recalled the passionate indifference of the girl, her teased brown hair electrified by the blankets on the double bed.

Many times after that, Jack would take advantage of his mother's need to support the family and sneak adventurous teenage girls up the stairs and into the world of oh that feels good! During those times, Chris was often the intruder, the unwanted, interfering child who was told to screw and come back in an hour. Once Chris almost froze to death, while his brother worked his magic inside the warmth of the Conley apartment. There was no resentment about this. Chris accepted his brother and his brother protected him.

Once Chris was coming home from school and approaching the projects when four older boys from Annunciation Way confronted him and demanded money, before he would be allowed on his way. Chris remembered the feeling of joy and power when he was chased into the courtyard of the projects in the midst of a stickball game with Jackie Conley fortuitously wielding a thick broom handled bat, a bat that he immediately applied to the heads and backs of his brother's pursuers.

Chris took great pleasure in their yelping retreat, knowing they wouldn't bother him ever again. That was a reputation maker in the projects. It allowed Chris more freedom to roam among older boys and to establish a reputation himself. For this, Chris loved and respected his older brother.

He had traveled, while in the Air Force. He was stationed first in Texas, then Okinawa, then England. He was even part of some classified group that inspected all of America's missile installations in the Orient and Africa.

It was while he was stationed in England that he began to think seriously about Hollywood and becoming a movie actor. His features reflected well in the few photographs that his father had taken before his death. Although his mother warned him repeatedly that he couldn't get by on his looks, Jack Conley's looks were precious keys that opened doors firmly closed to so many others.

Chris liked to brag about his brother to his friends in high school. He would show them photographs of some Mexican girl in San Antonio, seated lovingly on his brother's lap or some large breasted British stewardess, standing with her hands on her mini skirted hips, in front of Piccadilly Circus. The rest was left to the adolescent imaginations of boys controlled by the tedium and discipline of the Irish Christian Brothers.

Chris was ecstatic when his mother told him that Jack was going to be on television. Jack had taken acting lessons and landed a small part as a British soldier on the TV series *Rat Patrol*. Chris remembered sitting in front of the television and feeling his heart quicken, as he saw his brother's face and admired his authentic British accent. Of course the scene lasted approximately one minute, but nobody else in the projects or at Catholic Memorial had a brother on TV.

Since that time, he had seen him on TV a lot. He was always a soldier or an athlete whose parts were getting progressively larger. He saw him at the drive-in in a motorcycle movie and two or three horror films in which he was killed. There was no question that Chris loved it, when the women from the projects would ask him if he was going to be a movie star too.

As he stood on the sidewalk in front of the Olympia Hotel, Chris felt his eyes beginning to burn and water. The smell of the air was different from Boston. It was the sweet stench of an atmosphere permeated with car exhaust. Chris hadn't seen anybody walking all the way from the airport. He saw old cars, '55 Chevys, '50 Fords, in brand-new condition. The streets were called boulevards and they had names like Spanish boxers. It was all new. It was exciting. It was frightening, especially for someone running from uncertainty.

"Welcome to LA, man." The voice of Jack Conley called from a yellow Chevy convertible, as it pulled alongside of the curb in front of the hotel. He slid from behind the steering wheel and embraced Chris in one confident, fluid motion. He was dressed in powder blue dungarees and a red velour sweater. His thick, black hair was combed straight back and he appeared to be growing a mustache. His face was tanned and accentuated by a pair of sunglasses, even though sunset had occurred two hours earlier.

As Chris placed his suitcase in the back seat of the convertible, his brother reached out his hand and clasped Christopher's across the palm, pulling him toward him and hugging him. Once again his guardian angel had appeared.

"A little difficulty back in Beantown, huh?" Jack began. "How are ya holdin' up?"

"Okay," Chris replied, "I haven't seen anything about it in the paper, maybe I lucked out."

"You lucked out, all right, you're in LA now and you couldn't have come to a better place. Wait till you see the women out here, you're not gonna believe it. You'll never live back East again."

Chris detected the trace of a California accent as his brother spoke. He discovered on the trip from the hotel that Jack was living with a girl in a place called Los Feliz and that he had a place in Hollywood that Chris could crash at. Chris quickly learned that "crash" meant sleep and "bitchin'" was almost the equivalent of "pissa" back in Boston.

The Chevy soared from the freeway onto Hollywood Boulevard. The car radio reverberated with the gravelly dedication of Wolfman Jack and the sounds of a full throated black man singing "Tossin' and Turnin'."

As they waited for the light to change on Hollywood Boulevard, Christopher's eyes became fixed upon two of the largest, sexiest women he had ever seen. To his astonishment, they approached the convertible. The one wearing a short white skirt and heels seemed to jump with anticipation, as she called to Chris's brother.

"Hey baby, wanna take us for a ride?"

"Not tonight, fellas," Jack responded accelerating as the light turned green, away from the disappointed transvestites.

"Those were guys?" Chris asked incredulously. His brother simply nodded in affirmation. "Holy shit!"

"You know how you can tell?" Jack instructed, "Look at the forearms and the Adam's apple. Don't worry, it'll take a while, but you'll be able to tell almost every time. Hollywood is loaded with them."

As they took a right onto Sunset Boulevard, Chris spotted a statuesque blonde in a white leather fringed jacket and jeans. She looked about twenty to Chris and she was hitchhiking by herself. Jack slowed the Chevy down and asked the girl how far she was headed.

"I'm going to the strip."

Jack beckoned her to jump into the back seat and she complied. She seemed to pour herself over the side of the car, languidly positioning herself in the back seat.

"What a bitchin' car, man," she commented, spreading her arms across the top of the rear seat, "I love convertibles, they're so free." As the breeze of a June night swept through her hair, Chris could not help but admire the sun-splashed beauty of her face. She was as pretty as any girl he had seen. "Where are you dudes from?" she asked, apparently detecting Chris's accent from his conversation with Jack.

"I live here," Jack replied. "Meet my brother. He just flew in from Boston. He's gonna live here from now on."

"Groovy," she said, eyeing Christopher with a receptive smile. "My name is Crystal. What's your name?"

"Chris," he said shyly, smiling back at the suntanned blonde. As the convertible made its way West on Sunset, Christopher became immersed in the sights and sounds of LA. He was a world away from the fear and guilt of Boston and slowly beginning to enjoy it.

"Want to get high?" the blonde suddenly whispered, leaning toward the front seat and removing a marijuana joint from the pocket of her jacket.

"I don't think so," Jack interjected quickly, preventing his back seat passenger from igniting the multicolored paper surrounding the joint.

"How old are you, Crystal?" Jack asked, glancing in the rear view mirror at her face.

"Fourteen," the girl answered unashamedly, shocking Christopher with her response.

"You know, Crystal, you ought to be more careful," Jack warned. "I could be a narc."

"I never seen a narc look like you, man," she replied. "I just go with my feelings. I just let it hang out, dig it? I can get out here, man," she directed, pointing to a crowd congregated to their right. Chris observed a youthful, multicolored congregation of hair and beads and outlandish fashion beneath the billboard of the Whisky a Go Go.

The marquee above the nightclub told the world that the Chambers Brothers were now playing there. Across the street a smaller marquee announced that the Strawberry Alarm Clock was coming soon. Traffic crawled along that section of Sunset Boulevard known as the strip. Topless bars competed for customers with neon signs and sidewalk hucksters.

The blocks that comprised the strip possessed an energy, unlike any that Chris had seen. He thought to himself that he had lucked out. What a great place to hide! What a great place to escape! What a great place to forget cobblestones soaked in blood.

"How do you like it, Bro?" Jack asked, as he turned the convertible off of Sunset and headed back in the direction from which they came.

"It's wild," Chris responded, reveling in the vitality of his new surroundings.

"I told you, didn't I? You're gonna get laid more than fuckin' Frank Sinatra out here!" Jack shouted above the blaring car radio. At that moment, Chris wanted to embrace him like a grateful child embraces a generous parent. Instead he shouted, "I really appreciate you takin' me in, Jack. You know I..."

"Hey, wait a minute," his brother interrupted, suddenly silencing the blare of the car radio with a twist of his fingers. "Let's get something straight. I'm not taking you in; you're gonna be on your own."

Chris looked at Jack, attempting to conceal his shock and disappointment, as he reflected on his brother's words.

"I'm not gonna be taking care of you; you gonna be your own man."

"Yeah," Christopher said, feeling immediately uneasy about Los Angeles, and its myriad of differences from where he'd grown up.

"You know, I lived in a hundred different places, Chris," Jack continued, "all over the world. This is the best. Fuck Boston! Fuck that bullshit back there! You can be your own man out here. Just have to grow up quicker, that's all. Do you understand?"

Jack explained that they would not be living together. He was going to be living with his girlfriend and Chris would be living at Jack's house in Hollywood. It wasn't what he had expected. He really didn't know what he expected from his brother, but he didn't expect to be abandoned in such strange surroundings. His crash course in self-sufficiency had begun.

The convertible came to a stop in front of a cement walkway leading through a grove of trees to a one-story wood framed bungalow with a metal roof. As Chris removed his suitcase from the back seat and approached his new residence, he was reminded of the hut they put Alec Guinness into in *The Bridge on the River Kwai*. This place was a lot bigger, but he almost expected to hear the Colonel Bogey march at any moment.

"Here's the key," Jack instructed, "don't lose it. I only have one. The rent is eighty bucks a month and it's due in two weeks. You gotta get a job. I'll come by and see you in a couple of days."

Chris felt the back of his neck becoming white hot. His brother hadn't changed, he thought. It was just like when he was getting laid. He just wanted Chris to get lost, to screw. Chris instantly resolved that he would show his older brother that he could survive. He couldn't go back home anyway. He had no choice.

"You know, Chris," Jack added, as he slid back behind his car's steering wheel. "You better get into a college out here or they'll send your ass to Vietnam. I was over there in '63 and you don't want to get your ass shot in that fuckin' shit hole."

Chris barely listened to him. He knew that his words were true, but they didn't sink in just then. His mind was like an overloaded switchboard. As the convertible drove away he climbed the cement stairs and fumbled with the key in the unfamiliar door. The lock was entered and creaked as the key turned inside it. The light on the inside revealed a small three room layout filled with dust and stale air. The place hadn't been cleaned in months. It was a hell of a welcome. But it was better than a jail cell back in Boston.

CHAPTER 7

The rain pelted the pavement as he ran across the street from the subway into the Jordan Marsh department store. The weather made his mood even darker. He was obligated to speak to a girl that he didn't care about and make sure that she wasn't going to create any more problems for his best friend.

As he passed by the fragrant cosmetic counters where the sales girls in smocks wore too much makeup, his eyes searched for the annex and the record department, with its impressive array of long playing albums and 45 rpm singles. That was where Lorna worked as a sales girl after school and on Saturdays. He had only seen her once and that was from the back seat of a friend's Buick, as he and Chris rode through Egleston Square. He clutched a piece of paper with her name and Chris's phone number in California scribbled on it. He was a reluctant messenger, dispatched by loyalty to a friend thousands of miles away.

He saw her standing behind the counter, advising an older woman and a small boy with thick glasses about some unfamiliar long playing record. Michael McLean had more than a passing interest in records and music. As a child before his father stopped working, he had taken saxophone lessons at the Boys Club in Dudley Square. He stole to pay for his own saxophone, hiding it away from his father's rage and disapproval in the tiny closet he shared with his little brother.

27

Late at night he would sneak from his bed and climb to the roof of the community house located in the center of the projects and practice. He had been playing for six years. He loved Junior Walker and Stax records. Every once in a while he would even play in a small rock band at local church dances.

Glancing at her, he walked past the counter where she worked into a different department with bed spreads, pillows and old ladies. He waited there until Lorna was alone. She was writing something in a small leather-bound notebook when he approached the counter. His voice had a higher pitch than usual. "You're Lorna Shaw, right?" he began abruptly.

Lorna raised her eyes from her work; she seemed immediately offended by his manner and the tone of his voice. "Yes, my name is Lorna Shaw. Have I met you before?"

"Nah, I'm a friend of Chris Conley's." At the mention of the name, a look of sadness then uneasiness passed over Lorna's features. They stood facing each other, not knowing what to say or when to say it. Michael broke the uncomfortable silence as he looked around and leaned over her counter. "Ah, Chris was wonderin' if the cops came by and asked questions about the other night."

"Where is he?" Lorna asked, displaying both concern and resentment.

"Never mind where he is. Did the cops come by and ask about what happened?" Michael repeated, raising his voice above a whisper now.

"I don't have to speak to you," she protested. "Tell me, is Chris all right?"

Her question seemed to surprise Michael. Suddenly he changed the tone of his voice as well as his approach. "Look it, I'm Chris's best friend and he asked me to come by and see how you was doin'. He also wanted to know if the cops were looking for him, ya know?"

She stared at Michael for a moment. Then she suggested that they talk somewhere else. She was scheduled for a coffee break at 7:30. She told him to come back and they could talk during her break. Michael agreed.

He returned to the record department as Lorna was being replaced by an overweight, effeminate man in a blue tennis sweater. They walked out of the department store and scurried across the street toward Hayes Bickford's Coffee Shop. A steady drizzle soaked them.

After Lorna situated herself at a table in the corner of the shop next to the window, she resumed their aborted conversation. "Are you sure Chris is all right? He looked like he was really hurt the other night."

Again the concern in Lorna's voice unsettled Michael. "Don't worry about Chris. He's a tough bastard. One time we took on eleven kids at a party and he got beat up real bad. He never went to the doctor or nothin'. He's my man."

"Where is he?" Lorna asked again.

At first he ignored the question, changing the subject by asking her if he could get her something. She told him that the waitress would be by to take their order. After they were waited on he resumed the uncomfortable conversation. "Chris left for Florida. He has some friends down there. He asked me to come by and see you. I guess he really likes you."

Fighting back tears, Lorna jabbed her straw into the ice-filled Coca-Cola before her. She paused and then sighed for an instant. "The police did come by and ask questions about what happened, but I didn't tell them anything," she revealed in a quaking tone of voice. "I heard that the guy that Chris . . ." She stopped before saying the word "shot" as if the mention of the word itself caused her pain. "The guy that Chris shot had just got out of jail and he has a long record. He was on the danger list for a couple of days, but now he's doing okay."

"When the cops talked to you, did you tell them how it happened?" Michael pressed.

"They never talked to me. They never knew I was there; why would they?" Lorna stared out the rain spattered window toward the night, the street and the people passing by. The rain and the approaching night surrounded them. Neither of them spoke as they sat across from one another. The distance between them seemed immeasurable, even though they were almost touching. She was wearing a tan blouse and brown skirt. Michael couldn't help but notice how the moisture of the raindrops had nestled on her hair like dew on a beautiful hedge. Finally, she glanced at her watch. "I have to get back now," she said politely. "Could you tell Chris something for me?"

"Yeah, sure."

"Tell him that I'm sorry about what happened and I'm glad that he's okay." She stopped and took a deep breath before resuming. "Tell him that I miss him and I think about him every day. Will you tell him that?"

"Sure, I'll tell him," Michael promised, as Lorna excused herself from the table and hurried across the street and through the revolving door of the department store. Michael remained in the coffee shop until the driving rain changed to a mist. His eyes fastened upon the revolving door.

As he left the coffee shop his steps carried him across the street to the place where she had disappeared from his view. Suddenly he stopped, as if catching himself, then turning away. He pulled the collar of his coat up around his neck. It rained all the way back to Jamaica Plain.

CHAPTER 8

He sat there beneath an oversized scally cap with a shamrock on its brim, wearing a faded blue wind breaker. His eyes were fixed to the left, down the crowded corridor toward an auburn-haired girl. She stood with one leg bent up beneath her short skirt, smoking a cigarette, talking to a balding man with the face of a vulture. She was telling the man what to do.

He watched as she reached inside her blouse and from the area of her left breast removed something, placing it surreptitiously in the aging vulture's right hand. The vulture then turned and walked by him, confirming his suspicion that the young girl had just given him money for services to be rendered.

The crowd in the corridor began to line up outside of the Second Session Courtroom of the Boston Municipal Court. The man in the cap followed behind the young girl as she entered the double doors into the enormous courtroom. The creatures from the corridor took their seats in the long, brown wooden benches situated on either side of the aisle that led to a leather chair behind an elevated mahogany partition called a bench.

The man had removed his cap, revealing a head of thick black and gray curly hair, situating himself strategically so that he could observe the movements of the young girl. The cotton fabric of the yellow and green dress barely covered her buttocks. She wore purple platform shoes with a rhinestone bracelet encircling her left ankle. The man leaned forward in the bench that was situated behind her. He was in a position to hear whatever she would say and see the contours of her young body as it fidgeted in front of him.

The aging man with the features of a vulture returned. He sat beside her and whispered to her, while the man behind attempted to overhear. She and the vulture-like man came to their feet when the name Linda Pelligrini was called by the Court Clerk, seated in front of a white-haired Judge who was leaning back with his hands behind his head as she approached.

"Linda Pelligrini," the Clerk read in a baritone, "you have been charged with soliciting for the purpose of prostitution on July 23. What say you?"

The lawyer spoke for her. "Not guilty, your Honor."

"Is there a question of bail on this girl?" the Clerk asked toward the bench, to the left of where the Judge was sitting. There were a dozen police officers congregated. A red-haired bulldog of a man approached the microphone to his right and read from a piece of paper, responding, "No bail, your Honor."

The man watched with the trace of a smile as the young girl leaned down and whispered in the lawyer's hairy ear, then strolled defiantly from the courtroom. The man emerged from the bench as she passed and followed her onto the elevator and out of the courthouse.

As she spoke on the telephone across from the courthouse, the man in the cap watched her every movement from a position behind her. He pretended to be gazing at the magazines and newspapers at the stand where she hung up the telephone. She shot a glance in his direction. She walked over and almost brushed against him. She placed her hands on her hips and stared in the man's direction. As he passed in front of her, she spoke softly to him.

"Are you going out honey?"

The man didn't answer. He nodded in her direction and began to walk across the concourse, in front of the Suffolk Courthouse. She followed close behind as he turned the corner and approached the driver's door of a green, rusted Chevy Impala. She positioned herself at the passenger door as he slid behind the wheel. He reached across the torn upholstery and lifted the door lock. The young girl bent over before entering and scrutinized the man's face and the interior of the car.

"You want half and half, it's gonna cost you fifty," she said, looking from side to side for the approach of police.

"Is that all you're worth?" the man asked in a sarcastic voice that the young girl found vaguely familiar.

"I'm worth every cent, baby. Did we go out before?"

"I've seen you before, but we didn't get together," the man answered, removing money from the pocket of his windbreaker and showing it to the girl. She ducked into the car, positioning herself to offer a glimpse of her red panties.

The man drove carefully toward South Boston, glancing repeatedly in the rearview mirror. She turned on his radio and fondled its knobs, glancing at him from time to time until she came upon Aretha Franklin screaming for respect. She turned up the volume and slid next to the man as she chanted with the voices from the radio, "Sock it to me, sock it to me." The man smiled a curious smile and pulled the car into the rear of a triple decker on East Eight Street.

"Is this your place, honey?"

"This whole neighborhood's my place. Just wait here a minute. I promise I'll be right back," he said. He walked from the car and around the corner, out of sight. She sat and removed a Camel cigarette from her purse and lit it. It was late morning and beginning to become a hot and sticky July day.

After a while, the faces of an old man and a young man that resembled him appeared on either side of the rusted Chevy. The old man's hair and complexion made him resemble a large white rabbit. The young man was his son. The girl hadn't seen them in two years.

"Linda," the old man cried, "I thought I'd never see you again. Please stop breaking your mother's heart and come home. I've stopped drinking, please forgive me."

The man in the cap watched from behind the car as the three of them embraced in the front seat. He was standing with a smile faintly showing on his care-worn face. He listened to the sobs and promises of the father and his daughter. The father came to him after the girl had agreed to come home, and accompanied her brother toward a late model station wagon waiting at the curb.

"Well, you must feel good now," the man in the cap said.

"I never thought you'd find her," the father said, reaching out his hand to the man in the cap. He held the father's hand, pressing a black plastic rosary case in it.

"My family thanks you," the father said.

"God bless you always," the man in the cap whispered.

As the station wagon started from the curb, the man in the cap waved, placing his hands in his pockets and heading back to his car. He was running late. He knew there would be a crowd waiting for him back at St. Augustine's Rectory.

CHAPTER 9

Father McConnell was the pastor of a parish that needed him desperately. As he pulled out in front of the rectory, his people were there waiting for him. The parish held within its confines two housing projects, three half-way houses and an astonishing assortment of troubled lives that frequently found their way to the priest's door.

He was a large man, well over six feet, with a perpetually sad expression that camouflaged a serene disposition and a raucous sense of humor. He had been a lineman at Boston College High School before following in his older brother's footsteps and becoming a priest. Only once during his 53 years had he regretted that decision.

The people surrounded him as he entered the rectory. There were at least ten waiting to tell him their difficulties, in the hope of practical resolution or divine absolution. His eyes scanned the crowd, suddenly focusing on the woman sitting in the corner, waiting for a chance to speak to him, after the rest had made their pleas. He approached the lovely, familiar face, recognizing that it had grown old more gracefully than his own.

"May, it's a pleasure to see you again," he said sincerely. "Shall we go inside and talk?" He looked over his shoulder to the large Irish woman sitting at the table, motioning her to make peace with his parishioners while he spoke with Christopher Conley's mother.

Father McConnell and May had gone to the same grammar school and, if the truth be known, they were sweethearts up until high school. Each and every school day they would look forward to seeing each other. Their friendship was a release from the unhappiness in their homes. Father McConnell's mother was a widow afflicted with diabetes, while May's father afflicted her and her family with his drinking and his violent rages. They were two souls who found a refuge in each other's friendship.

Years before he had offered her all the comfort he could. That was when her beloved Tom died unexpectedly leaving her to raise her four children without a husband and father. From time to time he would stop by with donations of shoes and clothing for the family. She had once demanded to know why God had brought her so much pain. He had no answer, really. Perhaps it was true that the good died young. Perhaps God placed tests before us to see how we coped with adversity. If so, she had been tested enough.

"Well May, how is your family doing?" the priest inquired as she sat down in the red velvet chair reserved for the seekers of the priest's intercession.

"They are all well, Father. Tommy is at Georgetown Medical School and writes me every week. Jack is in California and wants to be a movie star. He has been on TV a lot. Did they tell you?"

"Yes, I heard something from Joe Zanuski about that. Isn't that grand! How are the two youngest?"

"Well, Patty was married last year and lives in Roslindale and Christopher . . ."At the mention of his name she stopped and bit her lip, revealing a saddened heart through her usually stoic expression.

"What is the matter with Christopher? May, is that why you've come to me?" he asked, pulling his chair toward her and caressing her hand reassuringly.

"Oh, Father, I have to tell someone. He has left home because of . . ." She was unable to continue without tears filling her eyes and clogging her throat.

"Go ahead May, please tell me. I'm here to help you."

"You know, Father, I've never asked for help. I guess I'm proud that way. But my Christopher's leaving has left me alone for the first time and I'm, I'm afraid," she said, bending her head, sobbing quietly.

The priest leaned over and put his arm around her shoulder tenderly. She had come to see him on her lunch break. Her hair was wrapped in a kerchief and her blouse bore the insignia of the laundry where she worked.

"Why did Christopher leave, May?"

"There was a fight with some colored men," she answered, "and my Christopher shot one of them." The aging priest patted the shoulder of his childhood sweetheart as she revealed the circumstances that caused her youngest son to flee Boston and leave her alone in the projects. She had become a prisoner there. Perhaps he could speak to some friends at City Hall. After all, her husband had been a police officer. He would speak for her, he resolved.

"It's okay, May," the priest whispered. "We'll look for a new home for you and I'm sure with God's help your Christopher will turn out fine. You know that Jesus will help you if you put it in his divine hands."

"Do you really believe that, Father?" she asked, her eyes allowing him a glimpse into the depths of her desperation.

"Yes I do, May. I do," he urged.

From a window of the place where he slept alone, he watched her leave St. Augustine's Rectory.

In his sermon that Sunday, he spoke to his congregation about the mystery of God's will and how faith alone allows us to accept it. After their meeting, he prayed for May Conley and her son, almost every day. He prayed she would keep her faith.

CHAPTER 10

The siren on the police car shrieked as it crossed Massachusetts Avenue onto Columbus. The boyish driver's perspiration made the navigation of the cruiser difficult. His hands were drenched and sliding along the fiberglass wheel. In the passenger seat sat an older cop with two muscled wrinkles in the back of his distended neck. He was shouting into the car's radio at the dispatcher for District 2. "High speed pursuit, Mass registration 276-304, two black male suspects, use without authority."

The black Buick bounced into the air as it crossed the uneven pavement of Columbus Avenue. The two occupants were young, black and frightened by the predicament that the theft of this car and its detection by the police, had brought upon them. The passenger screamed to the driver to pull over and stop. He was fifteen years old and he was crying. The driver's expression was that of a frightened deer running in terror from destructive hunters in blue uniforms. Alcohol and marijuana had increased his terror and his recklessness.

As the Buick took a left on to a street of boarded up brick warehouses, the police cruiser accelerated closer. From the passenger window, a hand extended with a revolver pointed at the rear window of the Buick. The boyish driver watched in disbelief as his partner fired his service revolver toward the speeding vehicle, two car lengths in front of them.

"What are ya doin'?"

"Shut the fuck up and drive," the passenger screamed. Again he fired at the car being driven by the black teenagers. Suddenly, the Buick veered to the left and to the right, signifying that the teenager was losing control of the vehicle.

The face of the police officer firing the gun was beaded with the sweat of an August afternoon, a face hardened by acne and premature wrinkles. His ears were large and his jaw was that of a mongrel dog. He glared as he discharged his weapon for the third time.

Suddenly the Buick's back window exploded into gray fog and disappeared. The back of the driver's head disintegrated like an egg full of red paint against the inside of the windshield. The car careened into a curb and somersaulted against the concrete foundation of an abandoned factory. The passenger's body was ejected from the vehicle and pulverized between the brown brick of the building and the chrome and steel of the demolished automobile. Both the driver and his passenger would never see another birthday.

From the passenger side of the cruiser, he approached, his service revolver still drawn. He surveyed the wreckage and its impact upon the youths tangled within it.

"Call it in, Mike, they're both dead," he bellowed toward the driver. The young cop did not move. He simply sat and stared vacantly at the carnage in front of him. The older cop slowly walked back to the cruiser, reached beyond its driver and called in a request for an ambulance.

After the message was received, the young driver suddenly screamed at him, "You shouldn't a done it, Hayes. You shouldn't a shot at those kids."

Through the cruiser window, without a word, he grabbed the driver around the neck with both hands and choked off the air in his windpipe. The driver's eyes were at first disbelieving, then terrified as they fastened onto the enraged face of the cop who called himself his partner.

"You say a fuckin' word out a turn and you'll end up like those fuckin' niggers, you understand?" the older cop threatened.

The driver nearly passed out before he released his grip. The look on his ashen face told the older cop that he would not be a problem. The older cop spoke, his tone detached, almost matter of fact. "Now Mikey, if you're gonna put in your twenty on this job, you better learn about the street, right now. These fuckin' niggers are no good! They're ruinin' the city and they're takin' over the country. It's them or us, ya understand?"

39

The young cop looked into the bloodshot, blue eyes of the older man without speaking. Disgust and resentment appeared on his face. The older cop barked at him again, "Maybe you didn't fuckin' hear me, mister. I asked if you fuckin' understand!"

"Yeah, I understand." The resignation in his reply seemed to temper the fury that had welled up inside the older cop. It was a lethal fury that would be supported and excused by authority. That was the way it was. That was the way it had always been.

CHAPTER 11

The enormous buttocks of the man standing to the left of the silver colored and chrome coffee truck hid the line of workers in front of him. The Cadillac Plastic Company employed 22 warehouse men, most of whom had difficulty with the English language as spoken in California in the summer of 1968. It was ten minutes past ten in the morning when Murray and his canteen coffee truck arrived, allowing the men to take a break from inhaling polypropylene and plexiglass chips, while following their routines inside the gigantic yellow doors of the factory.

"Murray, you pendejo, your burritos taste like dog shit," the young Mexican with the large white teeth cried in a good natured manner.

"You must like shit then Gonzalo, you eat two every day. I got those red hots just for your stomach. You'd eat Roberto's Volkswagen if we put hot sauce on it."

"You fuckin' gavacho, you must have eaten three fuckin' trucks to get so fat! You look like a pregnant fuckin' walrus," Gonzalo jousted, rising to the occasion of the ranking contest.

"Hey man, how come your donuts taste like soap?" the thin muscular black youth inquired jokingly of the fat man.

"Cause I just came from the car wash, asshole, what do ya think?"

The men in the line always laughed at the daily repartee that was likewise part of the routine at the company warehouse.

"Hey Murray," Gonzalo continued, his bristled black hair and broad grin making him look like a cartoon character, "I heard your wife drives a canteen truck, too. Is that bullshit or what, man?"

"Yeah, her father owns the company. She gets the Goddamn phone company on Alhambra and what do I get? The fuckin' United Nations on Beverly Boulevard!"

"But we know you love us, man," a middle-aged Jamaican with a flowered shirt and gold pants volunteered jokingly. "I tell you, Murray, some nights I dream about your truck, man, and all the good shit you sell us."

"That's 'cause all the weed you smoke, Bro," a grey-haired black man in the green warehouse uniform interjected with an amicable smile, patting the Jamaican's back.

"You know Jackson," he confided, "I smoked some of that Jamaican shit once and the next thing I knew I had fo' kids and gain 35 pounds."

"Best ganja in da world, from Jamaica, man. Best women too."

"Yeah, but that's all they fuckin' do is smoke dat shit. I had to put it down, man. If I didn't, I'd eat like Gonzalo over there," nodding his head in the direction of the Mexican with the grin, who was now sitting in a pocket of shade that the mid-morning sun had created from the incline of the factory roof. Christopher Conley was seated on the ground beside the young Mexican. He offered Gonzalo a bite of his green apple before beginning to eat it. Gonzalo shook his head and placed the reddish dripping burrito into his mouth, consuming almost half of it with one bite.

"How can you eat that shit this early?" Chris asked, marveling at the gastrointestinal prowess of his Chicano friend.

"Because I don't have a belly like you fuckin' gringos. I muy macho, man."

Christopher laughed as he watched the man devour the remainder of his breakfast. "You're unbelievable Gonzalo," he said, shaking his head and looking across the factory yard toward a tiny brown skinned man speaking to a portly Korean with a long black crew cut.

"Look at Roberto, man," Chris observed, "he got another ticket for driving too slow on the freeway. Can you believe that shit? The cop was walking beside the car when he pulled him over." He and Gonzalo laughed loudly at the exaggerated scenario.

Roberto, another warehouseman at the Cadillac Plastic Company, had recently arrived from Columbia and had a world of trouble coping with the freeways of Southern California. He drove an ancient pink Volkswagen with a tiny back window. The car had endured a dozen owners and infinite mileage by never quite exerting itself over thirty-five miles an hour, much to the consternation of the always compassionate California Highway Patrol.

"The poor bastard" Chris lamented. "He got three tickets in two weeks and he's talking to Kim about it. Can you imagine? Kim, a fuckin' Korean…been in the country for a year, telling him how to beat it!" He and Gonzalo continued to laugh for the remainder of the coffee break, until their foreman, a dignified middle-aged Cuban motioned them back inside the factory.

Chris had been working in the shipping department of the plastics factory for nearly an entire year. He had spoken to his mother four times since he had left Boston. She had reassured him that the police had not been looking for him. Although he had almost lost all fear of apprehension, his memories of the shooting continued to haunt his sleep. Michael had come by to visit with his mother, almost every week to see if she was all right, always asking for him.

Chris missed Michael almost as much as he missed his mother, but he couldn't go back to Boston. He had become accustomed to Los Angeles. He was taking courses at Los Angeles City College at night. He drove a '55 Chevy and dated three or four sun-splashed California girls. He hadn't seen his brother in three months.

Jack was supposedly making a movie in Europe. Once, Chris received a postcard from the South of France. Slowly, he had succeeded in conquering his loneliness and alienation, discovering horizons beyond the street corners of Boston. He thought of Lorna almost constantly at first, then her face had faded in his memory, like an old photograph in an attic.

That afternoon, a flatbed truck pulled onto the street outside of the factory. Six of the warehousemen were required to remove four enormous plexiglass sheets from the truck for shipment to Cam Ranh Bay in Vietnam. Chris was enlisted by the foreman to help unload and pack the hefty cargo. As the sheets were being unloaded from the truck by forklift, one of them slipped from the blades, falling onto Chris's right foot. Fortunately, his work boots were a size too big and the plexiglass severed just the toe off the boot, leaving his right foot badly bruised, but intact. Because he couldn't walk without pain, he was taken by his foreman to a clinic in downtown Los Angeles.

He wondered why he had to take off his shirt when the injury was to his foot. His nurse had hair the color of some of the red convertibles he had seen on Sunset Boulevard. It matched the lipstick and nail polish that she wore. The makeup on her face attempted to conceal the impact of too many summers in the California sun. As she ran her finger across Christopher's back beneath his shoulder length sun bleached hair, she remarked, "Well honey, you're not going back to work for a while on that foot."

"Are my toes broken?" Chris asked while attempting to move the painful extremities within the confines of a tiny examination room.

"No, but they'll feel like they are for about a week. Just think, you can collect workmen's comp and take your girlfriend to the beach. I bet the girls just love you, don't they?" the nurse probed.

For an instant, Christopher's mind flashed on the transvestites on Hollywood Boulevard. They would call to him on his way home from work, as he walked from the bus stop to his tiny bungalow three blocks away. The eagerness in their voices and the look on their faces revealed a simmering, scary sexuality that Christopher had no desire to partake of. "Am I all set?" he asked, while slipping his faded blue t-shirt over his head.

"Sure honey, just try to stay off the foot for a couple of days. The doctor gave you a prescription for Percocet. It's for the pain. Here's the number here, if you ever need anything, my name is Sharene."

Christopher glanced at the little white card she handed to him with her name written across the top. She smiled at him as he said goodbye to her and thanked her. He could see that she was disappointed at his lack of response to her less than veiled overtures. The loneliness in her eyes somehow reminded him of his mother, living in the projects all by herself. He wondered why there were so many lonely people.

As he got off the bus and limped down Highland Avenue toward his bungalow, he withstood a gauntlet of Jesus freaks and drug dealers, alternatively urging him to repent for his sins and soliciting him to commit new ones. Such was the underbelly of Hollywood then. He would be eighteen in two weeks.

CHAPTER 12

The saxophone had become his only release, an ally that injected passion and discipline into his disorganized life. He could become one with it. When the depths of his father's drunken rage created a nightmare for him and his family, he would flee to the roof of the community house and practice for hours. The sweet sounds that he and the sax could create seemed to soothe him and allow him to temporarily forget the pain that engulfed him.

He became proficient at blues riffs and Motown hooks, eventually leading him to become a full-time member of Little Johnny and the Royal Teens. Michael seemed to be searching for a rhythm to a life beyond the projects, beyond his graduation from English High School, beyond anything he was accustomed to.

"Your sound is hot; and I like ya style," Little Johnny, the black lead singer, had remarked at his audition in the garage that belonged to one of the guitar player's uncles. Johnny was a former middleweight club fighter out of Springfield who never talked about the ring or the time that he'd done for armed robbery.

His hair was tinted orange-brown and processed into an enormous pompadour. Michael had heard of Johnny through one of his friends and had spoken to him outside of Skippy White's record store on Mass. Avenue. He would go there almost every week to pick up a new rhythm and blues

45. He had managed to collect records made by the early Miracles, Wilson Pickett and the Rolling Stones.

He had seen Johnny perform at a church dance and had spoken to him between sets about his desire to join the band. Johnny had asked him to come by someday and show them what he could do. He practiced for a solid month before he felt ready. He could play Little Richard, Chuck Berry, and almost anything recorded on the Stax label.

The band accepted him. The sax had occupied him, kept him away from the simmering boredom of the street corner. He was eighteen and working part-time delivering shoes all over the city during the day. Three nights a week he would practice with the band and on weekends play with them at dances that drew hundreds of city kids, like metal chips to a magnet.

On this Saturday night he and the three other members of the band were playing at the Town and Country, a teenage dance hall located in Mattapan, a neighborhood that was fast becoming endangered by the predators of poverty, drugs and crime. Johnny was late and the crowd was restless.

Sid Berman, the obese, perpetually perspiring bookmaker and part-time proprietor of the establishment, ran a soiled handkerchief over his balding head and demanded that the band get started or their 200 bucks was long gone. A second band called the Harlem Rockers was scheduled to arrive from New York at 10:00 o'clock.

They immediately broke into "Green Onions," buying them time and allowing Michael to get his groove. Almost by design, Little Johnny arrived to the delight of the crowd. His skin-tight purple and white jump-suit clung to his small muscular form. His nod to the band told them where to go. Johnny cradled the microphone between his enormous fingers and moved to the front of the tiny plywood stage. He and the band began to rock the crowd. Their energy was commingled, fluid, electrifying.

The heat and exhilaration of the moment welled up in Michael's chest as he joyously blew through one tune after another. He loved to play. The sound that he shared with the crowd and their adulation was intoxicating to him. With the saxophone, Michael could overcome anything, anybody.

The crowd became more animated with every set. The climax of their night was a medley of "Rip It Up," "Johnny B. Goode" and "Jailhouse Rock." Michael's free-flowing sax and Johnny's wailing voice made love to each other. Together they led the crowd in a frenzied pace to a teenage nirvana. Two slow numbers provided the denouement, leading the crowd gently back to their senses and into each other's sweat drenched arms. It was the fall of 1968. It was a time of violent change and dashed hope.

Like an urban messiah, Johnny stood on the top step of the fire escape hanging from the back of the dance hall. The smoke from the joint in his sweat-soaked hand tantalized Michael's nostrils. Johnny passed the joint to him in a gesture of gratitude and respect.

Michael had smoked dope several times before, but never really enjoyed it until that night. Maybe he was older and could handle it better or maybe his brain was simply beginning to accommodate the disorientated thoughts and fertile rhythms that it activated there. That night, marijuana began to join the saxophone as an essential companion during Michael's sojourn through the city.

They arrived late in a dilapidated school bus bearing their stage name. The Harlem Rockers were a raucous amalgam of six oversized, sinewy black men cut from the iron of Harlem. Their sound and their choreography brought the crowd back to the frenzy created by Michael and Johnny. Michael watched with appreciation as the band moved deftly from one R 'n B standard to another. "Bony Maroni" and "Shake Your Tail Feathers" shook the crowd to the depths of their soul, releasing once again an energy that was absolutely exhilarating.

As Michael returned to the projects early that morning, he was careful not to disturb the stupor that enveloped his father's pathetic being, as it lay on the couch. Later that day, he learned that he had been summoned to the Boston Army Base for a draft physical.

CHAPTER 13

The blazing California sun reflected off the green metal flaked Chevy, as it meandered through the expansive, tree-lined boulevards of Beverly Hills. Christopher had scribbled the address given to him by his brother on a scrap of paper next to him on the red upholstered front seat.

As he drove, he marveled at the wealth and luxury of America's most successful colony. Here the Japanese gardeners and Hispanic housekeepers made more money than the office workers and middle-level managers in Santa Monica and Pasadena.

He was searching for DeCordova Boulevard. Never had he seen so many Porches, and Mercedes in one place. It certainly was a stark contrast from his desperate state the day before. For three weeks he had been waiting for his worker's compensation check to arrive. He had exhausted his meager bank account to pay the rent, believing that the check would come. Ten days without any money coming in and only peanut butter and sandwich bread to eat.

He was becoming weak, eventually spending the scorching days simply laying on his couch within his tiny bungalow, his mind in a stupor, yearning for food. His calls to the plastics company had received various unsatisfactory responses, including the paperwork hasn't arrived, the insurance company will be getting in touch with you and, of course the classic, the check is in the mail. Still the sun came up and he would stagger down to his mailbox and stagger back, cursing as he passed the windows of the elderly Hungarian sisters that were his landladies.

He wondered how long he could survive on the pocket change he had left. He had even contemplated calling his mother and asking her to wire him money, but his guilt at not calling and his concern at what she would think, wouldn't allow it.

As he spotted the sign for DeCordova Boulevard, his mind returned to the occurrences of the day before. He was sitting on the stoop in front of his sweltering bungalow, when a familiar, yellow Chevy Convertible pulled out in front. Incredibly, at the nadir of his predicament, there before him stood his older brother like the apparition of a conquering prince. He had returned from making commercials in Barcelona and Paris.

He was wearing a Nehru shirt and black jeans. The boots he wore were Italian and they sparkled like the onyx ring he wore on his baby finger. Suddenly all of Christopher's resentment and distrust disappeared. He was overjoyed; his guardian angel had shown up in the nick of time.

Jack listened as Chris told him about the injury to his foot and his desperation in not getting a check. Jack simply smiled and demanded that Chris come with him to get something to eat. Chris didn't hesitate. After devouring the steak and salad placed before him at the Sizzler, Chris became attentive to what his older brother had been trying to tell him.

"I have this new agent and he was telling me about this guy named Conroy from Chicago. He's looking for a driver and he usually hires college kids. I asked him if he would put in a word for you, man. He did, and the guy called and wants to interview you for the job. What do you say, Bro? No more fuckin' plastics up your nose, huh?"

Christopher was ecstatic. It was about time things started to come his way again. He knew things were looking up when the check finally arrived the following morning. Immediately, Chris drove to Hollywood Boulevard and shed his factory chic for a set of real clothes.

The smell of the lilacs in Beverly Hills suddenly registered a vivid recollection of Lorna and the Public Gardens in his brain. He wished he could see her. He felt that he was on a roll now.

The Museum of Fine Arts in Boston was the closest thing to the Conroy Mansion that Christopher Conley had experienced. The sweeping marble stairways, the statues, the expensive paintings and its variety of flowers, transported Christopher to a world he had never dreamed of, a world of privilege, of power and pride. It was a world far removed from that in which he lived. He wanted in. He could feel the comforting energy of it.

Christopher had grown since coming to Los Angeles. The thin boy who had fled Boston had become a slender, muscular young man. The sun of California had combined with the sweat of his labor in the factory yard to lighten his hair to the color of golden sand and darken his skin.

He was wearing a red and white striped short-sleeve shirt with dark green pants. He felt he needed the clean-cut college look for his job interview. He was right. His hair had just been cut and hung stylishly over his collar.

The housekeeper showed him through three sets of French doors out to the side of a crystal blue swimming pool. He waited for the master of the palace to arrive, aiming to please, yet not knowing exactly what to expect. He would not be disappointed.

Thomas Conroy entered the pool area of his twenty room home, dressed casually in a starched pink shirt and white chinos. His youthful appearance concealed the fact that this was his forty-second summer. He exuded confidence and class. His salt and pepper hair and athletic frame gave him the appearance of an erudite polo player.

Growing up in a large Irish family on the South side of Chicago, he had excelled in school, graduating third in his class from the University of Chicago and securing a master's degree from the Harvard Business School. He was the youngest member of the board of directors of Delano Fruits, a multinational company with offices in Los Angeles, New York and Honolulu.

As he approached Christopher he smiled and confidently extended his hand while scrutinizing the young man's eyes.

"Hello, I'm Tom Conroy, and you're Christopher Conley, correct?"

"Yes," Christopher replied, politely standing and shaking the man's hand.

"Can we get you something to drink, a soft drink, some lemonade?"

"No, I'm all set, thanks."

"Well, if you don't mind, I'm going to have some iced tea, are you sure you don't want any?"

"Yeah, I'll have some," Chris reconsidered, after realizing that the anxiety of the moment had made his throat parched.

"Did you have any trouble finding us?" Tom asked, reviewing the appearance of Christopher, as they sat down next to the swimming pool.

"No, a friend of my brother gave him very good directions. I can usually find anything though. I have a real good sense of direction." Christopher told himself not to appear too anxious or too eager to persuade this man to give him the job. He told himself to wait for the questions and answer them truthfully.

"Well, as you know, I'm looking for a driver, a chauffeur for myself and from time to time my wife and two children. I'm told you have no experience, is that correct."

"Do you mean as a driver?" Christopher asked.

"Of course."

"No, but I'm a very careful driver and I'll give it my best Mr. Conroy."

"They tell me you were working in a factory and you attend the City College at night."

"Yes, sir, that's right. I moved here from Boston a little over a year ago."

"I really love Boston," Tom stated, as he waited for his housekeeper to place the glasses of iced tea and an assortment of fruit between the two of them. "Gracias, Carmelita," he said, as the housekeeper smiled at him. "I always thought it was a very cosmopolitan city. Don't you agree?

"Well I've lived there since I was born and I liked it," Chris replied, hoping that was the right answer.

"Why did you leave?"

Christopher was stunned by the question, thinking for an instant that this man had uncovered the hidden reason for his departure from the city he had grown up in.

"Ah, I wanted to live near my brother and I thought I might as well do it right after I graduated."

"I understand your brother is an actor. Do you find that exciting?"

Christopher realized that this man was probing him for information in a nice way. He liked the way he talked, the way he assumed control without being a jerk about it. He began to feel comfortable with Tom Conroy, as they sat together next to a swimming pool, within a Beverly Hills mansion. He wished that Michael could see him now. He wouldn't believe it if he told him.

"Yeah, I think it's pretty cool. He just came back from making commercials in Europe. I guess you know the guy he works with. He's the one that told my brother about the job."

Christopher was conscious of Tom's intent observations as they spoke for almost an hour. He became relaxed and amazed that this sophisticated millionaire actually seemed to care about what he had to say. They spoke of many things at that first meeting — Christopher's mother, his school work, his work experience, the projects, the Red Sox. After leaving to receive a long distance phone call, Tom returned.

"Why do you want to work for us?" he inquired, leaning forward and resting himself on his elbows. The muscles displayed in his forearms convinced Christopher that Tom Conroy had been and continued to be, a very smart and a very tough customer.

He thought for a moment and responded, "Well, I figure I've been poor since I was born. I think that if I can work here in Beverly Hills I can learn how people become a success and I can do it too. Like I said Mr. Conroy, I'm a careful driver and I can find anything. I really need the job and I give you my word you won't be disappointed."

Conroy leaned back in the white wicker chair, watching Chris admiringly. He finished his iced tea and stared for a while into the clear blue expanse of the kidney shaped swimming pool before speaking once more. "You know what, I like you. You remind me of myself at your age. It's really quite refreshing to talk to someone like you. Tell you what, you write down two references with their phone numbers and if everything checks out, you can have the job, okay?"

Christopher was overjoyed. He really couldn't believe it. He was right there, in the richest town in the country, with a real live millionaire offering him a job. After writing the names of his foreman and the manager of the plastics factory, he said goodbye. There was a warmth between them as they shook hands.

All the way back to Hollywood, Chris blasted the Chevy's radio. As he turned on to La Brea Avenue, the sun was blinding and Stevie Wonder was singing Christopher's sentiments perfectly. "Baby, everything's all right, uptight, out of sight."

CHAPTER 14

His eighteenth birthday was his first day as a millionaire's chauffeur. He arrived at the enormous marble columns that flanked the wrought iron gate of the Conroy mansion as the sun spread itself like a red and orange quilt across the morning sky. It was going to be one of those broiling July days that brought the vapor up from the asphalt and scorched the remaining green from the hills surrounding Los Angeles, turning them an arid, flammable brown.

The pace of traffic on Wilshire Boulevard had already begun to crawl, as Christopher drove up from Hollywood. His body was electrified with excitement and anxiety as the master of the palace unlocked the castle-like doors leading to a cavernous garage. Within its expanse were contained a golden 1967 El Dorado and a recently delivered, cranberry 1968 Bentley that Christopher was instructed were to be his responsibility. He was to care for them like a groom cares for two magnificent stallions.

He was given a black log book to be kept daily. In it were to be included his destinations, his mileage and his expenses. He was also given the name of a clothier on Rodeo Drive where he was to purchase suitable chauffeur's clothing on account. He wondered if he was dreaming as he reflected upon the opportunities with which he was being presented.

His first day was one of adjustment and learning. He was introduced to the lady of the mansion as she dutifully kissed her husband on her way to a tennis match at the country club. She was tall with the look of exquisite breeding and intelligence. Her auburn hair and slender frame gave her the appearance of a college co-ed. She would not require Christopher's services on that day, but rather, was spirited away in a small Mercedes sedan, being driven by a tiny blonde woman wearing enormous sunglasses.

At the end of his first day, Christopher stared at himself admiringly in the rear view mirror of his '55 Chevy as he returned to Hollywood. He couldn't help but smile. Arrangements had been made to meet his brother at 8:30 that night so they could go to the Whisky a Go Go, a popular rock night club, located on the Sunset Strip. There Smokey Robinson and the Miracles would be performing. His brother had finagled the tickets from one of his many connections.

Between his new job and his plans for the night, he felt that a power beyond him was guiding him along the way and actually making his way easier. The comforting reassurance of these thoughts reminded him of his childhood days when he would attend the Novena of St. Francis at Sacred Heart Church. He could pray then, and believe completely that God was looking down upon him benevolently, making his path straight. Although the unfairness he had observed in his youth had dispersed these beliefs, he often longed for the reassurance they gave him.

Christopher waited in the foyer of Michelli's Restaurant for his brother's arrival. He was wearing a white long-sleeve cotton shirt with ruffles down the front and black jeans. His nearly blonde hair was still wet from his hasty shower and his black suede shoes had only been worn once before. He had situated himself on a long green leather couch that provided an excellent vantage point for observations of the restaurant's arriving guests. From there, he could gaze through the spacious front windows of the establishment for signs of his brother.

The signs that he observed astonished him. His brother and three beautiful women were making their way up the street outside the restaurant toward him. One of the women was a statuesque brunette in a short white dress that clung to her like a glove. Her arm was entwined with his brother's and she displayed an affectionate familiarity that attracted the attention of the continental maître d' as they entered.

"Four for dinner?" he inquired.

"No, five," replied Jack, as he smiled and beckoned to Christopher to come and be introduced to his companions. "Now didn't I tell you he was cute?" he announced, as the three women examined Christopher with approving eyes. "Well brother, this is your birthday present. Say hello to Fardya, Nina and Anastasia. They're from Iran and they don't speak English that good."

Christopher smiled and nodded, attempting not to appear shy. His brother went on to explain that he had met the girls at the Red Fez and that the tall brunette and he had been dating. The other girls, one a slender blonde with incredibly shapely legs and the other, a small auburn-haired girl with a tiny mole above her lip and alluring brown eyes, smiled and nodded in response.

At dinner, Chris admired the manner in which his brother interpreted the menu and took charge to make sure that everything was simply perfect. On the way to the nightclub, the voice of Wolfman Jack provided a backdrop to a series of radio dedications by friends and lovers throughout LA. The sidewalk was the site of a long line awaiting entrance to the show, as the yellow convertible containing the party of five arrived. Incredibly, a nod from his brother to the gigantic black doorman resulted in them being ushered into the dimly lit red and black interior of the Whisky a Go Go. Their seats were to the left of the runway-like stage.

In the darkness that permeated their location, Jack ordered drinks for all five, even though Christopher and the shapely blond girl who had nuzzled next to him, were clearly under age. Gin and ginger ale led into the show.

The Miracles appeared first, their melodies and Motown choreography thrilling the throng that had filled the nightclub to capacity. Then Smokey made his entrance as red and white spotlights ushered him down the runway to the front of the stage. He was wearing a white jumpsuit that the lighting made appear almost celestial. His voice and his lyrics succeeded in transporting the crowd to a region above the clouds that were gathering throughout America in the summer of 1968.

After the show, Jack showed Christopher the *piece de resistance,* a hotel key for a suite at the Beverly Wilshire. That night the brothers would soar on an intimate, erotic journey light years away from The Bromley Court Housing Project and cobblestones covered with blood. The sultry passion exhibited by their three female companions throughout the night and early morning was well beyond Christopher's fertile imagination.

With the morning, came a golden sun that entered the suite almost apologetically where the lovers slept. The intimacy of the night before had neither disappeared nor diminished. Later they drove up the California coastline with the top down on Jack's convertible. The hues of the panoramic ocean views dotted with athletic specks riding the crest of waves on multicolored surfboards furnished an indelible moment for the five that shared it. They embraced each other on the sand of Zuma Beach; the tide crashing, then approaching to caress the youth that blazed within them.

Christopher glanced at his brother locked in the arms of the statuesque brunette. Her languid figure oozed from a tiny orange bikini. He smiled and waved to him, lying between the nearly naked bodies of her two companions. He felt at that moment, if unexpected death came calling he would answer willingly, confident in the knowledge that he had not been cheated by the suddenness of its call. He hoped that his father had experienced something approaching that moment before his call came.

CHAPTER 15

*I*t had been almost two years since his flight from Boston. He had learned to live alone without loneliness and to earn his own way, first in a Los Angeles factory where English was a second language, and then at the knee of a millionaire. He had been an attentive, working class witness in chauffeur's clothing to Palm Springs polo matches, Wilshire Boulevard business meetings and all-night parties in the Hollywood Hills.

Thoughts of home were as rare as rusted automobiles on Rodeo Drive. Through his boss's intercession, he had become enrolled in his second semester at UCLA. Maybe it was the absence of catholic school restrictions and corporal punishment, but he actually began to like school, to see it as a worthwhile means to an unbridled end.

He had been with many women, but had not been in love. From distracted co-eds to fortune seeking office girls, he had enjoyed them all. He had matured and become a self-sufficient, confident, young aspirant in California. Boston, he thought, had confined him, limited his vision, stunted his dreams. Los Angeles, with its limitless expectations, had become his home. He would never live back East again. That was final. That was etched in stone. That was until the day that the letter arrived from Michael.

Michael McLean had been enrolled in a different school in the two years since Chris fled. The lack of college potential had predetermined that he experience a more sinister slice of the American dream. The streets of Boston in the late sixties were fertile fields for young patriotic hearts, mis-led by old men in Washington to the tormented hamlets of South Vietnam. Instead of being drafted, Michael had chosen to enlist in the regular Army and seek distinction and comradery in the company of Airborne Rangers.

The letter Chris received from his nearly-forgotten boyhood friend kindled in him a sudden, unexpected yearning to see Michael, especially before he shipped out to Vietnam. The letter told of a going away party at the Ukrainian Hall. Michael's family and most of their old neighborhood would be there.

As he read his misspelled words, he couldn't help but feel sorry for some reason for Michael. He really didn't know why, but Michael had been chosen by fate for a different, desperate journey. Christopher wondered if Michael had changed in the years since they parted.

It would have been easier for him to tear up the letter; forget he ever saw it and continue on with his life; close the book on his past. But he couldn't. Michael had been his best friend and he had written to Chris, asking him to come home and spend some time before he went overseas. Chris couldn't turn a deaf ear to the voice he had known so well. He couldn't forget that Michael McLean had, in a sense, saved his life that night on Parker Hill. It was Michael's gun that had administered justice and forced Christopher to find out who he really was.

The plane was delayed in its arrival at Logan Airport. Michael's going away party was already an hour old as Christopher passed through the terminal and traveled by bus, train and cab to the grey two-story wood building known to the residents of Jamaica Plain as the Ukrainian Club. It was a chilly October night and Chris felt unusually cold as he stepped from the cab and stood across the street, observing the blaring music and animated intoxication of the party.

Christopher's hair was almost platinum from the sun, it was combed straight back and touched his shoulders. He wore a brown leather jacket, jeans and black cowboy boots. He was now almost six feet three inches tall. He knew that he would probably not be recognized by many of his boyhood neighbors and friends. It was nearly his twentieth year.

He was anxious at being back in Boston. Even though the police had stopped looking for the shooter in the incident on Parker Hill, Christopher felt uneasy as he passed by the detail cop at the front door. He paid three dollars to enter the expansive hall, decorated with American flags and banners wishing Michael the very best. He stood just inside the crowded doorway, soaking in the setting and searching for Michael.

Christopher was right. He wasn't recognized by the people in the crowd, but he certainly was noticed. It seemed as he passed through the gyrating bodies responding to Creedence and "Down on the Corner," that every eye was fixed upon him. He thought that he would encounter somebody, anybody who would recognize or remember him.

Then he saw Michael's mother seated beside an uncomfortable, haggard man in an oversized suit. Christopher recognized him as Michael's father. He couldn't ever recall speaking to old man McLean. After all, he wasn't exactly what you would call approachable. He thought that he might as well do it that night.

"How are you Mrs. McLean?" Christopher began. The woman stared at Christopher's face for an uncomfortably long interval, finally recognizing who it was, that was speaking to her.

"Christopher Conley, I can't believe it. Oh, I hoped you would come. Do you know how much you've changed? My God, you're all grown up. How is your mother?"

"Oh, she's fine," Christopher replied, not wanting to open the subject of his not having seen his mother yet. "Have you seen Michael around?"

"I saw him a minute ago; he's with Peggy. That's his girlfriend; they're engaged you know. I think he went downstairs."

While he was speaking to Michael's mother, Chris noticed the surly stare of Michael's father from the corner of his eye. Attempting to conceal his contempt, Christopher spoke to him cordially. "How ya doin', Mr. McLean?"

"I'm doing okay. Why don't you get your hair cut? You look like a goddamn broad. What are you, a hippie or somethin'?"

It didn't take long for Christopher to discover that the years hadn't mellowed Michael's father's disposition. Not wanting a confrontation, Christopher ignored the remarks and quickly told Michael's parents that he would see them later. In fact, the only time Christopher wanted to see Michael's father again was in a casket. He continued to scan the crowd for a familiar, friendly face.

She was about twelve feet from him when he first saw her. She was dancing with a girlfriend and smiling. The smile was warm and inviting, like the cover of a beautiful book. She saw him almost immediately after he spotted her, then she shifted her attention to her girlfriend. With the loud music, the conversation that the two girls were having could not be heard by Christopher

He walked closer towards her, still looking for Michael, but hoping that an opportunity would arise to speak with her. Her hair was black and she was wearing a red mini skirt and black pumps. She had the features of an angel and the figure of a lovely, passionate flower. Christopher had never seen her before in his neighborhood. He smiled and slipped between her and her girlfriend as if he were cutting in. She smiled back as her girlfriend disappeared into the crowd.

"What's your name?" he asked, tenderly looking into the hazel eyes that looked into his.

"Linda, what's yours?"

"Chris."

"You're not from around here are you?" she asked, as they swayed with the rhythm of "Groovin" by the Young Rascals.

"I used to be, but I've been livin' in California."

"Really, what's it like?"

"What do you mean?"

"California, what's it like?"

"It's great. I'm going back in a couple of days. I'm an old friend of Mike McLean. Do you know him?"

"No, but my girlfriend knows Peggy, Mike's girlfriend."

"Yeah, I heard that Mike was engaged. Holy shit, that's unbelievable."

"Why is it unbelievable?" she inquired, as the song flowing through the crowd echoed throughout the hall, "The world is ours whenever we're together. There ain't no place I'd like to be instead of ——."

"No, I mean it's unbelievable that Michael is settling down with one girl. He must have changed a lot since I've seen him. How about if I get you a drink? Let's get out of this crowd."

She again smiled at Christopher, showing him an innocent willingness to accompany him and to get to know him. Christopher reached behind him for her soft, warm hand and she tendered it to him immediately. As he led the way through the crowd, he could hear his name being uttered by vaguely remembered faces. He had been recognized by them, despite his transformation. As they made their way toward the bar where the crowd was congregated three deep, a tall red-haired man with sweat dripping from his face was attempting to wait on everybody.

Suddenly, Christopher was nudged on his left side by an enormous barrel of a man whom Christopher had known since grammar school. Tom Wisnewski had always been bigger and older looking than other kids his age. His stature, however, had not added to his intellect. He had been the center on English High's football team and had never quite forgotten it. The school jacket that barely fit him told those who dared to look, that English High had been champions of their division in 1966 and "Snew" had worn number 66.

"Hey, Conley, where the hell have ya been?" he shouted above the dim of the crowd. "You were just a little shit when I saw you last."

"I've been in California for a couple of years. How ya been, Snew?" Chris answered, attempting to be respectful, yet wanting to escape from the unpredictable giant's focus. Wisnewski had been known to take offense over minor indications of disrespect and to unleash a savage beating in an instant upon the offender. Christopher didn't want to run that risk. "Have you seen Mike?" Chris inquired.

"What the fuck ya think we're here for? He's around."

"I'll catch ya later," Chris shouted, still holding the hand of his lovely companion. His attention was now directed toward her. "Let's get out of this and go over there," Chris directed, as he made their way to a corner of the crowded hall where they could be together, almost alone.

CHAPTER 16

The music reverberating throughout the hall suddenly ceased. Then the lights were turned up within the hall, as the four members of the band climbed the stairs on either side of the hall's stage. The black man in his late twenties reached his bony hand toward the microphone and addressed the crowd. "Ladies and gentlemen, boys and girls. I'm Johnny Wilson and I brought my new band here tonight to play for the best sax player in Boston, Mike McLean!"

The crowd of over three hundred erupted at the mention of Michael's name. The announcement also directed Christopher's attention away from the sweet, smiling face of the girl he had just met. They had managed to secure two seats in the far corner of the hall.

The way she spoke, the tilt of her head, as she listened to him admiringly, had mesmerized him. It was the first time he had felt like that. The first time in a long time, the first time since Lorna. Her name was Linda and she lived in Brighton. She was smart and oh, she was sexy in a clean and classy way. Chris wanted to learn more about her, but first things first.

The matter that had brought him back to Boston was Michael, the friend that Chris watched from across the crowd ascend the bandstand's stairs to a standing ovation. He too had changed. He too had grown in the two years they had been apart. He was tall, over six feet, and lean from months of advanced training. His head was shaved and the green uniform he wore with the gold eagle on the shoulder told Chris that he had done it. He had become a warrior attached to the 101st Airborne Division.

Christopher felt proud of Michael, yet deeply concerned about where he was headed. While in Los Angeles, his feelings about the war in Vietnam had changed 180 degrees. Before leaving Boston, he saw the war as something necessary, something just, something patriotic. But as the years passed, he saw it as such a tragic waste of so many lives.

He recalled speaking to the Chicanos from the barrio who had gone with bands playing and courage worn like a badge of honor. The ones that returned were disillusioned, addicted and damaged. Their silence and desperate need to become detached through drink or drugs spoke volumes. Few of them wanted others to go.

The war had divided America into separate distrustful camps, pitting the old against the young, the "for" versus the "against." The newspapers, the radio and the television stations saturated the country with the destruction and disruption of it all. Like gangrene, Vietnam was eating away at the extremities of the American consciousness.

Most didn't want to admit it; many didn't know how to combat it, and only a vocal few screamed for its termination, its immediate amputation before the soul of the country was lost. Christopher had spoken of these things to Tom Conroy. His boss, a former Navy man, had simply stated, "It is the wrong war in the wrong place, but there are an awful lot of people getting rich on it."

The black singer continued to address the crowd. "You know, Mike is in the 101st Airborne. He's the screamingest eagle you ever seen. Now I'm gonna ask him to scream with that sax over there. C'mon man, what d'ya say? Once them Viet Cong hear you blow that sax, they'll just lay down and surrender. C'mon, Mike, show the people our secret weapon."

Christopher stood and watched as Michael stepped to the front of the stage. He was accompanied by a petite girl with short, sandy hair and oversized hoop earrings. She kissed Michael as he waved to the exuberant crowd. Christopher applauded, fighting back the tears clogging his throat as Michael hugged Johnny Wilson and slipped the strap of the saxophone over his head. He waved again and smiled as the band began its version of Little Richard's "Rip It Up." The way he played, the sound his sax made, the response of those that came; every bit of it was indelible, unforgettable, just perfect.

Everyone in the crowd was in love with Michael. They kissed him, they caressed him, and they cried as they thought of the path that lay ahead of him.

As he was walking from the stage with the petite girl on his arm, Chris intercepted him. The joy on Michael's face and the depth of his embrace brought Christopher to tears immediately. They stood in suspended animation in the middle of the hall, locked in each other's arms, each of them crying. Christopher could feel the warmth of Michael's tears on his face. Michael whispered to him as they continued their vigorous embrace, "I missed you, man. Thanks for coming."

"I wouldn't miss it, Mike."

Michael reached for the girl to his left and brought her close to Christopher. "Peggy, this is Chris, the guy I told you about."

Christopher smiled as the young woman came close and held his hand momentarily. Her eyes were the green of a beautiful lagoon. Her face was attractive, but by no means beautiful. She was almost boyish in her appearance and yet there was something athletic and wholesome about her that made her pleasant to look at. Her hair was short and her earrings were enormous.

"Hi Chris, Mike has told me all about you." As she spoke she curled herself under Michael's muscular arm.

In the crush of the moment, Chris had forgotten that Linda was standing nearby. He glimpsed her expression as he and Michael stood with their arms on each other's shoulders. She was exquisite as she gazed lovingly at the embrace of the two friends. Suddenly, he remembered his manners and introduced her to his friend. "Hey Mike, this is Linda."

"Bianco," she volunteered as she reached her hand toward Michael and then hugged him. The way she touched his friend; the way she walked and most of all the way she laughed, caused him to stop and realize that she was something special. Something more than another languid body that Christopher could take to bed. They looked at each other and he kissed her softly, smelling the fragrance from her body.

He held her hand as they walked together to the parking lot outside of the Ukrainian Club. She was going home in her girlfriend's car. As she stood next to the passenger door beneath a street light, she wrote her telephone number on a napkin. He accepted her invitation to continue their encounter. He placed the napkin in the pocket of his jeans and looked again into her face. Suddenly the two of them were kissing deeply, passionately.

"You'll call me, won't you?" she whispered, as she opened the door to her friend's car.

"Definitely," Chris promised, "I'll call you tomorrow.

"I can't wait," she said, kissing him on the left cheek and hugging him. He stood on the sidewalk as the car drove away. The emotion-filled reunion with Michael and the promise of days ahead with Linda rekindled in Christopher a deep abiding feeling for the city of his birth. Los Angeles had changed him, allowed him to expand, but Boston somehow still held him, searching for answers, in the palm of its hand.

CHAPTER 17

The Bromley Court Housing Projects had kept pace with the changes that had taken place in the two years since he fled Boston, by going from bad to worse. Christopher sensed this when the cab driver refused to take him into the confines of the place that had been his home since shortly after his father died.

"This is as far as I go pal," the burly red-faced driver announced unexpectedly.

"What do you mean? I live over there," Christopher protested, pointing to the congregation of chocolate brown brick high rises in the darkened distance.

"That's your problem. The fare's three fifty."

"Cut the shit. I don't live here man, I live in there."

"Well, man," the driver replied mockingly, "I can't help that."

Rather than cause a fight, Chris threw four dollars at the driver and slammed the door as the cab roared away. It was beginning to get much colder. Chris zipped up his leather jacket and pulled up the collar.

As he walked through the darkened courtyard where he and his brothers had once played stickball, he could make out four or five stripped and burned out cars. Broken glass and boarded windows were everywhere. "The times they were a changing" and it wasn't good news for those forced to live at Bromley Court.

Chris had called his mother when he had arrived at Logan Airport and she was waiting up for him when he came home from Michael's party. The years had not been kind to her. Her hair was almost completely gray. Her face was more wrinkled and her eyes had a certain fatal sadness about them that caused him to feel guilty about his leaving her alone. As he viewed her surroundings, he thought of how he could get her out of that hopeless, dangerous place.

His mother was amazed by the transformation of her youngest son. She was disturbed by the length and color of his hair, accusing him in a good natured way of dying it to look like a beach boy. She was ecstatic that he had come home, sitting him down at her tiny Formica kitchen table and placing a tuna fish sandwich in front of him.

Despite his early morning arrival, she wanted to hear all about California, her son, Jack, and Christopher's going to college at UCLA. He could tell that she was so very proud of him. He could tell that she desperately needed his company to dispel her loneliness. She sat across from him, caressing his right hand in between bites of the sandwich. She was a sponge soaking in everything he said.

It was almost 3:00 in the morning when Chris kissed her goodnight and fell asleep in the once-familiar bed that he hadn't slept in for almost two years. As he slept, his mind flashed on Beverly Hills and UCLA, Michael McLean and a saxophone, his mother confined in a suffocating, lonely place and the loving face of Linda Bianco. Like the roller coaster at Paragon Park, his life was a dizzying jumble of faces and events that propelled him onward.

The sun of an October morning reflected off the tin roof of the Project's vandalized neighborhood house, as two friends sat side by side on a set of cement stairs near the site where they had first met and fought. They had come a long way together, a way filled with unexpected twists and turns. Their destinies were fashioned by where they lived and the times in which they lived them.

Michael had orders to report to Fort Campbell Kentucky that evening. From there he and his unit would fly to Fort Ord in California, then to Hawaii, then to the Philippines and then to war and South Vietnam. Christopher could see that Michael was anxious as he sat with his elbows resting on his knees, making a conscious effort to spit a design on the concrete in front of him. For a long interval neither of the friends spoke to each other. Suddenly, Michael broke the silence.

"You know, I ain't afraid of dyin' man. It's getting fucked up and endin' up in a wheelchair. If I get hit like that, I ain't comin' back."

"Just shut up," Chris interrupted, shaking his head. "I gotta feelin' you're gonna make it without a scratch. I swear to God, Mike, I do. Hey, look at all the shit you made it through already. Remember the time we got jumped by those assholes in Hyde Park? I thought we were fuckin' dead and then you punched that big asshole when he had his mouth open and broke his jaw. That was it. The rest of them had no balls and screwed. There musta been six of 'em and the two of us did 'em in. You 'member that?"

Michael smiled as he recalled the incident that Chris described encouragingly. From the pocket of his gray shirt, Michael produced a joint, asking Christopher if he wanted to get high. The two friends had smoked marijuana together before. The two of them had tried it before anybody white in the neighborhood knew what marijuana was. At that moment it was like a farewell bottle of champagne.

"Did you get into reefer in LA, Chris?"

"Not really, just once in a while, at a concert or a club."

"I love it, man. I used to smoke it before we'd play a set and I swear I could blow that sax like Junior Walker. It just relaxes me and makes me feel like it's gonna be alright."

For some reason, the way that Michael talked about marijuana made him uneasy. He had seen guys that spent all day getting high and they all seemed to love it too much. Like Michael's old man loved the booze. "You gettin' high a lot, Mike?"

"Every fuckin' chance I get, when I'm on leave, man. Don't worry 'bout it, it's natural. I'm cool with it. I don't do none of the other shit."

Considering where his friend was headed, Chris accepted his invitation and shared the joint with him. The two friends spoke of rock groups and girls they had known. Chris was asked about women in California and whether they were different from the girls in Boston. They were more open and much easier to get next to, Chris advised. Michael sat and stared for a moment, watching two pigeons scurrying across the Project's neglected courtyard.

"Who was that lady you were with last night?"

"Have you seen her around?" Chris inquired.

"No."

"Her name's Linda. She's from Brighton. She's fine, don't you think?" As Christopher spoke of the girl he had just met, he remembered Lorna and the conversation that he had with Michael before the night of the shooting. The marijuana began to have an effect, as Christopher watched intently while a flock of pigeons loitered on the roof of the incinerator building to their left.

"I'm gonna call her today, man. I'd like to see her again. Hey, what about Peggy. I heard someone say you were gonna get married."

"Yeah, she wanted to do it before I shipped out, but I told her no. We will when I get back; if I get back."

The effect of the marijuana was pronounced now. Michael's words made Christopher think of all the kids that had gone to Vietnam, all the TV news clips of the place, all the pain, all the protests. A profound sadness overcame him, as he dwelled on the destination of his best friend. He reached for him and hugged him forcefully. His words were choked by his tears. "You take care of yourself. I'm gonna miss you like a bastard, you crazy prick."

Michael too began to cry, enormous tears welling in his crazy Irish eyes. The picture they presented was incongruous as they sat embracing, perhaps for the last time.

"Promise me somethin' Chris," he said.

"Anything, man."

"Promise me you'll watch out for my mother and my little brother, no matter what happens."

Christopher hesitated. He was going back to LA, and didn't want to get tied down in Boston. He was free in LA, away from his mother and Michael and everybody that meant anything to him. He knew that the request came from the depths of Michael's heart. How could he refuse him? How could he possibly say no?

His mind was swirling now with everything that was happening. A debt owed to a best friend, a mother imprisoned in the place where she lived and Linda, lovely Linda, with the beautiful body and the smiling face. At that moment he made a decision that would change his life again. The roller coaster was suddenly changing direction. What was it gonna be, a dark tunnel, a frightening curve or a course back to the place where it all began.

"I promise, Mike. Swear to God."

"Thanks," Michael whispered. I knew you wouldn't let me down. You know what?"

"No, what?"

"I love the Airborne, man. I mean it's the first time I ever felt like I belonged to somethin'. I mean, it's kinda like the sax. It's parta me now. When you wear that uniform with that eagle on your shoulder, you feel like you can kick anybody's ass, you know. I mean, I figured if I was gonna get drafted anyway, why not go with the best, you know."

Unexpectedly he stood up and ran, climbing and balancing on the top railing of a cement and wooden bench across the way from where the two friends had been sitting. He stood erect and screamed, "I'm a fuckin' Airborne Ranger. I wanna kill some fuckin' Viet Cong."

His words echoed among the barracks-like brown brick and concrete buildings of the project. Chris approached Michael as he was screaming, extending his fist clenched arms above his head like a primitive priest performing a sacrifice. He was proud of Michael, but he couldn't help but feel that he was a small part of a great disaster, a miniature piece in a grotesque puzzle.

As his friend stood on the bench beside him, Chris sat and bent his head over his knees, silently praying that God would take care of Michael. It would be the first of many prayers that he would say for his friend in the months and years ahead.

CHAPTER 18

There was a soft, seductive excitement in her voice, when she agreed over the telephone to meet him outside the Forest Hills Subway Station. She was seated in a shiny, black 1963 Riviera that her father had kept in mint condition, when Christopher saw her from across the street. Their greeting was followed by a long, languorous kiss after Christopher slid into the passenger seat.

The slender beauty of her legs and the sheen of her silky black hair made Chris realize that his memory of their meeting three nights before had not been a dream. Linda Bianco possessed that rare combination of sensuality, and sensitivity that beckoned Chris to delve deeper into her mystique. The effervescent joy that shone from her face told him that she too had spent the night eagerly anticipating their rendezvous.

For a while they talked together, his hand instinctively holding hers, ecstatic to be in each other's company, together alone, without destination or distraction. Suddenly Chris thought of the perfect place for them to spend that crisp, golden October afternoon. "Hey, let's go to the Arboretum."

"Where is that?" Linda asked.

"You've never heard of it? he replied. "It's an unbelievable park. I used to go there all the time as a kid. It's full of trees from all over the world. It's right near here."

She was staring at him as he spoke. Her hazel eyes focused upon his face soaking in his intelligence and enthusiasm. Christopher paused, recognizing that this girl was a very special creature, appearing in his life like some magnificent present. They kissed again. The warmth of her mouth and the way she caressed the back of his head magnetized him. It had been a long time since he had felt this way. It had been a long time since that last night with Lorna in the Public Gardens.

"Do you want me to drive?" he asked, momentarily breaking the spell.

"What?" she whispered, having become lost in the passion of the moment.

"Can I drive?" he requested.

"Oh, yeah, sure," she responded.

As Chris came around to the driver's door, Linda slid across the car's console to the passenger seat. She was wearing a green mini skirt and a black cable knit sweater. Her hair was arranged in a French twist and she wore gold loops in her ears. She smiled and positioned her body as close as possible to him as he drove to their perfectly appropriate destination.

The Emerald Necklace was the name given years before to the chain of public parks that embraced the City of Boston. The Arnold Arboretum was the most magnificent gem in the chain. The October sun had painted its trees and rolling hills with a glorious amber glow, as Christopher and Linda roamed throughout. He was her guide, her teacher.

He spoke to her of California and the filthy rich of Beverly Hills. He reminisced of times when he alone and he in the company of Michael would come to the Arboretum to escape the stark confinement of Bromley Court, a confinement that he was determined to bring to an end. They walked together entwined, sharing dreams and memories, kissed by the crisp, October air that swirled amongst the falling leaves.

Chris told of his last encounter with Michael and how he prayed for his safe return from the hell of Southeast Asia. Linda's father had served in the Marines and had returned home after being wounded in World War II. She was the second of six children. Her father had come to this country from Sicily and had managed to support his family as a stone mason. Her mother was from a large Irish family. She fell in love with her husband and married him, following his return from the hell of war. Her family lived in a quiet Brighton neighborhood light years from Bromley Court. She was studying to be a dental assistant and was looking for a special someone with ambition and a sense of humor. On that day Christopher had made her laugh.

They stayed until sunset, not wanting the day to end. He asked Linda if she wanted to see him again. She told him that she wanted to see him every day. He knew that she meant it, as he kissed her outside of the train station. He would call her the next day.

On the train he sat alone, his thoughts insulating him from the others traveling through their lives. The staccato of the rails rocking him through the subway tunnel seemed to offer him some comfort. There must be a destination, there must exist a plan. He just had to find it. So much had happened, so much had changed. He had left Boston as a child, fleeing from a violent, justifiable act. He had returned, an unfinished work, seeking to stop the dizzying pace of it all, slow it down, break it down. Try to understand. Try to make sense of the unfathomable. Why had he come back? His life was taking shape in LA, a different life, a detached life, apart from family and commitments, away from friends asking for favors.

Linda was a reason. His mother was a reason and Michael made him promise, which he did. "Get out," his brother had said or it will be too late. But he wasn't his brother. He wasn't anybody. He had to find his own way apart, yet together with those he loved. Did he love Linda? He didn't know her. He hadn't seen her angry or disappointed. He hadn't made love to her. Yet somehow she seemed closer to him than all the others. Maybe he let her get close because it was time. Maybe she too would fade like a portrait in the sun. He had to stay awhile and find out where the ride would lead.

His mother was eating alone. Aluminum foil covered a plate across from her on the tiny table in her kitchen. The plate was waiting for him. He noticed such things now. Her eyes reflected her loneliness in that place. Age was coming fast now. He could see it. He could feel that she would never make him stay. She would simply endure it, like she had endured so much without deserving it. Why did he have to care for her? Why care for anyone really? Be an island, a rock. Hurtle through space and time. Be the sun. Get close but not too close. He loved them. That was it. He loved them, even though he knew that he couldn't be free and love them. Love came at a price.

"I want you to talk to Father McConnell," she had implored. "He will have some ideas."

"Ma, I haven't seen him in eight years. What's he gonna tell me? That I gotta come back to church?" he responded, staring at the supper she had covered in aluminum foil.

"He would never do that," she protested. "You don't know him. He's a good man. He was the only one, after your father died. He took care of all of you, without looking for anything."

Christopher knew she was right. He remembered the cold and the snow and Christmas without a tree. And that night when the priest came with a laundry bag full of presents. She was right. He didn't have to do that. So many priests didn't. So many priests were out of touch, pathetic creatures, hiding from who they truly were, or who they didn't want to be.

That night they spoke together of many things. She couldn't work at the laundry much longer. They were getting out and she knew it. The neighborhood had changed. The trucks were being vandalized. She was afraid to leave there in the darkness. There was a chance, another job in Mattapan Square, a real estate company looking for a bookkeeper.

She had been studying for the job late at night since she heard about it, using a high school book of Gregg Shorthand and Basic Bookkeeping, a green textbook checked out from the bookmobile. She was determined to have it change.

He agreed. He would go to see the priest he hadn't seen since he was a boy, the priest who once took him to the ocean with Michael. His ride on that roller coaster was taking a sudden turn now. He would hang on for dear life. Perhaps later, he would be able to jump off, before it was too late.

A large Irish woman with a thick brogue and thicker biceps showed him into a small room with an overstuffed chair, a small table and a rocking chair filling it thoroughly. Chris was directed to sit down in the green overstuffed chair. The priest arrived momentarily.

"Well, well, Christopher Conley all grown up and looking like a refugee from a California beach. How in the hell are you?"

"Fine, Father, how are you?"

"Well, I'm a day older than I was yesterday and just barely ahead of the creditors."

Christopher smiled as he reacquainted himself with the priest's appearance. He looked more like an aging middle weight than a man of the cloth. His black hair was like coiled wire and he possessed the forearms of a longshoreman.

"Your mother is well?"

"Yes, Father. She was the one that suggested I come to see you."

"Why didn't you want to come on your own?"

Chris hesitated before responding, not wanting to start their meeting off by lying to him. "No, I didn't want to come at first, but then things happened that made it seem like the right thing to do, Father, you know?"

"Sure, I know," said the priest, as he reached into a near-empty package of Lucky Strikes, retrieving the last cigarette and placing it in his mouth. "You know, you have a great mother. The things she did for you kids after your father died were remarkable. You owe it to her to become a success."

"I know, Father, that's why I'm here."

"Tell me that other business over on Parker Hill. That's all taken care of?"

He was shocked that the priest knew of the shooting that had made him leave Boston. He didn't know how to respond. The priest interjected before he could speak. "Of course, your mother came to see me afterwards. Didn't she tell you?"

"No, she didn't."

"Of course she didn't," the priest remarked, taking a long drag of his cigarette; then pausing to exhale before he continued. "Sometimes things happen for a reason, you know. Maybe you weren't supposed to hang around the projects for the last two years. I'm sure you've learned plenty out with your brother, Jack. Is he still a ladies' man?"

"Yeah, he does alright."

"How about you? Do you have a steady girl?"

Christopher thought for a moment about Linda and answered the priest as honestly as he could. "I'd like to Father. I met this girl the other night and she's unbelievable. She's somebody I could be steady with."

"So she's got that special something, huh Chris. Well, I hope it's more than just desire. I hope that your thoughts are about love for this girl."

Christopher listened but didn't respond. He didn't feel comfortable talking about his feelings for Linda. He hadn't quite sorted them all out yet and he hoped that the priest would change the subject. To his relief, he did.

"Let's see, your older brother, Tom, he's down at Georgetown Medical School. He was always so bright. Do you want to follow in his footsteps?"

He had never really thought about imitating his oldest brother's success. They were so very different. Tom was the perfect student, the first born boy who had been robbed of his childhood when his father died. In a way, Chris resented him trying to play the part of his older brother and his father. It wasn't fair to either of them. But fairness, he had learned, had nothing to do with it.

He knew that his brother Jack had rebelled at any thought of following in his older brother's footsteps. Chris was not intent on rebelling, but he didn't want to follow either. "I don't know father. I don't think I wanna be a doctor. I'm not real good at science you know."

"What are you good at, Chris?" Father McConnell asked, focusing upon him from across the small table. "What would you like to do?"

"I like to read about famous people. I like history. I like finding out how things work, how things get done."

"Like what things, Chris?"

Chris pondered the question for a moment. He could tell that the priest was trying to find out what made him tick. "I was working for this guy in LA and he was a millionaire business man. I used to see him talk to people about deals he was putting together and how he got them to do what he wanted. He was a master, Father, I mean it."

The priest focused on him with his right hand, touching his bottom lip. Christopher could see that he was concentrating. He seemed to be trying to decide something. "Have you ever thought about going to law school?"

"Law school! No, Father, I haven't."

"Well, it's something to think about then. I have this friend named Dan Featherstone, he's a criminal lawyer. Would you go to see him, if I arranged a meeting?"

Christopher paused, weighing the priest's proposal. He didn't think much of lawyers. He remembered the ones he had seen hanging around the juvenile court, when he and Michael got in trouble. They were bald men in glasses and cheap suits. In Los Angeles they were slick and slippery creatures that Tom Conroy attempted to avoid. Christopher was confronted by the priest's piercing stare.

"You know, they're not all shysters, Christopher," he remarked, seeming to read his mind.

"Sure, Father, why not?" he replied. "I might learn something."

"I'm sure you will, if I know Dan Featherstone. I'm sure you will," he said, standing up to signal the end of their meeting. "Please give your mother my regards."

"I will, Father. Thanks a lot."

CHAPTER 19

The turn of the century elevator rattled its way to the sixth floor of the office building at 83 Tremont Street. Christopher examined his recent haircut and blue corduroy suit in the distorted reflection of the elevator's doors. He thought he looked presentable for his first meeting with a lawyer.

Daniel Featherstone was once the most prominent criminal lawyer in Boston, before the death of his oldest son and a messy divorce drove him to distraction and absent-minded reminiscence of times lost. On occasion he would exhibit the old brilliance that made him a fortune defending crooked politicians, near-do-well Brahmins and even two of the Brinks holdup men. His was the misfortune of becoming a legend and then living long enough to become the legend's shadow.

Christopher fidgeted in one of the faded red leather chairs in the attorney's waiting room. Across from him, on a faded red leather couch, sat a young black boy and his worried mother. The smudged glass of the coffee table in front of him was strewn with outdated magazines whose covers screamed of America's preoccupation with Vietnam.

Christopher's eyes focused on a *Newsweek* that dealt with the Tet Offensive, an event that had badly shaken the faith of the American people in the conduct of the war and sent millions into the streets to demonstrate and to protest. Christopher thought of Michael standing on the bench in the projects, his voice echoing his pride at serving in the Airborne. He longed to hear Michael's voice again.

As he watched the black woman and her son being ushered into the inner office by the attorney's white-haired secretary, two bikers wearing studded motorcycle jackets, emblazoned with the insignias of the Devil's Disciples arrived. To Christopher's surprise they were polite and quiet, subdued perhaps by the predicament that brought them there.

He sat across from them, his eyes consciously averted to the magazines' pictures of death and misery in Southeast Asia. Soon after their arrival, a plain, young woman with brown hair tied in a bun and tortoise shell glasses, entered the waiting room from the attorney's office and introduced herself to the bikers as Mr. Featherstone's assistant.

Opening the mahogany door, she allowed them to enter into the inner sanctum where their cases would be discussed and prepared. There was a faint odor of perspiration that remained, after they left Christopher alone in the waiting room.

After a while, the white-haired secretary reappeared, accompanied by the black woman, who had been crying, and her son, who looked terrified as they left the office. Christopher surmised that whatever occurred behind closed doors had caused them terrible pain.

He felt like a sinner, waiting to confess to a priest of unknown disposition. Suddenly, the door opened and a small man with an unusually large head and unruly white hair confronted him where he sat. Before Christopher could stand up, the attorney reached for his hand, grasping only three of his fingers and introduced himself perfunctorily.

"Hi, I'm Dan Featherstone. Come on in for a minute."

Christopher received the initial impression that he was an imposition and as soon as he was shown into the spacious, sumptuous office of the attorney, he spoke.

"I'm real sorry I'm taking up your time. I can come back when you're not so busy, if it's okay."

The attorney sat down and lit a large cigar, then placed it in an orange glass ashtray that seemed enormous like everything else in the office. The attorney removed his thick horn-rimmed glasses and rubbed his eyes with both hands. He looked weary with steamer trunk bags under his eyes. Christopher guessed that he was in his mid-sixties and life had not been kind to him. He bellowed from across the expanse of the office for his secretary, "Martha, hold my calls, will you? I don't want Father McConnell saying I didn't give this kid the time of day."

Christopher sat there uncomfortably, not knowing whether to speak, to smile or to escape from the predicament he had been placed in by his mother and Father McConnell.

"If I don't have time to talk to young people like you, then I have my priorities in disarray," the old lawyer confided disarmingly. "I understand from my good friend that you're wondering about the law as a profession. Well, let me tell you, it can be a noble profession or it can be a license to steal. It just depends on your approach."

Christopher nodded in response to the old man's words, yet failed to grasp their significance. The old man scrutinized him and continued with his monologue.

"If you're looking for an easy way of life, don't even think about becoming a lawyer. Get into something else. If you're looking for a job that you can leave at the office, don't become a lawyer. Get into something else. But if you're looking for an opportunity to test yourself, your courage, your intelligence, and your concern for others, then becoming a lawyer is a way of doing that."

The old man stood up and crossed the office toward a credenza, removing a green leather-bound scrapbook from its top drawer. He approached Christopher and handed him the scrapbook. "Take a look at this kid," he said, "it's my life story in pictures. Maybe I'll write a book someday."

He left Christopher in the office with a giant cigar sending smoke signals from the ashtray. Chris perused the scrapbook that contained yellowed newspaper articles tracing Daniel Featherstone's career as a young Assistant District Attorney in the Thirties, prosecuting the landlord of a rooming house where twenty young women were burned to death. Then he was a young defense attorney representing a boy charged with killing his father, claiming self-defense. He was the focus of an article profiling the attorneys representing the Brinks holdup men, describing him as a genius in cross-examination. Christopher read through the scrapbook eagerly. He loved the history of it. He imagined the adventure and the personalities that this man must have encountered. He became thankful that Father McConnell had arranged this meeting with his old friend. The door opened and Attorney Featherstone returned.

"Well, kid, that's my sad story. Are you impressed?"

"Yes, sir," Chris answered sincerely.

"Well, don't be. I use that book to convince clients before I talk to them about my fee. Remember, people come to you because of your reputation and a book like that says a lot more than I have to. It's a lure, a lure to get and keep people coming through that door. Because, if they stop coming, you starve, pure and simple."

The "no bullshit" approach of the old man somehow made him feel grateful. He liked the fact that he didn't take himself too seriously. It was the same trait that he observed in Tom Conroy, while serving as his chauffeur. Maybe it was a trait of success, success without pretension. The old man took a long drag from his cigar and directed smoke rings toward the ceiling. He shot a look at Christopher and offered him an opportunity.

"You know, kid, in this business you're only as good as your last trial. I'm starting one tomorrow up in Suffolk Superior Court. If you have a chance, come on up. I'm in Room 806 before Judge McGuire. I'll be cross-examining the best liar on the Boston Police force. It should be quite a show."

Chris left the attorney's office and entered the evening darkness of the crowded sidewalk. As he made his way toward Park Street Station, he was intrigued at the idea of becoming a lawyer. As he approached the entrance to the subway, he stopped to buy a newspaper. It was November 7, 1969 and the headline story spoke of a major American offensive in the Central Highlands of Vietnam, an offensive that involved elements of the 101st Airborne Division.

All the way home on the trolley, Christopher thought again of Michael, standing on the bench screaming that he was an Airborne Ranger and that he wanted to kill some Viet Cong. Somehow, Christopher could feel that Michael was getting a bellyful of killing by then.

He prayed that he would be safe and reminded himself to call Michael's mother and see if she needed anything. After all, he had promised Michael that he would watch out for her and his little brother. A promise to a best friend was a promise he would keep.

CHAPTER 20

Fire Base Bastogne was a red dot on the map between Hill 461 and 463 in the South Central Highlands. It had taken Command three weeks to explode and bulldoze the wet, green hostility of a jungle mountainside into submission, so that Delta Company 357th Battalion of the 101st Airborne Division could set up an outpost to listen and await the approach of an unseen enemy, an enemy that thought of the jungle as its home.

Michael was a "fuckin' new guy" who hadn't slept more than two hours at any one time since he arrived "in country". In the lifetime that was his first month in Vietnam, he had endured three mortar attacks, two ambushes and a series of booby traps. While on search and destroy missions, boys he had known since boot camp had been killed and maimed. What he hadn't seen was a live Viet Cong or North Vietnamese regular. Now he and Delta Company were about to be the bait to lure an entire battalion of North Vietnamese from the jungle that concealed and protected them. Fear and diarrhea never left him.

The rain was relentless, causing the ground to erupt into a quagmire of oozing, stinking filth. The canopy of thick, grey monsoon clouds discouraged supply, evacuation and air support, but it encouraged the enemy to strike, to continue the war of nerves and attrition they had begun to win at Tet. The will of the enemy and his resolve to outlast the American presence was becoming evident.

Two days after Fire Base Bastogne was inhabited, it became a target for the enemy. Michael had spent almost every waking moment filling sandbags, cleaning his weapon and inspecting the perimeter for the appearance of "dinks". He seemed always to be burrowing deeper into the underground bunker where he and eleven other rangers sought shelter from the rocketing. They were like vermin concealing themselves from an exterminator. The battle, Michael's first, began on the night of the third day.

The claymores they had buried around the outside perimeter of concertina wire exploded suddenly, one after another. The agonized foreign cries that followed provoked terror-filled warnings of "Dinks in the wire! Dinks in the wire!" Short bursts of automatic weapons, M16's, M60's and AK47's reverberated in the oppressive, damp darkness. Mortar shells landed; lives and futures lost. Profanity and prayer mingled in the mud and blood of the attack.

Michael bolted from his bunker, wearing his steel pot and flak jacket. The ink black darkness was punctuated by the hot white light of tracers and the orange and red of mortar shells, scorching their way on and into groups of American boys, hiding underground. Their screams made him sick, terrified with a rage to kill something, anything in return. He would get his chance.

There were three of them, small and quick, running from his left and carrying a grenade launcher and automatic weapons. He concealed himself behind a rise in the terrain. It was covered by sandbags. He opened up on them; his weapon an extension of his rage. It spewed death. It splattered their brains and flesh into the air and from there into the mud.

The concussion of the mortar round lifted him into the air and propelled him sideways next to another bunker. There stood Miller. The angry Southern Sergeant was screaming at him, "McLean, you hit! You fuckin' hit, man!"

Michael rose from the mud and vomited on himself. There was blood trickling from his right ear, yet he didn't seem to be wounded. "Where's my weapon, where's my weapon?" he cried.

"We gotta set up a perimeter or we gonna get overrun. Dinks are fuckin' all over," Miller shouted, gathering three other rangers near him. They ran to the center of the firebase as one. Michael followed them, naked without a weapon.

Miller took command. He was twenty-two, a hard-ass regular army type from Arkansas. "Where the fuck is your weapon, McLean?" The rage of the Sergeant stunned him as much as the mortar round. Michael shook his head. "Here, take these fuckin' grenades and throw them right down their fuckin' throats when they come. You got it man?"

Michael nodded his head, indicating that he knew what was expected of him. In the meantime, more rangers had taken up position near the center of the firebase. They had formed two concentric circles on the crest of a small rise. Michael and ten others made up the inner circle with Miller directing fire. The outer circle had about twenty-five rangers spread out raggedly below them. Delgado, the crazy Mexican from San Antonio, had taken charge of this group. Michael could see that he had been wounded in the neck from the blotch of blood that oozed through the medic's tourniquet.

The shrill whistles of the enemy began the second phase of their attack. Michael could see pockets of rangers illuminated by a series of flares, fighting fiercely in the dismal darkness. Their shouts of derision for the enemy and encouragement to each other gave Michael and the other rangers in the two circles adrenalin-filled inspiration. They began to scream for the enemy to come. They were ready to kill or be killed at that moment.

The enemy came from two directions, North and West. They were well organized, courageous and disciplined. They were uniformed North Vietnamese Regulars. Michael saw approximately fifty of them deploying to his right. He could see that they were moving up to direct their mortar fire on the crest of the hill. He called to Miller, "They're settin' up to lob that shit right on top of us!"

Miller was busy directing fire toward another concentration of approximately two hundred enemy headed straight at them and did not see the danger on his right flank. He made no reply.

At that moment, Michael screamed to the rangers on either side and below him to direct their fire toward the mortar teams on their right. They too recognized the danger of a well-placed mortar round in the congregation of troops on the crest of the hill.

At least eight M16's sprayed the area where the mortar teams were setting up, killing several of their number. More enemy moved up to take their place. Their whistles were shrieking in the night. Now their shriek was accompanied by the terrible, agonizing wail of the wounded and dying on both sides. Despite the frantic focus of Ranger fire, the mortar teams continued to make progress toward a strategic flanking position, where they could deliver death to the Americans.

Michael and three others, Ferrioli, Franklin and Thomas, maneuvered across from the crest toward the mortar teams. The air was thick with lead and shrapnel. It smelled of cordite and death. Along the way, Michael retrieved an AK47 from an enemy soldier whose face and head had been blown to bits. His blood and brain tissue were rubbed from Michael's hands on to his flak jacket, so that he could manipulate the trigger. The sweet, sickening smell of the man lingered on the weapon, like a badge of death.

Suddenly, Michael saw a burst of a weapon from his left and felt Thomas's body career against him in its last moments of life. A second burst ripped through Ferrioli's legs, leaving him paralyzed and screaming for a medic in the thick blackness of the jungle mud. Michael and Franklin, the black gang member from the Cabrini Projects in Chicago, who hated white people and warfare, moved together toward the mortar teams. The enemy was receiving cover fire from the rear, as were Michael and Franklin.

At that moment, Franklin's left thigh was ripped open by a round and another passed through his right wrist. He belly flopped into the mud, managing to slide down a small embankment leading to a bunker. Michael slid behind him almost immediately.

"You hit Franklin?" Michael screamed.

"Yeah, man," Franklin groaned.

"How bad is it?"

"I got it in the leg. I can't feel my fuckin' hand."

Michael pulled Franklin's heavy body down the muddy embankment into the entrance of the bunker. Inside, all of the Rangers were dead, killed by a direct hit at the beginning of the battle. He tore off his flak jacket and t-shirt and swung the t-shirt into a crude tourniquet that he wrapped above the wound on Franklin's thigh. Bare-chested, he positioned himself at the top of the embankment and opened fire on the enemy who had just begun to direct their mortar fire toward the rangers encircled on the hill. His aim was deadly as he fired Franklin's M16. He emptied three clips into the determined enemy, before they began to fall back.

As they retreated, he and Franklin threw their grenades over the heads of the fleeing enemy, causing them to explode in their faces. At least twenty North Vietnamese corpses would be counted in the carnage that marked their retreat.

As dawn arrived, so did a break in the rainy weather. Michael wandered, surveying the surreal landscape of the battlefield. Many were dead and dying on both sides. There was no victory for either. He watched as Franklin and the others were finally evacuated by chopper from the firebase. He then slept a long, exhausted yet tormented sleep. That morning began his thirty-third day in Vietnam.

CHAPTER 21

uffolk Superior Court was the big show for criminal lawyers in Boston. It was the locus of famous trials for infamous cases. Daniel Featherstone had performed there brilliantly over the years, oftentimes with the cavernous courtrooms crowded with spectators. As he emerged from the always overcrowded elevator into the dimly lit corridor, where the family and friends of victims congregated in small groups, juxtaposed to the family and friends of the accused, he took a deep nervous breath.

That morning he was paid to defend an eighteen year-old boy from Charlestown accused with three other boys of conspiring to rob the Union Warren Savings Bank on Washington Street in downtown Boston. The evidence was mostly circumstantial; a money band discovered wedged in the rear seat of a seized automobile, two ski masks, a Smith & Wesson revolver obtained in a search of a suspect's apartment, a palm print on a getaway car's rear window and a confession allegedly obtained from Daniel Featherstone's client, implicating all the other boys in the armed robbery.

That confession had been obtained, according to the police reports, by Kenneth Hayes, a ruthless, ambitious, intelligent Sergeant, hurtling on a fast track up through the ranks.

Featherstone's client had come to the office with his father and the family's life savings. Their hope and the boy's fate rested in the old lawyer's hands like a tiny bird, capable of being crushed or set free, as he saw fit.

His face looked weary, as he made his opening to a jury of nervous, curious human beings who had been sifted and selected by the lawyers and deemed by the judge to be suitable peers for the trial of the four defendants.

The boys had denied their involvement in the crime but had not persuaded any of the lawyers representing them that they were innocent. All of them, however, were convinced that the confession was a fabrication to close the chain forged by circumstantial evidence around the necks of the accused. The credibility of Kenneth Hayes had to be destroyed in order for the boys to have a chance at being acquitted.

The Commonwealth was represented by Martin Reynolds, a graduate of Harvard Law School and the son of Judge Tom Reynolds, the recently retired Justice of the First Circuit Court of Appeals. He had graduated near the top of his class and had skied in the Alps every year since his twelfth birthday. He possessed the antiseptic good looks and pedigree necessary to dwell in the upper echelons of the Massachusetts' affluent.

Chris had skipped his afternoon class at UMass Boston, where he recently had been accepted into his junior year, in order to attend the trial to which he had been invited. The sights and sounds of the downtown courthouse, its magnitude and the vibrant variety of humanity that played out real life dramas on every floor, thrilled him.

He entered Room 806 and responded negatively to the court officer who immediately approached and asked if he were a witness. He sat in the mahogany pew in the back of the courtroom, just as Attorney Featherstone approached the key witness, a stocky cop in his early thirties with receding brown hair and the face of a South Boston boxer.

The old lawyer stood directly in front of the jury and fired questions at the witness like bursts from an automatic weapon.

"Officer Hayes, this is an extremely important case for you, isn't it?"

"Yes, sir."

"You received a commendation for your work on this case, didn't you?"

"Yes, sir."

"And a commendation can help your career, isn't that true?"

"I guess so, sir."

"You guess, Officer? There was no guesswork in this, was there Officer?"

"I don't know what you mean, sir."

"You knew that the Union Warren Savings Bank had been robbed on April 13, 1969, isn't that true?"

"Yes, I became aware of that."

"And you knew it was a front-page story, didn't you?"

"No sir."

"Well, you did read about the hold up in the newspapers, didn't you?"

"I don't recall if I did, sir."

"In any event, you were aware that an armed bank robbery in broad daylight in Boston was a noteworthy event."

"I heard about it in the cruiser while on patrol with Officer Dunn."

"And it was shortly afterwards that you observed my client, Mr. Shea, crossing Charles Street in the Back Bay?"

"Yes, sir, I did."

"And you knew Mr. Shea from before, didn't you?"

"Yes, sir, I had arrested him in the past."

"Yes, Officer, you had indeed arrested my client before, hadn't you? But it wasn't for bank robbery, was it?"

"No, it wasn't."

"In fact, you had arrested him for disorderly person and assault and battery on a police officer."

"I really don't recall the exact charges. I have arrested a number of people in thirteen years, Counselor."

"But Officer, you arrested my client for an assault and battery on you, didn't you?"

"Yes, sir, I believe I did."

"And it would be fair to say that there's not a good deal of warm feelings between you and him."

"You would have to ask him that, Counselor."

The old lawyer hesitated, cleared his throat and took a drink from a small Dixie cup that he had filled from a stainless steel pitcher situated on the table in front of his chair. He returned to his position in front of the jury box. The jurors' eyes were riveted on his movements. They seemed to be waiting on every word that he spoke.

"You told the prosecutor that Mr. Shea seemed nervous when you pulled up in front of him."

"Yes, sir, he was extremely nervous."

"Well, the last time that you had seen him before that, you had threatened to cripple him, hadn't you?"

"Objection!" the blonde-haired man sitting at the table in front of the old attorney shouted. Christopher surmised that this man must be the lawyer for the other side. He looked athletic and rich. He wore small steel-rimmed glasses and was staring at the jury when the judge stated, "I'll allow it. Continue Mr. Featherstone."

"Thank you very much, Your Honor. You had threatened Mr. Shea before this date, hadn't you Officer?"

"No, sir, I did not."

"You never told my client that if you had a chance you'd cripple him, Officer?"

"Absolutely not, sir."

"You say, Officer, that you stopped my client as he was crossing Charles Street?"

"Yes sir, running across Charles Street."

"Now, he wasn't really running, was he Officer?"

"He most definitely was running, Counselor."

"And you testified that you wanted to talk to him?"

"Yes, sir, I did."

"You had no cause to arrest him at that time, did you Officer?"

"No sir. I was checking him out to see where he had been during the bank robbery."

"In fact, Officer Hayes, without warning you threw him bodily across your patrol car and hand cuffed him."

"No, sir, I did not."

"And you placed your night stick against his testicles and told him that you were gonna make a bitch out of him."

"Objection!" The blond lawyer shouted again. At this time, Christopher watched as the two lawyers, along with a woman with a machine in her hand, came close to the Judge on the other side of the courtroom, away from the jury. Christopher noticed that Mr. Featherstone glanced in his direction and that his face appeared flushed and sweaty. The judge talked to the lawyers and then Featherstone thanked him. He returned to his position in front of the jury.

"Officer, you placed your nightstick against his testicles as he lay on the hood of your cruiser and threatened to emasculate him, isn't that true?"

"Absolutely not, Counselor."

"Then you forced him into the rear of your cruiser and threatened his life, isn't that true?"

"No, sir."

"Your testimony is that as you drove around, he suddenly said that he had nothing to do with the bank robbery?"

"Yes, sir. He brought it up right after he agreed to take a ride with us."

"And you want this jury to believe that without the slightest bit of coercion he decided to confess his guilt to this crime, despite the fact that moments before he had insisted he was completely innocent and knew nothing whatsoever about it?"

"That's just what happened, Counselor."

"Didn't you pull on to a side street, remove your service revolver and place it against his forehead with the hammer cocked?"

"I did not."

"You knew that you had no hard evidence against Mr. Shea, so you decided to fabricate this confession. Isn't that true, Sergeant Hayes?"

"I would never do that," the officer replied indignantly.

Christopher watched as the old attorney questioned the cop about every detail of the statement. Searching, hammering, always with a tone that told the jury that the witness was lying. Christopher marveled at the skill that the old man possessed, but he also could see that the cop was very smart, very cool under questioning.

It was a middleweight brawl and if anything, it looked like a split decision by the time the lawyers were through. Chris wondered if he had the makings of a lawyer who went to court and represented people in trouble. He looked at the four anxious faces of the boys, sitting beyond the mahogany rail, accused of robbing a bank at gunpoint. One of them reminded him of Michael. It was at that moment that he recalled the thunder of the gun and the blood of a screaming black man, spurting from wounds and drenching the cobblestones on Parker Hill.

He left the courthouse and sat by himself for almost an hour in the Boston Common. As the sun descended behind the buildings of Boston's Back Bay and the winter wind whipped through the fabric of his corduroy suit, he became convinced that he could become a trial lawyer, a trial lawyer who could defend people like those boys, boys like him and Michael McLean.

CHAPTER 22

*H*is sojourn in hell had lasted seven months when he received his orders. Ten days in Sydney, Australia, for rest and relaxation would keep the patient's soul from dying. Survival had required him to kill without caring, to observe without feeling and to encase himself in a primitive armor supported by the surreal, sadistic technology of corporate America.

In Sydney he would escape, but he would not forget, for this was merely an intermission in an unspeakably, horrid play of death and devastation. Michael had just turned twenty before he left Quang Tri Province for Australia.

The bar's name didn't matter, it was full of American boys wanting to spend money on Aussie girls willing to take a chance, try anything once. Some came from nowhere, sand-filled shacks bordering on the outback, bristling with boredom and frustration. Others worked at it, knowing that the opportunity for escape and adventure simply wouldn't last. A frenzy was brought on by war and a murky understanding that youth and life were passing faster than any of them wanted.

While he sat in the corner with Mayhew, he couldn't take his eyes from her. She was dancing close to a Marine Corps grunt who had been pawing her since she arrived. She didn't like it, but she didn't resist it either.

Michael's first move toward her was after the grunt went to the head. She greeted him, and accompanied him from the dance floor, down a dark hallway. It was not profound or romantic. It was just convenient and acceptable. Michael had been drinking Johnny Walker and water since seven that morning. Now it was time to smoke the rest of the joint in his pocket and try to take this girl to bed.

She was wearing a pair of tight-fitting shorts and platform shoes. Her hair was blonde from a bottle, but her body was the genuine article. Michael could see the contours of her firm breasts under her white cowboy shirt. She wasn't wearing a bra and she nuzzled against him as he ignited the joint. She shared it with him, taking a long drag to enhance the weed's impact.

Michael draped his arm over her shoulder and she slithered her hand behind his back, inserting her fingers into the loop of his jeans.

"What do you say we split this place and get a room somewhere?" Michael whispered; the alcohol and marijuana removing all inhibitions and pretense.

"Not so fast, sweetie," she replied, with an infectious Aussie accent, "I'm not in the habit of jumping into bed with someone I don't know. Besides, all you Yanks want is to get laid. We're not all tarts, you know."

"Yeah," Michael said, "I wanna get laid, but I just wanna be close to someone even more. I wanna wake up next to someone who knows that this fuckin' life is too fuckin' short and wants to make the most of it."

She looked at him with caring eyes, seeming to feel his pain. For a moment she seemed to share his despair, his need to say fuck it to anything and everything. Then she changed; she became deliberate and tried to manipulate wherever she could.

"Tell you what, luv. Let's have a drink and dance and then we'll see what happens. We've got all night to screw each other. Let's see if we like each other first, eh?"

Michael leaned back against the wall of the darkened hallway leading from the barroom to the back door. He smiled at her and pulled her close to him.

"Fair enough, mate," he said, "let's take it slow. Shit, I got nine more days."

At that time they caressed, while Michael kissed her on the right side of her neck. She responded momentarily, then pulled him down the hallway back toward the developing delirium of the bar's dance floor. An Aussie band was making a fair attempt at James Brown. They were loud enough and had enough horns. What they lacked was a sax player who could become one with American R&B. Michael and the girl swayed then grinded to the music.

"What's your name, luv?" she asked.

"Mike. What's yours?" he said.

"Sylvia."

"Hey Sylvia, what do you think of Americans?"

"I told you, all they want is to get laid," she replied jokingly.

"I tell you what. I wanna get laid a lot more than I wanna go back to that fuckin' jungle!"

"I don't blame you, luv. I don't blame you one bit."

It was then that she drew close to him and reached her arms around his neck and kissed him deeply. Her tongue was warm and wet as it darted back and forth in Michael's mouth.

Suddenly from the corner of his left eye, Michael saw the approach of someone moving quickly. He jerked his head away as the fist of the grunt flashed by his face, striking the girl a glancing blow to the side of her head. She crumpled to the floor, as Michael kicked their attacker squarely in the stomach with his right boot. He doubled up and presented an inviting target to both of Michael's fists. As Michael pummeled him, he was pulled away by the enormous forearms of Mayhew.

"Cool out, man, cool out," Mayhew cried, "You want to spend your fuckin' R&R in an Aussie jail!"

A group of GI's grappled with the battered grunt, pulling him to his feet and shoving him down the dark hallway and out into the humid night that enveloped Sydney. Michael then approached Sylvia as she sat near the bar with ice wrapped in a towel held to her right forehead. She was sobbing softly as he stood next to her and touched the hand resting on her lap.

"I'm so sorry, Sylvia," Michael said, "Are you all right?"

She glanced at him, the tears brimming from her dark blue eyes. "I've had worse, luv. It will be all right."

"What can I do for you?" he asked, commencing to stroke her head. The band, which had stopped playing during the fight, began again. This time they were playing "When a Man Loves a Woman" and still their sax player lacked fire, lacked the requisite soul.

Michael looked at Mayhew now standing beside him. The giant of a man from Tennessee had about the same time "in country" as Michael, but this was his second tour. He had been a Sergeant twice and lost his stripes both times. He hated "dinks" and officers, but he loved his wife and two boys. The pictures that he showed Michael revealed that the massive neck and red hair of their father would be passed on to both of his children.

"Hey, Mayhew," Michael shouted, above the blaring band.

"What?"

"Their sax player sucks, man. I can play that riff in my sleep."

"You play the sax, McLean?"

"Shit, yeah man. I played sax in a band in Boston for almost three years."

"Well fuckin' eh, then let's hear you son."

At that moment Mayhew began to scream like a master of ceremonies, trying to quiet a crowd at a banquet. "Ladies and gentlemen. Ladies and gentlemen! Could I please have your attention, please? I have an announcement and a request."

Slowly the band and the crowd grew quiet. "Thank you. Tonight we want to bring a little touch of the States to y'all. My friend here, who just came to the aid of this here beautiful Australian girl, would like the opportunity to play the sax in this here song. Now considering he's been in the bush for seven months and the "dinks" ain't killed him yet, I was wondering if y'all would give my buddy, Mclean, a chance to play here tonight. How 'bout it? Something for us Airborne boys. What do you say?"

The crowd erupted, causing the bar manager, a man in his fifties with strands of slicked back hair and a tan, wrinkled leisure suit, to ascend the three steps to the stage and talk with the tall, thin, blonde drummer of the band. The manager then approached the microphone and beckoned Michael to come on stage. He didn't hesitate.

Michael hadn't played the saxophone in almost a year. The band started again with "When a Man Loves a Woman," as Michael warmed to his opportunity, blowing the sax from the depths of his soul, embracing the crowd, wishing away the pain of the ones who had killed, the ones who would die, and the ones who likewise knew that this life is too fuckin' short.

CHAPTER 23

The summers of six years had come and gone. Lives and presidents had changed and the country with it. Christopher had married Linda the year before he graduated from Boston University Law School and their little girl was almost a year old. Money and prestige had beckoned him through offers from New York and Philadelphia law firms, but he had followed the advice of Dan Featherstone and accepted a position with the Public Defenders Officer for half the pay.

There in the criminal courts of Boston, he received a crash course in client relations, cross examination and the commitment necessary for becoming a trial lawyer.

His mother had finally escaped from the confinement of Bromley Court. The sweat of the laundry and bolted doors had been exchanged for a book-keeping position and the ability to sit on the tiny porch of her apartment house after supper, and converse with her neighbors. Joy and contentment were no longer futile aspirations. They were companions that came to visit her frequently, along with her children and grandchildren.

Michael had returned to the world from Vietnam, decorated for valor, yet disillusioned by what he had witnessed. He made no effort to contact Chris following his return. He spent his nights alone and his days without direction.

For a while, he was a regular at the VFW Post in Dorchester, cheap drinks and shared experience, twisting him toward the rim of oblivion.

For a while, he sought renewed solace in the tarnished saxophone that was stuffed in its black case in the back of his closet. Like the boy that he had been, he would climb to the top of another set of stairs and unlock the door to another roof. Standing alone, he would send his sorrow across the city's darkness. He would find no solace there. Even the sax had lost its magic.

Horrid dreams were sinking him deeper into the mud and blood of his memory. Months passed before he would return Christopher's repeated phone calls and respond to his avoided visits. He searched within himself, but found no answers. Why had it been so? Why had he been called upon to witness the horror of savage deaths and experience the depths of a bottomless despair? The lack of answers led him to breakfasts of vodka and amphetamines.

It was more than a year before he could hold a job. His father had died, and his mother had become despondent over the course that her life had taken. His brother had become a petty thief, running with a crowd that didn't listen and didn't care. Before it came apart at the seams, he married Peggy, his on again, off again girlfriend. Of course he only did so, after she became pregnant.

Eventually he took a job as an orderly at the Boston City Hospital. The low pay and lower profile afforded him a constant opportunity to escape and hide, sleepwalking in a pungent cloud imported from the high altitudes of Columbia. Eventually his third floor apartment in the South End of Boston began to strangle them. Perpetual combatants, their love for their son chained them together.

Necessity was his wake-up call. The time came to place the nightmares on a shelf. He had the responsibility. He had to take the weight. Back to reality, he roared, fearful of stopping and allowing his demons to overtake him.

As a decorated veteran trained in the art of killing, he was qualified to slide into the abyss or crawl out of it wearing a badge. He became a State Police cadet enduring the pettiness and the training necessary to make the grade. As a trooper patrolling the highways alone, he would approach vehicles filled with dark human forms on isolated stretches of dark highway. Any one of them could do it. End his life; seal the envelope, bringing an end to his pain.

There were times when he welcomed the solace that his sudden death would bring. There was a twisted adrenalin-soaked rush to it. For fleeting moments the intensity of combat was almost within reach. Living on the edge began to suit him. It became the only place he could reside with his torment.

His superiors began to notice him. Reports of his courage and his cunning preceded him. Before long his instincts for the street and his ease in the company of criminals catapulted him into the detective division of the Norfolk District Attorney's Office.

The job was the cure for a while. He could hide there like the gun nestled under his armpit. It was a masquerade for survival. But late at night, alone, after the lights had been turned off, so far away from his wife and child, sleeping in the next room, he wrestled in the darkness with the darkness in his soul.

Their meeting was happenstance, brought about by the demands of their professions. Christopher had been appointed to represent a small, frail ferret of a man who had used his genius and 43 aliases to outwit the airlines of America, swindling them out of millions through forged plane tickets. It had taken them four years to catch up to him. Christopher was his lawyer because of claimed indigence and feigned insanity.

As he climbed the shining white marble stairway that twisted its way to the second floor of the Norfolk County Superior Courthouse, Christopher failed to notice the congregation of unusually large uniformed state troopers that were filing into the room adjacent to the prisoner's lockup. A coiled spring, a cocked weapon, prepared to shoot forth and punish those who dared to mock the court and the system they had sworn to protect. Christopher would be a witness and Michael a participant in the lawful exercise of authority over prisoners on trial for a prison insurrection.

Christopher had been summoned the afternoon before to come to the courthouse, prepared to argue pre-trial motions and impanel a jury in Courtroom Six. Michael had been ordered by his superiors to coordinate the 12 member tactical squad of the State Police and unleash them if necessary upon the five inmates on trial in Courtroom Three for inciting a riot at the Walpole State Prison, eight months before.

It was not a coincidence that the five were black. Their leader was an athletic, handsome, psychotic who had served with the Green Berets in Vietnam. He had also been sentenced to three consecutive 45 to 60 year bids for the rape and mutilation of a 19 year-old girl.

"Did you hear what happened yesterday?" the swollen grey probation officer asked Christopher, as he sat perusing his client's yellow sheet prior to trial.

"No, what?" Christopher replied, while reviewing the progression of criminal offenses that brought him to that courthouse to represent a particularly mysterious little sociopath.

"Gabriel Martin, you ever heard of him?" the probation officer asked.

"No," Christopher responded, sensing that his preoccupation with his client's rap sheet would have to wait until the chain smoking middle-aged man had his say. Christopher put the yellow sheet on the desk and focused on the information he was being provided.

"Fucking Gabriel Martin was an all scholastic football and baseball player up in Lynn. He had offers from the pros and about ten colleges. Well, instead he enlists and goes to Vietnam. Well, he gets all fucked up over there and comes home. One night he pulls into a rest area where these two young kids are parking. He beats the fuck out of the guy, putting him in the hospital, then takes the girl into the woods and rapes and tortures her. Then he fucking tells her his name. McCormack sentenced him to serve ninety years."

Christopher sat transfixed by the story, wondering what had twisted a life from a path of promise to one of hopelessness and cruelty.

"Well, anyway," he continued, "he's going to trial for a riot up at Walpole, started by him and these other assholes that he tells what to do. Well, anyway, Martin comes into court yesterday and just after the judge comes on the bench, he lights up a fucking cigar in the courtroom. The judge sees it and orders him to put it out. You know what he fucking does?"

"What?"

"He fucking tells the judge, Your Honor, kiss my fucking black ass!"

"Holy shit!"

"So that's why they got the riot squad across the hall. Those fuckers act up and they're going to get it. You should see the size of those pricks over there. Stay tuned, stay fucking tuned," the swollen grey man repeated, his eyes betraying a perverse delight at the prospect.

Suddenly Christopher thought of Michael and followed the thought with an inquiry. "You know a detective assigned to the DA by the name of Michael McLean?"

"Oh yeah. He's been here about a year now. You know him?"

"He and I grew up together."

"He's a wild man," the probation officer remarked.

"Yeah," he murmured, "that's him."

Christopher nodded to the tall blonde court officer to allow him into the lockup. He was wearing the three-piece, grey, pinstriped suit he had wrestled from the rack during a Filene's Basement sale, and a starched white shirt. Linda had given him the red and blue silk tie for his birthday. She had thrown out two of his other ties, claiming that they needed to have their oil changed.

The years had chiseled his features. At twenty-six, he carried himself with a polite, but unmistakable confidence. His brown hair was stylishly long for 1975 and his body was lean and flexible from daily routines of Yoga and Tai Chi.

In the corner of the enormous metal cage behind the heavy steel door sat his client, a tiny emaciated looking man in his forties with blinding white skin and shaved red hair. In response to the appearance of his lawyer, he slowly made his way through the crowded lockup to the front of the cage. He was wearing a torn grey sweatshirt and faded jeans.

He didn't look like a criminal, let alone a criminal genius. For two years he had remained at Bridgewater, held there to determine whether he was competent to stand trial. Feigned insanity was better than hard time among wolves without mercy.

"How are you doing, Matthew?" Christopher asked.

"Quite well, considering," the little man answered.

"Well today's the day we get started. You all set?"

"Yes. Yes, of course. Have you seen my son? He's supposed to be here today."

"No, I haven't. I spoke with the DA."

"What did he have to say?"

"Seven to ten on a plea in this county and take your chances on the other charges out of Boston."

"Huh! That's ridiculous," the little man snorted, his face pressed against the wire mesh of the lockup. "Rapists don't get that."

"That's what he says. If you go to trial, all bets are off."

"So for exercising my constitutional rights to a trial by jury, I am to be penalized," he protested.

"What can I tell you? I think ..."

"You can tell me something I want to hear," he interjected angrily. "Tell me that the DA will take a plea to wrap up everything. I'll cop to five to six. Then I can wrap up with no parole for time served."

Christopher understood the method in the little man's madness. He had underestimated him. The little bastard who had outwitted the airlines was now attempting to do the same with the criminal justice system.

"You tell them that's what I will accept, five to six on all counts in both Norfolk and Suffolk County. If you can't get that for me, I'll fire you as my lawyer and will proceed pro se. Tell them that! Tell them that!" he shouted, "And if you see my son, tell him that I have refused to succumb to fascists."

With that he turned his back on Christopher and slowly made his way back to his perch in the corner of the lockup, away from the muggers and the derelicts that surrounded him. Christopher watched and shook his head. In a way he admired the little man, realizing that the last thing the DA wanted was to try a case where a gifted criminal could match wits with him and ramble on about the injustice being perpetrated upon him and his son. It was shaping up to be a special kind of show.

Suddenly he heard his name being called. It was a familiar voice from outside of the lockup. He turned and saw Michael standing there with the tall blonde court officer. Michael was smiling and beckoning him to join him outside in the courthouse corridor. Christopher's response was immediate and ecstatic. He was thrilled to see his old friend again, a friend likewise transformed by time.

Michael McLean exhibited the polish of a well-trained police officer. His neck and upper body had been sculpted by countless repetitions with free weights. Although he stood just over six feet, the erectness of his posture and the way he moved made him seem taller. It has been almost a year since he had seen Chris. During that time, he had grown a perfectly manicured mustache, now complemented by his close-cropped blonde hair. His blue eyes still possessed a gleam that could instantaneously become a glare. He was wearing a blue blazer with grey slacks and brown loafers, the perfectly appropriate attire for the youngest detective assigned by the Massachusetts State Police to the Norfolk District Attorney's Office.

"What is this shit? I bust 'em and you break 'em out? How ya' been, Chris?" Michael asked, clasping his friend's hand vigorously.

"I've been good, Mike. I've called you about ten times. Where the hell have you been?"

"Busy, man, I'm out with the job all the time. You look great. A real cracker jack too, that's what I hear."

"How's the family, Mike?" Christopher asked.

"Okay. How's yours?"

"Great. Kate is almost two now."

"I've been calling to invite you and the family over to our place for some lasagna. What do you say?"

"Sure, Chris," Michael answered, his attention suddenly diverted toward the stairway to his left as a phalanx of correctional officers escorted a group of shackled inmates slowly up toward the lockup.

"Coming up," Michael shouted authoritatively, signaling to Christopher that he had to address the business at hand. He then moved to clear the corridor in front of the courtroom for the passage of the prisoners into the lockup.

There were five, all of them shackled at the waist, hands and feet. One of them stood out from the rest. This must be Gabriel Martin, Christopher surmised. He was gigantic, almost six and a half feet tall. He wore a gold and green dashiki and an enormous Afro. He seemed to be scrutinizing the entire scene silently, sullenly watching everything and everyone. After he was led into the lockup, Michael ducked into the doorway adjacent to it.

Later that morning, Christopher met with the judge and the DA in chambers, informing them that his client had expressed a desire to represent himself and to dispense with his counsel. The news was greeted with an appropriate response. The case was continued for two weeks for a hearing on whether the mysterious little man, who had played the system like his own finely tuned instrument, would represent himself, with or without the assistance of the Public Defenders' Office in the person of one Christopher Conley.

Afterward, he searched the courthouse for the little man's son. There, outside of the room that the grand jury used to return indictments, he found him sitting on a long wooden bench, completely alone. He seemed no more than twelve, yet his eyes were much older, frail like his father. He was staring across the corridor toward a green chalkboard when Christopher approached. The children were always the ones who suffered the most from the sins of their fathers.

"You must be Ian. I'm Mr. Conley, your father's lawyer."

The boy nodded and glanced at Christopher momentarily and then returned his attention to the chalkboard.

"Your father has been asking for you. Are you all right?"

There was no response.

"His case was continued for two weeks. Do you want to go up and see him?"

The boy shook his head without altering his focus. There were no words. There was no emotion.

Christopher sat down beside him, not knowing exactly how to proceed. At that moment he followed the boy's trance-like stare to the chalkboard. On it, the boy had drawn a detailed depiction of the Titanic, its dimensions, the location of its boilers, its state rooms and its steerage. It was the product of a fertile, photographic memory. Chris thought about further inquiries, while soaking in the boy's appearance.

"Is there anything I can do for you? Drive you home? Make a phone call?" he asked out of concern, knowing full well what the response would be.

The boy again shook his head and stared, a tiny sphinx with a fathomless mind. As Christopher made his way back toward the lockup, he wondered what the future held for the mysterious little man and the son that barely spoke. Why a picture of the Titanic?

In the second floor courtroom of the Norfolk Superior Court, Sacco and Vanzetti had been tried and convicted as anarchists who had committed murder. On that day in the same place, a different drama was beginning to unfold.

Upon entering through the enormous swinging doors and taking a seat on one of the wooden pews, Christopher spotted Michael sitting within striking distance of the five inmates, situated side by side on the prisoner's bench. They were facing Judge Charles Mason, a no-nonsense Yankee from the Back Bay who seemed fully prepared for any eventuality.

At the time a defense lawyer for one of the inmates was arguing that certain evidence seized on the day of the riot should not be introduced to the jury. It was clear that the white-haired judge was not about to hamper the prosecution of those that stood accused before him.

"Do you have anything more to add, Mr. Grossman?" the judge asked.

"No, your Honor."

At that moment Gabriel Martin suddenly rose making a barely audible remark that caused the other inmates to glance furtively around the courtroom. There were six court officers in strategic locations and a large crowd of spectators who seemed to sense that something memorable was about to take place. Martin then slowly turned his body to either side, defiant and threatening, staring at those that were present. He spoke. "Your Honor, I have something to add."

There was an eerie silence that suddenly enveloped the courtroom. Christopher saw the muscles in Michael's jaw tighten. He knew what that meant. The judge, initially taken aback, responded in an attempt to control what was about to occur.

"Mr. Martin, you have an attorney who represents your interests. You are to address your remarks through him."

"I don't need no court appointed piece of shit to speak for me. I'm a man and I can speak for myself," Martin yelled, again reconnoitering the courtroom.

Christopher noticed at that moment that the riot squad was nowhere to be seen. Was this the design? He again watched Michael who had begun to lean forward within a few feet of the prisoner's bench.

The judge's voice rose to meet the inmate's contempt. "Mr. Martin, I am giving you fair warning that you are to address your remarks through counsel and this court will not tolerate any further outbursts during this proceeding."

The fuse had been lit. It was just about to reach the powder. Martin again turned his body, this time slowly confronting each and everyone within the courtroom, convincing them that he was unafraid, that he despised everything and everybody associated with that place. His voice was resonant and calm. "The reason I want to speak is that I want all of you to understand me when I tell you mother fuckers to suck my fucking cock."

"Remove the prisoner," the judge bellowed. Michael sprang. Martin's foot shot invisibly at his head. With one motion, ducking, grabbing, hauling the gigantic inmate's booted ankle into the air, Michael thrusted his knee up into his groin. Groaning, Martin crumpled to the floor like a wounded animal.

The riot squad crashed through the courtroom's swinging doors. There were twelve, brandishing large wooden bats. The other inmates turned, standing when struck. Bats flailing like mad lumber jacks chopping wood, screams and oaths. Martin was carried out first, shrieking he was sorry over and over, down the stairs and out of the building. Clumps of his hair were everywhere. The others followed like cause and effect. It was an overwhelming response. Hatred had been exhibited once again, in the hallowed halls where Sacco and Vanzetti had been tried and convicted.

Later, outside, the sun of an Indian summer afternoon warmed the peaceful neighborhood behind the courthouse. Nothing was shattered there. Christopher approached Michael as he spoke to two court officers on the rear steps of the courthouse. They were congratulating him.

"Are you okay, Mike," Christopher asked.

Michael's eyes again possessed the glare that he knew so well. It seemed almost like he was having fun.

"Yeah, shit Chris, I'm alright, a lot better than those pieces of shit. What do you think of that, counselor?"

"Unbelievable,"

"What do you say we do some partying tonight?" Michael asked, as he bummed a cigarette from one of the court officers. "For old times' sake?"

The request took Christopher by surprise. They had made plans twice before to get together, only to have Michael cancel them at the last minute. They really hadn't spoken for any length of time in years. Christopher welcomed the chance at again becoming the closest of close friends.

"That sounds great, Mike. You're gonna show this time, right?"

"Right, I'll take you to my special place, counselor."

"I'll call you later," Chris remarked, as he made his way down the courthouse steps into the still, quiet neighborhood.

"Tell Linda not to wait up," Michael shouted. Christopher waved and sprinted towards his car. It was just another day in the criminal courts.

CHAPTER 24

The thunder of the music triggered a frenzy of sight and sound. The strobe, a search light of distortion, snatched glimpses of contorting bodies on the discotheque's space age dance floor. They sat together at the corner of the bar, a fly ball's distance from Fenway Park. It was almost two a.m. at Lucifer's, Boston's most popular discotheque. They were both loaded by then, making a determined effort to capture time in a bottle, even though they both knew they were light years beyond where they had once been.

Mostly they had laughed, induced to a degree by the booze and the marijuana confiscated in Michael's lawful exercise of uncertain authority the week before. They were kids again. Project kids with a reputation to uphold after all, masquerading as up and coming members of a changing establishment. They barely noticed the tall, athletic looking man in the white suit and black silk shirt as he pulled his chair close to them at the bar.

"Two more," Michael responded to the bartender's notice of a last call.

"Jesus, I've had enough," Chris muttered, negating his friend's order for his fifth scotch and water. "I've got to be getting home. I'm not used to this shit, Mike. I guess I'm getting old."

"What's the matta? Forgot how to party? The night is young. I wanna take you to this after-hours joint in Southie," Michael insisted, "then I'll take your sorry ass home. How 'bout it?"

At that moment, the man in the white suit politely interjected himself into the two friend's repartee. "Excuse me fellas, I've been asked to invite you to a little get-together down on Comm. Ave. I'm Darrell Brown. Don't I know you?" he asked, extending his hand across Christopher toward Michael.

"You look familiar," Michael replied, accepting his handshake and introducing him to Chris. "Say hello to Chris Conley, the best criminal lawyer in Boston."

"How ya doin?" Chris muttered, shaking his hand.

"You know Mike Levange?" the man asked Christopher.

"Yeah, I know Mike. Is he a friend of yours?"

"A friend, shit, he's married to my sister."

"Mike's a good shit," Chris said. "He and I have had a lot of cases together. I'm a public defender.

"Yeah, I keep telling him, cut the shit with being a DA and go make some real money," the man said. "He could make a fortune working for one of those big outfits downtown. I know 'cause I sell real estate on Comm. Ave. Most of my clients are young lawyers and stock brokers making the big dough."

"I've seen you a couple of times at Daisy's," he remarked to Michael, who was just about to begin with his last Bourbon and soda. "What kind of business are you in?"

"I'm a detective."

"No shit," the man said, "I would never have figured that."

"He's fucking undercover," Chris interrupted, "way fucking undercover."

"What's your name?" the man inquired of Michael.

"Mike," he replied, his tone signaling an unwillingness to elaborate with a last name.

"How come you want us back at your place?" Michael asked curiously.

"I'm having a bunch of friends over. I just closed on a big deal and it's going to be a good time. I'll give you the address. It's 60 Commonwealth Ave, Suite Three. Come on by. You won't regret it. Believe me." With that the man slid his chair back from the bar and slowly disappeared into the crowd, as the disco's DJ announced that the last selection of the night was about to be spun.

"What d'ya think?" Michael asked Christopher.

"I don't know."

"Let's fuckin' go and see what it's about. Maybe we get lucky," Michael resolved.

"I'll go for a half hour. Then I got to go," Chris answered, not wanting the reunion with his best friend to end just yet.

The gold embossed elevator spirited them to the sixth floor of 60 Commonwealth Avenue. The plush orchid carpeting and the stunning murals adorning the hallway leading to the ornately crafted double doors marked with a Roman numeral three, reminded Christopher of suites at the Beverly Wilshire.

They entered unheralded and unannounced, yet not unnoticed. They found themselves in an enormous drawing room, dimly lit with Victorian table lamps. They stood together, their eyes attempting to adjust to the darkness of their surroundings. Simultaneously they began to make out human forms caressing, fondling and fornicating on and around a dozen or so leather love seats. Moaning passion and whispered exhortations of unbridled sexuality engulfed them. The smell of hashish and expensive perfume was mingled with stereophonic jazz in their commanding position overlooking the Back Bay skyline.

"Mike, Chris, can I get you a drink?" the athletic man in the white suit inquired, appearing as if on cue.

"Bourbon and soda," Michael replied while Christopher politely declined his invitation to imminent oblivion. He wanted to retain the modicum of sobriety he had wrestled to preserve, especially in such erotic surroundings.

"How do you like the place?" he asked, as he directed them to a hand-crafted mahogany bar that dominated the West corner of the suite.

"It's incredible," Chris said.

"How long you lived here?" Michael asked.

"Oh, about two years now, in my business I entertain a lot and I write off most of it. Why don't you guys grab that seat over there? I'm expecting some special guests in about a half hour. Make yourselves at home."

The nonchalance with which he spoke amused Christopher, reminding him of occasions in Hollywood and Beverly Hills when he would be called upon to witness and experience rights of passage through the late sixties. Now he was the attached observer, attached to a companion who seemed to be eager to participate in the swirling seduction of their surroundings.

"You wanna get high?" Michael whispered to him, as they settled into the comfort of a soft leather couch, placing his drink on the carpet next to them.

"Are you fucking crazy, Mike? You're a fucking cop, what if someone sees you smoking a bone in this place?"

"Relax, counselor. Anybody that's here wouldn't admit it. We're fuckin' golden." With that he removed a tightly wrapped party joint from his wallet and ignited it. He insisted that his friend join him, thrusting it in his direction.

He was right, Chris thought. Nobody in that place gave a shit who you were or what you were doing. Besides, it was so dark they couldn't tell who you were anyway. Why the fuck not! He took three hits and held them deeply in his throat, the warmth of the weed combined with his preexisting buzz to subdue him completely.

"What a fuckin' night, man!" Michael exclaimed. "I knew it was gonna be special. It's good to be with you, Chris."

"Same here," Chris muttered, suddenly focusing upon vague and distant shapes across the expansive chamber, a head bobbing, a woman's shapely, disrobed derriere thrusting back and forth like a metronome in heat, Miles Davis' music softly moaning.

"Check it out," Michael groaned, his eyes likewise observing the inflamed spectacle.

A spasm of anxiety suddenly began to grip Chris unexpectedly. What time was it? Were Linda and the baby safe? He was ashamed of where he had wandered. He glanced at Michael, unwilling to reveal his misgivings. His friend was enthralled by it all, eagerly soaking it in, reveling in it. Chris was not. It had gone too far. It wasn't right that he should be married and be there. It wasn't safe. Most of all, he longed to see his daughter, her face welcoming him, loving him unconditionally from her crib.

"C'mon Mike, let's get the fuck out of here," he demanded.

"What the fuck are you talkin' about, man," his friend replied incredulously.

"This ain't right, man. We're fuckin' married. Let's go home. What d'ya say?"

"No," he said bluntly, unwaveringly.

"Cut the shit, Mike! I got to get home. It's too late. Peggy and the baby will be missing you, too. What d'ya say?"

"No. You go, I'm stayin'," Michael insisted.

"What are you gonna do here?" Chris asked.

"What the fuck do you think?" Mike answered unashamedly.

CHAPTER 25

Plans had been made early in the week, a family dinner for two old friends. Following Linda's detailed written directions, he had stopped at the supermarket on the way home from the office and picked up ricotta and mozzarella cheese, two bottles of wine and a supply of Pampers. Chris was looking forward to that night during an exhausting day that included a visit to the Charles Street Jail, three bail hearings and preparation of two witnesses for a jury trial to begin the following Monday.

The phone call at seven o'clock was an unexpected disappointment for both him and his wife. Michael's anxious voice told them that he was sorry, but that Peggy had become sick during the day and she couldn't make it for dinner. He also asked if they could babysit his four month-old son, while he visited his mother in the Projects. Of course they couldn't refuse, besides, Linda loved little babies.

The expression on Michael's face imperfectly masked his distress. His eyes were wild and his conversation was disjointed and disturbing. He spoke of having to see his mother right away. He apologized for inconveniencing and disappointing his friend, especially when he saw the preparations that had been made by Linda for the evening. Although it was late October, his baby boy wore only a light cotton playsuit with no coat. Linda caressed the baby as Michael again apologized and left the Conley apartment.

"Something's really the matter," Linda said after Michael had left.

"Yeah, maybe his mother is sick. I heard she's been in and out of the hospital. It's too bad. He doesn't need any more trouble."

Instead of a reunion for old friends, Chris and Linda ate lasagna in the company of their daughter and Michael's baby. Throughout the evening, Christopher worried about his friend. There was something drastically different about him. Something untold eating him, making him run like a jacked deer.

After much coaxing, they put their little girl to bed. They then watched and waited for Michael to return for his baby as promised. Hours passed without a call. Night became early morning, an early morning punctuated by the crying of a baby, unfamiliar with his surroundings. The buzzer from the apartment building's front door jolted Christopher from his fitful sleep on the couch. Again the baby began to cry, while his exhausted wife attempted to soothe him. It was 4:30 in the morning.

Michael's appearance as he walked slowly down the apartment building's hallway triggered Christopher's unbridled rage. He was unquestionably loaded. His eyes were like that of an enormous insect, glistening from his skull. He scraped his body along the building's wall as he approached Christopher, standing in his apartment door. There was no apology and no remorse, only a defiant insolence.

"What's happenin', buddy?" Michael slurred, swaying in front of his friend.

"I don't believe you man," Christopher sputtered, shaking his head and shutting the apartment door as he slipped into the hallway and confronted him. "Are you crazy or what? You know what time it is?"

"Yeah, it's time I picked up my fuckin' kid," Michael sneered.

"Oh, you think so, huh? Well you ain't picking up shit the way you are, man," Chris challenged, the depth of Michael's irresponsibility flaming his fury like salt on a bleeding sore. "Let's take it outside, I wanna talk to you for a minute and I don't wanna wake up the whole building."

"Sure, buddy, let's take it fuckin' outside," Michael spat, leaning against the wall and placing a cigarette in his mouth. He lit it and threw the match on the carpet of the hallway, either not knowing or caring that this added insult to his friend's injury.

They crossed the parking lot. Christopher walked quickly in front while Michael staggered behind. He entered a small playground for the apartment building's children. He had pushed his daughter on the swings there two days before. He stood near the swings now, waiting as Michael slowly made his way into the playground, stumbling over a metal rocking horse near the entrance and cursing loudly as the cigarette dropped from his mouth.

Michael then gathered himself, his eyes glazed in the artificial light of the apartment complex, his hands extended, his head tilted defiantly. He began to scream with a thick, slow cadence to his voice.

"So what's the story counselor, a little fuckin' pissed off, huh?"

"What is it with you man?" Chris shouted, his finger thrusting inches away from his friend's smirking face. "You leave your baby with us until four fucking thirty in the morning and you don't call or nothing. What the fuck was you thinking?"

"I ain't thinking, I'm sick of fuckin' thinking, I'm just doin, man. You wanna get done?" Michael shot back without remorse.

"You're fucked up man," Chris sneered.

"You bet your fuckin' ass I am! You want a fuckin' piece of me or what?" Michael shrieked.

The assessment was made suddenly. The situation was spiraling out of control. Chris attempted to retrieve it before circumstance dictated a violent response. His manhood was being challenged by the contempt of a best friend; a horrible, ugly episode to be avoided, despite his rage.

He stopped and looked at the clear, star-filled October sky. He attempted to compose himself, not wanting to look in the direction of Michael's surly face. The transformed creature that stood before him was frighteningly foreign to his experience. The threat persisted.

"What's a matta, counselor? Do all your fightin' in court now? Too educated to get down to it, or did you just lose your balls?"

Christopher glared at him, then unexpectedly, without explanation, felt sorry for him. Loyalty and affection had reappeared at the last moment, pulling him from the dangling edge of his emotions. He sucked a deep breath and sat down on the bench, used by parents to watch their kids at play. Michael stared blankly at him now, again swaying with intoxication. Christopher spoke deliberately, choosing his words carefully.

"Hey, Mike, what are we doing? Tell me, what's the matter? I'll help you."

Christopher's consolation seemed to sting Michael. He reeled back and leaned against the metal cross bars on the end of the swings.

"I don't need your fuckin' help; I don't want your fuckin' sympathy. I wanna get my kid and get the fuck out of here, alright?"

Christopher knew that it would be folly to have Michael take the baby in his condition. He tried to reason with him.

"How about you stay awhile and then you can take the baby. I don't want you driving like this with the baby in the car. Come on, how 'bout it? Maybe we'll do something tomorrow with you and Peggy."

"I ain't doin' shit with Peggy, man. She's all fuckin' done," Michael interjected.

"What d'ya mean?"

"She gave me some shit and I popped her. I broke her fuckin' nose when I hit her. Good fuckin' riddance to the bitch!"

Now shock and revulsion tightened their grip on Chris. What had Michael done? A clearer, more chilling portrait was being painted of the friend that he thought he knew. Contempt awakened, bearings lost. Michael McLean was a ticking bomb that needed defusing. Did he have the courage to do the job? Chris had to try. He owed him that much.

"Hey, Mike, cut the shit. I'm your friend. Listen to me!"

"I ain't listenin' to any fuckin' lawyer. Shit, just get my kid and I'm fuckin' out of here!"

"I can't let that happen, Mike" he stated purposefully, attempting to once again regain control of the situation.

"Oh, you can't huh?" Michael responded, suddenly bending over and removing a snub-nose .38 concealed under his pants above his right ankle. Christopher stared in disbelief as Michael approached him, deliberately cocking the gun and placing it against the middle of Christopher's forehead. "Does this fuckin' change your mind, mother fucker?" Michael demanded in a resolute and detached tone. Chris sat transfixed, terrified that his wife and baby would never see him again.

"You know how many mother fuckers I've blown away man? I can do you just like I did them. You know that?" he threatened, pulling Christopher's head back and pressing the cold black barrel of the gun against his perspiration-soaked forehead.

"I know it," Chris whispered, looking up at Michael's vacant expression.

"You never went to Nam. You lucked out with college and the lottery. Well, I seen shit there that you wouldn't believe man; shit that made me dead inside; shit that pricks like you missed while we were gettin' wasted.

Now you're a fuckin' muff, a fuckin' lawyer who twists the fuckin' truth. I hate fuckin' lawyers, man! They all suck! Now get me my fuckin' kid or you're fuckin' dead!"

Mortal fear choked Christopher's voice to a moan. He stared at Michael and begged, tears rapidly running down his cheeks. "Please God, please Mike, don't do this. There's something wrong with you. You don't know what you're doing. Please Mike, I'm scared shit you're going to kill me, but I can't let you have the baby. You're too fucked up! Please Mike, I love you, you're my best friend, stop what you're doing. You need help, please don't kill me. Please!"

Michael stood over his friend, like a man standing on the edge of a deep canyon. He stared at the gun and then at Christopher's face. He didn't speak, tears suddenly causing him to blink repeatedly. He jerked the gun away and placed it in his mouth. The hammer was cocked as his finger began to depress the trigger. Christopher reached for the hand that held the gun. He held it gently. The words came spontaneously from his heart.

"Michael, your baby needs you alive."

The words froze him. Slowly he removed the iron from within his mouth and dropped it into the sand of the playground. He turned from Christopher without speaking. He staggered from the playground to his car and drove away. Christopher picked up the gun, his hands shaking. He sobbed in the moonlight until dawn appeared. The dawn of the day that Michael McLean disappeared.

CHAPTER 26

The burnished gold 1989 Mercedes purred as it climbed Beacon Street toward the Federal Courthouse. Christopher glanced at the face of his Rolex watch purchased in Marigot on the Island of Saint Martin two months before. He and Linda had gone there to celebrate their fifteenth wedding anniversary, leaving their two children with a French au pair for a week of sun and renewed passion.

It was ten minutes to nine. He had made good time from his home in Wellesley Hills. His experts were waiting as he turned the corner to the corridor that led to Judge Forte's courtroom. It was the third day of trial in a case where the insurance company had offered $500,000 to settle all claims against its insured. He had rejected their offer out of hand.

The years had brought silver to his hair and paper-cut wrinkles to the skin under his eyes. His skill as a trial lawyer had increased with the hard-learned lesson that there was a correct way to present cases, a way of making a jury of strangers visualize the fault and feel the pain it caused. The lesson had served him and his law firm well. He was within striking distance of the pinnacle and he had thoroughly enjoyed the climb. He would turn forty one that summer. The summer of 1991.

That morning he had made arrangements to present two prestigious doctors who would provide expert testimony that the obstetrical care received by his client was negligent and caused brain damage to her son who was now seven years old. The doctor's mistakes had condemned her child to a life in a wheelchair.

The nervous tension he felt as he waited to begin his presentation that morning had formed patches of perspiration beneath his designer shirt and stolen his appetite. It was the same fear, the same anxiety in every case. That was the price of admission to a club that gambled on their ability to communicate with juries and persuade them that fairness required a verdict of seven figures.

It was difficult with expert doctors. Down deep, he knew they resented him for pursuing and blaming one of their own. It was necessary for him to convince them that they were acting righteously and that he was not a predator, poised to plunge his teeth into the unfortunate neck of a fellow physician and suck until satiated. The fact that his brother was a well-known physician gave him threshold credibility. The fact that he paid their fees and expenses by return mail solidified their responsiveness and loyalty.

Because of the length of the trial, the judge had empaneled fourteen jurors. Eight men and six women listened intently as Dr. Max Allen, the Chief of Obstetrics at the Parkway Hospital in New York, testified with the hint of a Brooklyn accent, by pointing to blow-ups of the fetal monitor tracings, that the failure of the obstetrician to perform an emergency Cesarean section resulted in this baby suffering a deprivation of oxygen and brain damage.

Chris had learned to watch juries intently while he presented his cases. Their eyes, their expressions and their body language were signals of success or failure as the trial progressed. He had learned that in order to succeed he had to stimulate their visual senses and imbue their brains with photographs, videotapes and magnifications of documents that reiterated his theme like the refrain of a haunting melody.

He stood at the very end of the jury box in a grey three-piece suit from Hart Schaffner Marx. The starched collar of his light pink shirt cradled a conservative blue and grey tie that was matched by a blue and grey silk handkerchief peeking from the pocket to the left of his lapels. His black Italian shoes had been polished vigorously two days before in the lobby of his office building. The aging black shoe shine man had spoken of the Celtics and wished Christopher good fortune. He had tipped him five dollars.

"Doctor," he inquired, "do you have an opinion based upon a reasonable degree of medical certainty as to whether or not the obstetrical care and treatment received by Mrs. Orlandi from Dr. Lippman fell below the acceptable standard of care for the average qualified physician practicing in the field of obstetrics?"

"Yes, I do," the doctor replied, taking his horn-rimmed glasses off and speaking directly to the jury foreman.

"What is that opinion?"

"In my opinion, Dr. Lippman's obstetrical care of this patient was negligent and fell below the acceptable standards for the average qualified obstetrician."

"What is the basis of your opinion, Doctor?"

Christopher watched the jury as the white-haired, handsome New Yorker explained in great detail the reasons he had come to Massachusetts to point the finger of blame at another physician. Christopher was delighted to see the heads of the foreman and two other jurors nod in affirmation as the doctor explained how the fetal monitor tracings and the notes of the nurse attending the mother's labor showed that the baby was in distress and how the doctor delayed in responding to this distress until it was too late. Christopher sensed that the jury believed his expert and, more importantly, he sensed that they saw the truth that had brought him there to testify.

That afternoon, he presented the Chief of Pediatric Neurology at the Tufts Medical Center to explain to the jury how the delay in performing an emergency cesarean section had caused a deprivation of oxygen and brain damage evident from a CT scan of the baby's brain. Again the jury was shown the evidence. He could almost feel their pulse now. They were that close. This family's misery could have been prevented. His confidence was beginning to take hold. His exhilaration was simmering deep in his heart. Would they do what he would ask? Would they follow his lead to justice for his client?

As he emerged from the red leather-covered doors of the courtroom with his client, a small, plain woman with thinning black hair, whose face betrayed the depths of her and her son's ordeal, he was asked to wait a few minutes by Steven Bloom, the attorney representing the doctor being sued.

Steve Bloom and Christopher liked each other very much. In fact, they had once played on the same basketball team when Steve was with the Attorney General's Office and Chris was a public defender. Bloom was a small man with thick black hair and pointed features. He was also an extremely capable trial attorney who never over tried a case or alienated a jury.

As Christopher watched his opposing counsel conversing with an overweight, sweaty bald man in a blue suit that was a size too small and a woman in her twenties with brown hair and glasses, stylishly attired in a green tweed jacket and skirt, he asked his client to have a seat on one of the benches at the far end of the deserted courthouse corridor. She complied with his instructions without hesitation, as Bloom approached him from behind and whispered in his ear.

"We have to stop meeting like this. It's not good for my image."

"Then you should pay us the money, you cheap prick," he replied good-naturedly.

"That's what I want to talk to you about," Bloom said.

"Why is it you guys only want to talk, after we start kicking your ass? Can you tell me that?" Chris asked sarcastically.

"Because that's the way it works, you putz! Don't you understand that yet?"

"Okay, what's the story?" he asked, momentarily glancing at his client situated all alone at the end of the corridor.

"We are prepared to increase our pre-trial offer on this case, but we want to know if you will recommend it before we do." His recitation was based upon his instructions from the sweaty man in the suit that didn't fit, conversing with his young attentive assistant at the other end of the courthouse corridor.

"Steven," Christopher responded, his tone calm and carefully measured. "You know how it is with me. Make me an offer in good faith or try the case. Don't give me that bullshit about what you're prepared to do. Tell me what you've got and I'll convey it to my client."

"Well, this is the way they want me to present it and since I don't sign the checks, this is the way I have to present it. If you will recommend it, we will offer $900,000 to settle this case. Not a dollar more."

Christopher paused after hearing the dollar amount decided upon by the insurance company. He couldn't help but feel irritation at their cynical attempt at manipulation of the tragedy that had enveloped his client and her child, and yet he knew that it was an old strategy that had worked before with countless other attorneys. He pressed the issue to protect himself and his client.

"Unless you tell me that there is an offer on the table of $900,000, I will not convey it to my client. Now go back and tell those two that we don't play this game. Put an offer on the table or take your best shot. I've gotta go. You have my number at the office, I'll be there tonight."

With that, he walked down the corridor toward the anxious face of the woman sitting alone. He hoped, as he saw the pain in her eyes, mingled with the desire for an end to her public outcry for relief, that he hadn't made the wrong move in this high-stakes game of chess. He was fully prepared for another night of troubled sleep.

CHAPTER 27

As a public defender he had learned to appeal to a jury's humanity; to somehow personalize even the most despicable and portray them in a light that allowed the "better angels" of the jury's nature to reach out and redeem. For almost four years the wretched came and went, all of them prisoners of one type or another. At first it was almost noble, he and his client pitted against it all; then it became old, like being at an absurd carnival of mayhem without being able to go home. Saturation set in, the defendants became maggots in the jargon of the callous. Desensitized, he became disenchanted, the burning desire began to flicker and he escaped before it stole his spirit.

The decision was made to take a new direction, to find new fulfillment on another avenue in the law. His decision shocked those that knew him. He spurned overtures to throw in with up and comers with a clientele steeped in the tradition of the damned, drugs and money, blood and high interest loans, cashmere coats and concealed weapons. He simply didn't want to be ashamed of the way he made his living.

His experience and talent made him a viable commodity. He looked for and found a position with a small, suburban law firm where he could inconspicuously grow and prosper, where he could learn a new lyric and sing his own song.

As an associate in Murphy, Carrington and Costello, Christopher represented union laborers, carpenters, electricians and plumbers. He learned to negotiate contracts and argue grievances before arbitrators. It was a welcome change that elevated his perspective from the bottom of the dark, green criminal well.

Instead of atomized, angry indigents, he would champion the causes of working men and women organized to speak and wield power as one. Instead of descending, he sprinted up the escalator of respectability. He found himself telling others that he used to be a criminal lawyer. Like the projects, criminals and criminal law became a previous chapter, a nearly-forgotten form that had shaped his being.

He didn't expect his career to reach another crossroads so soon, but it did. It occurred following an all-night negotiation session for a new contract between an electricians' local and an electrical contractor. As the orange traces of dawn invaded the upstairs conference room of the union hall, cigarette smoke and stale coffee caused him to escape to the welcome frigidity of the February morning air. He was accompanied by the business agent for Local 602 of the International Brotherhood of Electrical Workers, John McManus.

McManus was an intriguing figure. He loved the opera and Bruce Catton's Civil War histories. He had fathered eight children and had put six of them through college. His lack of stature at five foot six made his lion heart even more impressive. Chris had never met a man who was as respected and as honest as this man. His only vice was an absolutely rabid devotion to the Boston Red Sox, the team most likely to break the hearts of its disciples. It was John McManus who provided him with the means to become his own boss.

"Do you know anything about medical malpractice?" the aging business agent inquired, as the wind whipped across the expressway from Dorchester Bay and rearranged his grey receding hair.

"I've worked on a couple of malpractice cases," Chris answered, recalling the research he had done when he first came to Murphy, Carrington and Costello for the senior partner, Peter Murphy. Cases that were eventually referred to other law firms because of their complexity.

"Well my brother-in-law had a lump in the back of his leg and he went to a doctor who told him not to worry about it," McManus explained. "Eight months later it's still bothering him and he goes back to the doctor again and this time they remove it and find out he's got cancer. He's dying now. It's all over his body. He and my sister have three kids. He went to some lawyers in town and they told him they couldn't do anything."

Chris was flattered, knowing that John McManus was reaching out to him, to help his sister's children. McManus knew a hundred lawyers and yet he picked him. Chris promised to do whatever he could to help. Of course he meant it. His respect ran deep for this man who had helped so many achieve dignity in the work place.

Three years later, having learned the lexicon of medical negligence, its fundamentals and its nuances, he settled the case on a Friday afternoon, in a quiet courtroom, light years away from the din of the criminal milieu. Afterward, he made reservations at Emile's overlooking Boston Harbor, delighting Linda with the news. He had succeeded in securing a million and a half dollars for John McManus' widowed sister.

The rise from there was rapid, almost breathtaking. There were featured newspaper articles, appearances on evening news telecasts, his phone ringing, his options and horizons expanding. Eight years after he turned away from the lure of being a criminal lawyer, he had become the president of his own six member law firm, concentrating in sophisticated and lucrative personal injury cases. Conley, DeCoste and Joyce soon became a front runner, an established player in the fertile fields of medical negligence, product liability and seven figure jury awards.

That night, within his spacious downtown law office, Christopher watched as the mother wheeled her brain-damaged son toward him. The child's body was twisted in the wheelchair like a used pipe cleaner, but his face was hauntingly angelic. The mother who had placed her faith in the doctor that delivered her son was now, and for the rest of her life, his nurse, his caretaker and his devoted companion.

The desperate condition of her child had shattered her marriage. Perhaps there wasn't enough love and dedication to make it all work under such trying circumstances. Too much expended in accomplishing what other children did without pain, without struggle and without wondering what might have been.

The eyes of the child and the considered opinions of the doctors who treated him, convinced Christopher that their case was righteous. Had this child not been deprived of oxygen through the negligence of the doctor, there would have been no need for a trial, no final argument, no sleepless night wrestling with his decision to reject a $900,000 overture from a formidable adversary.

He had informed the mother of his discussions with Attorney Bloom concerning settlement. He had advised her how insurance companies conducted the business of defending physicians accused of malpractice, and recognized that she was too anxious to begin to understand. She had left it completely up to him. He prayed that he would not let her down. He couldn't bear to think of what would happen to the two of them if he failed.

"They must know they did this to my boy, Mr. Conley," the mother said, passing her right hand through the thinning black hair that managed to barely cover her head. Tears like crystals seeping from her eyes.

"I'm sure they do, Mrs. Orlandi," Chris replied.

"Well, why don't they admit it and help me take care of him. They must know I can't do it by myself."

"I don't think they care about that. It's not the doctor who makes the decisions. It's the insurance company and it's just a business transaction to them. That's all."

"Well, it's so unfair. My boy would be normal if the doctor had only done things right. There's nobody in my family with these problems. Don't they see that?"

"I don't know what they see, maybe they're blind. All I know is that we have to prepare you to testify tomorrow and show them the videotape of a day in your son's life and then our case will be almost over."

"I hope I can do this, Mr. Conley. You've helped me so much. I just hope I don't screw it up. Do you think that they will settle the case before I testify?"

"I doubt it," he said matter-of-factly, not wishing to give her false hope and decrease her resolve to do whatever it took to help her son, including the baring of her soul before a jury of fourteen strangers the following morning.

For the next two hours he sat in his office with her, preparing her testimony while her twisted child stared from his wheelchair at the city below. His face pressed against the glass. The depth of her love and the dimensions of her dauntless courage inspired him, spurring him to prevail, to be their avenging angel.

In his office, in the dark, long after she and her child had departed, he prayed and meditated on what he would say to the jury. When he came home to a darkened house he kissed his sleeping daughter and son and curled next to his devoted wife. The tears slid down the sides of his face as he prayed for the courage to be their champion, recalling over and over what the mother had said.

"It's so unfair, my boy would be normal if the doctor had only done things right."

CHAPTER 28

There was no turning back. No compassionate overtures from the defense that eased the pain of the mother and child, no noble gesture that removed the burden from Christopher's mind that he alone could help them. The jury had watched and listened to the mother's testimony and viewed the videotape of the daily obstacles both mother and child encountered, a child unable to dress and care for his basic needs, a child who required an hour to do that which the normal child did without effort.

He rested his case on the morning of the fifth day, after presenting a medical economist who explained the costs of caring for this child, leaving his calculations on the courtroom blackboard, calculations that dwarfed the offers made by the insurance company.

The defendant, a man in his fifties with black hair and glasses, testified that he did all he could for the mother and child. His testimony was corroborated by the best experts the insurance company could buy. Men in grey suits with the looks of central casting actors, equipped with stellar credentials and visual aids, challenged the case presented by Christopher and his witnesses.

He watched the jury as he cross-examined the defendant and his experts. He saw them respond. He felt their support. He prayed they would not be swayed by the skill and confidence of the defense experts.

Judge Albert Forte was a bald, cantankerous man whose raspy voice and quick temper purposefully kept all before him in a perpetual state of uneasiness. He met with the lawyers in his chambers to discuss the instructions concerning the law that he would give to the jury.

"Have you gentlemen gotten any closer to settling this matter?" Judge Forte asked.

"Not really, your Honor," Chris replied, glancing in Steve Bloom's direction.

"What has been offered by the company, Mr. Bloom?"

"We offered $900,000, your Honor, and are not prepared to increase that amount in light of the evidence."

"What do you say to that, Mr. Conley?" the Judge inquired, smoking a large cigar and adjusting his shirt and suspenders.

"It's not acceptable, your Honor. You've heard the value our expert has placed just on future medical care, never mind the pain and suffering in this case."

"Well, I've presided over eight of these cases and everyone has come back with a verdict for the defendant," the Judge said, looking directly at Christopher with an expression that told him he was being foolhardy. "I trust you've fully explained the chances of success in this type of a case to your client, Mr. Conley."

"I have, your Honor," Chris responded, fighting a burst of anxiety as he reflected on the impending final argument he would present, praying that it would be successful.

After they discussed the charge to be given by the Judge, the lawyers and stenographer emerged from the confinement of his smoke-choked chambers into the courtroom.

"You should take the money, Chris," Bloom whispered as he shook his head, "Your experts were out-classed."

"We'll see, man," Chris muttered, resenting the last attempt of his adversary to break his concentration just before final argument. "We'll see," he repeated, staring and winking at him defiantly.

The jury waited restlessly for the judge to enter the courtroom. Chris approached his client who was sitting alone in the front row behind the rail partitioning the courtroom. Her face was that of a small frightened animal, uncertain of its fate as he sat beside her. "Are you ready, Mary?" Christopher asked, touching the hand that she rested on her lap and discovering rosary beads gripped within.

"I am," she answered meekly.

"Well, so am I," he affirmed. "I just want to tell you that it is a great honor representing you and your son in this case. Please pray that the right words come to me."

"I have," she whispered, momentarily clutching his extended hand.

As he returned to his seat behind the plaintiff's table, he whispered to himself a portion of his meditations. "Please let it flow through me. Let me be an instrument for your light. Help me God."

The courtroom was commanded to rise and the Judge asked the lawyers if they were prepared to deliver their summations. Steve Bloom, resplendent in a dark blue three-piece suit, argued first, skillfully sympathizing with the plight of the plaintiffs, yet distancing that sympathy from any fault on the part of the doctor. He spoke about the credentials of their doctors and their testimony. He also demanded they do justice for everyone in the case, including his client. It was a flawless performance.

As Christopher stood in front of the jury, he paused, examining the expressions of each of the fourteen faces before him. He began deliberately, grasping for the right words at first and then the power appeared and took over.

"Ladies and gentlemen, you have heard the evidence, you have seen the exhibits and you will use your collective intelligence and common sense to determine the truth. Truth is what we seek here today. For with the truth will come justice, the two are intertwined in a case like this.

The truth is that Anthony Orlandi's brain has been forever damaged because of the inattention and delay of this doctor. A life has been altered, foreclosed and restricted, by negligence. As I prepared these closing remarks, I couldn't help but remember Mrs. Orlandi's words to me before she testified in this case. She said, 'It's so unfair. My boy would be normal if the doctor had done things right.'

Well that's it, isn't it? That's what this case is all about, the unfairness to this mother and her son's life and the fact that it was all so avoidable. All that had to be done was for this doctor to do what was right, what he was taught, what an average, qualified obstetrician should have done. When he was told by the nurses that the fetal monitor tracings weren't good, he should have taken this baby by emergency Caesarean section, not wait, not delay, not allow the deprivation of oxygen to be so great that a portion of this child's precious brain would die and be lost forever.

And what does forever mean, ladies and gentlemen? It means that this child will outlive his mother and be left without a caretaker, a loving, comforting hand to assist him through his years of pain and decades of frustration.

Today you, all of you, can be that loving, comforting hand, a righteous hand that acts only after your heads and your hearts have decided that justice demands it. We ask for your loving, comforting hand in assisting Anthony Orlandi and his mother today. You have that power, the power of a jury, people who have become the conscience of our community. Ladies and gentlemen of this jury, this child needs your loving, comforting hand. This mother needs your loving, comforting hand. Please do justice."

They sat in the corridor together. Christopher, the mother and her twisted son confined to his chair. The buzzer sounded from the jury room, shattering the stillness that had enveloped the courthouse at that hour, signifying that the jury, after almost six hours of deliberations, had reached a verdict. This was always the time of the most anxiety for Christopher.

His heart beat uncontrollably, reverberating in his ears. The palms of his hands were rubbed repeatedly on the sleeves of his suit, as he sat and waited for the jury to file in and take their assigned seats within the jury box.

The clerk spoke with the loud, ceremonial voice of federal authority. "Ladies and gentlemen, have you reached a verdict?"

The forelady, an impeccably dressed, middle-aged woman with short brown hair, wearing a solemn, sad expression, spoke for herself as well as the other jurors. "Yes, we have."

"What say you, ladies and gentlemen? Was the defendant negligent?"

"Yes," the forelady responded emphatically.

"Did the defendant's negligence cause damage to the plaintiffs?"

"Yes," she repeated.

"What is the amount of the jury's award on behalf of the plaintiffs?"

"Three million five hundred thousand dollars."

There was a calming finality to it. The years of research and painstaking preparation had not been in vain this time. He reflected on it all, detached from the uproar that engulfed him, spectators gathered to witness an authentic drama being played out. His overriding emotion was one of profound relief, not exhilaration. The face of the mother was its own reward, her embrace punctuated by expressions of sobbing gratitude. He could say nothing, his throat choked with tears.

In that courtroom on that day, a precious almost supernatural occurrence had taken place. Justice had appeared with its balancing touch.

CHAPTER 29

The uneven wooden stairs were strewn with broken syringes and burned bottle caps as he cautiously ascended, placing one foot in front of the other in the dim light. His investigation had taken turns and twists like an amusement ride run by a madman. Foreign suppliers, New York distributors and Boston's Black and Hispanic underbelly of narcotics traffic had reached their tentacles into this Grove Hall triple-decker.

Jack Panton had been assigned to the Boston Police Drug Unit for four years. He was now a Sergeant, having been promoted for meritorious service in daring to reach into the recesses of Boston's worst ghetto in order to identify and eradicate the vermin who lured the young and the desperate with white powder, stealing their souls and perpetuating the misery and viciousness that had combined to make the area a free fire zone of criminality.

The day before, his snitch had told him of a shipment of heroin that was almost 70% pure, arriving from New York and being targeted for Boston, Springfield and New Bedford. A major deal was coming through and the junkies were ready. They were always ready, to shoot more powdered poison into their veins, and kill everything else in their lives. He hadn't had time to tell anybody except his partner and leave a message for the detective in charge of the Drug Unit, Detective Kenneth Hayes.

That afternoon, he had secured a warrant for 37 Martindale Street, Roxbury, the location that his snitch had told him would be the stepping off point for local distribution. Experience told him that he could waste no time. The junk would be there and gone in a flash. A judge was encouraged to sign the warrant that would make the arrests stick. His partner, Ronnie Domenico, watched anxiously on the landing below, making sure that they wouldn't be surprised from behind as they crashed through the door to the apartment specified in the warrant. Time and circumstance dictated that Panton and Domenico would strike without backup.

Jack Panton had served as a "recon" marine in Vietnam. He had been wounded in the battle of Hue and returned to action a month later, earning a purple heart and silver star for his valor. He was a mass of muscle and tenacity, towering over his peers and able to bench press two hundred and fifty pounds. His buddies in the Drug Unit were happy for him when he made Sergeant. They knew the extra pay would help him care for his little girl who was afflicted with cystic fibrosis.

As he reached the hallway in front of apartment six, he snapped his fingers to his partner, who was watching the landing below them. The signal brought Domenico up the stairs and beside him, as he knocked on the door before splitting it with a sledgehammer above the New York police lock bolted to the floor inside.

The thunder of their entrance was followed by their screams announcing their presence, followed by their demands that whoever lurked inside should come out with their hands on their heads or be shot. They heard nothing; they could barely see in the apartment, illuminated by one hallway light. Panton kicked the debris of the door and the police lock aside, dropping the sledgehammer and gripping his weapon with both hands, while making his way slowly down the narrow hallway. His partner was right behind him, clutching a shotgun and shouting again for the occupants to come out with their hands on their heads. No response, no voluntary submission to their intrusive authority.

A child, a black female no more than three years old, suddenly appeared before them and was almost shot. A face too young to be terrified, a victim of circumstance, she began to cry hysterically. All she was wearing was a filthy tee shirt with Big Bird on the front. Panton shifted his weapon to his left hand and snatched the screaming child with his right. He handed her to Domenico, who immediately placed her behind a hallway radiator and out of harm's way.

Panton continued to move slowly down the hallway with rooms on either side. Suddenly he heard a barely audible whisper in the bedroom up ahead on his left. This caused him to once again identify who they were and command whoever was inside to come out with their hands on their head into the dimly lit hallway.

He positioned himself in the hallway against the wall, his weapon held with two hands extended from his chest, his heart pounding in the ominous silence. Domenico was a few feet to his right. Both of them prepared to enter the room that contained the whispered voice. The burst of a semi-automatic from the ink-black darkness of the room across the hall spewed three rounds, shattering his jaw and severing his throat. Gurgling and choking, Panton slid down the apartment's blood-splattered wall, dead as he hit the floor.

Domenico dropped to the floor, discharging one barrel of the shotgun toward the location of the shooter, splintering the doorway with buckshot. Sweat dripping down the back of his neck, he crawled through the hallway's trash toward his partner, feeling the ooze of Panton's shattered neck for a pulse. There was none. Suddenly the hand that had killed his partner reached around the door jam, finger squeezing off an additional burst of three rounds into Domenico's prone torso. He could only roll on his side and blast a hole through the ceiling's crumbling plaster.

The hand then grabbed for the shotgun clenched in Domenico's bloody grip. He resisted, momentarily catching a glimpse of the face of the man that killed his partner and intended to kill him. The semi-automatic was pointed at his head, the face in the shadows staring down at him, no expression, detached, devoid of emotion. Trigger being pulled, no eruption from an empty clip. Domenico was staring up from the hallway's floor, registering the killer's face in his memory before his consciousness was obliterated under the sole of the killer's boot.

Searching for the plastic wrapped bag containing the morning paper, Christopher stepped barefoot onto the flagstone staircase leading from his front door toward the circular driveway and remote control gate that opened to his property. He had returned from a trial lawyer's convention in San Francisco the night before. His plans were to catch up on his yoga and tai chi, read the paper and return to the office around noon. The headlines of the *Boston Globe*, "Two Cops Shot in Drug Raid," caused him to shudder in the November morning mist.

As Christopher discovered that one drug detective had been killed while another was fighting for his life at Brigham and Women's Hospital, he reflected upon his years in the Public Defenders' Office. He felt fortunate that he was no longer involved with the kind of maggots who were capable of such a crime.

CHAPTER 30

At the end of a dead-end street, among the rat-infested remains of houses that had been abandoned by people, too sick, too poor or too scared to stay, stood the St. Dismas House. Years ago it had been an orphanage for Italian children, displaying the outward appearance of a brown brick private school. It was surrounded by a concrete courtyard and a black wrought-iron fence that kept its inhabitants in and the rest of the world out.

Now it was a halfway house for inmates from prisons like Deer Island, Norfolk and Walpole, men desperately attempting to reenter the world from the jungle of confinement and mayhem that was the Massachusetts correctional system.

That night, within an enormous, drafty second-floor room, a meeting was taking place. The old priest stood in front of the inmates' hardened faces and spoke softly yet forcefully.

"All of you are here because you have lost your way. Through acts of evil you have descended to the darkest depths of our society. But in that darkness there is light, the light of love. I want all of you to come into the light and love. For only through the light of love will you find your way again."

The congregation was unique. It was black, Hispanic and white. It was young and it was middle-aged. It was the dregs, the convicted, the incarcerated. They were there because they had to be. And yet they seemed to be listening to the old priest as he spoke to them in a deep baritone rasp occasioned by too many Lucky Strike cigarettes.

"A poet by the name of William Blake, who wrestled with his own demons for his entire life, once wrote, that the road of excess leads to the palace of wisdom. I believe that. I believe that after you have followed the path of excess and almost destroyed yourself, that is when The Spirit either lets you die or provides you with the opportunity to see and to feel reality, to understand that we are all one.

We are all part of the one Spirit that exists in everything and everybody. Each of you can partake of this Spirit if you love enough. If you want to love and have peace of mind, please raise your hand."

Of the twenty-three that sat on the metal chairs arranged by the priest in a circle surrounding his own, the response was meager at first. It was a black hand that had robbed and beaten other human beings that grasped the air making a fist as it was elevated. Then reluctantly two more followed his lead, then six, then eighteen.

There were only three who didn't raise their hands. One of them sat there, sullenly, his arms folded across his heart. His piercing blue eyes were clouded by a sorrowful indifference. His face had the recognizable imprint of one who had been inside and had withdrawn from the emotion of it all; one determined to survive alone.

His look was that of an intelligent, battered animal; a look that the old priest had seen on many faces over many years. The old priest's eyes besieged his soul. He sat transfixed. Their eyes communicated as he sat there, unwilling and unable to signify his need by the raising of his hand. The priest continued; his voice crackling and echoing against the walls.

"The starting point on the way back to light is to be harmless, to give yourself up to the Spirit, or the energy that binds the universe together and love. Love the screws that imprison you. Love the friends and family who may have forsaken you, and most of all, love yourselves."

"So many of us are our own worst enemies. We torture ourselves daily for things we have done or haven't done. The Spirit doesn't want you to torture yourself. The Spirit wants your company along the lighted way, the way of the truth and life eternal. Please come with us. It is not too late."

The convict's hardened expression gradually began to soften. The words of the old priest pierced his armor, touching his soul. The inmate had seen the priest before. It was a Christmas Eve many years ago at the Conley apartment in the Bromley Court housing project. The priest was old now, almost fragile, with pure white hair and stooped shoulders. The lion was beginning to fade, to become increasingly fatigued by the struggle. The force of evil was relentless.

As he spoke, Michael McLean, the inmate with the piercing eyes, began to relent and to dwell upon the old priest's words, as if they were intended for him and him alone.

"We all have feet of clay. We all have evil within us. All of us, if pushed enough, can become evil. But we also have the power to be good; to be a force for the righteous Spirit that dwells in all of us. For those of us who have known evil, walked with it and in some cases been possessed by it, there is an advantage. We have been to the mountain top. We have looked over the edge and we know that the only real chance for all of us is to love one another."

The old priest paused, gathering his breath to roar. His hands were raised in prayer, the inmates devoutly attentive in a circle around him. "Will you all, on this night, make a promise to love yourselves and to love others? Please, each of you promise me."

The voices of the fallen responded to him at their own pace and in their own way. Some were crying. Some called out, as if to reassure themselves that they could do it.

The priest focused on each of their faces. He didn't judge. He didn't condemn. He only cared deeply for each of the twenty-three in that room. His focus finally returned to Michael McLean, the inmate with the piercing eyes and anguished face, as he sat there across the room from him, wrestling with the demons that had dragged him into addiction and prison.

Slowly he raised his hand into the air, making his arm taught and erect. He hadn't cried in seven and a half years. Prison and tears can be a fatal combination. His tears seemed to awaken him, to release him from all that he had been through. Tears that brought him back. Tears through which he moaned, "I promise, Father, I promise."

CHAPTER 31

He came to the realization that his mother was dying almost a year before. Her cheekbones were protruding from her wrinkled face, encasing the deep, dim lights of her faded blue eyes as she held his hands.

"Was I a good son to you?" Christopher had beseeched her, as he reached across the narrow maple table that afforded her a place to eat alone in her tiny kitchen.

"Yes, Chris," she sighed, mustering a smile through the pain occasioned by her leukemia. She was seventy-six then and she would eventually welcome the death that would end her suffering.

Christopher was waiting for a jury to come in when he received the call he knew would come. His partner would receive the jury's verdict, awarding another injured human being compensation for misery and remuneration for preparation and eloquence that had almost become automatic when he delivered his summations in the courthouses of the Northeast. His success had made him wealthier than he ever dreamed. As he drove through the rain-soaked streets of the city toward his mother's home in Dedham, he thought about the unfairness of her life.

She had endured an alcoholic father and his rages, fleeing lovingly to her husband, who at a young age, choked and died from a blood clot in his lung in front of her and her crying children, thirty-five years before. She had cried and prayed that God would give her the strength to withstand the world and its indifference to a widow with four young children and no skills to earn a living.

Twenty years in the projects, worrying and struggling through the daily despair that infested the tiny apartments behind those heavy, green, metal doors. She would make her escape. Her children would escape as well. It was her love and her courage that had accomplished it.

Her children visited her and supported her, but they never completely removed her loneliness and her conviction, that life was unfair to so many for no justifiable reason. Then age and finally illness came to stay with her, though unwanted and rejected by all of her strength. They remained, weakening her, changing her temperament and making her bitter toward the futility of the struggle. Christopher, his two brothers and his sister all realized that it was a matter of hours before this unknown, untold story of courage would come to an end.

When he arrived she was comatose, pouring sweat; her breathing labored; her body emaciated and frail. She didn't speak, but she understood those who spoke to her.

Arrangements had been made for Jack Conley to arrive that evening from Los Angeles. Christopher's oldest brother was on the phone telling the hospital that someone would have to cover his patients, while he watched and waited for the drama to end. Chris hadn't spoken to his oldest brother for almost a month. His law practice provided few social occasions when they could talk.

Christopher's sister sat in her mother's kitchen, saddened and sympathetic, greeting Chris with a kiss and a long, desperate embrace, which needed no explanation.

"What time is Jack coming in?" his sister asked, as she poured herself a cup of tea, resembling her mother in the dignified manner in which she held her head. She was a thin, athletic woman with thick, auburn hair and a round, angelic face.

"Six-thirty," Chris answered, watching as his brother prescribed a course of treatment to the nurses responsible for his patients' care at the hospital, marveling at the youthfulness of his appearance. His close-cropped hair was still a chestnut brown and his face was that of a middle-aged choir boy.

He had always admired his oldest brother. As a boy, he had been robbed of his youth by his father's death, having to become a father figure at thirteen to his younger brothers and sister. It had made him wiser, it seemed, but it had taken its toll on his outlook on life. Chris had often found him too serious, too driven, too opinionated. His saving grace was that he genuinely loved his family and his patients and despite being doctrinaire, he won people's hearts with his caring nature and his skill as a physician.

Christopher left the two in the kitchen and entered his mother's bedroom. She looked troubled and in pain, lying on the bed below him. His hand touched her forehead gently and then he bent over and kissed her, whispering to her as she struggled to catch her fading breath.

"Hang in there, Ma, Jack's coming to see you. I'm picking him up at six-thirty. Please hang in there till then."

She seemed to respond with an imperceptible nod of her head. He caressed her hand, remembering her face on that night years before, when he told her that he shot another human being and would have to leave her alone in the projects. He regretted that he had caused her pain; that he had ever caused her to worry. He turned from her before breaking down. He passed into the living room, where his children used to sit with their grandmother on the couch, while she read to them and reminisced about the grandfather, they would never know.

The plane was late. Chris stood at the gate looking at the monitors that listed the number of Jack's flight and told those that were interested that it would be delayed. Christopher prayed that they would not be too late.

Jack arrived in a long brown leather coat. His hair was streaked with gray, yet his face was that of a young man. He had given up acting and had become involved in film making. He and his company had produced two of the year's biggest movies. He had been married twice and had fathered three children. Perhaps it was the restlessness of his nature that had cost him his marriages, Christopher didn't know.

He did know that it was the restlessness of his nature that had caused him to become one of Hollywood's elite, whether happiness embraced him at any time was anybody's guess. He was still an enigma.

The Mercedes pulled into the driveway of May Conley's house with two of her sons knowing that this was her last day on earth. She was still breathing as Jack knelt beside her bed, whispering to her and clutching both her hands in both of his. It was remarkable that she had held on that long.

When Jack had said his peace, he joined his brothers and sister in the living room. They sat together for the first time in years, each looking at the others, simply reflecting, but not speaking.

Finally the oldest broke the silence, "You know, she's quite a woman. I don't know if she's even in her right mind right now. But do you know what she asked me the two times she spoke in the last three hours?"

"What?" Jack asked.

"Is it six-thirty yet?" She was holding on for you to get here. That's amazing, isn't it?" the doctor's eyes suddenly began blinking back the tears forming within.

While they were talking, Christopher suddenly stood up and entered his mother's bedroom for the last time. He didn't know why he had done so until he saw his mother on the bed. She was rising up, unsupported by the pillows beneath her.

Suddenly, her face seemed to change from an anguished, distorted expression, punctuated by short gasps of labored breathing, to that of apprehension, then joyful astonishment and finally wonder. Her breathing increased as she sat straight up, transfixed by something the living are not meant to witness. Her eyes flashed open as the rapidity of her breathing increased, gasping yet grateful at what was finally taking place. Then her body, its life extinguished, fell back on the bed.

Christopher was the recipient of his mother's last gift. Her last moments on earth convinced him that she had seen the face of the Almighty.

CHAPTER 32

*H*er death was of little consequence really, except to those who loved her or admired her courage. She had never attained worldly notoriety or wealth and yet they came to pay their respects with her passing, to stand in line in whispered silence outside the funeral home. Some came and renewed old acquaintances, marking time by her death on their own mortal calendars. Others came because they knew her children, the reflected glow of her quiet flame.

The priest who had helped and comforted her during her struggle, the man who loved her and but for his vows would have sought to spend his life with her, raised himself from his position behind the altar to speak the words; a sermon delivered from the heart, perfectly capturing her essence and touching those seated and standing in the church, the place from which she would be buried.

Christopher sat surrounded by his family and the families of her children. The rhythmic rumbling of Father McConnell's voice pierced him, conjuring in him memories of her. He dared not look at the faces of those she loved, those she had helped to bring to life. He had promised them that he would also speak to those that gathered there. Instead, in reverie, he reflected upon her life and her passing. He had shifted suddenly from the blur of the present to memories of the past. There he found her floating unrestricted by time and space, in the recessed protection of his mind's eye.

Her attractive face bore the trace of a smile, her raven black hair, her hands folded almost in silent supplication, elbows nesting on a table in front of her. She was again a tragic heroine, tested by misfortune yet determined to persevere, to survive with her dignity, and that of her children, intact.

Since he was only two when his father died, he had no personal recollection of the night that altered the course of all of their lives. Yet the indelible recitations of those who had witnessed the horrid occurrences of that episode had created a vivid series of composites in his imagination. It was a collage of thoughts, combined with remembrances that preserved the defining event, the anguished past.

It was a grey spring evening, indistinguishable from all of the others at the outset. A supper table set with a white embroidered tablecloth and five settings, a high chair in place for the youngest. The '48 Desoto glided over the crushed stone of the apartment building's driveway. The unmistakable pattern of his footsteps traversed the walk adjacent to the building and bounded up the wooden stairs that led to the back door.

Suddenly he appeared, tall and manly handsome, with wavy chestnut hair and eyes that bore just a hint of mischief. Attired in a dark blue Boston Police uniform with gold buttons running up either side of his torso, he was proud of his occupation. He was proud of his loving wife and family even more. He kissed his wife first and then each of his four children. They were a perfect ensemble soon to be shattered by the unfathomable hand of fate.

There had been no warning; no chance to recognize and cherish how precious their moments spent together had been before they were gone. He had never been sick. Months before there had been a train wreck outside of South Station and he had injured his left leg while rescuing a young girl. He had stumbled and fallen on a railroad track while carrying her unconscious body to a waiting ambulance. He was a shift commander then, admired and respected by the men he worked with. He was just forty-four.

His dedication to his profession and the stamina of his constitution had persuaded him to forget the intermittent throbbing and numbness that was traveling slowly up his left leg.

The table had been cleared and the children had departed from the tiny kitchen, leaving the two of them there alone. She told him of her day with the children and he recited the occurrences of his. A pot of tea was all that separated them. Suddenly, a flash of excruciating pain gripped him. Her cries attracted the attention of the three oldest children. They ran toward her alarming anguish, confronting the cruelty of their drastically changing circumstance.

"Mother of God, Tom!" she screamed, attempting to comfort him as he stood and pushed himself away from the table. His contorted face passed from lime green to ashen white. The children were screaming now, "Oh, Daddy. What's the matter?" There was a look of terror in his eyes as he attempted to speak to them through the excruciating pain in his left lung.

"Call the ambu—" he moaned, gripping his throat and falling to the floor in front of those that loved him. She knew he was gone as she knelt beside him, sobbing uncontrollably. Her children were shrieking and holding each other. The youngest in his crib in the bedroom, unaware of the turn his life has just taken. The oldest composing himself, calling the police. It would be the first of many such instances in his now short-circuited childhood. They took him from their midst with a red oblong tag dangling from his foot, signaling to the world outside that Tom Conley was dead on arrival.

In the pew in front of him sat his oldest brother and his family. He was thirteen when his father died and immediately recognized that he and his mother had been dealt a dismal hand for no explainable reason. His religion was his mainstay, at one time contemplating the priesthood as his vocation, but later settling on medicine.

Like the father he never knew, Christopher's oldest brother taught him how to fight, how to ride a bike, how to throw a baseball. He also taught him that hard work was the only avenue out of the projects. Christopher admired and loved him for all that he had forsaken, all that he had done and all that he had endured.

Beside him sat his brother Jack. The death of his father had affected him perhaps the most. He was eight years old at the time and refused to believe that the man he loved most in the world had been taken so unexpectedly away from him. For a week after the funeral, he remained at the top of the tallest tree in the neighborhood, refusing to come to earth, an earth so unfair to one so young.

His sister and her family sat behind him. She had become her mother's constant companion after her father's death. They seemed to understand every thought, every sentiment that the other possessed. It was his sister who had cared for his mother during her illness, bathing her, changing her, wrestling with the injustice of her suffering.

All of these reflections embraced him as he sat with his family and the families of her other children in the church from which she would be buried. At that moment Father McConnell's remaining words awakened him from his remembrance.

"May Conley is gone, and for those who knew her struggle it may seem unfair that one so caring should have had such a life. But keep in mind that her beauty and her self-sacrifice were not of this world. Her soul now resides where it belongs, in paradise with her Savior."

He knew that it would soon be his time to speak. He prayed that the words would come, that they would inspire and give testament to her simple greatness.

After the priests had distributed Communion to the crowd, Father McConnell, his body bent by the years and his thick white hair beginning to thin in spots, revealing his pink Irish skull, nodded at Christopher, signaling him to proceed. Although he had made a living speaking in public, portraying pain and presenting his positions, this was different. He wanted it to be brief. He wanted it to be perfect. He began nervously.

"This is not a day for mourning. It is not a time for sorrow. It is rather a time to rejoice, rejoice in the knowledge that my mother's soul has been set free. Set free from a life of heartache and from a diseased and aged body."

His voice had now become clear and resonant, oblivious to the crowd that gathered there, soaring with the Spirit engulfing him.

"My mother lived her life unselfishly. The cornerstones of her being were the success and comfort of her children. The Bible says that greater love hath no one than one who gives his life for another. My mother's life was given up to us."

The faces from her life were attentive in the church from which she was buried; tears in eyes that had looked into hers. Her youngest saying the words they would not soon forget.

"Let us go forward from this place, inspired by her love and her unselfishness, for if we truly do that, she will have no greater legacy. Oh Mary, may your soul soar like a dove to the mountain top and may God bless you and keep you in the palm of his hand."

In the end, the tears came to him also. He had resisted them just long enough. He returned to his seat beside his wife and his sobbing children.

He could say no more. His brothers nodded their approval and their pride. He bent his head and genuflected, as Father McConnell blessed the crowd and then the casket carrying her body to its place of rest.

As the family followed the casket slowly down the center aisle of the suburban church, with its interior painted light blue and white like the sky on a beautiful summer day, they passed the figures that had played parts in her life. Chris scanned their faces, wanting to remember those that came to say farewell.

Unexpectedly, a face was seen that was barely recognizable. It was a face that had suffered; that had aged prematurely, yet maintained its strength; a face that Christopher remembered from the Bromley Court projects. It was the face of Michael McLean.

He stood like an interloper, in the last pew on the far left hand corner of the church. He was alone, wearing a worn, loose fitting tweed jacket, a wrinkled white shirt with a frayed collar and a tie that didn't match. His grey hair was worn long, combed straight back and knotted in a ponytail by an elastic. Christopher stared at him momentarily, catching his eye, nodding his acceptance and gratitude for coming there on his own, so all alone.

Chris had been told that Michael had gone to prison. He had spoken to neighborhood friends who told him that his marriage had fallen apart and his child had been adopted by the man his ex-wife had married. Twice he had thought about visiting him, but he didn't. The last time they had been together had been so painful for both of them. He couldn't do it. He couldn't confront the ghosts of whom they had been. Besides, he had his own life and its demands to meet, just too many deadlines, too many commitments to take the time necessary to make the effort.

It was at the cemetery that they spoke to each other for the first time in so many years. It was Father McConnell who brought them together, after he led the crowd in the Lord's prayer at the grave side.

"Christopher, I asked that an old friend come to the service. I hope you don't mind," the priest said, holding his hand gently against Michael's elbow, steering him toward his boyhood friend.

Michael smiled and spoke hesitantly. "You look great, Chris. It's real good to see you again."

"It's good to see you too, Mike," Chris whispered, opening his arms spontaneously and embracing the lost soul that had been his best friend.

The priest stood next to them and glanced at the grave to their left, a slight smile touched his lips as he nodded his head in silent satisfaction.

142

CHAPTER 33

From the window of the halfway house bearing the name of the good thief who had managed to break into heaven on the day Christ died, Michael was able to glimpse the skyscraper where Chris had his law office. His reflection from a cracked pane of glass stared unmercifully back at him, as he anxiously prepared himself for his meeting with Chris that afternoon.

The bony angularity of his face had become a fortress from which the sentinels of his deadly eyes kept vigil. He had been in prison for almost eight years and divorced from any semblance of a family life for seven more. His body and his disposition were hickory hard, despite having recently turned forty one.

His free fall into oblivion had begun long before he had threatened to kill his best friend and then himself, a myriad of lifetimes before. It had begun when the seeds of his simmering hatred and gnawing resentment began to take root in the fabric of his being, slowly suffocating the decency within him.

To those who attempted to reach him in the depths of his descent he lashed out with vitriol, lies and finally violence. Before being sentenced to twelve to fifteen years at MCI Walpole for robbing a supermarket and shooting a security guard, the elderly trial judge had asked him rhetorically how he had come to such a place in his life. His years in prison had afforded him ample opportunity to reflect upon a satisfactory response, yet none was forthcoming.

Perhaps it was his upbringing, a father who had lost hope and found his only consolation at the bottom of a bottle, a mother who progressively withdrew from the pain that engulfed her, finally losing contact with reality itself. Yet others had overcome worse, without finding themselves so far from reason and human kindness.

Maybe it was Vietnam and the insane cruelty that he had witnessed there. Yet others had gone and come back without plummeting into the abyss.

Undoubtedly drugs played a part. First it was the affair with marijuana, then the addiction to cocaine and heroin with their voracious demands of unequivocal servitude. But why was there the craving in the first place? Why was there the need?

Perhaps it was as simple as a character flaw or a genetic defect bestowed generations before, leading him inevitably to stumble and so swiftly descend. What difference did it make after all? Who cared anyway? Excuses were as bountiful as autumn leaves in prison.

As an ex-cop facing the hardest of hard time, Michael was given an opportunity to dwell in the protective custody section of the state prison, a place reserved for informants, child molesters and other associated vermin. He refused and was transferred to population as Inmate 851, taking up residence in Cell 56, an eight by twelve concrete crevice within Cell Block B. He didn't have to wait long to receive the neighborhood's welcoming committee.

There were four of them, one to act as a lookout and three to apply their special brand of affection to the new fish. Their design was to brutalize him and make him their bitch, their special piece of community property. Before long they realized they had dialed the wrong number. The Airborne Ranger, taught by his government to kill so efficiently, reappeared when his survival was at stake.

From the springs of his cell's bed frame he had hastily fashioned a stiletto-like shank that he applied to the faces and necks of his attackers with surgical precision. Thereafter he struck like lightning with the weaponry of his hands and feet, focusing on their windpipes and kneecaps, sending them reeling from his cell out onto the third tier. From there, among the bleeding forms of his assailants, he shrieked his notice to all who cared to listen within the cell block.

"I ain't nobody's fuckin' punk! I ain't nobody's fuckin' punk! I just want to do my time and be left alone!"

After two D Board hearings and sixty days in the hole for putting three of his fellow inmates in the prison infirmary, Michael McLean would grudgingly be left alone, to count the days, months and years of his dwindling life in a concrete cesspool so far from care and kindness.

It wasn't until his encounter with Father McConnell and their subsequent prayer-filled sessions at the halfway house that Michael began to think and feel like a human being once again. He knew that the old priest had gone out on a limb for him with the parole board. He didn't want to let him down. That was one of the reasons he was nervously awaiting the meeting that afternoon with Chris, a meeting that the old priest had prevailed upon Chris to arrange. The wake of Ed Brennan served as the perfect backdrop for just such a meeting.

Ed Brennan had been a legend in Boston, long before Chris and Michael had seen the inside of the Bromley Court Housing Project. He was a two-fisted, hard-drinking hydrant of a man, who had landed at Normandy and fought at Bastogne before his twenty-first birthday. While stationed down South during the war, he had developed a love affair with the blues music of the Mississippi Delta. Ed Brennan had given many a fledgling blues man the opportunity to perfect his craft and earn enough money to eat and find a place to sleep.

His bar at the base of Mission Hill and the blues music that poured through its walls out into the crowded streets had become a Boston tradition. His energy and generosity had succeeded in bringing a vibrant foreign slice of Americana to the working class of Boston. His wake in the middle of the dimly lit back room where craps had been shot, cards had been dealt and an army of blues men had rehearsed their riffs and hooks for the demanding masses in the barroom next door, was an indelible event for those fortunate enough to attend.

Christopher had chosen Ed Brennan's as the locus of his reunion with Michael, because it was a trolley ride from the halfway house and a familiar setting for a former sax player. Besides, Father McConnell had implored him to be patient with Michael and to meet his old friend more than halfway upon the path of his return.

He was seated inconspicuously in a booth in the far left corner of the barroom, wearing jeans and a leather jacket. He blended imperceptibly into the smoke-filled surroundings that Michael encountered when he ducked into the front door. Chris spotted him almost immediately, scrutinizing him as he made his way through the crowd that had gathered to pay its respects to the deceased and to hear the Stanley Carter trio.

Chris suddenly felt both pity and resentment toward his boyhood friend, now so much older and so visibly beaten by life, as he made his way toward him through the crowd. Had they not started from the same place? Why had Michael traveled such a hard road? Was it simply the cruelty of fate or a choice made to turn away from the light of self-sacrifice? How had the old priest prevailed upon him to become his brother's keeper?

Father McConnell had browbeaten Chris into considering Michael for a position as an investigator with his law firm. "After all," he could hear the priest repeating with his unmistakable rasp, "He was one of the youngest detectives on the State Police before his troubles."

Chris had run the suggestion by his partners, hoping they would turn him down and help him close the door on charitable commitment that the old priest had pried open. Perhaps an Irish wake punctuated by the blues was the perfect setting for such a decision.

Stanley Carter, a white-haired black man with the face and frame of an aging dancer, stepped to the front of the tiny bandstand and began to blow the strains of "St. James Infirmary" on his cornet. Gradually, the old companions began to traverse the distance toward reconciliation.

Their conversation began with small talk and shifted slowly to sports. Could the Celtics regain their championship stature? Would the Red Sox win one in their lifetimes? Would there ever be another Bobby Orr? Eventually the questions and the topics became more serious, more probing. It was after all an uncompromising job interview and Christopher Conley was an employer who needed to be convinced of the qualifications of the applicant, particularly after so much water had passed beneath each of their bridges.

"Are you still involved with drugs, Michael?" he asked, his tone suddenly shifting to that of an interrogator. He could tell the question stung like a slap. In fact, he wanted it to. A slight smirk of resentment appeared on Michael's face as he responded.

"What do you mean, do I crave it?"

"You tell me, man. Can you live without it?"

Michael paused, examining the label surrounding the green glass of the Rolling Rock bottle on the table in front of Chris. He stared back at his inquisitor's face.

"You want the truth?"

"Yeah, the truth is a good place to start, don't you think?"

"I crave it every fuckin' day, but I haven't touched it in over three years."

Christopher glanced away from Michael and changed the subject. He had developed a sixth sense for recognizing the truth and was satisfied with Michael's answer. He ordered another beer and a ginger ale from the waitress and then began to reminisce with his boyhood friend.

"Remember the time we went to that party in Milton and you stole the records from the cellar?"

"Yeah," Michael answered.

"And they came looking for you and found me."

"Shit! You really got a beatin' that night," Michael remarked, pausing momentarily to ignite the Marlboro cigarette in his mouth.

"You know what I'll never forget?" Chris continued, "Those idiots closing in around me and I knew what was coming and I remember saying to about six of them, 'You got a lot of balls jumping me. I'm all by myself here.' You remember what happened?" Michael shook his head. "You came out of nowhere and stood right beside me and said, 'No, he's not. He's with me.' Then you sucker punched the one who was doing all the talking and all hell broke loose. You remember that?"

"I remember some of it. I was probably high or loaded or somethin' at the time."

"What happened to you, man?" How did you get all fucked up?"

Michael stared at Christopher for a moment and then at the table in front of him. There was a long interval before he responded. "I don't know. Before I went to Nam it didn't seem like it was all comin' apart. But afterward, I was goin' downhill fast and I knew it. It was almost like I wanted it all to crash. The dope and the booze were used to dull the pain"

"What was Vietnam like?" Chris asked, searching for a reason, hoping for an explanation.

"It wasn't like anything that I ever saw before or since. It was like a nightmare but it stuck with you when you turned on the lights. There isn't a day that goes by that I don't think about it. You know that?"

Christopher sat silently nursing the beer before him. He watched intently as Michael reflected on his life in a barroom full of booze and blues music. Stanley Carter, with a face full of sweat, sang to the crowd about

Stormy Monday and the days that followed. The friends talked and listened to each other as they had so many times as kids. As the nearly forgotten bonds of friendship began to be forged once again, Christopher became almost apologetic.

"I wish we hadn't had a falling out for so many years, Mike. You were always my best friend."

"I figure that's the way it had to be, Chris. When I was in Nam and I received your letters from home, I hated the thought of you bein' there and me bein' where I was. I remember one day I was reading one of your letters."

"My platoon was supposed to evacuate a village because the NVA were moving up. I remember bein' in a boat and this mama san is on the shore with a pig in one hand and a baby in the other. We tell her to throw us the kid and let go of the pig and jump for the boat. You know what she fuckin' does? She throws the baby in the fuckin' river, then throws us the pig and jumps for the boat. I couldn't fuckin' believe it! Right then I wanted to waste her and waste everybody near me that had a part in me bein' there. After that, it just seemed like nuthin' mattered."

"What about prison, Mike? What did you do to end up there?"

"I guess I was supposed to. I was freakin 'cause I didn't have any cash and needed to get high. So I take a fuckin' gun and I stick up a supermarket in Medfield, in the middle of the fuckin' day. As I'm comin' out the door, this toy cop comes out of nowhere. I just started shootin'. The next thing everybody and their brother's chasin' me. I got a twelve to fifteen for armed robbery and attempted murder from old Judge Donahue."

"You wanna know about prison? You gotta pretty good idea what it's like from being a p.d. You know what's the worst part? It's the routine of it. You do anything to break the monotony, even become an animal. The whole prison system is a complete failure. If it was a business, it would've been bankrupt a long time ago. But nobody really gives a fuck. That's really it, man. Nobody gives a fuck, man!"

"What do you want to do with the rest of your life?" Chris asked, resting his head on his right hand and concentrating on the expression and eyes of the boy turned old before his time.

After a deliberate interval, Michael's response came in a torrent. "I wanna feel alive. I wanna feel like I made a difference by bein' here. I wanna make up for shit that I did and I wanna stay straight."

Slowly, Christopher raised his beer to his old friend and smiled, nodding his head in silent acceptance and appreciation. He would offer Michael a job as his investigator. He figured that he was worth the risk.

As the crowd listened to spontaneous sober and drunken tributes from the many that came to pay homage to Ed Brennan, two old friends began their last journey together.

CHAPTER 34

He didn't recognize the name. His secretary had made an appointment with just another voice looking for help, beseeching Christopher for legal representation. It was only when she came through the front door of his law office that he recognized her. Her beauty hadn't faded. Her style had changed, but her dignity was as evident as the gleam of a sapphire.

It had been twenty-four years since he had seen Lorna. It seemed like another life and yet, it seemed like it had just happened. The excitement, the affection, the violent episode on Parker Hill that would change the direction of his life. He wondered what she had been doing and why she had come to see him.

She sat on the red leather couch in the waiting room, surrounded by other clients, anxious to speak with the lawyers in Christopher's office, now one of the busiest law firms in Boston. She wore a pink and black skirt and jacket. Her hair was stylishly short and natural. The light in her eyes had not diminished, but merely required the assistance of glasses that made her appear refined. She had managed to preserve her shape over the years and maintain the unmistakable bearing of a lady.

As Chris approached her, she stood and extended her hand with the rectitude of royalty. The touch of her palm warmed him, as she smiled and expressed her sincere appreciation at seeing him once again. Chris ushered her into the conference room that overlooked the Boston

Common and captured the golden dome of the State House within its panoramic view.

"You've certainly come a long way," Lorna remarked, as she stood at the enormous window, gazing at the city below.

"I've had some good fortune," he answered, momentarily examining the contours of her figure, as she stood with her back to him. "Tell me what you've been doing, Lorna?" he asked, as he sat down in the ornate leather chair that commanded the conference room.

"I'm the Director of the Dorchester Counseling Center," she replied, as she seated herself at the opposite end of the conference room table. "Our agency assists in crisis intervention for people in the community. I've been the Director for five years."

"Do you enjoy your work?"

"I wouldn't want to be doing anything else with my life," she answered confidently, while leaning forward, her hands clasped together on the imported mahogany of the table between them.

"Are you married?" he asked without hesitation, curious as to the specifics of her personal life.

"I'm divorced."

"Any kids?"

"Yes, I have two daughters. They live with me in Cambridge."

She asked him about his life following their night together so many years before. He told her of his sojourn in California and the way in which he decided to become a lawyer. He recalled his work in the Public Defenders' Office and how he had begun his involvement with personal injury work. He spoke of his wife and children. She listened attentively to his recitation, all the while focusing on his face.

Christopher was surprised at the degree to which he had opened up to Lorna. After all, they really had barely known each other, he thought to himself. He glanced at the face of his Rolex watch and noted the time on the intake sheet in front of him. He knew that he had three other appointments scheduled that afternoon.

"What can I do for you, Lorna?" he asked pointedly, suddenly shifting from a personal tone to that of a professional advocate.

She paused before responding. Her eyes shifting their focus to the brochure describing Christopher's law firm situated on the table in front of her. She looked up and he observed her eyes to be brimming with tears.

Something deep and destructive was bothering her. He encouraged her to tell him why she had come to see him.

"I really hope you can help us," she began haltingly, doing her best to maintain her composure, "My sister, Eunice, died in 1980. She was mixed up with this guy and he used to beat her up. He beat her up so badly one night, he caused a hemorrhage on her brain and she died after about three weeks in the hospital. Well he was sent to prison, but she had a son and he's my godchild."

The burden that brought her to him began to take shape. She started to cry unexpectedly at the mention of the child. He reassured her and told her to take her time. He could almost feel her anguish as she continued.

"He just turned twenty-two in March. You probably read about it in the paper. He's the one they say killed . . . they say he killed that police officer and he didn't do it."

She began to sob uncontrollably. Christopher sat staring at her. He had read about the case alright. The television and newspapers were saturated with it. One cop killed and one crippled by a drug dealer, a maggot. He was hoping that she wasn't going to ask him to get involved in it. It looked like it was open and shut from the papers, a couple of eye witnesses and a murder weapon with his fingerprints on it.

He had heard that the DA was seeking the death penalty which the Governor had succeeded in getting the legislature to reenact, supposedly in response to the Commonwealth's soaring crime rate.

"Will you please help us?" Lorna pleaded. "I didn't know who else to ask."

He knew what his answer would be, but he just couldn't bring himself to say it to her, face to face, there and then. Over the years he had developed a facility for turning down cases without appearing callous or indifferent. It was part of his job, his stock in trade. As she sat across from him with her face stained by tears of desperation, he searched for a way to let her down easily.

"You know, Lorna, I really don't get involved in criminal cases anymore. I'd be like a fish out of water in the criminal court now. Didn't the court appoint him a lawyer?"

"Yes, but Booker, his name is Booker Edward Webb. Booker tells us the lawyer that was appointed doesn't believe him and he's down there at Charles Street rotting away and the lawyer never visits him or tells him what he's been doing. I've called him twice and he never calls back. I'm so afraid he's going to be convicted and that they'll want to make an example of him. They even said that they could execute him. I just can't bear to think about him being down there all alone. Lord help us," she muttered, before breaking down again.

Christopher approached her and tendered his white silk handkerchief, placing his hand gently on her shoulder. "Have you spoken with any experienced criminal lawyers about undertaking the case?" he inquired, standing over her, seeking an avenue of escape from her sorrowful petition.

"I talked to three of them and two wouldn't touch it and the third wanted a hundred thousand dollars. There's no way we could raise that kind of money. That's why I came here. Please help us."

He gazed at her. Her face was beautiful. For a moment he recalled the first time that he had seen her waiting for the bus in Egleston Square. Like the "Rose in Spanish Harlem" she was a beautiful flower growing up through the concrete. He couldn't bring himself to say no, but there was no way he could take the case. A case like that could undo everything he had built over the years. The bad publicity, the effect on the firm's clients, it would be a disaster. Besides, the little maggot was probably going to get what he deserved. He had decided how he would handle her.

"Lorna, I'll tell you what I can do. I'll put my investigator on it and we'll see if we can help you. If there's a way out from under this mess, he'll find it. Give me a month or so to look into it. If I can't undertake it, I'll see if I can put you in touch with someone who can, okay? Please, in the meantime, don't torture yourself. You've got kids of your own to take care of. You can only do so much, you know."

Slowly she composed herself and thanked him for his time and his words. She shook his hand after wiping the tears from her face and eyes. Her expression told him that she was at wits end and just desperate enough to believe that he would actually try to help her and her godchild. Chris would assign the case to Michael with the admonition that he didn't want the firm involved in defending a cop killer.

CHAPTER 35

He was buzzed into the lobby that led to two enormous metal doors that accessed the stairs that led to a gate that opened into the Charles Street Jail. A puffy, red-faced guard scrutinized him through the bullet proof glass of a faded yellow brick cubicle that served as the control center for the entire facility.

He was required to fill out a green questionnaire that asked him his name, address, purpose of his visit and whether he had been convicted of a crime. Michael reluctantly answered yes to this last question and, after being thoroughly patted down by a matron and passing through a metal detector, he was permitted to wait in a large concrete room behind a wire mesh partition for the arrival of Booker Edward Webb, prisoner number 362.

At first, he had resisted Christopher's request to go to Charles Street. He had been removed from the lock and key existence of prison life for nearly three months and was reluctant to reenter the suffocating confines of the incarcerated.

Christopher insisted that he go, explaining that he had given his word to Lorna, Booker Webb's godmother, and Michael would make good his promise. Christopher also made it clear that Michael was an employee and thus expected to carry out the commands of the law firm's senior partner. There was no mistaking his meaning. Michael was an ex-con on parole and on probationary status with his new employer.

As Michael waited behind the long wooden table and screen, carved with the initials and messages of a generation of jail visitors, he reviewed the newspaper clippings he had obtained from the Boston Public Library detailing the murder of Officer Panton and the circumstances surrounding the apprehension of the man he was to meet.

The evidence against him appeared overwhelming. There had been an eyewitness identification by Panton's partner who was still recuperating from his wounds, an identification by a Boston Edison worker who had seen the suspect running from the apartment, the suspect's prints were on the murder weapon which was discovered a week afterward near the scene and there had been admissions. The recent re-institution of the death penalty by the forces of law and order in the Commonwealth seemed to be fatefully timed to the arrest and prosecution of Booker Webb.

The sight of the man described in the newspapers surprised Michael. He had an intimate knowledge of hardened criminals. In fact, he had been one. The appearance of Booker Webb was not what he expected. He looked like a frightened boy. His skin was a deep brown. His hair was cut short with a part running up the middle of his head. He had a broad nose with large nostrils and scared, suspicious dark brown eyes set back in his head. His right arm was in a sling and his left arm was bandaged at the wrist. He was small, about five feet six and had what appeared to be a razor scar on his left forearm that also bore his initials.

Michael introduced himself to the young prisoner who nodded without looking at him directly. As they sat across from each other, separated by the wire mesh screen, Michael could see that this accused cop killer was a kid just about to come apart at the seams. With the assistance of the guard positioned to observe all prisoner visits, Michael was able to pass a cigarette to him. The tell-tale tremor of the prisoner's hands as he took a drag of it, spoke volumes to Michael.

"How you holdin' up?" Michael asked.

"I be awright," he answered, as he leaned back in the wooden chair, eyeing Michael warily.

"You know why I'm here?"

"Yeah, my aunt said you was with that lawyer she knows."

"Yeah, I'm an investigator for Attorney Christopher Conley and I have permission from your court-appointed attorney, Mr. Downey, to speak with you."

"Yeah, I called that dude's office four times last week and he never called nor come by to see me. Shit, he got me already convicted, man."

"Well, the evidence against you appears to be very strong."

"It's fuckin' bullshit, man. I never wasted that cop. I didn't have nuthin to do with no shootin'," he protested, his voice and his body rising from the chair in concert, calling attention to himself to the point where the guard moved in his direction.

"Well, that's why I'm here," Michael continued matter-of-factly, discounting the indignation of the young man. "I want you to tell me everything you remember about that night and I'll stop you and ask you questions as it goes, okay?"

"Sure man, and you and your lawyer buddy gonna walk on fuckin' water for me and walk me the fuck outta here, right?" he responded, shaking his head, displaying his contempt for Michael and the methodology of his mission.

Michael paused, looking directly into the insolent black face that confronted him through the wire. He beckoned him to draw closer to the screen to speak in confidence, thus allowing his emotions to simmer, before setting him straight in a voice of whispered strength.

"Listen homey, I don't give a fuck what you think of me. I'm here on a fuckin' job and I might just want to help your sorry fuckin' ass, if I can. But you give me some mother fuckin' shit and I'll walk right the fuck outta here and you can write to me while they're dusting off the electric chair for you. How's that? Are we straight on this fuckin' thing?"

The young man glared at the hardened middle-aged white man across from him. There was a long interval where he just sat and stared at Michael. Michael stared back without saying a word. Finally Michael broke the ice-like silence.

"You gonna let me help you or what? It looks like you need all the help you can get."

"You got that fuckin' right!" the young man replied dejectedly, lowering his eyes from Michael's face to the linoleum floor of the jail's visiting room. With that, Booker Webb began to recite the recollections he had of the night that the cops were shot. He and Michael spoke for more than an hour about where he was, where he had been and what happened when the police arrested him.

Slowly, the two of them became comfortable with one another. Perhaps it was a level of understanding and commiseration that only the imprisoned can understand. Its form was barely perceptible at first, not quite recognizable, yet present. It smelled like the animal, it left tracks like the animal and hid its cry.

Perhaps this thoroughly abject human being, all but convicted and sentenced in the hysteria and revenge that followed the murder and attempted murder of two men whom the newspapers and television had canonized, was an innocent man. His instincts and his suspicions caused Michael to phone Christopher at home after leaving the Charles Street Jail and tell him that he needed ten days to check out Booker Webb's story.

CHAPTER 36

All of the energy, all the effort, all the experiences, Michael McLean had accumulated, provided him with a rat-like sixth sense about people. The expressions of Booker Webb, the way he carried himself were that of the street, the badge one needed to carry just to get over without privilege, without education, without any prospects for the future. Yet there was a certain vulnerability that betrayed his veneer.

The night that Michael left Charles Street he began to piece together the strands of Booker's life, attempting to see and feel for the truth. His investigation ironically took him back to the Bromley Court Housing Project where Booker's mother had been beaten to death by his father. That was the turning point, the terrible traumatic occurrence that transformed a child of hope into one of fear and despair.

As Booker related it, it appeared to Michael that he and his mother were a matched pair, pitted against the world by circumstance, a world dominated by the hulking, violent bear of a man that terrorized Booker and his mother. He was an abusive monster, who called the roach-infested three rooms inhabited by Booker and his mother behind the blood-red brick and green metal door of the projects his home, whenever it suited him.

Michael visited the schools that Booker attended, examining his records, deciphering the impact of his mother's death on a child who had been a gifted student. A child once described as delightful, attentive and hard-working who slowly became disinterested and incorrigible.

He obtained his criminal record from the department of probation. He spoke with his probation officer, an aging, Hispanic man with a bald head and a look of world-weariness. Booker's history was that of a shoplifter, a junkie and a pickpocket, but he was never vicious, never destructive to anybody but himself.

He met with Lorna. She had attempted to help Booker when she discovered his addiction to heroin. She remembered that he was fifteen at the time and that he promised her he would stop so many times she lost track. He never could. She told Michael that it was his way of escaping. The treacherous avenue of getting high had twisted him, yet eased the pain of his crumbling life. Michael could see now what Christopher had seen in Lorna so many years before. Her dignity, her loving, caring honesty shone through her like a beautiful, warm light.

He gathered the police reports, the grand jury testimony, the eyewitness accounts, the ballistics reports, the fingerprint analyses. All of them succeeded in creating an air-tight package around Booker Webb. The case for the Commonwealth was overwhelming and it was being prosecuted by Lloyd Sorett, the politically astute avenging angel, who was District Attorney Martin Babcock's First Assistant.

Michael had become acquainted with Sorett when he was a state police detective assigned temporarily to the major crimes unit in Suffolk County. Sorett was ambitious, ruthless and undeniably the most thoroughly prepared assistant district attorney that Michael had ever met. It was believed that Martin Babcock was slated to be the next Attorney General and Lloyd Sorett was the heir apparent to the position he had always aspired to, District Attorney for Suffolk County.

Michael had worked feverishly for almost two weeks on the case when he met with Christopher at Dolan's in Jamaica Plain, a classic neighborhood bar where generations of Boston politicians had made and broken many a promise over the years. He sat in the booth in the rear of the interior dining room, nursing a ginger ale with a splash of cranberry. His graying hair was tied back with an elastic band into a small ponytail. He hadn't shaved in two days.

Christopher was almost an hour late. It had not been one of his better days. His wife had called to tell him that his oldest son had been hit in the mouth with a bat during a Little League practice and he had just received notification from the Court that he was to commence the trial of a medical malpractice case without his expert witness, the following afternoon.

The crowd of working class regulars in their scaly caps and tanned, tattooed forearms paused and stared from their beer and conversation while seated at the turn of the century bar that ran the length of the main bar room. Christopher was indeed a sight in his tailor-made double-breasted suit, monogrammed shirt and gold cuff links, as he stood in the doorway under the elevated tracks, searching for Michael's face through the cigarette smoke.

Although he had grown up less than three miles away, his attire made him suspect, a subject of derision, until he wore the face that he had developed on the street and made his way confidently, yet politely, through the bar's curious patrons. After spotting Michael, he ordered a Dewars and water from the waitress and made his way to the booth. His greeting was like a left jab stopping just shy of the tip of Michael's nose.

"We couldn't do this at the office? I have to walk down memory lane with you? It's not like I have nothing better to do, Mike. You know what I mean?"

"Sorry Chris, but I wanted to meet you here 'cause I'm supposed to meet someone else, someone that knows a little more about the murder."

"I'm having one drink and I'm out of here. Adam got hit in the mouth with a bat and Linda's all upset. Besides, fuckin' Judge Sullivan wants me to start the Drummy case tomorrow and my neurologist is testifying in Cleveland." After he slid into the dark wooden booth across the table from Michael, he cut to the chase. "What's up?"

"I don't believe this kid killed this cop, Chris, honest to God."

"Why do you say that?" Christopher said disbelievingly.

"I get the word from the street that he was set up, but I need to go to New Haven and I'll need three grand to spread around."

"You what! Are you fuckin' shitting me?" Christopher fumed. "I told you from the outset I didn't want to get involved in this case. I don't give a fuck about this kid. It's somebody else's problem. Now you're telling me you want three thousand dollars, you have to be crazy."

After receiving his drink from the waitress and taking a sip of the scotch, Christopher pointed his finger at Michael's face, barely controlling his temper. "Now I want you to write up a report and that's going be the end of it, understand? You've spent too much of the firm's money already."

"I can't do that, Chris," Michael protested, the veins in his neck distended by his simmering indignation.

"Well, you better fuckin' do it or get yourself another fuckin' job! Is that crystal clear enough for you?"

Michael suddenly excused himself from the table, asserting that he had to go to the head. In reality, he needed the time to compose himself. He passed through the crowd to the men's room, forcing himself to urinate, slowly returning to his agitated boss after calming himself. He placed his forearms on the table in front of him and began to speak in a measured manner.

"Let me just talk to you a minute before you get all pissed off, will ya?"

"I don't want this case, Mike. Don't try to persuade me."

"Please, just listen to me, will ya?"

"Okay, I'll give you ten minutes and then I'm gone." Christopher stared at Michael with his head propped on his right fist. He, too, was attempting to calm himself down. The effect of the scotch and the sincerity in Michael's eyes temporarily cut the hostile edge from his mood, while Michael pleaded his case.

"You know, Chris, I did some checkin' on this kid. You know he was a straight A student before his mother died? He was fifteen years old when his old man beat her to death. Can you imagine how that would fuck with your mind at that age?"

"Yeah, fuck you up enough to kill a cop without giving a shit," Christopher replied sarcastically.

"But that's just it. I checked this kid's record and talked to two of his PO's. There's no violent shit on it."

"What's his record like?" Chris demanded, finishing off his scotch and water.

"No A&Bs, no unarmed robberies, not even a disorderly person. You know what he is? He's a fuckin' junkie and that's it! He's got some store larcenies and two larcenies from a person. He's a fuckin' pickpocket, man. He's not a shooter."

"So maybe he was strung out and didn't know what he was doing. Don't they have prints on the weapon? Don't they have two positive IDs?" Christopher argued.

"Yeah, they do."

"So that's ball game, man. We're not talking about three to five here. We're talking about murder one and it's a cop who died. You think a jury's not going to want to hang him? Come on. Who's the DA on it?"

"Lloyd Sorett."

"Yeah, he'll be kicking the fuckin' jury box, screaming for the death penalty with that choirboy's face. The jury will be out maybe an hour, with lunch. You're not convincing me, Mike."

"He didn't fuckin' do it, Chris!" Michael insisted, raising his voice so that the crowd looked in their direction to see what was going on.

"What makes you say that?"

"I can feel it, man."

"Oh, great! We'll tell the jury that they should find him not guilty of murdering this dedicated, courageous police officer in cold blood because my investigator 'feels he's innocent.' Cut the shit."

The waitress returned to see if another round was in order. Chris abruptly asked for the check. As she left, Michael lit a cigarette and continued his efforts to convince his skeptical boss why his instincts were right.

"You know when I was in Nam, I met guys who were stone killers. They liked it. They got off to killin'. And then when I was in the joint, you knew who the killers were. They didn't need to advertise. This wasn't a junkie shooting. This was a fuckin' execution! This cop was wasted by someone who liked it. Someone who knew what he was doin'. The other cop is all fucked up and his ID sucks. He took two rounds and he's bleeding like a stuck pig in a fuckin' dimly lit hallway. His partner is dead and the shooter stomps him because he's got no more rounds left. This fuckin' kid is incapable of this shit. I know him. He's a fuckin' victim, man!"

"The world is full of victims, Mike. I represent them every day, fucked up in car wrecks, mangled by machines, burned in fires. You want victims? My office has hundreds of them, and they didn't bring it on themselves. I don't need to reach out and look for victims to represent, they're already there. I have a trial starting tomorrow involving one. Fucked up by a doctor who didn't take the time to do what he was supposed to do. I'm sorry, Mike, let somebody else take this one."

The boiling point had been reached, the mercury pushed to the top of the thermometer. Michael sought to restrain himself, but he couldn't. His hands stabbed the air as he spoke angrily.

"So that's it, write the fucker off. That sucks Chris. What happened to you? Too many nights sleepin' on satin sheets in Wellesley? Too many fuckin' zeros on those checks you get from insurance companies? I never thought I'd see it. You're fuckin' bought and sold! You used to be a fuckin' street smart mother fucker, now you're a fuckin' rich guy. You don't want to get involved because it will hurt your image. Fuck your fuckin' image! I'm tellin' you this kid is gonna fuckin' fry for somethin' he didn't do and I can't let it happen! You can't let it happen!"

"Yeah," Chris responded defiantly, "I am a fuckin' rich guy. But nobody handed it to me. I earned it and managed to keep my shit out of prison. Remember me, we fuckin' grew up together in the same shit hole, and now I'm payin' your fuckin' salary! You're on fuckin' parole and you're fuckin' telling me what I have to do?"

The words scalded Michael. Chris wanted them to. There was a period of silence where the two looked away from each other. Michael finally made a last attempt at convincing his old companion. He was subdued as he spoke.

"You know, Chris, nobody knows better than me how much of a mess I made of my life. But this kid and what's happenin' to him gives me a chance to do somethin' right. I know in my soul that he's innocent. He couldn't have killed this cop. It's not in him. This kid wouldn't even know how to do what was done. The ID sucks, like I said, and the admissions just sound like bullshit to seal his coffin."

"Who did he make the admissions to anyway?" Chris asked.

"The head of the Drug Unit, a detective by the name of Hayes."

The name triggered a memory like a switch turning on a light. Featherstone cross-examining a street cop in the Suffolk Superior Court many years before; a cop named Hayes, a confession that was fabricated to seal a case, the best liar on the Boston Police force. Was it the same Hayes now?

"What kind of a weapon was used in the shooting?" he asked.

"A semi-automatic biretta," Michael replied, lifting his eyes to look into the engaged expression of his friend.

"Where was the weapon found?"

"In a cellar, near the scene. It was in the bottom of an old bureau, wrapped in newspaper."

"Did they get prints?"

"Yeah, they say his prints were all over it."

Chris sat reflecting, turning over the scene in his mind, a turbine beginning to whirl and roar.

"Does the kid remember anything about that night?"

"He remembers getting high in the building, then leaving when he heard the sirens from the police and ambulance.

"Does he remember talking to this cop, Hayes?"

"Yeah, he was high, he says, but knows he never said the shit laid out in the police reports."

"Does he ever remember somebody handing him a gun after the shooting?"

"I asked him that. He doesn't remember it."

"Did Hayes find the weapon?"

"Yeah, I think he did," Michael answered, "What are you thinking about, Chris?"

"You say that Hayes is the head of the Drug Unit? How old is he? Is he in his mid-fifties?"

"Yeah, he's a fuckin' hard charger, been shot twice and decorated for meritorious service. That's the thing. This guy I know says he's dirty, man. He likes the hookers, the younger the better, and he's got snitches all over the city. That's why I need the three grand."

"For what?"

"This friend of mine from the joint tells me that Hayes is out searchin' for one of his snitches now. One that he tried to waste after the cops were shot."

"Where is he?"

"He's supposed to be in New Haven. He's hidin' out. He knows about the cops being shot and that the kid they grabbed is being railroaded."

"When are you supposed to see your friend?" Chris asked.

"In about an hour, I'm supposed to meet him at South Station."

"And you need the three thousand for what?"

"Two grand for him, my friend and the rest for the snitch. He says he needs to buy some protection and stay in a place out of sight. They live together. They're gay."

"You believe this kid didn't do it?" Chris asked earnestly, staring at Michael from across the years of their friendship.

"I know he didn't do it."

"Come by tomorrow and pick up the cash. But don't get me wrong, I'm not making any commitments."

Michael smiled as he extended his right hand, gripping that of his friend in a gesture of renewed commitment.

"I promise you, you won't regret it, Chris."

"Fuck you, Mike. I regret it already. I'll see you tomorrow. Don't get your ass shot off!"

The bar had only a few regulars left, as Christopher stepped on to the sidewalk under the elevated tracks and looked to his right. For a moment he thought about Lorna and Egleston Square so many years before. It was funny, he thought, how she had come back into his life and brought with her a mirror of his past, a mirror that he hadn't yet been able to confront.

CHAPTER 37

As a blazing, orange dawn forced its way into the Venetian blinded room, it found him sitting on the edge of his bed, anxiously smoking the morning's fifth cigarette. The growth of a two day beard marked his face with patches of white and grey as his small blue eyes darted from side to side in their sockets, driven by the rapid fire of his desperate thoughts.

There was to be an urgent meeting that morning, one that had been made necessary because their business relationship was in jeopardy. A loose end had developed and it had to be burned or torn off, before the fabric of their clandestine alliance unraveled. To the public they were mere acquaintances, but to each other and the inner circle in Providence they were much more. They were accomplices.

The old men who congregated in the back of the inconspicuous garage near the top of Federal Hill in Providence had granted them a license, a very special permit, accompanied by protection to engage in the business of supplying lost souls with imported powder for their self-destruction. They were conspirators in a dark endeavor.

Kenneth Hayes was the detective in charge of the Boston Police Drug Unit and the philanthropic Everett Kane, with his GQ looks and Ivy League pedigree, was a black prince and one of Boston's most prominent entrepreneurs. In concert, they supplied Boston's underbelly with heroin and cocaine.

As the July sun ascended between the thick white morning clouds, it placed a hazy, hot and humid envelope over the city. People moved like ants immersed in oil, as he drove his blue Crown Victoria through the streets of his West Roxbury neighborhood, framed by vinyl sided duplexes squeezed behind small, adjacent green yards.

The time and place of their meeting had appeared on a note in his weekly envelope, containing the customary thousand in small bills. There was no phone call. The telephone had been used to forge too many links in too many chains around the unsuspecting necks of careless, criminal customers. Contacts were made by note or by personal contact with a variety of obedient lieutenants.

Their arrangement had worked perfectly for six years. He was periodically supplied with sufficient information on their competition in the drug trade to allow him to excel in making arrests and securing convictions. In the process, a monopoly was being fashioned; a monopoly presided over by Everett Kane. His public altruism and legitimate business acumen was only surpassed by his confidential yet ruthless participation in the multi-million dollar world of narcotics trafficking.

The murder of Jack Panton had complicated matters tremendously. The public outcry for the apprehension of his killer caused the doors and windows of the drug unit's operations to be flung open to the light of day. There in the crevice created from years of desperate deception stood Jack Panton's boss, the man whose alliance with the very forces that controlled the supply of narcotics to Boston had helped cause Panton's death.

He had lost his way about the same time that he lost his family. There were too many nights with too many junkies, his ship sailing closer to the rocks. The nether world and the life of those who dwelled in it, and those who invaded it with a badge and a gun had begun to consume him. His wife divorced him. The myriad of times that he watched the apprehended walk away, rich and contemptuous, had taken its toll. His conscience steadily decomposed amid the darkness.

Maybe he was set up. Maybe he was always available for the right price, twenty six thousand dollars strewn on a coffee table along with a kilo of coke. It was a test for his battered integrity to avoid an error in addition. Ten thousand untraceable dollars, placed in an envelope that he stuffed in the back of his dresser drawer for two months, before partaking of it. That was the turning point.

They found out. A man with a brief case visited him and explained how they could expose him, unless he got his head straight and opened his eyes to opportunity. That was how it was presented to him, very persuasive, very effective, very much in his financial interests at the time.

They provided him with perks too. After he was in too deep to escape, they cemented his allegiance with a thousand a week. He was well worth it. They controlled his snitches. They fed him insider information on other dealers whose busts propelled him up the ladder to Detective in charge of eight others.

He received accolades and meritorious citations from the Mayor. From the dark side, he received money that filled his needs, an occasional eight ball for exhilaration and anonymous encounters with teenage whores in out-of-state hotels.

On the afternoon before the night he was murdered, Jack Panton had left him a note. Hayes didn't come on duty until four that day. Panton and Domenico were already working a double shift. They had gone on their own to get the warrant. Information secured of a shipment that was to arrive that would make all the junkies well. A shipment orchestrated and approved by Everett Kane, and not that of a competitor.

Signals were crossed and traceable loose ends were ultimately created. Hayes knew who the shooter was. He was one of Kane's closest associates. In fact, he used to deliver the weekly envelopes that Hayes had grown to rely on.

News of Panton's murder and Domenico's struggle to survive had galvanized the City. How could he deflect the attention of the detectives assigned to this homicide? —By demanding a role in the investigation. As the knowledgeable and dedicated detective, whose obsession to catch the maggot who murdered one friend and maimed another, he was both convincing and inspiring. After all, Detective Sergeant Kenneth Hayes was identified as one of Jack Panton's pallbearers in the photograph that appeared on the front page of the *Boston Globe* following his funeral mass.

It didn't take him long to devise a plan, to construct a web that entrapped another, thereby protecting his domain and that of Everett Kane. He emphatically swore to God that he wouldn't rest, wouldn't take any time from the job until Jack Panton's killer was caught. Booker Webb came along at the perfect time. He was a ready-made suspect. All that would be required was to seal the container shut. Booker and his addiction had taken care of the rest.

Hayes sat on one of the metal and wooden benches under the trees near the Providence City Hall. His jaw bone pounded three sticks of chewing gum like a pile driver, after he finished his first pack of cigarettes that morning. He appeared to be reading the *Providence Journal* while his eyes peered from beneath bushy brown eyebrows, scanning the location for the approach of Everett Kane.

A .38 caliber pistol was wedged into a shoulder holster under his left arm pit and a snub nose .38 was strapped to his right shin. A loose fitting blue wind breaker comfortably encased his expanding mid-section and stretched over the top of a pair of black jeans.

He had situated himself so that he could observe traffic driving by. He observed the black Mercedes as it approached the area. Its windows were tinted, making observation of its occupants impossible. He characteristically clenched his left arm against the holstered .38 as the vehicle slowed and then passed by him, traveling up the hill leading to the rear of the white domed City Hall.

He ran his left hand over the unsettling bald spot beginning to appear in the back of his salt and pepper head. His thick neck rotated periodically, allowing him to scan the faces of the pedestrians as they walked slowly by, oppressed by the climbing mercury and increasing humidity of the morning. He focused again as the Mercedes reappeared, this time maneuvering next to the curb to the right of where he was sitting.

From the passenger door, a tall, elegantly dressed black male emerged, smoothing the wrinkles from the rear of his double breasted, green, silk suit; wrinkles obtained in traveling from Boston. He wore wrap around designer sunglasses and carried himself with the confidence of an NFL corner back. He too scanned the area, before moving fluidly toward the vigilant detective.

"Let's take a walk," he said, his tone bordering on that of a command as he stood in front of the seated police officer. Hayes rose slowly, folding the paper under his right arm and accompanied the young man as he walked away from the Mercedes.

"My employer would like to know the purpose of this meeting," he began, removing the sunglasses and flashing a perfunctory smile toward the aging detective. Hayes stopped short on the sidewalk. The muscles in his neck were tense and the corners of his thin lips signaled his irritation.

"Listen, pal," he responded quietly, "I want to talk to the man and I wouldn't have asked for this meet if it wasn't important to our interests. Now tell him that I want to talk to him, and him alone, not to you."

The young man glared at the detective. A glare that disturbed the professional image he had attempted to present, like a stone tossed into a serene pool of water. He stood there staring, appearing uncertain as to his next move. Suddenly, the tinted rear window of the nearby Mercedes came down and a large black hand emerged, snapping its fingers loudly. The young man's head turned instantly in the direction of the vehicle. He moved toward the snapping fingers like a well-trained Doberman.

Hayes wasn't close enough to hear what was being said, yet he recognized the soothing confidence of Everett Kane's voice coming from the vehicle's back seat. Hayes stood, again caressing the .38 under his left armpit. The young man suddenly reentered the front passenger seat and from the rear driver's side door there appeared another envoy.

He had the features of a seasoned performer with thick grey hair combed back, like a middle-aged soap opera actor. His demeanor was deliberate and deadly serious. He walked briskly over to Hayes and looked around for an inconspicuous opportunity. He then apologized and patted the detective down, inconspicuously seizing the .38 without protest and placing it in the pocket of his Armani suit. The Feds frisked people the same way. He then asked Hayes if they could speak in confidence, informing him that he was one of Mr. Kane's closest advisors.

"So let's talk," Hayes muttered, as he and the man sat down on the bench where Hayes had been sitting.

The man offered Hayes a cigarette, commenting that his son had begged him to quit smoking. Hayes said nothing. The man stared straight ahead, without looking at Hayes, as he spoke reassuringly. "We are aware of your difficulties and we appreciate how they affect our mutual interests. "Please", he paused, shooting a momentary glance at the detective, "accept our condolences for the unfortunate episode involving the two detectives." He explained that the condolences came not only from "Mr. Kane" but also from the "gentlemen" that he reported to.

He then inquired of the purpose of Hayes' repeated requests to have a meeting. They spoke for several minutes. Hayes assured him that he had managed to take care of the matter up to that point without assistance. He explained to him the seamless web that he had devised to shift the focus of the investigation away from supply and ultimately himself and how he had discovered a perfect patsy for the crime that they all had participated in.

He told how he had known Booker Webb before the shooting; how he was a stone junkie who was always hanging around the neighborhood where the cops were shot, looking to get high. He had checked Webb's record. He lived sometimes with a grandmother on welfare and sometimes with an aunt that worked for some social service agency. He was too stupid to present a problem.

He recited how he recovered the murder weapon from one of Kane's men and managed to get one of his snitches to get Webb's fingerprints on it, while he was nodding out in one of the neighborhood's shooting galleries. He also explained how he had held off on having the weapon discovered until he could get the witnesses to identify Webb as the shooter.

One of the witnesses was an Edison repairman who had seen someone running from the shooting. It didn't take him long to convince the guy that Webb, who was always in the area anyway, was the one he had seen. He then went to the hospital to visit Ronnie Domenico, who had just been released from intensive care. Through photographs, he likewise convinced the officer that Webb was the man who did the shooting. After Webb was picked up, the murder weapon was conveniently discovered in one of the places where the junkies hung out.

It had all fit so perfectly, except for one small detail. The snitch that Hayes had used to get Webb's prints on the weapon had disappeared before Hayes could pay him off. Hayes had it planned, he explained, to supply this junkie with just enough eighty percent pure heroin to blow up every vein in his body. His death would be just another anonymous John Doe who overdosed.

But the snitch had split, disappeared before his fatal payoff. Hayes had heard on the street that he was somewhere in New Haven holed up with his boyfriend. Then he came to the punch line. He needed help in whacking the snitch and his boyfriend out.

The grey-haired man listened intently to what had been said and in particular to what was being requested. He complimented Hayes on the way he had managed to handle things and reassured him that they would assist him in this difficult time.

After advising him that someone would be contacting him in the next couple of days, he returned the .38 to Hayes during a departing embrace. He then returned to the Mercedes that awaited him and the man who commanded and controlled a small army of loyal lieutenants. Before doing so, he handed Hayes a matchbook from a Rhode Island hotel with the date, time and room number of a very young and very willing companion. Such were the fringe benefits of such a dark endeavor.

CHAPTER 38

he ambience of the place provided a perfect setting for reminiscence. The enduring emerald ball yard located behind a brown brick edifice within the abdomen of Boston, presented them with a symphony of sight and sound that spoke of a simpler time. It was a special place where a seemingly carefree present saluted the nostalgia of the past.

"A lyric bandbox," a monument, a shrine to the game of baseball where grown men could capture the essence of youth and hang onto it for nine full innings. In the place known to those who cherished it as Fenway, Christopher sat with his short sleeved right arm embracing the shoulder of his ten year-old son.

Because he had worked there as a boy, Fenway was a veritable treasure chest of memory, vividly preserved and available during yearly pilgrimages. The eternal underdog, Boston Red Sox, called it their home, always raising and inevitably dashing the resilient hopes and aspirations of their faithful, fateful following.

That day they watched from box seats behind the visitor's dugout, a vantage point within conversational distance of the manicured playing field. Red Sox versus Detroit and the sun of a June afternoon bathing them in its warmth. A father and son held in suspended animation.

With the innocence and optimism of undiminished youth bursting from his ten year-old form, Christopher's son, Adam, gripped his baseball glove, hoping for an errant fly ball to float its way into his eager grasp. The sight of his adoring blonde child nestled next to him, proudly wearing the cap of his little league team, unleashed a torrent of reflection within Christopher's brain.

He had come so far, achieved so much, more than what was expected of him. He had been the youngest of four and he had grown up poor, brushed by the back hand of tragedy. Yet somehow he had been preserved and protected by happenstance, circumstance or providence. His thoughts were of his mother and the cruel injustice of the hand she had been dealt. The dignified manner in which she coped, persevered and fleetingly overcame her fate through the success and happiness of her children. She had been their safe harbor, their shining light.

How had they been spared, he wondered? Why had they not succumbed, despite their mother's love and sacrifice? Was it all meant to be? Was it predetermined, predestined? Was it etched on some tablet in some karmic attic aeons before? Or was it self-determined? The product of unfettered choice, the reward for rectitude and righteousness. He knew better. He had seen evil suffocate innocence and goodness. He coped with injustice. He was painfully aware that life wasn't fair.

What did he really believe, he asked himself? That few were called and even fewer were chosen. As he sat staring at the profile of his affectionate son, he pondered upon the cause and effect that had brought him to that place in his life, a place of contentment and self-satisfaction, bordering on vanity.

As a child brought forth from the influence of nuns and priests, his religion had instilled in him an abiding belief in a plan, a paradigm, a design. As a youth, his agnosticism had called all of this into question. Yet, as a man with children, he had wanted to believe again with the innocence of a child. Perhaps that was the key; perhaps that is what was meant by being as a little child in entering heaven. He wondered.

He remembered that after the shooting that sent him fleeing to Los Angeles, he had lost his inclination for the Spirit, immersed instead in the experimental excesses of the Sixties. But this too had passed and he continued to search. He read Confucius in college, then Buddha, then Lao Tzu. He began to meditate, practice yoga and eventually taught Tai Chi. He was still searching. He was searching still.

While admiring the face of his child enthralled in the game, he couldn't help but believe that there was a rhythm to it all, if only one could reach it and became one with it. All of it made sense if you believed. There had to be a meaning, he thought, a reason for tortuous ways of hardship. After all, it was only through suffering that wisdom could be attained. Through loss and hardship he had learned and he had grown.

In a way, he had received wondrous gifts as a child. He had not been shackled by auspicious beginnings and he and his siblings had been exposed to the imminence of unexpected death. This was a keynote in his life. His father's untimely passing had fostered in him a self-reliance, a motivation to overcome, borne of necessity. He considered these to be the characteristics of his liberation. He was not weighed down by the mundane concerns of the petty or the privileged.

He remembered being in the second grade on Father's Day. The matronly teacher with hair that smelled like kerosene, forcing her class to cut and paste mementos to fatherhood. Waiting until the appropriate moment in the back of the class, he raised his hand to remind her that he alone was without a father and thus distinguishable from all the rest. In a way, it had always set him apart, made him special, made him strong. Of course, his teacher would catch herself and allow him the opportunity to work apart from the crowd, to create on his own. The memory was emblematic of his life, an anecdote for posterity.

Adversity at an early age had ironically spared him from other adversities later on. Like other boys, he had enjoyed the comradery and exhilaration of sports. From time to time, he had even excelled at them. Yet he was never required to compete, to excel, to outdo his peers by the prodding of persistent paternal pride and expectation. No, he was allowed by circumstance to reach and discover his own level, his own likes and dislikes, his own salvation, without an authoritative presence to mark the way or a diminished one to block it.

Such had not been the case with Michael McLean. Michael, the child, had indeed been diminished by the pessimism and brutality of his father. He was so very bright, even brighter than Christopher, and yet his school work suffered. He preferred to escape to the roof and play the saxophone, drowning out the cries of his mother in the project building below. Christopher had been thinking about Michael almost constantly since their rendezvous at Dolan's the week before.

Why had Michael become so obsessed with the case of Booker Webb? Maybe Michael saw himself in Booker? Christopher's mind hovered and soared through a myriad of recollections now. He didn't want to dwell on the matter of Commonwealth versus Booker Webb. In the setting of that afternoon, he wanted only pleasurable memories to invade his mind.

He suddenly became immersed in the flashbacks of a multitude of summer nights from long before. Errant faces on familiar street corners, fleeting vignettes of acquaintances, conquests and conflict. His mind was soaring over the landscape of his life now.

There he was, bare-chested in the back of a 1963 Oldsmobile, his body sticking to its upholstered seat. There he was in the presence of older, tougher boys, wanting to impress, passing a joint. Boys who had been laid. Boys who had been in jail. Boys who had taught him about the intimacies of girls and instructed him on the rhythm of the streets.

All the while the radio blared, through the Sixties, Seventies and Eighties, through war, through protests and through assassinations. Sporadically, he began to glimpse the steadily aging face of Michael calling him, smiling at him, advising him to take a cold, black pistol with him for protection. And then there was Lorna of the past and Lorna of the present. A face of passionate promise suddenly transformed into one of desperate disappointment, beseeching him for assistance. There she was, standing with Michael now, crying. Michael's words were ringing in his ears from across the booth at Dolan's. He was bought and sold. He was bought and sold by his own success.

He wrestled with the voices; he denied the truth of the words. Why should he get involved? Why should he be the one who was called? Somebody else would be there to help, somebody else other than him. But the words in his thoughts rang hollow.

He recognized that Booker Webb was standing on the edge of oblivion and Michael and Lorna were calling upon him in their powerlessness. Those vivid characters from his now vivid past had come to him and him alone to do what they knew he could do best; to step down from the comfortable pedestal that he had created for himself and to take the risk, enter the fray, intercede once more for a lost son.

He knew now that he was well within the firm grasp of his troubled conscience. He gazed once more at the son he so dearly loved, seated beside him. Then, in a split second, he reflected upon all the sons who suffered from the sins of their fathers, sons like Michael, like Booker Webb. It was at that moment that he made his decision to undertake the criminal defense of an accused cop killer.

CHAPTER 39

The hours that had once crawled across the confines of his cell like a crippled cockroach had taught him to cope with the frustration of waiting. It had been an acquired, simmering patience that had proven useful in his new found occupation as Christopher's investigator.

He had been sitting, smoking for almost two hours looking through the rain spattered window of the New Haven House of Pizza from behind the orange Formica table of the last booth on the left. He had stopped looking at the Seiko watch, given to him by Christopher, with the instruction that time was indeed money. He was there to meet Kim DeSimone, the transvestite boyfriend of the witness, who could help acquit Booker Webb.

Michael had met Kim in prison. The two were outcasts in a sea of outcasts. He had been a cop and Kim wanted to change his sex to accommodate his sexual preference. Michael had protected Kim from the wolves that roamed the third tier of their cell block. Both had been convicted of armed robbery.

When Michael was paroled, Kim was left alone, without Michael's demonstrated ability to deliver on both his threats and his promises. Michael's path had recently returned him to the semblance of a normal existence, while Kim was utterly lost and in love with one of Detective Hayes' "reliable informants."

Michael's hair was combed back, almost touching his shoulders. He was wearing a green t-shirt beneath a faded green sweater. His eyes had begun to tell him that they needed assistance in making out faces from a distance. He had no trouble recognizing Kim, as he passed through the door.

His hair had been dyed blonde and a small amount of blush had been applied to his pale white cheeks. He was wearing skin-tight jeans and red high heels. The convincing success of his transformation was evident from the suggestive stares of two construction workers, passing their lunch break, encouraging the rain to continue.

Kim looked around warily, then strutted toward his former guardian with just the trace of a vulnerable smile. "I'm so sorry I'm late, Mike" he began, snatching a glimpse of himself in the pizza shop's mirror, then fixing his coiffure. "Ricardo was so afraid that I would be followed, he made me take the Goddamn bus from across town. How do you like my hair? I was a brunette the last time you saw me, wasn't I?"

"Yeah, you look good, Kim," Michael answered, feigning sincerity. "I like the look. It kinda reminds me of Marilyn Monroe."

"Do you really think so? You know that Marilyn is my idol. Have you ever heard "Candle in the Wind" by Elton John?"

"Yeah, sure."

"It just says it all. She was so misunderstood. It was such a tragedy. Did you know that she was Robert Kennedy's mistress? I saw a picture of them in the *Star*."

"You don't really believe that bullshit, do you? I mean, I saw one where they had Elvis getting married and he's been dead for about ten years."

"You know, he really could be alive," Kim argued. "There have been a lot of people who have seen him since he died."

"C'mon, will ya? Have you had anything to eat?" Michael asked, seeking to change the subject to something more significant.

"No, I'm trying to lose weight. Ricardo likes me in a size seven and he says I'm starting to get chunky. What d'ya think?"

"You look great. Are those new?" Michael asked, focusing on the protrusions from Kim's chest.

"Yeah, I forgot that the last time I saw you, I was wearing a heavy sweater and you probably didn't notice."

"No, I didn't."

"Of course, you were never interested in me anyway, were you Mike? I mean all those years in prison and you never even tried to..."

"Forget it, Kim," he insisted, not wanting to resurrect the decisions he had made in his past. "You and me were friends and we helped each other. That's enough, isn't it? I need you to help me again, Kim. Will you help me out on this case?"

"You know I'd do anything I could, but it's up to Ricardo. He's the one that's gonna decide. I told him that you were a stand-up guy and that you helped me in the joint. He's real sorry about what's happening to that kid and he hates that fucking Hayes."

"Are we gonna meet with him today? I mean, I came all the way down here. If I can just sit down with him, I can help both of you. What d'ya say?"

"Well, I can take you to him, but you can't know where he is. I mean, he made me promise that you wouldn't be able to find him. He's afraid of Hayes. He already tried to kill him, you know. He knows that Hayes has been looking for him."

"So what do you want me to do?"

"Leave your car here and we take the bus. Then you gotta wear a blind-fold and I'll take you in my car to where he is. That's the only way it will go down. Okay Mike?"

Michael thought it over and agreed to the conditions of the meeting. He really had no other choice. The desperate state of Booker Webb and the fact that this was the only avenue that could lead to his acquittal caused him to go along for the ride.

The bus transported them to a part of the City on the other side of the world from Yale and its privileged, protective ivy covered walls. Walls of a different kind predominated there, walls of poverty, of prejudice and indifference. The bus seemed to gasp as it came to a halt next to the curb. During the trip, the driver kept focusing on Kim with a look of uncertainty appearing from his overhead mirror. Michael, too, was uncertain. A steady drizzle pelted them, as they approached a white Subaru wagon with the look of a mobile domicile. Rust had eaten the passenger door just beneath the window. It smelled of crack.

"Now, you have to put this on," Kim insisted, as she presented Michael with a brown rag that appeared to be the torn right arm from a disco shirt. "Now you have to lay down in the back with your face down on the seat."

179

"You know Kim, I'm against fuckin' Hayes too. Isn't the blindfold enough? I give you my word I won't look. I don't give a fuck where your boyfriend is. I just want him to talk with me."

"I can't help it Mike, Ricardo made me promise and he can always tell when I'm not telling the truth. You know that I'm a terrible liar."

The ride lasted about seven minutes according to Michael's estimation. Kim escorted him swiftly from the back door through a thick grassy area down four stairs and through a narrow cellar hallway that smelled of mildew and coal dust.

As his eyes adjusted to the dimly lit room that appeared, after the rag had been removed from around his forehead, he was confronted by a small, slender Hispanic man, wearing a cut-off sweatshirt and black jeans, seated on a dilapidated grey couch directly across from him.

His oily, angular face was accentuated by an enormous, imitation gold chain and medallion, dangling from his neck. His expression and the languid, distant glare of his coffee brown eyes informed Michael that he had removed himself from his pathetic surroundings by the powder that steals the soul. When he spoke, there was the trace of a stutter. "You come a-a long way to talk and I pr-promise Kim I talk to you. So tell me what you want. I be straight wit you, man."

"What do you know about Booker Webb?" Michael began.

"I know he don't shoot dose cops. I know he b-been set up by that mutha fuckin' Hayes."

"How do you know that?" Michael asked.

"Cuz he use me to get him high and put the piece in his right hand, so they get his prints on it."

"Who's in it with him?"

"I don't know, somebody big, man. Someone wit a lot of fuckin' juice. Dat's all I know."

"Why did he want to set up Booker?" Michael asked, lighting a cigarette after offering one to his reluctant host.

"I heard on the street he makin' a score and dose cops be fuckin it up. So dey get shot. Hayes, he don' do the shoot, but somebody he know do. Dat's what day say. Dis Booker, he there, man, dat's all it took."

"What did he say to you before settin' Booker up?" Michael continued.

"I real sorry about dat kid," he moaned, adjusting his small, wiry body on the couch. "I can help him now. I want to. Hayes tell me he need a favor. He give me some shit and I do it. I done a lot of things for him. He used to take care of me, sometime. Den I find he lookin' to do me. It sucks man. I no want dis shit. How I make it right and fix dat mutha fucka?"

"You're gonna have to come back and testify in Boston. That's the only way to make it right, Ricardo."

The look on his face told Michael how terrified he was of Hayes. It was the look he had seen in the faces of the Vietnamese when they were hoarded on to choppers for relocation, a deep anguished look of primal fear, a fear of annihilation and extinction.

There was a long silence as Ricardo stared vacantly at the floor. Suddenly, he began to shake his head and clutch the medallion dangling from around his neck. The muttered words that came from his mouth could not be deciphered. He was crying now. Sobbing like a brutalized child.

"I wan' to make dis right, but I go back, I gotta get protected. You gotta make sure. Kim says you look out for her in the joint. You gotta look out for me wit dis cop, man. He the craziest fuck I seen. You gotta get some juice and I ain't gonna get locked up for dis shit. You take care of it, I come and help dis boy. I wasn't gonna let him burn. He just a fuckin' junkie like me. Can you take care of dis business?"

Michael stared at the agony on the face of the twisted creature before him. He felt neither contempt nor pity. His own life had brought him to the point where he no longer sat in judgment upon the abject. Instead, he offered his assistance along with a solemn promise, if Ricardo came back to testify, he would protect him with his own life if necessary.

The sincerity in his words sealed the bargain. An alliance was forged in the bowels of a New Haven cellar. A congregation of lost souls would come together to aid one of their own. As he drove his rust-infested Chevy back to Boston, Michael turned up the radio and sang for the first time in years.

CHAPTER 40

$\mathscr{Y}$ears before, his training as a criminal lawyer had taught him to encase himself within a protective shell whenever he was required to visit a client in the joint. The overwhelming bang and blab of the place, the surly indifference of the guards and the hopeless predicaments of those he came to see were all part of the criminal mosaic.

Each and every time he had been inside he imagined what it was like to be a prisoner, to be at the mercy of others with an eternity to dwell upon the disasters that landed you there. Such was the case when he went with Michael to see Booker Webb for the first time at Charles Street.

The almost child-like dependence of his client was upsetting. It was apparent as Christopher, Michael and Booker sat together in the tiny cubicle reserved for attorney-client consultations that Booker Webb had been transformed by his situation.

His appearance was more that of a college freshmen than a career criminal. His forced withdrawal from the world of white powder had restored his innate intelligence and the doe-like disposition that Lorna had described to Christopher. Christopher sensed that if Booker Webb was convicted of murdering Jack Panton he would lose all hope and rob the executioner of the opportunity to take his life.

The belief in a particular client's uncompromising guilt was liberating. It provided a ready-made rationalization, a safety valve that relieved the pressure and reaffirmed one's belief in the system, a system where the innocent were supposed to be acquitted and the guilty were punished. Cops were not supposed to do the things that Hayes had done and compound it by framing a perfect victim. There had been a thousand criminals that he had represented, but none of them were absolutely, unequivocally innocent like Booker Webb.

The following morning, he filed his appearance in the First Session of the Suffolk Superior Court. A commitment was made, a pledge had been taken. He was to represent a man whom Michael had confirmed had no role in an unspeakable tragedy other than that of being available and vulnerable. Booker Webb was a junkie, the absolute dregs of a society that had recently returned the death penalty to the statute books and dusted off the electric chair for convicted cop killers.

The news of his involvement in the case spread throughout the city like flies on an abandoned piece of meat. An established player, an invited guest to the table of the elite, had spurned their society by undertaking the criminal defense of Booker Webb. Despite the years of expended energy and effort put forth, Christopher recognized that he would soon become an interloper in places where propriety was paramount.

Instead, he had chosen to return to those corridors of the courthouse where the beasts of despair and resentment appeared daily. He had attempted to prepare himself for the hostile tide that would rise even faster than he expected.

He met with the First Assistant District Attorney in his office behind the metal doors and buzzers that protected him from the violent and the vicious. Lloyd Sorett was a graduate of the Yale Law School who had positioned himself politically to accept the mantle of leadership when the powers that be felt he was ready. The conviction and execution of a drug addicted cop killer could accelerate their decision in his favor. He had assigned two members of his expanded staff to develop a dossier on Christopher as soon as he had received official word that his appearance had been filed on Booker Webb's behalf.

Lloyd Sorett was a descendent of the Sorett's, who had settled and controlled the North Shore community of Beverly Farms since before the American Revolution. His father had been appointed by Nixon as Ambassador to Luxembourg after a distinguished career as the Republican Senator from Massachusetts.

While Christopher and Michael were learning how to hot wire cars in the Bromley Court Projects, Sorett and his companions were perfecting their backhands and sailing techniques in Marblehead. His unrelenting good looks and patrician bearing had made him a favorite of the *Boston Globe* society pages.

During his tenure in the District Attorney's Office he had commanded the Career Criminal Unit. An individual was selected as a career criminal, if the case against him was insurmountable and notorious enough to appear on the front pages of the *Boston Herald*. Booker Webb's designation as a member of this ignominious club was a foregone conclusion.

Christopher had met Sorett socially on at least three occasions. They had conversed about forgettable subjects at charitable functions. He had never seen him try a case, but only preside at guilty pleas and appear thereafter for stirring pronouncements on the six o'clock news. Sorett was absolutely convinced of Booker Webb's guilt, based upon the overwhelming evidence gathered by the Boston Police Department.

Chris had been receiving updated reports from Michael as to just how formidable the Commonwealth's case was. The fact that Ricardo Calderon had been found and had agreed to cooperate with the defense had been a source of cautious optimism to him. Sorett had no idea what kind of hand Christopher possessed, as he introduced himself from behind the antique desk upon which he had just placed his pipe in the gold embossed ashtray, presented to him by the Boston Bar Association.

Sorett was a tall man who always stood erect. He appeared much younger than his forty-two years, with close-cropped reddish blonde hair. He had a prominent nose and penetrating green eyes. His chin and jaw were resolute in their appearance and his teeth were impeccably white and perfectly straight. He was wearing a coordinated ensemble that included a blue Brooks Brothers suit, a white shirt and striped red tie, along with a pair of inherited suspenders. His greeting was perfunctory and ceremonial. Christopher was cordial.

"Good morning," Sorett began, extending his hand and grasping Christopher's firmly. "Haven't we met before?"

"As a matter of fact, I was thinking about that on the elevator. I met you at a Children's Hospital fund raiser a couple of years ago."

"Oh, yes, now I recall. You're that personal injury lawyer, aren't you?" The rhetorical nature of his question and its import were obvious to Christopher.

"For the last few years, I've pretty much concentrated in that area," Christopher replied, sinking into the black leather chair facing Sorett's desk and recognizing, upon staring up at the experienced prosecutor, the strategic advantage of his office furniture.

"I'm told it's a lot more lucrative than criminal work," the prosecutor remarked, examining Christopher's appearance and apparel with an eye for detail, as he settled comfortably into an
enormous, black leather chair.

"I suppose it depends on the brand of criminal law you practice, and the clients you're called upon to ..."

"I was just curious as to why someone with your type of experience would become involved in a case like this." The tone of the prosecutor's voice bore just a trace of disdain.

"I don't know whether to take that as a compliment or not," For a moment, Christopher stared at the prosecutor without speaking, trying to decide just how much he wanted to reveal to a committed adversary. He leaned back in the chair and brought his hands together across the buckle of his belt. He measured his words as he spoke. "You know; I've asked myself the very same question, believe me. I suppose I'm involved because this kid is completely innocent and way too many people want to see him dead. Besides, I owe it to some old friends."

"You don't really believe we have the wrong man, do you?" Sorett asked incredulously.

"No," Christopher challenged, "I know you have the wrong man," his voice rising to a decibel above a determined whisper.

The prosecutor's expression was quizzical yet unremitting. It was as if he had come across some rare form of flora at the Gardner Museum. He probed further. "Tell me what makes you so sure of that."

Christopher knew that he had more than piqued Sorett's curiosity. Yet he also knew that further revelations to someone, so obviously intent upon the conviction of his client, would be fruitless, if not foolhardy. He decided he'd rather play his cards close to the vest. "Because I know this kid and he couldn't have done something like this."

"That's it?" "That's your defense?" Well, you're going to need a lot more than that to convince a Suffolk County Jury."

"That's funny. I must have been away from criminal work longer than I thought." Slowly he sat forward in the black leather chair, staring across the desk top into the determined eyes of his opponent. "It used to be that you guys had to do the convincing, that people like my client had to be proven guilty in court. Remember the presumption of innocence, counselor?"

Sorett stared back and spoke like a cop confronting an insolent criminal. "Don't you preach to me! Save it for the jury. Let's get down to business."

"By all means."

"Pursuant to the standard discovery rules, my office will provide you with all police reports, all forensic reports and the names and addresses of all witnesses, both lay and expert. A package is presently being prepared for delivery to your law office by messenger before the close of business this evening."

"Thank you for the courtesy," It was now his turn to demonstrate his proficiency in a field where he had become comfortable and conversational many years before. "I have prepared a Consolidated Motion for Discovery and if I could, I would like to address certain specific areas that we can discuss to see whether further motions and a hearing is required."

"Let's see your motion." "Do you mind if I smoke?"

"No, it doesn't bother me."

"I always ask nowadays," Sorett remarked, igniting his pipe and perusing the two page document that Christopher had devised from his years as a public defender.

"Now, let's see, "number four, a statement of identification procedure. You know that there are two eyewitnesses in this case?"

"Eyewitnesses to what?" Chris asked, attempting to conceal his contempt for the Commonwealth's case.

"As detailed in the police report, Officer Ronald Domenico and a civilian by the name of Daniel Sheehan have identified your client as the perpetrator."

"What was the name of the officer, who obtained these identifications?"

"Let me see," Sorett answered, reading from the police report, "Sergeant Kenneth Hayes."

"Hayes, Hayes. Isn't he the head of the Drug Unit?" Chris probed, feigning unfamiliarity with the workings behind the scenes.

"Yes, he is. He supervised both Officer Panton and Officer Domenico at the time of the shooting."

"I thought this was a homicide investigation?" Christopher remarked.

"The entire resources of the Boston Police Department were utilized in apprehending this individual. I don't have to remind you that this case involves the murder of one police officer and the maiming of another," Sorett exclaimed, his voice rising.

"Now who's preaching? You don't have to remind me or my client of that. Remember, he's spent the last three months in that shit hole at Charles Street on no bail status. I fully appreciate the dimensions of the tragedy that we're dealing with. My father was a Boston Police Officer. And he died when I was two. Believe me, sir; you don't have to remind me as to what is involved in this case."

"Fair enough, I hope that we can conduct ourselves as gentleman throughout this case, despite the magnitude of what is at stake."

"I hope so, too. Why don't you examine my motion and I'll call you later to discuss it."

"Fine, do you want to discuss your client's options on a guilty plea?"

"Sure."

"He can plead to First Degree Murder and Assault to Murder Officer Domenico. In return, my recommendation will be life without parole and fifteen to twenty from and after. If he goes to trial and is convicted, I will ask for the death penalty." The confidence and determination in the prosecutor's voice struck Christopher like a blow to the nose.

The fact that his client could die as the result of what he did or did not do had never been so painfully presented to him. The responsibility and its ramifications splashed over him like a wave of cold ocean water.

He sat there, momentarily pondering the magnitude of his undertaking, flashing upon Booker languishing at Charles Street, and Lorna with a beseeching expression, sobbing in his office. He then remembered Dan Featherstone, the seasoned trial lawyer who had inspired him to follow his profession. He knew that he had been tested many times before and he had not failed. But this, this was different. This was indeed a matter of life and death and he prayed that he was up to it. His words rose straight from the chamber in his soul that contained his courage. Intuitively, instinctively, he accepted the challenge.

"There will be no plea on this case. We will be going to trial."

CHAPTER 41

He took delight in the laughter of children. It was a tonic, an elixir that had often replenished him during the six decades that he had been a priest. Every year he would repeat the ritual, taking twenty underprivileged kids on a chartered school bus to another world, ninety miles away on Cape Cod. This was the summer of his seventy ninth year and the "Sunshine Weekend" he was about to conduct would be his last.

Thirty-five years before, Michael and Christopher had been on the bus, their clothes and toothbrushes squeezed into the green and white cloth bags distributed the week before by Father McConnell and two other priests. Neither had been to the verdant luxury and serenity of that part of the Cape before then. Each remembered the trip as if it was yesterday. A yesterday that had been totally transformed into a treacherous present for the twenty tiny pilgrims gathered together to collectively experience a sliver of life apart from their worlds of fear and diminished opportunity.

It was a simpler time when Michael and Christopher were children on the bus. Kids, even those from the projects, remained kids longer then. But times had undeniably changed and the children of the alienated, living where the alienated were forced to live, were robbed of something precious, something necessary. Within the crevices of urban decay, American children were being robbed of their innocence on a daily basis, and being devoured by the pestilence of indifference.

Christopher had marked his crowded calendar two months before and insisted that Michael come along. He did not resist. The chance to relive boyhood, to pause among the turmoil and reminisce upon a time of few complications was worth the effort. This time they were the chaperons, the counselors who directed the children, as they climbed upon the bus outside of St. Augustine's Rectory. Like the neighborhood surrounding them, they were black, Hispanic and white. Like the neighborhood confining them, they were poor. All of them were simply delighted to be there.

As was his custom, Father McConnell would appear like Moses, after the bus had been loaded and the children mollified with ice cream sandwiches and Hoodsies. It was the last weekend in August and the weather was cooperating by providing them with a benevolent forecast.

Michael and Christopher sat up front, behind the enormous, white haired driver, whose coffee colored hands caressed the steering wheel like the shoulders of a tender woman. It was his fifteenth year as the driver of the bus. They called him Cyril.

"Cyril, did you ever come on this trip as a kid?" Michael asked, leaning forward and gently touching the driver's shoulder.

"I sure did."

"When was that?"

"1953."

"How old were you then?" Chris asked.

"Eleven years old."

"Do you remember much of it?" Chris probed, curious as to the depth of the man's memory.

"I remember it was the first time I was out of Boston and the first time I ever been to the beach. I couldn't swim a lick. Still can't." The memory caused the man to smile and then to laugh, shaking his enormous head, while his belly rolled like a large lovable animal.

Michael walked down the aisle of the bus, asking the children, whose faces stared curiously at his, if they wanted a lollipop. The bus was almost ready to depart. Christopher watched as Father McConnell made his way slowly down the concrete stairs leading from the parish house. He was frail and bent. His thinning white hair was easily rearranged by the soft August breeze. The lion was fading fast.

Christopher studied him as he stopped to speak with an elderly woman, just beyond the brick wall that surrounded his church. His hands signaled his comfort and condolence to the anguished face before him. Chris admired him as much as any he had met. He was a disciple, much closer to the light and further ahead on the path.

"Hey, Father. Hurry up or I'll highjack this thing!" Michael shouted from the last window in the back of the bus.

The old priest smiled and hurried up the stairs into the bus. The children cheered spontaneously as he stood in the aisle behind the driver and addressed them. He whispered a short prayer and blessed each of the children before the bus pulled up the hill and past the projects where many of them lived from day to day. To those tiny pilgrims, exuberant in their escapade, the Sunshine Weekend was like salvation. The old priest had planned it that way.

The Cape Cod community of Quivet Neck is an anachronism. It is as if time had stopped at its boundaries, preserving it unchanged, undeveloped like a vivid snapshot that didn't fade. The bus traveled up a narrow lane, bordered by stone walls and wild roses that led to the retreat, a gigantic white farm house with green shutters within walking distance from a magnificent beach, reassuring those that visited it, that in some places there was a rhythm, in some places there was a rhyme.

Michael hadn't returned there until that day. Christopher had taken his children there on a number of occasions, relating to them how he had nearly drowned while swimming near the jetty, until Father McConnell pulled him from the water and screamed at him for disobeying his commands to stay close.

The children were in awe at first, then gradually adapted to the harmony of their spectacular surroundings, like minnows to a tide pool. Michael shepherded those that wanted to swim, while Christopher arranged their blankets and borrowed umbrellas in a gigantic circle, watching with delight as his charges laughed and frolicked in the surf before him.

Father McConnell told them that he would catch up with them after he took a short nap. The bus trip from Boston had made him "a bit queasy."

His absence from the beach gave Christopher and Michael the opportunity to get to know the children. To share in the wonder and excitement that delighted them. It also allowed the children the time to grow comfortable with them.

The splendor of the day was punctuated by the symphonic reassurance of the tide. To those children, living lives that dangled from threads of uncertainty, the comfort and tenderness of Father McConnell and the two grey-haired men who had come so far in so many different way to appear there together, provided them with reassurance.

Christopher watched as Michael led the children from the beach and onto the jetty that reached like a bony arm out to the sea. It was a day of blinding sunlight, the different hues of the sea and the sails that dotted Cape Cod Bay made it perfectly indelible.

Eventually Christopher walked toward the sea, slowly immersing himself and swimming like a careless child out toward the Bay. As he floated on his back with his eyes closed, he recalled another summer day, so many years before, when he was led to that place by a vital, indestructible man in a Roman collar.

He recalled his fear and his loneliness. He recalled how Father McConnell had made him feel significant, worthy of the priest's attention. He remembered Michael as a child, now standing visible on the rocks, his unmistakable figure, standing surrounded by the children.

As Christopher submerged and reappeared, he felt an inner warmth, a near perfect peacefulness. He was eleven for an instant, and in the midst of another reminiscence, following older boys off the heights of a granite quarry into deep green fathoms below. He could barely swim then, yet he couldn't refuse the challenge. His mother had forbidden it. His oldest brother had even threatened him with a beating, if he discovered he had gone there. Didn't they realize that their warnings made it even more enticing? He couldn't miss the chance. It was that way with him. It was that way with Michael. Now they were together again. The more things change, he thought, again submerging in the refreshing waters.

He was on his back, arms outstretched in the deep, surrendering to the sun and the surf. It was indelible. Again he was transported, back to being a frightened boy, fearful of drowning in the depths of the rock quarry's fathoms. It was terrifying, it was comforting. There he was, surrendering again, eyes closed, whispering to God to save him, to save those near him. He hadn't prayed as fervently in a long time.

When he emerged from the surf, he saw the old priest standing in the distance, surveying Michael's interaction with the children. They were returning from their exploration of the jetty. Michael was singing "The Saints Go Marching In." Chris had never seen him so happy.

The children were the chorus led by a tiny black boy with a giant's voice, bearing the name of an African King. Chris guessed that he was ten. How totally alive he seemed in the sunlight. Suddenly, Chris thought of Booker, then Lorna. He prayed for the strength to be their champion, to be their salvation.

After a cookout where the children ate like hungry bear cubs, they returned to the beach. Father McConnell organized a Wiffle ball game on the firm white sand, exposed by the receding tide. Michael's team made a valiant run in the seventh inning, but Christopher's stalwarts withstood the challenge. Any disappointment on the part of the defeated quickly evaporated with the distribution of one more round of ice cream sandwiches.

The sunset captured them sitting in a circle around their patron. The old priest spoke to each of them in a soft, soothing voice. "You know kids, Jesus always said let the little children come next to me, even when his friends, who were called the Apostles, didn't want them to. He says that to you today. Come next to him and be like him, loving and kind."

"All of you have seen bad things, things that you probably can't understand. Remember what Jesus said. In order to enter into heaven you must be like a child, like you are today, joyful and innocent. Be close to Jesus and say the prayer that He taught us."

With that, the priest had the children repeat the words of the Our Father after him. Both Chris and Michael repeated the words as well. Michael's eyes were closed as he did so. The enormous red ball that was the sun descended beyond the horizon as they left the beach. It would be their last time with Father McConnell.

CHAPTER 42

He slipped away in his sleep without suffering, without a sound. The lion's heart that had bestowed love upon so many had simply stopped beating. His passing was marked by thousands. They came to the church where he had comforted and inspired them, asking only that they walk closer with the Spirit. The lowly and the well-to-do, the famous and the infamous, passed by his open casket surrounded by a sea of flowers, each of them remembering his role in their lives.

Michael and Christopher carried his coffin along with four others whose lives he touched. He was buried in the New Calvary Cemetery, lowered into a rectangular plot that was a stone's throw away from the place where Christopher's mother rested. As they drove away together from where they had buried him, they were silent. Words had been said, thoughts had been registered. His life had been lived for others. That's all that mattered after all.

The demands of Booker Webb's defense caused the two friends to spend countless hours together, hours that reestablished their friendship and devotion. All of Boston knew that Christopher was Booker's lawyer. The sensationalism surrounding the case flowed through every rivulet that the media controlled. Radio, television and newspapers endlessly recited the chain of incriminating links fashioned around Booker's neck.

The courage and dedication of Jack Panton was profiled. The sorrow of his loving wife and children was indelibly captured in a haunting photograph of his disconsolate son and widow, while leaving his funeral mass. The charismatic Lloyd Sorett was portrayed as the righteous First Assistant whose track record of brilliant success in prosecuting the forces of evil in Suffolk County was only surpassed by the dismal background of the accused, a drug addicted career criminal.

They were right. Booker Webb was a drug addict and his criminal record exposed him to the scornful judgment of the public. Yet he was not the villain in the piece. Jack Panton had been murdered by forces co-ordinated and controlled by persons unknown to Michael and Christopher, forces that somehow had succeeded in manipulating Panton's boss like a laboratory rat. Only a handful knew the truth. Only a few would bother to peer through the haze of an expertly orchestrated illusion.

Christopher needed an ally. The newspapers had profiled him as well. He was like a heavyweight fighter measured to the inch. They described his pedigree, pointing out that he had finished in the middle of his class at Boston University Law School. They interviewed legal scholars brimming with negative perspectives on the outcome of the trial, scholars who had never tried a criminal case to a jury. Who was this personal injury lawyer? They demanded indignantly. Why had he taken a sabbatical from chasing ambulances to come to the aid of someone like Booker Webb? How dare he defend someone so despicable, so utterly guilty, and do so without the slightest hint of remorse?

Christopher had become friendly with Ron Shapiro in law school. They began as classmates and soon became companions. Instead of practicing law, Shapiro had embarked on a career as an investigative reporter affiliated with Channel Six. His brother was a state trooper who knew Michael from the State Police Academy and had even written to him in prison. Christopher needed his old friend to even the playing field from its decidedly disadvantageous slant. He hoped that he had the courage to do so.

Shapiro had agreed to meet Chris and Michael at Dolan's. He was hardly prepared for the revelations presented. He was a cynic by profession, yet even he found the intricate web which his old friend described, totally unbelievable. That was the problem. That was the need. Could he help make the incredible worthy of belief? Could he assist in persuading the public that the wretched accused had been framed for the murder by one of Boston's finest.

"You got to be shitting me," the veteran reporter exclaimed from the booth in the rear of the saloon, as the story was pieced together by first Christopher and then Michael. His angular features and photogenic grey eyes made good copy on the nightly news. Flecks of grey had begun to appear in his thick black hair. He appeared much younger than Christopher though their birthdays were just ten days apart.

His manicured mustache and baritone speaking voice were insignias that his viewers recognized. "I will need a double to cope with this. Hey, Liz, bring me a large soda water," he shouted to the barmaid. "Look it guys, I like you and I know you're not naive, but what you're telling me will blow the lid off this city. Channel Six won't touch this without a truck load of reliable sources. They don't like lawyers and libel suits. I don't either."

As the afternoon passed, the three of them sat together contemplating strategies and suggesting avenues of recourse that would give Booker Webb a chance. "How about it, if Michael takes you down to New Haven, so you can talk to this guy yourself?" Christopher implored, from across the booth's red and white checkered table cloth. "Would that be...?"

"No way," Michael interrupted. "He's scared shit about gettin' wacked. I bring a stranger down there, we might lose him completely."

"Hey, Mike," Chris argued, "we need all the help we can get. We have to somehow get the truth out. Everything you see, everything you read. Forget the presumption of fucking innocence. I bet there's about ten thousand people out there right now who would volunteer to pull the switch on this kid."

"You got that right," the reporter agreed, "I wouldn't want to try and pick a jury for this kid. You really believe he's innocent, huh?"

"I know he's innocent," Michael insisted, "and Chris knows he's innocent. More important, fuckin' Hayes knows he's innocent. The only trouble is everybody else wants to hang him by the balls."

"Wait a minute," the reporter remarked, as the wheels of experience rolled within his brain, "Maybe I can't run the story just yet, but maybe I can make things a little interesting for your friend, Hayes. How about I meet with him and tell him I want to do a piece on Jack Panton and the dangers of being a drug cop. Who knows? Maybe we can shake something loose?"

"It's definitely worth a shot," Chris urged.

"It's the best I can do for you," Shapiro promised, staring across the bar room table at the hopeful expressions of his two hosts.

Although disappointed, Christopher fully understood the risks that prohibited his friend from committing himself and his television station to the crusade for Booker Webb. He took comfort in the fact that Shapiro seemed convinced that an injustice had in fact occurred. He knew his friend well enough to leave the rest to his devices. Ron Shapiro was not only a man of his word; he was inordinately resourceful in delving into the depths of deception.

On the drive back to his home in Wellesley, Christopher's mind was beset by the difficulties that presented themselves at every turn in the defense of Booker Webb. There was the precarious nature of keeping Ricardo Calderon alive and on ice, until just the right moment. There was the apparent certainty of Webb's identification by both a civilian and an experienced police detective. And last, there was the unremitting tide of sympathy that arose around Jack Panton's memory. If only he could chip away with a well-placed story, a timely sound bite that might just create a crack in the dam, a chink in the armor.

He thought about Hayes, the battler, a crafty middleweight with the head of a mastiff. He remembered how he withstood the cross-examination of Dan Featherstone twenty years before; how convincing he could be, even while lying through his teeth. It was the first week in November and the hearing on his Motion to Suppress was scheduled for the middle of the following week.

He reminded himself to get in touch with Dan Featherstone before the date of the hearing, in order to gain an insight, an advantage in his approach to destroying the credibility of one of the Boston Police Department's finest fabricators. He prayed that Ron Shapiro would help in delivering some overdue karma to Detective Sergeant Kenneth Hayes.

CHAPTER 43

When he was younger it didn't bother him, he was mostly swept away in the adventure of it all. It had been like so many other things that age had eroded. It used to be that he could walk with them, talk with them, even joke with them and then after he had done his best for them, watch with detachment as they were led away in shock, sometimes screaming their innocence or crying to a loved one that had come to see the trial.

The trials, there had been so many. He had become proficient at juggling lives like little blue rubber balls. He never thought too much about it. He took satisfaction and comfort in the fact that few could have done better in the representation of the wretched. Losing was perceived as one of the inevitable consequences of trying to defend the indigent criminal. He tried to recapture the detachment so necessary for his self-preservation in defending Booker Webb. He simply could not do it.

Perhaps the wisdom derived from his struggle for success was in this instance a liability, robbing him of his power to refrain from caring too much. He understood how his own children were given an advantage that removed them from the daily struggle of the dispossessed, a struggle that he had managed to escape by threads of fate and circumstance. What about those whom fate had ignored? What about those that spent their lives clawing and sliding down the walls of an American nightmare?

From his home in Wellesley, he couldn't see the Bromley Court Housing Project and as Michael had said, he had almost forgotten that it ever existed among the promise and privilege that he had earned for himself and his family. Michael had been the messenger, but Booker Webb was the message.

Booker Webb had brought him to see the awful reality that was America, like a grotesque apparition in shards of broken glass. In virtually every American city, there were thousands of Booker Webbs. Thousands who were born without hope, without a chance of awakening from a nightmare of indifference, thousands who would grow to fill the prisons of America, or die on its streets with their youth and their hope seeping into the sewer that surrounded them.

He had never really been able to reconcile it, the notion that God cared and dwelled close enough to influence our daily lives and the terrible agony that fell upon so many of the innocent, so many of the defenseless. It was Booker Webb who made him ponder and protest against the injustice of it all.

The night before the beginning of the end, Chris visited Booker at the Charles Street Jail. Twice before they had met and spoken with Michael present and participating in their trial preparation sessions. But this was different. It was the first time that Chris and Booker had been alone together. It was the first time that Chris came, simply to spend time with his deeply devoted client.

He had been ushered into the rectangular concrete conference room perched above the enormous expanse of the jail's flats, by an overweight, oily guard who made no attempt to conceal his contempt for both Booker Webb and his lawyer.

"You just wait right here, counselor," the guard sneered, as Chris pulled a rusted metal chair up to the battered wooden conference table, scarred with the initials and messages of a thousand idle visitors. "I'll make sure and send your boy right up. Hey, did you talk to him about what kind of casket he wants?"

Christopher choked back a profane response, while attempting to restrain his fury. Instead, he stared icily at the combative countenance of the screw. There was really no mileage in matching wits with an imbecile, he told himself, as the guard slammed the steel door to the conference room shut, effectively sealing Christopher off from the relentless din that engulfed the joint outside. During the half hour that transpired before

Booker arrived in the company of two enormous guards, Christopher reviewed the Grand Jury testimony of Hayes and Domenico.

Before allowing Booker to confer with his attorney, the older of the two guards, a red-faced, red haired bear of a man explained that a pat down was required of Christopher by jail regulation. Although Christopher had never heard of such a regulation, he submitted to the search and accepted the perfunctory apology of the younger guard.

After they departed, locking the conference room door behind them, Christopher pulled up two chairs in the far corner of the room and invited Booker to sit next to him. The gesture seemed to signal the beginning of a new phase in their uncertain relationship.

"How are you holding up?" Christopher inquired, leaning over and looking into the shattered brown eyes of his client.

"I've been alright," Booker muttered in a near whisper, betraying the insincerity of his response.

"Has Lorna been by to see you?"

Booker shook his head, remarking in the same subdued tone; "I don't want her coming round no more. It's been hard. She be crying and shit. It's bad enough in here without that." His hands seemed to be searching nervously for a place to remain stationary.

Spontaneously, Christopher reached out to Booker, his right palm outstretched. Momentarily, Booker glanced at the white skin of Christopher's beseeching hand and then at the face of his only hope. Slowly, hesitatingly, he reached and grasped the offering presented to him, holding on like a frightened child. Neither of them spoke. Words were superfluous.

In a voice choked with the emotion of months of preparation and anticipation, Christopher eventually spoke.

"I'm going to give you the best I got, man. I can't do any more than what I've done to get ready for this. You've got to promise me you won't lose hope."

Booker stared back at Chris. His expression was twisted by a multitude of emotions. His eyes were brimming with tears. His mouth quivered as he attempted to form the words that shivered through him.

"We got any kind of a shot in this thing, Mr. Conley? Tell me the truth. I can't handle any more bullshit."

Christopher reached again for the cold, sweaty hand of his young client and gripped it firmly. He couldn't help but think about how young he appeared, how frail, how completely lost he looked in the faded denim issue of the jail where he was slowly deteriorating. If Christopher had been more detached, he could have given him the standard response. But this case had expanded beyond the realm of standard responses. His response was the complete, unvarnished truth.

"Our only shot is Calderon. He comes in and the jury believes him, we've got a fighting chance."

Booker pondered the response as he stared at the floor beneath his feet. His head began to sway back and forth as the rage welled up within him. His voice rose from a whisper to a near desperate shriek.

"What a mother fucker, man! What a fucking mess I'm in. The only hope I got is the word of a junkie, like me. That ain't much, Mr. Conley."

Without thinking, Christopher draped his right arm over Booker's slender shoulder and pulled him to him in an affectionate, desperate embrace. The young prisoner clung to him like a lost son. For a moment, the two of them were one in each other's arms. Sensing that Booker's hope was oozing from him and knowing that hope was essential to any chance of an acquittal, Christopher mustered his strength and spoke.

"Sometimes, when everything looks like shit, when everything you do, everything you see seems to be against you, it's like a test and if you don't lose hope and believe that somewhere, somehow, something's going to happen that's going to make it right, all of a sudden it turns. And things start breaking your way. I have to believe that's what's going to happen here. You have to believe it too."

Before the guards came for him, the look in Booker's eyes told Chris that a spark of hope was still alive, just a spark.

CHAPTER 44

As he approached the Center Plaza Garage, he listened to the nine o'clock news on the radio of his Mercedes. The announcer told those that listened that preliminary hearings were set to begin on Booker Webb's murder case. As he walked across the concourse toward the courthouse, he spotted Michael pacing impatiently on the courthouse steps. Something was bothering him, he could always tell.

"What is it?" Chris inquired, with a tone of impending doom. His observations of Michael had been correct.

"I can't find our friend in New Haven."

"Since when?"

"Since two days ago."

"You think they wacked him?" Christopher asked, the desperation in his voice coming through loud and clear.

"I don't know. I don't think so. I think he just split. What the fuck are we gonna do, man?

Chris felt sick. He could see the waiting horde of reporters, positioned to pounce within the confines of the courthouse lobby. He had to compose himself. He had received bad news at the last moment before. It was an occupational hazard in medical malpractice cases to have an expert witness "go south" without warning.

This was different though. This wasn't about damages, or the embarrassment of revealing a weakened hand to an insurance company. This was life and death, Booker's life and death. Chris instructed Michael. "Let's just walk in there like we got them by the balls. I don't want the front page of tomorrow's newspapers telling the world, we know we're fucked."

After a collective deep breath, the two friends entered the courthouse lobby and were immediately besieged by the waiting rabble. Questions being shouted, camera mechanisms whining like angry rodents, the frantic crowd of reporters confining them, inquiring, probing, before they escaped on the elevator to the ninth floor. As the doors opened, more reporters awaited. Chris smiled politely, promising the throng that he would speak to them following the proceedings of that day. He hoped that his expression had not revealed the hopeless predicament he and his client were in.

Why had he become involved in this case anyway, he again began to ask himself, as he opened the leather covered doors into Courtroom 906. When he saw Booker sitting handcuffed between two court officers, surrounded by a hostile host of eager spectators, he knew the answer.

He walked over to Booker and placed his hand on his right arm, reassuring him. The expression on his face of utter faith and dependence, made Chris angry and aggressive. He would need to be both and he knew it. If the truth was worth anything, he would win, he tried to tell himself. Michael stood on the other side of the oak partition that marked the boundaries of Chris's arena. He beckoned Christopher and grasped his hand forcefully, as he whispered his encouragement to his old friend, "Give it your best, man."

"You got it," Chris replied, looking into the face that was unable to mask its disappointment, at Calderon's disappearance.

From the corridor leading to the back stairs that provided access for the lawyers and court officers to the courtrooms on the floors below, emerged Lloyd Sorett. He was accompanied by a young black man and an attractive brunette. They each carried a briefcase and a file under their right arms. By the expression on their faces, Christopher's opposition appeared prepared and formidable. He wondered if they could tell how desperate he felt at that moment.

Judge Hector Aubregon was a Cuban refugee whose family had escaped the Castro regime thirty years before. He was the first Hispanic Judge appointed to the Superior Court and had developed an impressive reputation as an incisive and impartial jurist. He was a small man with a muscular build and thick, curly black hair. His olive complexion and oval face made him appear almost angelic above his black robe.

His voice was that of a tenor, capable of leading an inspired choir. His appointment to the case was the only beneficial development that Booker's defense had received. Judge Aubregon would stop the circus from coming to Courtroom 906.

The clerk addressed the lawyers and the crowd that filled the enormous drafty courtroom. The television stations had commissioned two court-room artists to memorialize the scene. They sat across from each other, their charcoal pencils recreating the moment for the six o'clock news. The clerk cried out, "Calling Case Number 92-2061, Commonwealth v. Booker Webb. Would counsel identify themselves for the record?"

Chris stood erect wearing a grey pin striped suit and white shirt. His grey hair had been recently cut and his imported shoes had been vigorously polished a golden brown.

"Your Honor, Attorney Christopher Conley representing the accused."

He never liked to refer to his criminal clients as defendants. At least the appellation of accused preserved the fiction that Booker Webb was presumed to be innocent of killing Jack Panton.

The Assistant District Attorney then addressed the Court and the crowd that had come to that place on that day, "Assistant District Attorney Lloyd Sorett representing the Commonwealth."

Judge Aubregon glanced at Booker as he sat nervously, repeatedly rubbing his forefinger in the crevice beneath his bottom lip. Lorna had purchased a dark blue suit for him at Filene's Basement. He wore a white shirt and a red and grey striped tie. The suit was too large for his painfully thin body. Booker looked like a terminally ill patient waiting for death to end his agony.

Christopher prayed that the image was not an omen, as he stood and began to present his evidence at the Motion to Suppress Hearing. He realized that Booker's appearance was anything but confident. "Damn", Chris thought to himself, he looks guilty as shit.

"Your Honor, may I proceed?" he asked, exhibiting an appropriate tone of respect and obsequiousness. The judge nodded to him, then focused on the Affidavit and Memorandum of Law which his overweight, disheveled clerk had placed before him.

At the outset, Christopher's voice seemed to quake, as he began to become reacquainted with the subtleties of criminal work. The Motion was a chance for him to question the accuracy and reliability of the identifications made by two pivotal witnesses for the prosecution.

Chris was convinced before he began that the identification of Booker by Daniel Sheehan, a middle-aged Boston Edison lineman, who had reportedly seen a black man in his twenties running from the tenement where Jack Panton had been murdered had been engineered by the suggestions of Detective Hayes. He also felt that Jack Panton's partner could not have identified anybody, considering his predicament at the time of his observations.

The Motion to Suppress was an attempt at getting these identifications knocked out of the case before the jury heard them. He knew the chances of doing that were remote. The Motion also afforded him an opportunity to cross-examine three pivotal witnesses for the prosecution and test the accuracy of the identifications, without the jury being present.

In a way, the Motion was a dress rehearsal for the cross-examination of these witnesses at trial. Gradually, Christopher began to become more comfortable, as if he were returning to an old neighborhood, where the streets and the alleyways were very familiar. He was a criminal lawyer once again.

"Your Honor, prior to proceeding on the accused's Motion to Suppress Identifications, I am asking that the Court act on my Motion to Sequester the witnesses I have subpoenaed, Daniel Sheehan, Detective Ronald Domenico and Detective Sergeant Kenneth Hayes. I ask that they be sequestered and instructed not to discuss their testimony with each other, during the pendency of this hearing."

"Any objection?" the Judge asked the Assistant District Attorney, who was standing erect with his arms folded behind his back. Sorett made good copy for the illustrators in that pose.

"No, your Honor."

"Motion allowed as to Sequestration. Call your first witness, Mr. Conley."

"The accused calls Daniel Sheehan."

CHAPTER 45

From his seat at the end of the battered bench that looked to be a remnant from an ancient cathedral, Dan Sheehan was beckoned by an enormous black court officer. He was a simple man, thrust momentarily into the limelight by circumstances irrevocably beyond his control.

Dan Sheehan had worked for the Edison Company since being discharged from the Army in the late sixties. Because his older brother was sent to Vietnam, his fate was to be stationed in Korea. A tall man with acne scars, he had worked his way up to a supervisory position after twenty years. He was on Martindale Street the night that Jack Panton was murdered.

The dark blue suit he wore was uncomfortable, even though he had owned it for eleven years. Funerals were the only time he had worn a tie since the service. The crowd that gathered within the canyon-like courtroom intimidated him into a swagger, as he strode through the leather-bound double doors with tiny rectangular windows designed to permit observation from the corridor outside.

As he approached the Judge, he was confronted by the Clerk who made him swear an oath that he would tell nothing but the truth, so help him God. He declined the Judge's invitation to sit down, since he preferred to play his part in the drama while standing. The wrinkles in the corners of his eyes and the trace of broken blood vessels on his nose and cheeks were part of the price he paid for steady employment outdoors. His gray thinning hair was shaved close to his long, narrow head. For years, he had been recognized on the job by his grey herringbone scaly cap with the green shamrock on the brim.

Michael had interviewed Dan Sheehan regarding his identification of Booker Webb months before the hearing. He had been cordial but not cooperative. He had become acquainted with Jack Panton while working for Boston Edison over the years and had enjoyed his conversation and company on long winter nights. Sheehan was convinced that Booker Webb was the man he had seen running from the scene of the crime.

Michael had discovered that Detective Kenneth Hayes had showed Sheehan the photographs from which he had identified Booker. He insisted that the source of his certainty was his memory of that night and not the suggestions of the Detective in charge of the Drug Unit. Nevertheless, he did admit that Hayes had visited with him twice, since he had been determined to be an important witness for the prosecution.

"Good morning, Mr. Sheehan," Chris began, standing within striking distance of the Edison supervisor. Sheehan nodded without saying anything. The narrowing of his eyes told Chris he was preparing for his initial thrust. "I'm going to direct your attention to the evening of November 2, 1991. Were you working that evening, sir?"

"Yes, I was."

"Where were you working?"

"I was at the corner of Geneva Avenue and Martindale Street in Roxbury."

"What were you doing at the time?"

"I was supervising the installation of an electrical cable."

Christopher had subpoenaed the Edison records from its business office and quickly established that Sheehan had been working a double shift that night. By nine o'clock, he was working his twelfth hour that day. Fatigue and preoccupation with the business at hand were trails he would explore in testing the accuracy and reliability of this man's testimony.

"How often do you work double shifts, Mr. Sheehan?"

"As often as I can with two kids in college," the witness responded wryly, evoking a ripple of nervous laughter from the audience that crowded the courtroom.

"I can understand that," Christopher added with a broad smile. The witness in turn relaxed the arms that were folded across his chest. Chris detected an opening. He continued. "Wasn't that a particularly hectic day, Mr. Sheehan?"

"I don't remember," was his honest answer.

Christopher crossed the courtroom and retrieved what appeared to be a pink sheet of paper from a manila envelope, clearly marked as belonging to the Boston Edison Company.

"I show you this document, sir, and ask you if you can identify it?" The witness looked at the paper presented to him with considerable interest. He was studying it when Christopher inquired further, "What is that, sir?"

"It's my time sheet for that day."

"The date of November 2nd, 1991?"

"Yes."

"Can you describe to us your itinerary on that date?"

Slowly the witness began to decipher the times and locations of the places he had worked on that day. He translated Edison jargon where necessary at Christopher's request. The brush strokes of a recognizable picture began to appear. He supervised five jobs over a twelve hour period. Christopher could feel the stage being set for dramatic testimony to come. He shifted his focus to another avenue.

"Do you have a yearly physical at the Boston Edison Company, Mr. Sheehan?"

"Yeah, once a year."

"And when was your last physical prior to November 2, 1991?"

"I don't remember."

"Would it refresh your recollection if I suggested that your physical was in August of that year?"

The witness paused for a moment, briefly scratching the trace of a beard on his right cheek. "I would say that it could have been August, I'm just not sure."

Again Christopher crossed the courtroom and retrieved some documents from the manila Edison envelope. "I show you this document and ask you if you can identify it? What is it, sir?"

"It looks like a form concerning my physical," the witness responded, seemingly perturbed by the invasive thoroughness of Christopher's preparation.

"Thank you, sir. Do you wear glasses, Mr. Sheehan?"

"Only for reading."

"Do you wear them when you drive?"

"No, sir, I don't."

"Wasn't it suggested to you during your physical in August that you should get some glasses, sir?"

"No, it wasn't."

"Didn't the August physical include an eye exam?"

"I think so, yeah, it did."

"And what were the results of that eye exam, sir?"

"They never told me I needed glasses all the time."

"Your vision is 20/50 isn't it, sir?"

"I think that's what they said."

"That means you're nearsighted, doesn't it?"

"I object!" Sorett exclaimed, again standing erect with his hands folded behind his back.

"Overruled," the Judge said, "you may ask him if he knows the difference between nearsightedness and farsightedness, Mr. Conley."

"Do you know what nearsightedness is, Mr. Sheehan?"

"It means you can see things near, but not far away."

"Doesn't 20/50 vision mean you're nearsighted, sir?"

"Objection, your Honor," Sorett's tone of voice appeared both agitated and concerned.

"He may have it," the Judge replied.

"I don't know what it means. All I know is that I don't wear glasses, except when I'm reading."

"Thank you, Mr. Sheehan."

Christopher paused for a moment and collected his thoughts. The spadework had been done, the foundation had been laid. Now was the time to focus on the substance of this witness's testimony; his ability to observe and recognize the assailant on the night in question.

"Sir, on November 2, 1991, could you tell us whether you were wearing glasses at the time that you allegedly saw the accused, running from the building at 31 Martindale Street?"

"No, I told you I only wear them for reading."

"And, it would be fair to say that it was dark at 9:15 on that night?"

"Yeah, but where I was standing was directly under a street light."

"Nevertheless, it was dark in the sense that the sun had set and it was nighttime, correct?"

"Yeah, 9:15 is nighttime in November."

The witness was beginning to become perturbed and began to measure his responses, looking for traps in the questions to come. Christopher could understand his irritation, but needed to exploit it, if he could.

"You told the police that you heard what you thought was gunfire and you looked in the direction of 31 Martindale Street, correct?"

"Yeah, that's what I said."

"And then you said that you saw a light skinned, black male in his early twenties appear on the porch and jump across the stairs to the sidewalk and down an alleyway. Is that correct?"

"Yeah, I saw him come on the porch and I knew something was up, so I focused on his face. Then I saw him jump off the porch and run like hell out of there."

"How far away were you from him, when he was on the porch?"

"I don't know distances."

"Was it 100 feet, 200 feet?"

"It wasn't 100 feet; it was less than 100 feet. I told you, I don't know distances."

"Can you point out the distance by something in this courtroom?"

The witness stopped and looked around the crowded courtroom. Small beads of sweat had appeared above his upper lip. He asked for a cup of water. Slowly he sipped from the tiny Dixie cup handed to him by the court officer.

"What was your question again, I'm sorry?"

"Can you point out the distance you were, from the alleged assailant, when you observed him on the porch?"

Again the witness looked around the cavernous courtroom and pointed to the farthest wall directly across from the witness box. Before speaking, he looked for an instant at the Assistant District Attorney. "I would say he was about that far away."

"How long did you observe his face?"

"About a minute, I guess."

"May that be stricken, your Honor?" Christopher requested.

"I'll let the answer stand, Mr. Conley."

"In reality, Mr. Sheehan, you only observed this individual for a few seconds, isn't that true?"

"I saw him long enough so that I'll never forget that face," Sheehan replied defiantly.

Christopher stood in front of the witness, waiting for his intuition to take him to the next line of questions. He didn't know how this happened; it just seemed to kick in without thought, without deliberation, a spontaneous, active formulation that flowed from his lips, seeking reality, searching for truth.

"What was the description you provided to the police of the man you observed on the porch, Mr. Sheehan?"

"Black man, about twenty years old, very thin, wearing a dark shirt and dungarees."

"That's a pretty general description, isn't it, sir?"

"You asked me what I told the police and that's what I told them."

"Did you ever tell the police that he was a light-skinned black man?"

"I think I did."

"Did you tell them anything else about his face?"

"What do you mean?"

"Did you describe his facial characteristics?"

"No."

"Did you describe his hair?"

"No, I didn't."

"Did you tell them anything distinctive about his appearance other than that he was light skinned?"

"I don't remember."

"Did you estimate his height and his weight?"

"No, I think the police officer asked me whether he was heavy set or thin and I said that he was thin."

"Had you ever been in the vicinity of Martindale Street and Geneva Avenue prior to the date when Officer Panton was shot?"

"Yeah," Sheehan thought, "once or twice before."

"Could you have observed Booker Webb in that area before the date in question?"

"What do you mean?"

"Could you have observed my client in the vicinity of Martindale and Geneva Avenue before November 2, 1991?"

"I don't think so," Sheehan answered, scrutinizing Christopher in an effort to decipher his reasons for the question.

"Were you aware that Booker Webb was a drug addict who frequented that area on a regular basis?"

"I didn't know that."

"And you identified Mr. Webb as you drove by with Detective Hayes some three days after the shooting?"

"No, I identified his photograph before that."

"Let me see if I can get the sequence of events correct, Mr. Sheehan. You were working a double shift when you heard what you believed to be gun shots, correct?"

"Yes."

"And at that time you saw what you described to the police as a light-skinned, thin black male appear on the porch and jump off of it on to the sidewalk and run down an alleyway?"

"Yeah."

"And you say that he was about the distance of that far wall away from you, when you saw him?"

"Yeah."

"And it was nighttime, correct?" And you weren't wearing your glasses?

"No."

"And thereafter you were shown eight photographs of black males by Detective Kenneth Hayes."

"I don't remember how many photographs I was shown."

"Sir, I show you Defense Exhibits A-H and ask you if you can iden-tify them?" With that, Christopher approached Sheehan and spread the photographs from which Sheehan had identified Booker on the thick, wooden rail in front of him. "Looking at these photographs, Mr. Sheehan, these are color photographs, correct? And they are photographs of black males?"

"Yeah," the witness answered, examining the photographs presented to him.

"And those are the array of photographs from which you made your initial identification of Booker Webb?"

"Yeah."

Christopher again approached the witness and gathered the photo-graphs in his right hand, like a dealer with a lethal hand of cards.

"Sir, you described the man you observed as a light-skinned, black male, correct?"

"I already said that I did," Sheehan responded, beginning to display an irritation with Christopher's persistent questioning. At that time

Christopher separated five of the photographs from the eight and showed them to the witness.

"I show you these five photographs and ask you to look at them closely for a moment."

Sheehan suddenly began to display an open resentment to Chris, by snatching the photos from his grasp and examining them with an insolent expression. The witness stared at the photographs and then pushed them away from him ever so slightly. Chris raised his voice an octave for effect. He had remembered Dan Featherstone doing this the first time he had seen a criminal trial.

"Sir, the men depicted in those five photographs are not light-skinned black males, are they?"

"What do you mean?"

"Those men in those photographs are dark-skinned black males, isn't that true?"

There was a pause, a silence within the courtroom. Christopher knew that the answer about to be given was vital to the defense. Deliberately, while examining the photographs once more, in a cadence that was slow and pensive, the witness spoke the truth.

"Yeah, they are dark-skinned."

Christopher felt a rush of satisfaction, a reinforced belief in the innocence of Booker Webb. "And I show you these two photographs here, Mr. Sheehan. As I recall, you told us that the man you observed for a matter of seconds, running from the scene of this terrible crime, was thin. Is that correct?"

"Yeah,"

"And the men that are depicted in these two photographs are heavy set black men, are they not?"

Again, the Edison supervisor examined the photographs handed to him, sincerely, trying to tell the truth, so help him God. The pause that occurred was filled with nervous apprehension. Slowly, the witness began to shake his balding, grey head ever so slightly from side to side. Christopher glanced at Sorett. He appeared to be holding back his concern, as his chin rested within his right hand. Finally, the answer came.

"I would say yes, they are heavy set."

Christopher was ready for the coup de grace now. He stared at Judge Aubregon and turned his back to the witness, facing the crowd of spectators transfixed within the enormous courtroom. His voice was confident and certain as he spoke.

"So, of the eight photographs that you were shown by Detective Kenneth Hayes, only the one of Booker Webb matched your initial description of a light-skinned, thin black male in his early twenties. Isn't that true, Mr. Sheehan?"

"Yes," Sheehan conceded, lowering his eyes to the floor and away from the eyes of Booker Webb, whose face for the first time since his arrest, began to brighten with the distinct trace of hope.

CHAPTER 46

*I*t had taken him just over two hours to drive like a maniac to New Haven, switching the stations on the old Chevy's radio repeatedly, while filling its ashtray with half-smoked Camel cigarettes. As he accelerated and maneuvered through the afternoon traffic along Route 95, the pressure of the case had caused him to play out the circumstances of Booker Webb's predicament in his brain. He knew that Booker was a dead man without Ricardo Calderon's testimony.

He had managed to get in touch with Kim Desimone from Christopher's office. The news was not good. Ricardo was still nowhere to be found. Kim had come home three days before and discovered he had vanished, no note, no signs of struggle. Ricardo had been careful not to sleep outside their hideaway, since he had fled from Hayes.

Michael had arranged to meet Kim at the same pizza house as before. This time Kim was there when he arrived. Michael could see that the twisted man that he had befriended in prison was devastated by his companion's disappearance.

"Oh, Michael, Michael, I know something awful has happened, I know it," Kim sobbed, hugging him like a terrified child.

Michael embraced his friend and guided him to the last booth in the rear of the pizza place. A Greek boy with bad skin stood behind the counter, watching the two of them curiously. Michael ordered two cups of coffee to cut the chill from the November night then sat across an orange Formica table from the distraught transvestite.

"Did you talk to the police?" Michael asked.

"Of course not," Kim snapped, "Who knows who that Hayes is involved with. We can't trust anyone. You didn't speak to anybody about Ricardo, did you?"

"No," Michael answered, blowing gently on the scalding coffee. "You know me better than that."

Kim glanced admiringly at Michael and then continued. "We heard that two guys were looking for him, a black dude and an older white dude. He was scared to death about that. There's no way he would let anybody in without putting up a fight."

Michael rubbed his left wrist across his chin. The glare in his eyes betrayed the desperation of his thinking. "Is there anybody else he would contact, any relative that he'd get in touch with?" Michael asked. Kim answered in the negative. "What about his connection?"

"What about him?"

"Was he usin' every day?"

Kim sobbed again, burying his head between his arms resting on the table top. "I told him not to use so much. I told him. But he wouldn't listen to me. He was freaking out when he heard about those dudes. He could have gone to get high. I don't know. I just don't."

Michael stared at Kim's tormented face. There was no disguising it anymore, no question about his identity. Even an adolescent boy could tell that Kim was trapped in a twilight sphere between being male and female. He looked deranged, out of control. Michael attempted to console him and lead him in some way to help him find Ricardo, if he was still alive.

"Would you know where we could find him?"

"Find who?"

"Ricardo's connection, his dd."

"He hangs out at the Caribe. It's a Spanish bar on Connecticut Avenue."

"Would he be there tonight?"

"I don't know. What day of the week is it?"

"Thursday," Michael answered impatiently, "and tomorrow is Friday and before you know it, we're gonna be on trial without a prayer if we don't find Ricardo."

"Fuck the trial! Fuck everything! I don't want to live anymore," Kim moaned, choking off his voice with tears.

Suddenly, Michael thrust his hands across the table like the flash from a pistol. He grabbed Kim and shook him violently. He was dangling on the edge. "Don't tell me to fuck this trial! I gave this fucking kid my word. I gave my best friend my word. If Ricardo is alive, we gotta find him. Now snap the fuck out of it and help me find him!"

Kim's shoulders heaved as he attempted to control himself. The flowing tears had dissolved the pancake makeup that camouflaged his telltale masculinity. Slowly, he stopped sobbing and started nodding. He promised Michael that he would take him to find Ricardo's drug dealer.

The Club Caribe was an outpost in the jungle. Those that roamed there were on the lowest rung of the ladder leading to hell. Nightly incidents of mayhem went uninterrupted and unnoticed in an area of New Haven that even the police tried to

forget. Michael knew that he would be violating his parole by placing the unlicensed .38 in the rear waistband of his charcoal grey pants. The suit coat he had worn to court that morning effectively concealed the deadly weapon from the curious, as he and Kim entered through the club's grey metallic doors. Inside sat two Hispanic men, one in his early fifties with the look of an over the hill prize fighter and the other a tall, slender man in his late twenties with a small tattoo of what appeared to be a bat on his left cheekbone. It was apparent they were both armed and they were both extremely dangerous.

The two men studied Kim and then Michael. Their eyes delivered the message that they were going to be watched very closely while they remained on the premises. Michael escorted Kim down the narrow aisle between two rows of booths. He situated himself beside Kim within the second to last booth on the right. From there, he had a strategic observation point. Slowly, his eyes adjusted to the dimly lit interior. As they did, he began to observe the subterranean activity that was taking place around him.

The dive was nearly filled to capacity. In each booth there was a different detail in a portrait of criminality. A young girl, no older than sixteen, sat between two inebriated men in their late thirties, pretending to enjoy their company, and fondling each of their genitals under the table. An older woman with rotten front teeth seemed to be encouraging the young girl in Spanish, as the man to the right of the young girl ordered another round of drinks for the booth.

Across the way sat a group of young men, three Hispanic and one black, gyrating in a stupor to the deafening Latin music that permeated the confines of the place. It was obvious to Michael that each of the four had done time and would do more before their abbreviated life expectancy ran out. Behind them, a dark skinned grey haired man in an enormous fedora with gold jewelry hanging from him like ornaments from an imitation Christmas tree sat speaking intently to two well-dressed younger men. It appeared that the lesson he was delivering was not lost on the eager young faces that nodded to his every word.

Suddenly, through the darkness, Kim noticed a familiar face sitting at the bar speaking to an overweight woman in a red dress. He was in his late twenties wearing a long white leather coat and black and white cowboy boots. An oversized medallion hung from his muscular neck down an open shirt. His hair was curly and jet black. His beige skin was marked on the right cheek by a long, thin razor scar. It was a face of destruction.

When he saw Kim he stared. Kim in turn grabbed Michael's forearm, as he sat surveying the occurrences before him.

"Don't look at him, but he's at the bar," Kim whispered, attempting to be discreet.

"Whereabouts?" Michael inquired, not wanting to make eye contact until he could focus quickly and thoroughly.

"Over to your left. He's wearing a long, white coat."

Michael glanced and then glanced away. As he did, the man stood up from the bar and started to move nonchalantly, but deliberately, toward the front door. Michael in turn moved quickly. The man accelerated. Michael gave chase.

The two men at the front door attempted to obstruct Michael from reaching the front door until the man made it to the street. Michael reached behind him and snatched the revolver from the back of his pants. Suddenly he confronted the two men standing before him. He flashed what appeared to be a badge in the darkness of the bar. He pointed the revolver first at the older man and then his younger companion. He screamed, "Forget it, gentleman. I'm a federal agent with a warrant for this man's arrest."

They hesitated, long enough to allow them past the door. The unquestioned authority in his tone of voice and the words he had uttered had been perfect. He had carried it off. He had avoided a violent, blood-letting with experience. Kim scurried after him as he emerged onto the street. He caught a glimpse of the dealer's white coat as it flapped behind his sprinting form in the November darkness. Michael pursued with a vengeance. Breathless and exhausted, he finally succeeded in overtaking and collaring the last man to see Calderon before he vanished.

CHAPTER 47

*H*is sleep was snatched in unsatisfying segments. Thoughts and images kaleidoscopically whirled within his brain. In all his other cases he had been able to calm the beast and entice unwilling sleep, confronting the next day renewed. This was different. This was without precedent. A sentence of death was hanging over the head of an innocent man, an innocent man whose only hope of acquittal was unceremoniously dropped squarely in his lap.

Perhaps it was his age, now forty one, the years of stress had begun to manifest themselves on his face and in the white hair that gave the juries reassurance that he would not lead them astray. He remembered Dan Featherstone telling him years before that the law was a profession where his courage would be tested. Oh, Christopher thought, as he stared through the frost-glazed windows of his study, awaiting the orange traces of dawn, was he ever right.

The first day had gone well. He had begun to chip away at the formidable gray wall that the Commonwealth had erected around Booker Webb. As he shook his young client's hand and told him that so far it was so good, he felt inadequate, disturbed by Michael's inability to locate Ricardo Calderon.

Christopher knew that Sorett was right, when he told him that he would have to produce something dramatic for Booker to go free. If Ricardo was lost, so was the case. He couldn't bring himself to contemplate the outcome —— years of imprisonment and then an execution, an innocent man, an outrage against truth.

Images returned again and again. Lorna in a grey and black dress holding Booker in prison denim, caressing his head like a baby, as it rested on her shoulder. She was the most haunting apparition of them all. He had seen her in the dimly lit corner of the courthouse corridor, signaling her encouragement with a smile of admiration, before the lights of the television cameras and the hostile inquiries of reporters descended upon him.

He also caught a glimpse of Ron Shapiro, his one ally within the media, but couldn't speak to him. He looked for Michael and found out later that he had gone to New Haven to find Calderon. Why hadn't he called? What had happened? Alone with his anxious thoughts, he reviewed the Grand Jury testimony of Ron Domenico, the next witness to be cross-examined in his Motion to Suppress.

Ronnie Domenico was a large, handsome man in his early thirties. His muscular neck and shoulders and dark, boyish features gave him the appearance of an Ivy League linebacker. He had never recovered from the gunshot wounds he received. He delivered his testimony to a hushed and overflowing courtroom from a black and red motorized wheelchair. Christopher could almost taste the public's hatred for him and his client, as he began his presentation on the second day of the hearing.

"Good morning, Detective Domenico," Christopher began in a tone both measured and compassionate.

"Good morning," the detective replied, adjusting his body as erect and attentive as he could in the chair that was his detested companion.

"Sir, if at any time you need a break in your testimony, please tell me. I will attempt to make my questioning brief and to the point.

Are you in pain at the present time?"

"Yes, sir," he answered, his eyes giving convincing corroboration of this fact as he focused on Christopher's face.

"Are you presently on medication for this pain, Officer?"

"Yes, sir."

"What medication do you take?" Chris asked.

"Percocet"

"How often do you take this medication, sir?"

"Four times a day," Domenico answered, with a hint of shame in his deep, masculine voice.

"Following the incidents of November 2nd, 1991, you remained in the hospital for approximately eleven weeks, isn't that true?"

"Yes."

"And three separate operations were performed upon you at the Brigham & Women's Hospital, isn't that true?"

"Yes."

"And you were in the intensive care unit because of gunshot wounds, were you not?"

"Yes."

"And it was following these gunshot wounds that you made the observations that led you to identify Mr. Webb as your alleged assailant. Isn't that true?"

"Mr. Webb was my assailant," Domenico answered, the tone of his voice betraying conviction and hostility.

"I'm sure you believe that, sir. Would you please bear with me, while I ask you a few more questions? As I understand the occurrences of that night, you were on duty, in the company of Detective John Panton, before his tragic demise?"

"Yes."

"And you were there pursuant to a search warrant for 31 Martindale Street in the Grove Hall section of Roxbury?"

"Yes."

"And while executing this warrant, Detective Panton was shot to death in your presence?"

"Yes," the witness replied, choking back his emotions within the crowded hush of the courtroom.

"And it would be fair to say that the murder of your friend and partner has had a terrible impact upon you, isn't that true?"

"What do you think?"

"And almost immediately after witnessing this horrid occurrence, you yourself were shot repeatedly, were you not?"

"Yes," he muttered.

"And up until that point, you hadn't seen the face of your assailant, had you Officer?"

"I saw his face," the witness replied sullenly, "and I'll never forget it."

"May that be stricken as unresponsive, Your Honor."

"It may," Judge Aubregon said, quietly measuring his words to the agitated witness. "I recognize that this is very difficult Detective, but please answer the questions without editorializing, if you could."

"I'm sorry, your Honor," Domenico responded, composing himself. "What was your question again?"

"You didn't make any observation of your assailant on the night of November 2, 1991 until after you witnessed the horrible event of your partner's murder, and after you were brutally shot, yourself?"

"Yes, I only saw him after that."

"And Officer, it would be fair to say that you were in mortal fear of losing your life, just as your partner had lost his, before your very eyes, at the time you made your initial observation of the perpetrator of this crime."

"I don't recall," Domenico muttered sorrowfully.

"And Detective, these observations that did occur took place in a dimly lit hallway for only a few seconds, isn't that true?"

"It was more than a few seconds and it was long enough," Domenico insisted, his voice brimming with pain and outrage.

Christopher stopped and stood in front of his notes which had been placed carefully on the counsel table below him. The courtroom was silent except for a cough here and there. He paused for a moment. Should he continue digging or make his final thrust? His heart ached for the crippled man confined to the mechanical chair in front of him, yet his duty to the accused boy situated behind him, caused him to wade deeper into the muck and mire of the case.

"Detective, when was the first time that you became aware that my client had been identified as the man who shot you?"

"I don't understand," Domenico answered quizzically.

"Strike the previous question," Chris said, while attempting to formulate a more expansive presentation of his point.

"Detective, following your observations in the hallway on Martindale Street, you were taken by ambulance to the Brigham & Women's Hospital where you fought for your life over the next three days in the intensive care unit. And it was after being transferred from the intensive care unit, while under medication, that you made a photographic identification of Booker Webb, correct?"

"Yes."

"And your identification of Mr. Webb was in the presence of Detective Hayes, who showed you these eight photographs, correct?" Chris pressed, presenting the photographs previously identified by Dan Sheehan the day before.

Slowly, Domenico examined the photographs handed to him. A long, pregnant silence had fallen over the courtroom, as he methodically repeated a review of the photos before speaking. "Yes, I made the identification from these photographs."

Chris would leave the rest to argument. He had established enough suggestiveness in the identifications for the present. Following Sorett's questions, Judge Aubregon called for the morning recess. Christopher's last witness in the Motion to Suppress hearing would be the most important one, Detective Sergeant Kenneth Hayes.

CHAPTER 48

There was no need for conversation. Michael wore the depths of his disappointment like a badge, as he waited among the overflow crowd, outside of the courtroom for the morning recess. The mosaic that Christopher had attempted to construct would never be completed. Ricardo Calderon was dead from an overdose.

The news was devastating to Christopher and absolutely fatal to Booker Webb. There would be no happy ending, no buzzing crowd, whipped into a frenzy by the testimony of a coerced accomplice. There would be only deep, unremitting pain, followed by an annihilating defeat and the eventual destruction of an innocent victim of circumstance.

Christopher attempted to speak, after he learned the grim details of Michael's discovery on the little-used back stairway leading from the courtroom. The words wouldn't come. His brain was suddenly a jumble of diffuse thoughts, his voice box frozen. The air within the courthouse was now not sufficient to sustain his consciousness.

He had to flee, to escape, collect himself, preserve his sanity. With the gesture of one slapping at a fly from in front of his face, he left the company of his friend and bounded down the back stairway out into the grey chill of a mid-November morning.

His heart was beating uncontrollably as he wove through the indifferent crowd that hurried passed him on the sidewalk. The anguish of being utterly alone and incapable of preventing an inevitable disaster swept over him. How could it be, he kept asking himself, as he broke into a trot and then a sprint. Where was the justice he had been taught to expect?

Before, he had always been able to control the conditions and somehow achieve at least a satisfactory result. But this was uncontrollable, beyond comprehension. Had he lost it by not doing more? He had failed Booker and Lorna, sweet, long-suffering Lorna. How could he face her with the knowledge that he had no hope of saving her flesh and blood? How could he face a world that despised him and his efforts to prevail against injustice?

Suddenly, he longed for the embrace and comfort of his wife and children. He had gambled with their fate as well. He had devoted himself to Booker's case, Booker's cause, to the detriment of all that he had built, all that he had achieved. The animosity he had incurred in defending an accused cop killer was more than he had even imagined. He knew that his partners had suffered a loss of their business as the result of his decision to defend Booker Webb. He cursed himself for ever undertaking the risk.

He found himself on the stairway leading down to the Boston Common from Beacon Street. Even the golden dome of the State House had lost its gleam in the gloom of that dark November morning. He stumbled trance-like down the stairs into the Common, suddenly realizing that his coat-less form was no match for the bitter cold of the wind that swirled through the rolling hills around him. A refuge was required from the storm that was about to break.

To his left across Park Street he spied the Paulist Center, a Roman Catholic chapel, wedged inconspicuously on the side of the hill leading from the State House. There he could be alone with his misery and his anxiety.

He ducked through the two sets of double doors into the tiny darkness of the chapel. There was no one there to disturb him except for a balding white-haired old man seated with his back to him in one of the front pews. He fell to his knees within the back pew of the chapel. The pounding in his head would not stop. His attempts to calm himself, to think in other than disjointed thoughts were fruitless. He could not release himself from the grip of his self-induced terror.

He had failed, utterly, undeniably. He could not bear the thought of it. He could not face the world that had turned so hostile, so hopeless. He began to shake, to cry. He was in the throes of a breakdown. Thoughts of self-destruction flashed uncontrollably across his brain. Fragments of disjointed and disturbed images engulfed his mind. He was tumbling, falling, hurtling downward into the abyss.

He prayed like a beseeching child, as the drumbeat of his pulse throbbed in his temples. He was terrified, lost in the grip of defeat and desperation. Only the oblivion of death could release him from the burden of his torment. He contemplated forms of self-destruction, while trembling and sobbing. Where was the way out? Where was the path away from the pain? He was hanging by a thread, when he heard what he thought was music, a faint ethereal melody.

At that moment he raised his head from his agonizing prayer and saw a tiny wheel of light, reflecting through the stained glass. It was dim at first and then increasingly bright, toward the front of the chapel. He looked for the old man who had been sitting in front of him; he was no longer there. He had moved. He was standing, facing Christopher from across the chapel.

That face! Christopher stared in disbelief. Could it be? Was it possible? The wheel of light became rays of different hues and colors, brilliant, mesmerizing colors. The old man suddenly smiled at Christopher, but did not speak. He seemed to be waiting for someone or something to arrive, to make its presence felt within the chapel. Christopher was certain now. He knew the old man's face. It was the face of a dead priest. It was the face of Father McConnell.

He could not remember afterwards, whether he ever stopped crying during the encounter with the Spirit. That is the way he remembered it, an encounter with the Spirit that surrounds us all; the Spirit that dwells in us all; an angel or a presence that seemed to infuse him, as the melody played and the light shone within the chapel. Then undeniably, there seemed to be a voice, coming from within and without him, touching him in a profound way, reaching a part of him that he had never felt before. The voice was so completely harmless, so unashamedly loving. It was the voice of one crying in the wilderness.

"Why are you afraid? Have you lost the faith of the child that sustains you? The path is always treacherous for those who love. Have the courage to love, to give of yourself completely, and your path will lead to the kingdom."

Suddenly, he was no longer in the chapel. He was outside, standing in front of the sculpture of Robert Gould Shaw, the Civil War hero who gave his life leading a regiment of black soldiers in battle. It was snowing heavily, blanketing the world around him in white. He had somehow been released from the pit of his own despair and with that release came renewal.

Whatever happened —- he knew he could withstand it, endure it, cope with it all: the scorn of the people, the failure of a guilty verdict, even the destruction of Booker Webb. Whatever happened —- he took comfort in the fact that he had loved and, even if he failed, it was in daring to care for another human being, an innocent man.

As he emerged from the back stairs, leading to the ninth floor courtroom, in the vestibule where the lawyers negotiated pleas and settled cases, he saw another old man seated on a padded courthouse chair, the feeble fingers of his knurled right hand caressing a cane. As Christopher approached, he could make out the features of Dan Featherstone. Had the mentor come to see his pupil perform, confront an old adversary?

Christopher had not remembered him as being so small, so human, so vulnerable, as he sat there chatting with one of the older court officers. His head was large, perched like a boulder upon his tiny shoulders. Gold wire spectacles dangled from a chain around his frail neck. It was obvious that the old lawyer was dying, succumbing slowly to age and disease.

Christopher greeted him warmly, receiving the old man's delayed recognition. He asked him if they could talk privately before Judge Aubregon reconvened the morning's proceedings.

On the stairwell behind the metal door, Chris explained his desperate predicament to the old man. He listened carefully, squinting through the gold wire glasses that now clung to his massive face. Perhaps, age had taken too much of a toll. Maybe the giant that once seemed to dwell in the body of the old man had departed, leaving only a shadow to answer when his name was called. As soon as Featherstone spoke about his craft, Christopher knew that he was a gift from God.

"Does this bum know that your star witness has taken a permanent vacation?" the old man demanded, in a throated rasp.

"The DA?"

"No, not the goddamn DA! Hayes, for Christ sakes...that sorry excuse for a police officer!"

"I don't know. I don't know whether they got to him or he did it himself."

"Well, what were you going to do before the shit hit the fan?"

"I was going to cross-examine Hayes about our information and bring Calderon in, while he was testifying. Then keep Calderon protected, until he testified at the trial."

The old man nodded in affirmation at Christopher's strategy. Christopher could see that his mind had not lost its incisiveness with the years. He observed his arthritic right hand, fondling the head of a lion on the cane he required for walking. What a generation of giants! Christopher thought, as he reflected momentarily on the lives of Dan Featherstone, Father McConnell and May Conley. The old lawyer took a deep breath and spoke in a tone that required Christopher to bend over close to him.

"Remember the old saying, son. 'If you got the law, beat on the law. If you got the facts, beat on the facts. If you ain't got nuthin', beat on the fuckin' table!' Now, from what I've been told, you got a few facts that you can emphasize and a lot of good poker you've got to play. Now go in there, like you've got this son of a bitch by the balls and maybe, just maybe, he'll do the rest himself. Never, ever, underestimate the power of the truth."

The old man's words were so right, so utterly simple, yet undeniable. The confidence that flowed within him from the encounter in the chapel made even Michael believe that a new ace in the hole had been discovered. He sat in the rear of the courtroom squeezed between two elderly women who came to the courthouse daily to watch real life soap operas. The drama began when Christopher's called for the court officer to beckon his next witness.

"Your Honor, the accused calls Detective Sergeant Kenneth Hayes to the stand."

From the bench outside the courtroom, where the witnesses had been sequestered, Hayes rose, dropping a cigarette to the floor and extinguishing it with his heel. Christopher had not seen him in over twenty years. His demeanor as he walked slowly to the clerk and recited the oath that had become meaningless so many years before was confident and controlled.

He wore a pair of glasses with black rims that softened the hardened contours of his ruddy face. Deep wrinkled grooves from fifty-eight winters and thousands of cigarettes ran from the sides of his nostrils to the corners of his mouth. Christopher could only imagine the expressions of that face when bent upon a dark endeavor. He looked Christopher directly in the eye, as he approached to begin his interrogation. His tone was polite with a trace of condescension.

"Would you state your name for the record, Sergeant?"

"Kenneth Hayes."

"And what is your occupation, Sergeant?"

"I am a Sergeant with the Boston Police Department."

"How long have you been a police officer, Sergeant?"

"Thirty-four years."

"And you are presently the Detective in charge of the Boston Drug Unit?"

"Yes," Hayes answered in a proud and accomplished tone of voice.

"How long have you been in charge of that Unit, Sergeant?"

"Nine years."

"Over the course of your involvement with the Drug Unit have you become acquainted with Booker Webb?"

"Yes," Hayes answered, glaring at Booker, who was seated to the left and behind Christopher. The iciness in his eyes left no doubt as to his contempt and hatred for the accused. Hayes seemed to know exactly what the sentiments were within the crowded courtroom and played to them perfectly. Christopher knew that his adversary was accomplished at reaching for every advantage and slipping punches whenever the opportunity presented.

"In fact," Christopher continued, "you had attempted to enlist him as an informant, hadn't you?"

"Not that I know of, sir," Hayes said deliberately.

"You had seen Mr. Webb in the vicinity of Martindale Street prior to November 2nd, 1991, didn't you?"

"Do you mean had I seen him in the area before the night Jack Panton was shot, counselor?" Hayes sparred.

"Yes, that's what I mean, Sergeant," Chris said.

"Yes, he appeared on surveillance in the area on a number of occasions."

"In fact, in June of 1990, he was arrested not two blocks from the 31 Martindale Street address, isn't that true?"

"I don't recall."

"Prior to November 2nd, 1991 and, in light of your prior experience with Mr. Webb, had you ever known him to be a violent criminal?"

"I can't answer that counselor. I am not aware of all of his criminal activity, nor am I aware of whether he possesses violent tendencies."

"You knew him to be a drug addicted person with no history of violence on his criminal record, isn't that true?"

"I wouldn't know counselor," Hayes answered, exhibiting a slight trace of contempt, consistent with the mood of the audience that surrounded him.

"Whenever he was seen in the area, was he considered to be an individual who could be armed and dangerous?"

"That's difficult to say with drug addicted individuals counselor. They're not what you call predictable."

Chris realized he was in a battle with a street fighter, a witness who knew full well how to maneuver in the clinches and relished it. It was essential that he alter his attack, change his tactics to keep him off balance.

"Detective Hayes, you were the officer who discovered the murder weapon, were you not?"

"Yes."

"And in your report following the homicide of Detective Panton, you described the circumstances under which you discovered the weapon, correct?"

"Yes."

"I show you this document and ask you if you can identify it?"

"That's my report regarding the weapon."

"And this is a Continuation Report, is it not, Detective? Following on the heels of your reports on the identification of Mr. Webb by the previous witness, Mr. Sheehan, and your report of the identification by Officer Domenico, correct? You were very involved in this investigation, weren't you, Detective Hayes?"

"Yes, two of my detectives had been shot, counselor," Hayes replied. The tone of his voice was that of a bereaved father who had done his best to protect his children.

"And Detective Hayes, you also obtained certain statements from Mr. Webb which you and the District Attorney assert implicate Mr. Webb in this homicide, isn't that true?"

"Yes, he denied ever being in the area," Hayes replied, playing to the crowded courtroom with the reason for Booker's deception.

"Wasn't this a homicide investigation, Detective?"

"Yes, it was."

"And you're not a homicide detective, are you?"

"No, I'm not."

"Yet you almost single-handedly developed this case against Booker Webb, isn't that true?"

"I worked day and night to find the man responsible for this murder, along with several other police officers, counselor."

"Isn't objectivity a necessary ingredient for good police work?" Chris pressed.

"I don't understand the question," Hayes responded, shaking his head ever so slightly for effect.

"I mean, Jack Panton was like a son to you, wasn't he?"

Hayes sat there momentarily staring at Christopher. He seemed transfixed by his memory of the slain policeman.

"Did you hear my question, sir?"

The face of the detective was wrenched with emotion. He seemed to have gone blank, unable to speak, unable to maneuver from Christopher's onslaught of truth.

"What was the question, sir?" Hayes stammered, his eyes blinking rapidly, as if he were attempting to dispel a swarm of flies from his brain.

Christopher stared out into the audience that choked the courtroom. There was a silence, a hush that came over the spectators, like a circus crowd watching a man balancing on a wire above them.

"You wanted to apprehend the man responsible for the death of your friend and brother officer more than anything, didn't you?"

Hayes again paused, his eyes continued to blink. A ripple of conversation could be heard among the curious spectators. Finally, he gathered himself and focused on Christopher, almost as if he had been awakened from a troubled sleep.

"I'm sorry, counselor, could you repeat the question?"

Christopher began to lead now with his right hand, hoping to confuse and disable the man facing him from the confines of the turn-of-the-century witness box.

"I'll withdraw it, Detective. Let me ask you this. You are acquainted with a man by the name of Ricardo Calderon, isn't that true?"

The name seemed to disturb the detective. Christopher could see it. Slowly, he moved toward Hayes as he seemed to retreat ever so slightly in his seat. Chris removed a photograph of Calderon copied from the State Police mug books and showed it to him.

"You know this man, don't you?"

Hayes stared at the photograph presented to him. He seemed to be buying time to develop an appropriate response. Finally he answered. "Yes, I've become acquainted with him over the years."

"Oh, he's much more than an acquaintance! Isn't he?"

"I don't understand the question."

"You know what an accessory after the fact of murder is, don't you, Sergeant?"

"Objection, your Honor," Sorett shouted — not quite understanding the import or the intent of Christopher's question.

"Overruled," Judge Aubregon ruled, staring at the witness and focusing on the slight tremor of his left hand.

Christopher again paused and scanned the arena of rapt spectators. He could see Michael now, a smile of admiration and encouragement on his face. He saw Dan Featherstone seated like an aged dignitary inside the rail that separated the inner circle of lawyers and court personnel from the public. He too signaled his encouragement.

Chris stood directly in front of the man who had woven this intricate web of lies. A man, who himself appeared to be ever so slightly unraveling. Maybe it was the guilt. Maybe it was the truth. Whatever it was, Chris saw the advantage and made the best of the opportunity.

"Detective, I want to remind you that you have sworn before God to tell the truth in this case, a case that involves the death of a friend, a father and husband. The photograph before you is that of a man that you coerced into becoming an accessory after the fact of murder, a murder for which you are responsible, isn't that true?"

For a moment, Hayes looked disoriented. His eyes darted back and forth between blinks. He was a cornered rat, a desperate flailing animal. He attempted to compose himself. His voice could barely be heard. "I have no idea what you're talking about, sir."

Chris knew he had reached pay dirt. There was a second, an instant when Hayes stared at Christopher with the look of a weary sinner wishing for a reprieve from his guilt. There was one more thrust and he would leave the rest for trial.

"You know what I'm talking about, Detective. I'm talking about your role in causing the death of Detective Jack Panton and the crippling of Detective Ron Domenico, your role in framing an innocent man!"

Hayes sat shaking his head, repeating that Christopher was crazy. Lloyd Sorett stood, screaming his objection. The crowd within the courtroom erupted. Judge Aubregon and the court officers attempted to restore order. Christopher thought to himself, after he had cried no more questions, that Dan Featherstone was right. Never underestimate the power of truth.

CHAPTER 49

A nerve that vitalized the city and allowed it to function had been exposed and aggravated. A decorated veteran police detective had been accused in open court of participating in the murder of a brother officer and a friend. The reaction was swift and determined.

Lloyd Sorett had summoned the press to the District Attorney's Office to issue a statement in time for the evening news. His role as the avenging angel, called upon to prosecute a vicious killer whose lawyer had made preposterous and reckless accusations against a respected law enforcement official suited him perfectly. The indignation and determination to mete out justice shone through his angular handsome face. Christopher could tell that Sorett recognized an opportunity to be a media darling like he was born to it. He sat flanked by Hayes and the politically astute District Attorney, for Suffolk County, Martin Babcock. The seal of the Commonwealth and the American flag were positioned appropriately in the background. It was a master stroke of adverse publicity against Christopher and Booker Webb.

Michael and Chris sat in the conference room where Lorna had requested their assistance, watching the press conference on television. The performance of Sorett was measured and flawless. He had spoken of an overwhelming case that involved two eyewitness identifications, forensic evidence linking Booker Webb to the murder and a statement by the accused that betrayed a consciousness of guilt.

"It is inconceivable to me," he proclaimed, "that the attorney representing Mr. Webb would seek to defend his client by smearing the flawless reputation of a heroic and dedicated police detective who cared for these men as if they were his own sons. It is a desperate and despicable tactic that is unparalleled in all my years of prosecuting criminal cases."

A feeling of being alone without allies, without options, gripped Christopher momentarily as Michael clicked the remote, shutting the television off. The two friends of so many years sat alone in the darkness. Michael finally broke the silence.

"Well, every fuckin' one of them is against us now, man."

"You got that right," Chris replied, recognizing full well the almost certain fate of Booker, waiting and hoping in the bowels of the Charles Street Jail. "That poor fucking kid! It's going to take a fucking miracle to get him acquitted."

"But you could tell the son-of-a-bitch was lying. I could see you were getting to him. Maybe at trial he'll come apart. Maybe he'll fuck up beforehand," Michael said encouragingly, turning on the lights in the conference room that overlooked the Boston Common and the golden dome of the State House.

A wet, slushy snowstorm gripped the world outside the windows, amplifying the dreariness of the moment. It would be another night away from his family for Christopher. The day's events had totally exhausted him. He hated the voracious demands of trial work at that point.

He sat staring, as if he were alone, wondering about the fate of his client and his own resolve in representing him —- wondering also about the occurrences within the chapel. Had he been witness to an apparition or was it a hallucination induced by anxiety and oxygen deprivation? He couldn't be sure. It really didn't matter. The strange serenity he experienced afterward was worth a brush with madness. Michael was seated across from him now, likewise lost in thought, attempting to figure an avenue toward the public presentation of the truth.

"You know what, Mike?" Chris said, staring across the conference room table out into the snow pelting the sky line of the city he so desperately loved. "We have to keep the pressure on Hayes. Shadow him. I want to know where he fuckin' eats, where he sleeps. I want to know everything about the prick. I want you to know him, like you know yourself."

Michael nodded and smiled at the irony of the request. In a way, Hayes was like Michael. They were both cops who went bad. Chris could detect Michael's determination to see the case through. The cause of Booker Webb had become his personal crusade. The wheels were turning feverishly now.

"We got to get in touch with Ron Shapiro," Chris advised. "He's got to give us at least a fighting chance on the TV. He's got to put the pressure on Hayes, too. I'll give him a call in the morning. We've got a week before trial. I better go down to the jail and see Booker before I go home. Whatever you do, Mike, don't tell him that Calderon is dead. I don't think he could handle it. I don't want him cheating the executioner just yet."

Michael nodded again without speaking. Words were superfluous. He could see the commitment and the dedication of his friend and it reinforced him as well. He spoke to him like a brother, gently touching his shoulder.

"You know, Chris, whatever happens in this thing, I'm just real proud to be doing it with you."

Chris looked into Michael's aging face. He flashed a half smile. "Will you get the fuck out of here and find some way to get out of this mess you talked me into?"

With that, Michael slipped into the faded green raincoat with the missing buttons that he had grown comfortable with since his release from prison. He would get something to eat and spend the night parked in a row of cars down the street from Hayes' house, watching, waiting for a lead, for a break.

After visiting with Booker and returning his devoted embrace before saying goodnight, Chris slumped into the soft, brown leather seat of his Mercedes to begin his journey home. It was almost eleven o'clock and although he was fatigued, he knew that it would be hours before troubled snatches of sleep would arrive. The snow storm that had descended upon the city had made the roads treacherous.

He recognized that Linda would be worried about him and used the car phone to speak with her. She too had suffered from the ordeal of the case. Her voice was soothing and reassuring, as she told him she had seen the news reports about the day's events. He told her how much he loved her and the kids; how much all of them meant to him. She was disturbed by his words, asking him if he was alright. He would not tell her about the occurrences within the chapel. He wouldn't tell anybody.

He scanned the dial of the car's radio, looking for a song to match his mood and there it was. The soothing female voice telling him, *"What the world needs now, is love, sweet love."* Suddenly, he was transported by a kaleidoscopic series of reminiscence: Booker's embrace, Lorna in the courthouse corridor, signaling her support through a crowd of hostile reporters, Michael telling him that Calderon was dead, Hayes staring at him with confidence and hatred.

The snow splattered continually upon the windshield from the deserted streets. Snow plows were everywhere, dispersing sand and salt, his windshield wipers throbbing rhythmically to provide some visibility. He was utterly alone again, anxiety creeping up inside of him. He tried to reassure himself, saying he was doing his best and that was all he could do. Please, God, that's all he could do. He was in the chapel again, the face of a dead priest smiling at him. Was he really there? Was he really the recipient of some divine intervention?

Again he was walking with Lorna up Parker Hill toward her house, the windshield wipers almost deafening in his head. Then suddenly, the face of a black male appeared, contorted by mortal fear, shrieking, while lying on a street of cobblestones, the dark red thickness of his blood spurting and covering his hands and belly. The face was indelible and then became transformed into the face of Booker Webb. Chris saw himself reaching for Lorna, the gun smoking in his hand, the smell of spent shells stinging his nostrils, crying to her in inexplicable circumstance.

Lorna was transfixed, staring at what he had done. Slowly the face of Booker was transformed to that of Jack Panton and then to that of Hayes, smiling and sneering. Then Hayes was holding the smoking gun. Oh yeah, the lyric was right, the melody perfect. What the world needed more than anything was love, sweet love.

His house was dark as he turned into the driveway. His wife and children were safe and still unharmed from the turmoil that engulfed him. A small, yellow note of love and support, a picture drawn by his son and an "A" on a math quiz received by his daughter, stuck to the refrigerator with a magnet bearing a smiling clown's face.

He prayed that all would not be lost, all that he had built, all that he had dreamed of. He remembered his mother, sitting alone behind bolted doors in the projects, watching him leave, watching him flee, leaving her so completely alone. He could feel her loneliness deep within his soul. He prayed then he fell asleep.

CHAPTER 50

*T*he dawn of another dreary, November morning stretched itself across the interior of the spacious master bedroom revealing Christopher with his eyes wide open and his mind already engaged. He had six days to get ready for the trial. All the preliminaries had been completed. Six days that would pass in a blur and then it would begin —- the most significant case of his career.

Linda was lying beside him, still fast asleep, her left arm outstretched across his bare chest. He stared at her in slumber, gently caressing her cheek with the tips of his fingers, admiring the features that had captivated him and the contours of her still lithe body. With all that was swirling around him, he needed her more than ever before. She was his refuge in the storm.

Ron Shapiro smiled, shaking his head as Christopher searched for him in the crowd having breakfast within the Marriott Hotel. Shapiro was prepared for another afternoon and evening before Klieg lights and television cameras. He sat in a booth behind two tiny glasses of orange juice and a pair of dark glasses that served to create uncertainty amongst those who thought they recognized him.

He wore a powder blue shirt and a grey Pierre Cardin double-breasted suit. His pointed features and his styled brown hair glistened with a fragrant gel. His lack of wrinkles and his olive complexion had assisted him in avoiding the daily tedium of the make-up room. He beckoned Christopher with the wave of his left hand.

"You look like you've been up all night, my friend," Shapiro remarked.

"I just couldn't get to sleep with all that's going on," Chris confided. "How have you been?"

"I'm fine. How's our friend holding up in Charles Street?"

"He'll be alright. I spent some time with him last night."

"Good, because we are going to strike a small blow for social justice with my report on the news tonight. Here, take a look at this," he said, presenting Christopher with two pages for the Teleprompter that described Ricardo Calderon's involvement in entrapping Booker Webb under Hayes' direction.

Christopher grew cold as he read the report that his friend intended to present, a report that spoke of Ricardo Calderon as a witness who would appear and testify at trial. Shapiro knew from Christopher's facial expression that something was terribly wrong.

"What's the matter? It's what you wanted, isn't it?"

"It's unbelievable. I can't tell you how much I appreciate what you're trying to do, Ronnie."

Christopher suddenly paused, glanced at the glass of orange juice on the table before him and downed it like a shot of peppermint Schnapps. He cleared his throat and leaned over to confide to the reporter the stark reality of his and Booker's predicament.

"Calderon is not going to testify."

"Why not?" Shapiro snapped, removing his dark glasses, revealing the piercing grey eyes that had endeared him to the housewives of suburbia.

"Because he's dead!"

The news struck the reporter like a blow to the forehead.

"Michael found out yesterday. He's down in the morgue in New Haven under a John Doe."

Shapiro sat back slowly against the red leather of the restaurant booth. He sighed and ran the long, bony fingers of his right hand across his forehead. His voice was almost a whisper.

"Do you think it was Hayes who killed him?"

Christopher stared at his friend, shaking his head for a moment. "I don't know. Mike talked to the paramedic that picked him up. They're treating it as an overdose. Who knows? Maybe he did it to himself or they did it to him. All I know is he ain't gonna be around to testify."

"What are you going to do now?" Shapiro asked, searching Christopher's face for a sign of hope, a glimmer of confidence.

"I guess I have to play it out like he's still alive and pray that they don't know it yet."

"That's it? That's all you've got? What about his boyfriend or whatever she is, the one that Michael knew in prison? What about her testifying?" Shapiro asked.

"It's all hearsay. Besides, she's all fucked up. The only thing I can hope for is that the truth will come out somehow."

"Holy shit, Chris! How about the U.S. Attorney, the FBI? What about going to them?"

"No. They're on the same team, man. They're not going to touch a cop shooting. When was the last time you heard of the Feds going out of their way to help a junkie?"

Christopher knew that the death of Ricardo Calderon had hamstrung his old friend. He couldn't possibly go public with the story now that Calderon was gone. He needed him to be around for backup in order to make the allegations in person. Yet he wanted Shapiro to do something offensively, something that would help Booker Webb in some way. Maybe he could try to reach Hayes like he had suggested at Dolan's. Maybe if Hayes believed that Calderon was alive and willing to testify, he would do something desperate, something that would tip his hand, seal his fate.

He explained this to his old law school buddy, pointing out that Hayes seemed to be visibly shaken for a few moments during the Motion to Suppress hearing the day before. Shapiro nodded. His mind was racing with Christopher's in a common endeavor. Maybe if he and Michael and Christopher kept pressing, searching for that weak link in Hayes' chain of deception, a miracle would transpire. The only commitment he could get from Shapiro was that he would see what he could do from his end. No promises made. With everything that had happened, Chris couldn't expect more.

For four days Michael stalked his unsuspecting subject. His obsession with Hayes and the innocence of Booker Webb had transformed him. He became a specter that shadowed the veteran detective relentlessly. He lived on cold coffee, stale pizza and Pepto-Bismol. He snatched sleep at isolated intervals across the front seat of his Chevy. The second night outside of Hayes' home he had shaved his face and his head to streamline his person and eliminate his concerns for anything except his prey. Like a tortured voyeur, he longed for a glimpse of the concealed, the secretive recesses of Hayes' life that would lead to revelation and hopefully redemption for Booker and his best friend.

He was parked on Appleton Street in the late afternoon in front of a row of brownstones when the opera glasses he had picked up at a yard sale fixed on Hayes and another cop conversing behind the District Four Police Station. He could see that Hayes was agitated and angry.

The cop was young and seemed apologetic. Hayes pushed him aside and entered his blue Crown Victoria double parked nearby. Michael followed cautiously, allowing two other vehicles to remain between his vehicle and the detective's car. Michael expected to follow him home as he had done on the three previous afternoons. The weather had turned bitter cold with the setting sun when Hayes began to show himself.

His car traveled through the city where the wind and temperature had succeeded in removing all but a few pedestrians from the streets. Michael followed as Hayes jumped on the expressway heading south from Boston and sped toward Route 128. Michael watched and photographed Hayes as he made a telephone call from outside of a gas station in Canton. He then followed him as he traveled onto Route 95 toward Providence and took the McCoy Stadium cutoff. Slowly, he lagged behind as Hayes parked his vehicle in the parking lot behind the Holiday Inn in Pawtucket, Rhode Island.

Hayes remained in the vehicle as if he were waiting for somebody. Michael slid behind the Chevy's dashboard, allowing just enough room to observe the occurrences that followed. Two women in a white Camaro entered the parking lot about ten minutes later. They too seemed to be looking for someone. They drove by the Crown Victoria. Michael saw Hayes' mastiff head nod. The Camaro drove once around the lot and pulled into a parking space located near the rear entrance of the hotel.

Michael watched as Hayes slowly got out of his vehicle and glanced around the parking lot. He pulled the collar of his brown leather jacket up around his thick, muscular neck and removed a grey gym bag from the passenger seat. He trotted across the windswept parking lot as the women got out of the Camaro.

The driver had long red hair and looked to be in her mid-thirties. She wore a raccoon jacket, jeans and red pumps. She said something to the other woman who was with her. She appeared very young, early twenties or even younger. She had short blonde hair spiked up with long earrings, a red suede jacket, a short red skirt and black heels.

The redhead greeted Hayes outside the rear entryway of the hotel. She shook his hand and seemed to introduce him to her young companion. Hayes draped his arm over the young blonde's shoulder and ushered her through the door and down the hallway. She did not return his embrace.

Michael would wait and watch for an interval and then call the front desk and see if Hayes had checked in under his own name. It was obvious that Detective Sergeant Kenneth Hayes had traveled to Rhode Island to party with two working girls. Maybe the worm was finally beginning to turn. Hayes had indeed checked in under his own name.

Rather than risk detection in the lobby of the hotel, Michael returned to his station wagon and slept on and off until he observed the women leaving the hotel. The redhead seemed to be consoling the young woman who appeared to be crying. The young woman was now wearing sunglasses and she was helped into the passenger seat by the redhead. The light of the fast approaching dawn allowed Michael to squeeze off five photographs of the departing women.

Hayes left the hotel mid-morning. His thinning grey hair had not been combed and his face was swollen and fatigued. As he walked across the parking lot to his car, he paused to look around and zip up his leather jacket. He seemed to stagger ever so slightly, as Michael's camera clicked away from a distance.

On the way back to Boston, the city that Hayes had vowed to protect and serve, Michael struggled to stay awake. After he made sure that Hayes had returned home, he telephoned Chris at the office.

"Are you getting anywhere?" Chris inquired anxiously.

"I'm following a lead in Rhode Island."

"I don't have to tell you we've got five days until trial. Have you seen the *Globe* this morning?"

"No, I've been down in Rhode Island."

"Check it out, Mike. They devoted two and a half pages to our favorite detective. Saying what a great fuckin' cop he is. Fuckin' Sorett, he's not leaving anything to chance. He's got the firing squad ready, man. You got to come through for me. I'm dying here."

"I hear ya. I'll call you tonight."

"Make sure you do," Christopher demanded, the tone of his voice betraying his anxiety.

Michael needed to contact some old friends in the State Police so that he could pay a visit to a certain redhead that drove a white Camaro. Maybe she and her girlfriend could tell him something more than the newspapers, about Detective Kenneth Hayes.

Cynthia Evans, also known as Cynthia Taylor, also known as Claire Burke, was thirty-two years old and hadn't been arrested since 1984. The Rhode Island State Police had provided Michael's contact at the Major Crimes Unit of the Mass State Police with her criminal history and her present address in North Providence. At one time, she had been a personal favorite of Sal Butera, one of the enforcers for the Rhode Island mob, before he took a fall for loan sharking and was sentenced to the Federal Penitentiary at Atlanta. Since then she had pretty much been freelancing between Providence and Atlantic City.

Her apartment was located on a quiet tree-lined street of two family homes about three blocks from the Amtrak railroad station that provided convenient transportation to points south, including New Jersey. Michael parked his station wagon a couple of blocks away and walked toward the address provided, 86 Hazelton Court.

The white Camaro was parked in the driveway adjacent to a two family stucco home. It was almost six in the evening. Michael had managed to take a shower and grab a couple of hours sleep in his own bed after calling Chris. He had been going almost nonstop for more than four days. The chimes of the doorbell provoked the barking of a dog located somewhere inside.

"Who is it?" the female voice inquired.

"I have a delivery for Ms. Cynthia Evans," Michael feigned.

"Just leave it inside the door," the voice demanded.

"I'm sorry, ma'am. Ms. Evans has to sign for it."

"I'll be right down."

As soon as she opened the door, she knew that Michael had not come with a delivery but wanted something from her. Michael wasted little time in getting to the point, inserting his foot into the threshold of her door to prevent a quick rejection.

"Ms. Evans, I'm Michael McLean and I'm a private investigator hired by an attorney representing a young boy accused of killing someone he didn't kill."

"I don't want any," the woman muttered angrily as she clutched the aluminum handle of her front door and attempted to slam it shut in Michael's face. She was wearing a tan terry cloth bathrobe with her thick, auburn hair piled near the top of her head. Her left hand grasped a dark brown cigarillo.

By that time Michael had succeeded in wedging his right shoulder between the door and the door jamb, preventing the woman from rejecting his overtures without further explanation. The woman's tone was cold and deliberate, the tone of a whore who had been short-changed by a John.

"You want me to call the fucking police, Jack, or would you rather I scream rape for the neighbors? Now take your business somewhere else and get fucked!"

Michael's voice was soft and pleading. He attempted to win her over within a matter of seconds. "Please Cynthia, listen to me for a moment. I promise I will never bother you after this, if you can just listen to me, please."

She hesitated, looking into the eyes that had always seemed to say more than he ever could. He had his chance but it was a fleeting one.

"The man you were with this morning is suspected of being involved with the murder of a Boston police officer and the father of three kids. He framed a young black kid up in Boston and I work for the lawyer who represents him in the murder case."

The woman stood in the doorway, stunned by the words and the sincerity with which Michael delivered them. She slowly took a drag from the dark brown cigarillo and blew the smoke away from Michael's face. The harshness of her voice had changed to cool calculation.

"From what the son-of-a-bitch did to one of my girls, I wouldn't be surprised if he was mixed up with some shit like that."

She then paused and stared at Michael, sizing up his appearance while the mechanism of her brain worked deliberately. Slowly she removed her right hand from the handle of the door and beckoned Michael inside with the gesture of a woman who knew how to control men. As he followed her up the stairway into her apartment, he continued to solidify the chance.

"Look, I used to be a cop and I'm an ex-con. I know this kid is innocent and I just need some leads to figure out things. Nobody will know about this. I promise you won't get in any shit by talking to me."

The woman led him into an elegantly decorated living room with white leather chairs and an enormous glass coffee table. It was a place of business and pleasure, a site of entertainment where she had negotiated and consummated a number of illicit contracts.

After she poured herself a drink from a smoked amber pitcher, she poured herself into one of the white leather chairs, exposing her right thigh in the process. From this receptive pose she and Michael spoke of Detective Sergeant Kenneth Hayes and his affinity for the dark side of human existence.

CHAPTER 51

on Shapiro had always been a disbeliever, a cynic with a knight's sense of honor, shaped and sometimes distorted by city newsrooms and surreptitious encounters to snatch a story. His grandparents had been seized and slaughtered by the Nazis. He grew up in Asbury Park, New Jersey. His gods were Walter Lippmann and Saul Alinsky. Television had come calling him and he had forsaken the written word for a six figure bank account. Yet he still longed for a Pulitzer. Maybe Chris Conley, his moot court partner from law school, would give him the chance to get one.

He had met Chris outside of the Sherman Union at Boston University. They stood near to each other, listening to an emaciated teenager scream and imitate Mick Jagger, both of them marveling later on, when the teenager grew to dominate the record industry in the early eighties. It was just another instance of counting out a hidden winner.

They had liked each other from the beginning. Shapiro was the only law school friend that Christopher had, who seemed to possess the same sixth sense on how to survive and prosper in a world of unfairness. Michael had always learned the hard way. Shapiro and Christopher were smart enough to recognize the path of least resistance and follow it whenever their consciences would permit. Booker Webb's case had become the catalyst for activating their consciences to travel on a path of no return.

Since their meeting at the Marriott, Shapiro had been required to retrench and reassess his options. After law school, he had become a columnist for nine years with his own by-line at the *Record American*, the competition to the *Boston Globe* in the City. He had learned where all the bodies were buried and nothing surprised him about the capacity of human beings to be something other than what they seemed.

His sixth sense told him that Hayes was a case in point, a diabolical, walking, talking contradiction, made all the more lethal because of his power. Shapiro had learned to trust Chris Conley's instincts almost as much as he had learned to distrust authority.

The plan had been to report the other side of the story on Booker Webb, to champion his wretched cause and that of his lawyer. The death of Ricardo Calderon had wrecked those plans. Shapiro would be exposing himself and his television station to a lawsuit, without a warm body prepared to testify under oath about the machinations of Kenneth Hayes. Pragmatic idealism had its metes and bounds.

Instead, he and Christopher had devised a new plan, a different stratagem to enter the edifice from the back door and see what lay inside. His first call was to Steven Rossman, an old friend who worked with him at the *American,* and who was now the Information Director for the District Attorney of Suffolk County.

He told Steve that he wanted to do a story on the character and careers of the police officers involved in the Booker Webb case. Neither the District Attorney nor his ambitious First Assistant, Lloyd Sorett, suspected that the actual focus of his inquiries would be the hidden side of Kenneth Hayes. He was granted permission to converse with Hayes in a matter of hours. Hayes returned the third call that Shapiro made to him, four days before Booker Webb's trial was to begin.

The meeting had to be at a location where Hayes would feel relaxed and comfortable, a place where he and Shapiro could speak without interruption, a place where Shapiro could slowly and deliberately work on lowering Hayes' guard and then attack. He had arranged to meet Hayes at Charlie's on Newbury Street, a watering hole for mostly locals with turn of the century decor and decent food. Hayes had politely insisted that Shapiro come alone, before the after work crowd arrived.

When he walked through the doors, Hayes was already seated in a booth to the right and behind the bar. Shapiro shook Hayes' hand vigorously.

The hand was unusually warm and slightly clammy. The detective glanced into Shapiro's eyes briefly and then sat down behind the bourbon that he had been nursing.

"What are you drinking?" the detective asked, lighting a cigarette. His voice was cordial and cooperative. He wore a tweed overcoat and a black turtleneck. His face had the wrinkles of an old baseball glove; his thinning grey hair was parted well on the left side of his head and swept over the expanding scalp of his large head. His nose had obviously been broken more than once and his hooded blue eyes darted back and forth before fixing upon the reporter. His eyes overlooked pouches of skin that told those that observed such things that he had not been sleeping well.

Shapiro ordered a white wine from the blonde college girl waiting on the tables in that section of the restaurant. He spied the detective's perusal of her rear-end as she walked from the table after delivering his drink.

"Thanks for taking the time to meet with me, Detective. I know with everything that's going on you must be flat out," Shapiro began.

"No problem. Call me Ken, will ya?" Hayes insisted.

"Okay, Ken. I'm Ron. You know, I've seen you around a hundred times in the City but we've never really met, have we?"

"I think I was introduced to you a few years ago at Bill Burton's retirement party over at Jimmy's Harborside. You remember that?"

"Sure, now I remember. How's Bill doing anyway?" Shapiro inquired, feigning a recollection of one of a thousand required gatherings, useful in establishing the contacts and relationships so necessary for a successful TV reporter's career.

"I heard he shot himself a year ago down the Cape," Hayes stated matter-of-factly. Shapiro momentarily looked at the eyes of the detective. They were without light, without emotion; as if he were speaking about somebody he hadn't known except from an obituary.

"Oh, that's awful," Shapiro said.

"It's a tough fuckin' life."

"Can I ask you something personal?" the reporter asked.

"Maybe," the detective said defensively with the bourbon on the rocks cocked in his right hand and ready to swallow.

"How do you deal with the murder of a close friend?

Hayes gulped the drink down and placed the empty glass on the table. He then took a long drag on the cigarette in his left hand, exhaling slowly through his nostrils. The fingers of his right hand then stroked his grizzled chin as he stared at the reporter. His expression was distant, detached, encased within an inscrutable personality.

"How would you feel if your younger brother was murdered? I've seen a lot of good men go down on this job. Jackie Panton was the best cop I ever knew and the son-of-a-bitch that killed him should die like a fuckin' mad dog."

"Does that make it easier?" Shapiro asked, pointedly attempting to win the detective's confidence through commiseration.

"What?"

"Working to bring his killer to justice," Shapiro explained, measuring Hayes' responses with an expression of utmost respect.

"It's not gonna bring him back, but maybe it will make it easier on his wife and kids," Hayes replied, as if it were a mental reflex.

There was still no hint that the truth was something other than what appeared to be the case. Maybe he had told the story so much he was like an actor playing a part, rehearsed and presented a thousand times. Detective Kenneth Hayes was a thoroughly prepared player in a real life tragedy.

Another round of drinks was requested along with two orders of chicken fingers. Shapiro devoured the appetizer since he hadn't had the time to grab lunch. Hayes never touched his food. He looked older and more worn down as their meeting dragged on. They spoke of Jack Panton and the crippled Detective Domenico. Another round of drinks and emotion slowly began to dominate their conversation.

"I've been speaking with Lloyd Sorett and he tells me that you were relentless in catching Panton's killer," Shapiro remarked.

Hayes sat staring at him impassively, his fingers caressing the heavy glass that held the bourbon. Slowly Shapiro noticed an almost imperceptible change in the detective's disposition, as the subject of Booker Webb was again placed before him.

"It must be almost impossible to restrain yourself from doing harm to this maggot when you see him in court," the reporter commented, focusing on the expressions of the detective's world weary face. Shapiro continued with his feint.

"Of course, you've probably dealt with enough maggots to fill a hundred prisons. What do you think makes them tick anyway?"

Hayes raised his eyes from the table during Shapiro's remarks. He knew that Shapiro's brother was a detective with the State Police and seemed to see a bond, a link with an ally that understood the jungle that was the street. Hayes' speech was now animated, with a higher pitch and a more rapid rhythm.

"Pricks like that aren't fit to be part of this society. They're like rats carrying the plague. Sometimes I just wish our government would give us a free hand without the fuckin' lawyers and bleedin' hearts working off their fuckin' guilt. If I had one year in this City to clean it up, I would make it like it used to be, when people, decent people could walk the street. We gotta stop 'em. Wipe 'em out or they'll be runnin' the show and white people will be fucked. I'm tellin' ya."

Shapiro recognized the animal well. The scent was the same, the stripes had not changed, only the uniform. There before him was the same danger, the same state of mind that had gone unchecked in Europe decades before. The focus on scapegoats, the bigotry, the hatred that poisoned even intelligent, educated, human beings to commit atrocious acts of violence and deception. Chris was right about Hayes. He was capable of most anything.

Shapiro sat there seething, attempting to compose himself in the face of the evil he knew so well. He was ready to push the button that hopefully would dispatch a lethal torpedo below the unsuspecting detective's water line. Shapiro measured his words carefully, watching and hoping for Hayes to show himself, to lower his defenses even more.

"You know, my people have spoken with Webb's lawyer and he tells them they're going to produce a witness who will implicate you in the death of Jack Panton. Can you believe that?" Shapiro said, feigning incredulity and outrage at the prospect.

Hayes shifted in his seat at the statement. His eyes darted in his massive head, the jaw of his battered and pock-marked face tightened. His tone was cold and bitter, the tone of a killer.

"I think that fuck is desperate and him and his lawyer will do anything to save his fucking black ass. Did he tell you where this star witness is located?" Hayes inquired, his face betraying a desperate, calculating attempt at discovery.

"Yeah, he's right here in town somewhere. He's going to hold a press conference during the trial and have the guy tell everything he knows. I guess his lawyer has a connection with someone at one of the television stations," Shapiro reported, talking pleasure in the irony of his statement.

Hayes attempted to mask his reaction. His eyes again began to blink and his yellow teeth bit his lower lip ever so slightly. He then began to turn his cards slowly over for the veteran reporter to view.

"Listen," Hayes confided, "if you hear where Calderon is, let me know. There's a warrant outstanding for him. I know that he and Webb were sweethearts, but I can't believe he'd have the balls to come in and fuckin' testify to this bullshit."

Hayes continued, his voice dripping with venom. "I'll tell ya, this fuckin' Conley is dangerous. If he thinks he can pull this shit, he's in the wrong fuckin' league. We'll fuckin' bury him and that fuckin' nigger junkie he represents!"

From the sides of Hayes' mouth, Shapiro observed a trace of white saliva. His words were amplified by the contortions of his face. Shapiro could see that Hayes was lost, beyond retrieval, a violent, vicious monster, intent upon covering his tracks, but the tracks had been left for Shapiro to see. Hayes, not he, had been the one to mention the name of Calderon.

Shapiro was certain that Hayes and not Booker Webb should be the one rotting in the Charles Street Jail. He was also certain that Hayes was unaware that Calderon was dead.

CHAPTER 52

The dedication of the Dorchester Youth Center was an event to which the media had been invited. It was an opportunity for Mayor Ryan, the darling of the newly-constituted Democratic coalition to speak about the City and the needs of its children. Everett Kane and the Mayor had posed together a year before with shovels loaded with gravel at the undeveloped site of the three-story brick and glass facility. Kane was there once again, this time to accept the Mayor's accolades for his generosity and commitment in the completion of the project.

After the purple and white ribbon that was strung across the front door had been cut and all of the speeches had been recited, the gathering began to dissolve amongst the first flakes of another November snow storm. Everett Kane was conspicuous and striking in a perfectly tailored grey Armani suit and black cashmere coat.

His degree from Dartmouth and the refinement he consciously sought to develop while residing in Hanover, New Hampshire had helped to propel him to dizzying heights in real estate development. But success in that sphere had not satisfied him. He had been a creature of the streets and it was in controlling them that he felt omnipotent and satisfied.

Through a network of underworld connections and a myriad of legitimate business pursuits, he had become almost mythic in his ability to manage and launder enormous sums of illicit money. Corporations with twenty separate divisions, each leading to a maze of additional trusts and limited partnerships presented would-be investigators with a confounding shell game of deception and frustration. Bank accounts in Geneva, Barbados, Trinidad and Buenos Aires were opened and closed by wire transfers from numbered accounts. His talents in this regard were recognized and appreciated by the old school of grab and enforce in New York, Newark and Providence.

The manner in which he had monopolized the distribution of narcotics in the City of Boston was masterful. His political contributions, his apparent dedication to his community and the legitimate success he had obtained in real estate development had combined to create an alternate reality that successfully camouflaged his dark endeavors. He was the head of a small army of hand-picked associates who were made wealthy by their leader's ruthless expertise.

Hayes had fallen into his lap, like a gift from the god of greed and corruption to insure his prominence. The mob and Kane had reached an understanding. He would control drugs in Boston and they would not interfere. They would control all other areas of the criminal spectrum and he would launder the money generated by it. Hayes had proven to be a manageable, effective marionette, manipulated from a distance by Kane and the mob, a partnership from hell.

But, suddenly something had gone wrong. A corpse had been created that couldn't be ignored. A Boston cop had been killed. An associate of Kane's had pulled the trigger during an unexpected and unannounced drug raid. Hayes hadn't been told and neither had they. A scapegoat had been found and was about to be sacrificed. In two days Booker Webb's trial would begin in the Suffolk County Superior Court.

The charade of Ron Shapiro had flushed the jackal from his lair. As Everett Kane strolled to his waiting limousine across the street from the newly-dedicated youth center, Hayes watched from behind the wheel of his car parked on a side street within view of the ceremonies and Kane's participation in them. Hayes was desperate. He wanted a personal assurance from his surreptitious employer that the promise made of tying off a loose end by the name of Ricardo Calderon would be kept. If not, he would become a loose end himself, an end that could unravel the fabric of Kane's kingdom.

Besides his driver, Kane was accompanied by his personal bodyguard, Ellory Riggs. Riggs had known Kane since the Boys Club in Dudley Square. Riggs was always the best athlete in whatever sport he chose to play. A dozen colleges had recruited him in both football and basketball.

Instead, he chose the Army and the Special Forces. It was there that he became proficient in small weapons, demolition and the martial arts. Since Vietnam he had worked with or for only Everett Kane. He was an intimidating presence who could back it up and then some, standing six foot five in his stocking feet. He had killed people for Everett Kane.

As the limousine pulled away from the curb, the snow began to fall more intensely. Hayes had been chain smoking and drinking coffee since four in the morning. As Booker Webb's trial approached, his anxiety increased. Nights alone were endless. The sights and sounds of his job and the daily reminders of his double life were closing in from all sides. He had just spent two and a half hours meeting with Lloyd Sorett, preparing his testimony and repeatedly responding to a simulated cross-examination that anticipated the outlandish allegations which Webb's attorney had promised to present through one Ricardo Calderon.

His plans were uncertain. He waited to confront Kane somewhere that was inconspicuous and make him realize that Calderon's elimination was absolutely essential. He followed Kane's limousine through the streets of the City they had conspired to control, a servant stalking his master, waiting for an opening to develop.

Kane's offices were located on the thirty-second floor of a glistening architectural marvel that commanded panoramic views of Boston and its environs. Sixty State Street was the business setting for the cutting edge of Boston's commercial elite. It was a mini-metropolis possessing its own health club, pharmacy, and exclusive clothing stores. The parking facility beneath it provided an excellent opportunity for an unexpected, impromptu meeting of two netherworld associates.

Hayes remained in his car as Riggs, Kane's bodyguard, emerged from the lengthy black limousine to beckon the elevator with the middle finger of his massive gloved hand. Kane alighted slowly from the rear door on the driver's side. Hayes slid his vehicle into a nearby space and sprang from it, catching Kane with his back to him, as he reached to gather his briefcase from the limousine. Hayes had succeeded in catching the entrepreneur off balance and unprepared. The tenor of the detective's voice was authoritative and resolute.

"Excuse me, Mr. Kane, but it's time that you and me had a sit down."

Kane whirled and confronted the determined detective. His chauffeur called to Riggs as he stood awaiting the arrival of the express elevator to those floors above the twenty-fifth. Riggs reached under his left arm for the .38 caliber Beretta, sprinting to the vehicle only to be confronted by Hayes' service revolver perched within his hands and directed at his mid-section. Hayes' voice was uncompromising and convincing as he addressed Kane's cohort.

"You don't want to do what you're thinking. I want to have a short discussion with your boss without interruption. Why don't the both of you take a walk? Nothing's gonna happen unless you act like assholes."

Riggs could see the eyes peering at him from deep within Hayes' massive skull. They were cold, like the radiators in an abandoned tenement. He glanced at his employer for direction. Kane was cool and spoke without emotion.

"Ellory, it's all right. I'm sure Detective Hayes wouldn't be so foolish as to cause an incident to occur. Neither should you. You and Patterson go up to the office. I'm sure our discussion will only take a matter of minutes. Isn't that correct, Detective?"

Kane's calm and controlled response eased the danger of the confrontation. The emphatic nod of Kane's head toward the elevator demanded compliance from his loyal subordinates. They obeyed like good children, leaving Kane and Hayes alone at the rear of the limousine. Hayes waited until the elevator had taken them away before accompanying Kane in the back seat. Without missing a beat, Kane removed a bottle of Perrier water from the limousine's refrigerated compartment. He offered a glass of the beverage to his uninvited guest.

"Would you like some, Detective?"

"No thanks," Hayes replied abruptly, as he slid his body sideways to observe Kane, his service revolver clutched within the right hand pocket of his overcoat.

"You know that you could have contacted me through the regular channels. There was really no necessity for such a dramatic encounter. I would hope we could..."

"Come on, pal," Hayes interjected scornfully, "you can pull that sophisticated shit with the Mayor and his fuckin' flunkies, but don't bullshit me. You know that I've been tryin' to get in touch with you for almost a month now."

All pretenses had been discarded. They were now simply two criminals discussing a mutuality of concern arising from mislaid plans and dark intentions. The creature of the ghetto appeared from the depths of the entrepreneur's person. Being confronted by angry, insolent white cops had been something he had once become used to, growing up in Dudley Square. Kane's disdain was tempered by his instinct for survival. He was firm, not foolhardy. After all, he could see the bulge of the detective's gun in his overcoat pocket. Hayes' reputation for using his gun with or without authority was well known. Again, Kane's tone was measured and direct.

"No bullshit, Detective. That's not what you're here for. Tell me how I can make things easier on you."

Hayes smiled ruefully at the request. He was insulted by the lack of Kane's understanding. Nothing would really make it easier. Nothing could. Hayes was dangling from the limb of Kane's tree and both of them knew it. If Hayes exposed Kane, he destroyed himself. He wasn't prepared to do that.

He had grown accustomed to the dance of the damned and didn't want it to end. He wanted a promise from a man that had escaped the neighborhoods that Hayes despised and terrorized. It was a bitter irony that the detective's predicament required assistance from a proud, successful black man.

Hayes spoke with the voice of a killer, just above a whisper. They were the words of a cornered animal. "I want this fuckin' Calderon dead. He's on ice somewhere in the City and he's gonna spill his fuckin' guts during this trial. You and your friends from Providence were supposed to take care of this problem. I'm not gonna go down alone. You understand me?"

Kane stared at the Detective's desperate face. The danger he presented to the operation Kane had worked so diligently to develop was crystal clear. The testimony of Ricardo Calderon could bring unwanted inquiries that could ultimately topple Kane's empire like a house of cards. Kane's response was adamant and brought a measure of fleeting reassurance to the tormented detective.

"I've been told that Calderon is not in the City and that he's still somewhere in New Haven. Within the next forty-eight hours our people feel confident that he will be found and taken care of. Don't you think he's of great concern to all of us, Detective? He will never testify. You have my assurance on that."

At that point, Kane reached his hand toward Hayes in a gesture of friendship and common purpose. Hayes glanced at the black hand extended in his direction. He stared directly at Kane's face and shook his head, slowly, contemptuously. Kane seethed as the detective gathered himself and departed from the limousine, leaving him there alone.

As Hayes walked to his car, the eyes of Michael McLean were riveted upon him from across the parking garage. The occurrences Michael had observed between Hayes and Everett Kane on that day would allow him to bring Christopher to one of hell's windows for a good, long look.

CHAPTER 53

On the eve of the trial, the four of them gathered in the tiny meeting room that looked through the bars and smoked plexiglass of a rectangular aperture upon the three hundred and eighty cells of the Charles Street Jail.

The relentless din of the place with its blaring music and profane screams of anger and derision competed with the howl of another wind-blown November snow storm blanketing the City. It was three days after Thanksgiving and Booker Webb was to go to trial for first degree murder the following morning. Only his life hung in the balance.

Since his arrest, Booker had been transformed. In his first month walled off from the street, he had been forced to wrestle and writhe with the demons of his addiction. After a month his physical being had been cleansed but the lethal powder still tampered with his mind and battled for his soul.

Michael had visited him repeatedly without Christopher's knowledge, seeking to assist in the battle that he too had fought and almost lost, years before. At first Michael's overtures were rejected, yet slowly, surprisingly, Michael had become Booker's confidante, perhaps even an inspiration to the receptive, intelligent young man that had emerged from an addict's ashes.

Lorna had been relentless in her support of Booker. She alone had known the depths of his childhood sorrow, the loss of his mother and best friend. She had watched helplessly as the bitterness slowly seeped through his being and took root, like a cancer coursing through its victim. He had been a child of so much hope, so beautiful and alive, running from the school bus; his papers marked with praise from his teachers, into the arms of his devoted mother, her sister.

Now he stood along the wall of the jail's meeting room, anxiously smoking a cigarette. Christopher and Michael had spent the afternoon preparing and informing Booker that Calderon was dead. The news had its anticipated impact. Booker sat sullenly, stood uncertainly, then sobbed quietly. There were really no words of consolation. They all knew that the die was cast. It would take a miracle for Booker to be acquitted.

As Booker's attorney, Chris was required to discuss his client's options on a change of plea. A plea to the murder of Jack Panton could save Booker from the executioner, yet condemn him to life imprisonment, without a chance at parole. A trial on the merits could mean certain death.

Michael's surveillance of Hayes had uncovered a connection with organized crime generated from Providence. The encounter he witnessed between Hayes and Kane was the part that didn't fit. The puzzle was still a jumble of disjointed and meaningless pieces. What did it mean? What story did it tell? Why would a respected member of the community, like Kane, allow someone so antagonistic to what he appeared to be, to confront him and point a gun at his companion?

Was that the proper introduction to a meeting with one of Boston's most successful entrepreneurs and respected community activists? —- a meeting that took place underground in a parking garage, behind the closed doors of a limousine's rear seat —- a meeting that lasted almost ten minutes —- a meeting from which both participants emerged with anxiety and concern evident on their faces.

Chris had attempted to make sense of it after sitting silently and staring at the photographs Michael had taken of the occurrences in the garage. He had spoken with Ron Shapiro who advised him that Hayes seemed to be at the end of his rope, primed and ready to do something desperate to save his neck.

Was it all an elaborate charade, designed to confuse or conceal evil? Or a large, seamless web, that had hopelessly ensnared the man he represented? A web created by the Mob that had succeeded in ensnaring Kane and Hayes as well. A web that had entangled Jack Panton, and choked off his life, a web that had crippled Ron Domenico, and condemned him to a lifetime in a wheelchair.

Chris had never really dealt with criminality that was so calculated, so devious and devastating. He had known criminals who never could act in concert, ignorant, inept creatures, too atomized to be cooperative, too sociopathic to be sophisticated. Maybe he was in a different league, as Hayes had told Shapiro. A league where crime did pay and paid very, very well, provided you didn't mind losing your soul in the bargain.

Chris sat at the heavy battered, wooden table scarred with the initials of a thousand indolent criminals who had come and gone from the Charles Street Jail. Lorna sat in a metal folding chair next to Michael, her face wrenched with worry, yet still startlingly beautiful. She had never really trusted Everett Kane. There was something almost sinister about him. She recalled a remark he made, several years before, of wanting to gain control of the entire community, including its shadows. She recalled that Kane's companions seemed too willing to follow, too programmed to do his bidding without question. He seemed to hold their allegiance with something more than respect. They seemed to be genuinely afraid of him.

Christopher's head was reeling from the magnitude of the confusing information he had received, attempting to assimilate it all into a viable defense for his devoted client. He had a case to try. How could he incorporate it all into the creation of a reasonable doubt as to Booker's guilt? How long could he stay in the game, pretending to hold a trump card by the name of Ricardo Calderon without producing him?

All of this recent information was intriguing, even astounding, but it did not an acquittal of Booker Webb make. Christopher and Michael knew this. Lorna and Booker suspected it. Without Ricardo Calderon, Booker Webb would be executed for a murder he didn't commit.

After they had all spoken of their theories as to what it all meant, they were left with the reality. It was hard not to be realistic, even morose, within the confines of a jailhouse, awaiting trial for the murder of a cop. The world outside had already convicted him. In the court of public opinion, Booker Webb was vermin and society would be protected by his efficient extermination. After a long silence, it was the condemned who spoke. His words were chosen carefully.

"You know, I've been thinking about dying and I figure that I've already been dead. I figure I've been worse than dead, living life like I was. So whatever happens, I'll be ready for it. All of you have been real good, trying to help me. Maybe, I had to start helping myself, and this place, and even getting killed, like other brothers been killed, is how I get over."

Christopher sat transfixed, fighting back tears of rage. Lorna buried her head in her hands and sobbed, while Michael spontaneously reached and touched her heaving shoulder. Chris could see that his old friend was fighting back tears, as well. He thought of his mother kneeling beside him on the floor of the tiny Bromley Court apartment, beseeching heaven for divine intercession.

He thought about the encounter in the chapel and was momentarily comforted. Then he returned to the reality of the moment. Chris and those who sat with him were as helpless as little children, in desperate need of something impossible to occur and deliver them from evil.

Christopher thought of all the victims he had represented. The truth as he saw it, at that moment, on that snowy November night was that life would once again prove to be unfair. That Booker Webb, a tragic child, would simply join the ranks of so many other tragic children, ranks that seemed to grow more numerous each and every day. Despite all of this, he could not give up. He had to fight. He had to improvise on a grand scale with the courage and abandon of one who knows that the game is lost. Some of his best work had been done from such a position.

Suddenly the words of the man he was defending brought a wave of resignation that swept his worried state away. He had reached the point where he could do no more. Intuition and the flow of forces he had tapped but had not understood must now take over. He would appear the following morning and pick a jury that would stand impartial, he prayed, a jury that would listen to the evidence that was presented, without being poisoned by the sensationalism that the case had provoked.

He must have faith. He must believe that truth would prevail or the jury would sense his disbelief and convict. His faith was his only hope. He must not underestimate the power of truth.

After the guard knocked on the plexiglass covered aperture, located near the top of the thick, metal door, signifying that their time together had elapsed, Michael stood and made a startling request. He asked that each of them stand and form a circle, a circle of truth and love that could withstand the evil that surrounded them, the evil that threatened them all.

The circle was formed. The four of them stood together, hand in hand. With his eyes closed in the fervent aspiration of one who had been lost and had somehow been found, the man whose path had caused him to walk hand in hand with evil, led them in the Lord' Prayer, praying as a little child Each of the four knew that the drama would soon be over.

CHAPTER 54

The morning light invaded his bedroom, causing his heart to race. There would be no more time for misgivings. He didn't know what would transpire. He only knew the end was near. It seemed that the world had become obsessed by the Booker Webb case. The fountains of the national media had sprayed its vapor over the country. A murder committed, racial hostility simmering beneath the surface, corruption alleged, righteous outcries for execution. It was a surreal slice of urban America and there Chris stood, like a soap opera villain in a three-piece suit

Parking near the courthouse was impossible. All the lots had been filled since shortly after eight. They had all come, caught by the lures of the sensational and the sordid. The Mayor had spoken on a nationwide, breakfast talk show, assuring the world that Boston would survive this ordeal, and return to a semblance of normalcy, once the case was concluded. As he replayed vignettes of what had taken place, Chris wondered whether normalcy was ever attainable again.

Once again, before the trial commenced, Sorett had denounced Christopher's tactics as desperate and divisive, while flanked by his boss and Hayes. To the world at large, he was an avenging angel, armed with the truth and searching for a just retribution. Careers were to be made. Worlds were to be conquered. An unworthy life was to be taken.

Chris was driven to the courthouse by Michael. Together they had gone over the inquiries to be asked of the prospective jurors. A limited "voir dire" would be allowed by Judge Aubregon, because of the racial undertones of the case. Each side would be allowed five minutes to inquire of each prospective juror whether publicity or prejudice would prevent them from being impartial. Christopher had contemplated whether a change of venue, a transfer of the case to another county, would be more conducive to Booker's fate. No, Suffolk County jurors were as good as any for a criminal caught in a web of police impropriety.

The snow had continued intermittently for three days. The cold, wet flakes settled upon Christopher's nearly white head as he emerged from the passenger side of his purring vehicle. From the trunk he retrieved an enormous black leather valise that contained blow-ups of the murder scene and excerpts from the pre-trial testimony of Dan Sheehan and Ron Domenico.

The valise also contained recently blown-up photographs of Hayes in the company of two Rhode Island whores and another of him pointing his service revolver at Everett Kane's bodyguard. Above and beyond what the rules required, he had also delivered a list of rebuttal witnesses to the District Attorney. It included Ricardo Calderon and Everett Kane. Shock waves would be felt where they were supposed to be felt.

He had selected a blue, three-piece, pinstripe suit and a white shirt from his expansive closet. His black shoes were polished and ready. His red and grey striped tie added an appropriate splash of accentuation. His face was beginning to develop wrinkles across his forehead and between his blue eyes, the eyes that had focused their attention upon so many juries and witnesses in the past, the eyes that had peered through an elaborate deception, perceiving the truth. He had kissed his wife and two children before leaving. Linda had stopped herself from remarking that he looked like a handsome undertaker.

The courthouse corridor was as crowded as he had ever remembered it. It was like the Boston Garden before the final game of a championship series. He could hear the surly remarks and pointed inquiries from the waiting press, as he struggled to make his way through the brown leather covered doors of Courtroom 906. Finally, he was in the arena once again, a place where real-life dramas occurred, a place where he had reigned victorious. Then he saw Lorna sitting to the far left of the enormous courtroom.

He could tell that she was barely holding on. Her beauty and youth had disappeared from her loving face, cruelly evicted by worry, bordering on despair. Sitting on the bench, almost directly behind her, Chris could see the hulking form of Detective Kenneth Hayes. Their eyes met. Hayes wore a look of grim determination. Christopher smiled slightly and avoided his deadly stare. The drama was set to begin.

The arrival of the Assistant District Attorney was marked by the uproar of the crowd, gathered outside of the ninth floor elevators. Sorett had seized the opportunity presented by the case for all it was worth. He had skillfully orchestrated a blitzkrieg upon the media. His message was merciless. Execution was the only remedy for the premeditated murder of a policeman. As he had planned since his graduation from law school, he was now the heir apparent to Martin Babcock's position as District Attorney for Suffolk County.

Sorett was accompanied by three of his staff, each carrying an enormous brown leather briefcase, full of fatal arrows to be directed at Booker Webb. Sorett was impeccable in his appearance, not a hair was misplaced on his blonde scalp. His Brooks Brothers tweed was complemented by a starched, pale blue, button down shirt and a brown and yellow polka dot tie. His associates and he presented the perfect image of what the best and the brightest wore and did for a living.

The approach of Booker Webb was likewise heard from within the crowded courtroom. From the hallway leading to the lockup, behind a green metal door that reminded Christopher of the Bromley Court Projects, came the sound of chains and leg irons being unfastened. Suddenly, the door opened and Booker emerged, flanked by two muscular court officers. They escorted him to the chair next to Christopher, thereafter removing his handcuffs.

Booker's diminutive, boyish appearance was in sharp contrast to the accusations of the Grand Jury and the charge of first degree murder that hung the penalty of death from the ceiling above him. Booker looked at Chris, momentarily signaling his resignation to whatever fate had in store. Chris touched his client's left wrist reassuringly.

Christopher was situated with Booker in the middle of the turn-of-the-century courtroom, behind an enormous, ornate table, while Sorett and his entourage were located almost beneath the enclosure that would encase the Judge and his clerk. The hushed audience was crammed into the space provided by five wooden pews that ran almost the width of the canyon-like courtroom. After a white-haired court officer bellowed like an ancient town crier for all to rise and attend to the proceedings, the erudite and distinguished Judge Aubregon called for the jury pool to be examined on "voir dire".

It had taken Michael several minutes to find a parking garage for Christopher's Mercedes. The snow was pelting the City relentlessly now, slowing traffic to a crawl and adding significantly to the gloom that surrounded the first day of Booker Webb's trial. Michael hurried to the courthouse, barely retaining his footing on the treacherous white sidewalks. As he emerged from the elevator, the crowd in the corridor had all but disappeared, except for a small congregation of reporters smoking cigarettes and sharing war stories.

He had waited patiently among a handful of spectators for a fleeting opportunity to peer through the small rectangular window located on the courtroom's door. As he did, he could see Christopher questioning a small bald man with glasses in his late thirties. He could tell that the man was extremely nervous and finding it difficult to answer Christopher's questions.

"Mr. Goldstein, do you consider yourself open minded about the issue of race in this case?"

"What do you mean?" the tiny man inquired.

"Could you believe a black witness whose testimony was contradicted by two or three white witnesses?"

"That depends."

"Depends on what?" Christopher pressed.

"It depends on the believability of the witnesses."

"Are you conscious of any racial bias or prejudice that would cause you to disbelieve the black witness simply because of the color of his skin?"

"I don't think so," the man answered, staring earnestly at Christopher and then nervously glancing at the Judge.

"Then, Mr. Goldstein, you could decide the guilt or innocence of my client, Booker Webb, solely on the evidence without consideration of race or what you have seen or heard about this case?" Christopher continued, looking for the surefire signs of the juror's sincerity.

"Yes, sir, I think I could."

"And you're telling us under oath here today, that if the evidence presented by the prosecution is not believable and does not amount to proof beyond a reasonable doubt, you could fulfill your duty and acquit Mr. Webb of the murder of Officer Panton?"

"Yes, sir, if I didn't believe it, I could do that."

"Thank you, Mr. Goldstein," Chris declared. "This juror is acceptable to the accused, your Honor."

As Michael stood near the courtroom's doors, they were suddenly shoved open by the hands of Hayes. Michael then watched intently as the detective made his way toward the dimly lit corridor, following him at a distance, curious as to the destination of the Commonwealth's star witness. As he watched Hayes stop, Michael attempted to be inconspicuous, standing with two others in the corridor. Hayes was pacing, waiting impatiently, after pressing the down button for the elevator.

When the elevator finally arrived, Michael boarded it in the company of the two strangers, turning his back to Hayes as he stood inside. After the elevator stopped at the fourth floor, Hayes brushed by Michael. Just before the doors closed, Michael exited, catching a glimpse of Hayes as he turned to the right, down the corridor toward the Detective's Room. Michael had been there twice before, when he was a state police detective waiting to transport interstate fugitives.

Michael remembered that the Detective's Room was a small rectangular area located at the end of a deserted corridor, near the lockup for the Boston Municipal Court. It was removed from the daily traffic that descended upon the courthouse and if nobody else was around, it was an ideal location for a violent confrontation. A confrontation that was a long time coming between Michael and the man he had shadowed for what seemed an eternity. The hunter was about to come face to face with his quarry.

The timing was right. The room was deserted except for Michael and Hayes. Hayes had retreated into its recesses and appeared to be using the toilet. Michael could hear what sounded like the Detective puking inside. He checked once more to make sure their impending "tete-a-tete" would not be intruded upon, locking the wood and smoked glass door that read Squad Room behind him. Michael then sat down on the wooden bench beside the door and fixed his eyes on the location from which Hayes would emerge. As the door opened, Michael stood up.

"Can I help you, pal?" Hayes demanded, upon seeing Michael. He did not recognize him. Michael appeared almost innocuous in a suit and tie.

"I'm sorry," Michael replied, "I used to be a detective with the State Police and I just wanted to see the place. I mean ——"

"Take a walk down memory lane some other time, will ya?" Hayes interrupted. "I'm in the midst of somethin' and I gotta use the phone. See ya later."

"I know you," Michael feigned. "You're Hayes, the one involved in that cop shooting. That's going on now, isn't it?"

"Yeah, don't let the door hit you in the ass on the way out, okay?" Hayes remarked, while drawing closer.

Michael persisted, standing erect and blocking the door that had been locked behind him. "You know, I met Jack Panton once. What a good shit he was. What a good fuckin' cop, just tryin' to do what was right! It's a fuckin' shame, isn't it?"

"Yeah, it's a shame," Hayes said, impatiently moving toward the door in an effort to usher Michael from it. Michael stood immovable in front of Hayes, their faces inches apart. Michael could smell the stale odor of his breath.

"What is it, pal? What do you want?" Hayes demanded, staring into the face of the man who had grown to know him and despise him.

"I wanna know how it feels," Michael sneered.

"How what feels?"

"How it feels to get a friend killed because you're dirty."

Hayes tried to grab Michael by the throat in a rage, but Michael's hands smashed upward, breaking his grip. With one motion his two fists drove into Hayes' throat sending him sprawling backward across the room and onto the floor. In a flash, Hayes reached for the service revolver located under his left armpit. Michael was quicker. He drew a .9 millimeter biretta from his waistband. It was registered to Christopher. Michael had taken it without permission. He trained it on the prone detective, ordering him to remove his weapon slowly with his left hand and slide it across the floor. Hayes complied. Michael then trained both guns on Hayes.

"You're in deep fuckin' shit, asshole," Hayes cried. His face was the color of red Christmas candy.

"No, you're the one in deep fuckin' shit, Hayes, not me," Michael screamed, standing above Hayes, hatred oozing from every pore. "You're fuckin' number is up, man. You're gonna go down for what you done to Panton and Domenico and what you're trying to do to this fuckin' kid upstairs."

"Go ahead, do it," Hayes urged, as he stared directly into the barrels of the promise of death.

Suddenly, Michael came to his senses. He restrained himself from killing again, even though the creature before him deserved it. He lowered the weapons to his sides and sat down once again on the wooden bench.

"What are you, one of those fuckin' bleeding-heart mother fuckers, working off your fuckin' guilt for this fuckin' nigger?" Hayes challenged, tempting fate and self-annihilation. "You got no balls. That fuckin' punk deserves to die! He's a fuckin' nigger and a junkie. They all deserve to die and maggots like you feel sorry for them. Fuck you! Fuck you!" Hayes screamed, rising to his feet.

Michael's rage returned. He again pointed the weapons directly at Hayes, grinding his teeth till they hurt. His eyes were ablaze. His breathing was quick, as the sweat poured down the back of his neck.

"You no good fuck," he muttered, as he slashed toward Hayes and kicked him squarely in the groin. The detective crumpled to the floor, puking up blood.

"Now sit there and listen," Michael commanded, focusing the guns on Hayes like two lethal cameras. Slowly he began to describe his intimate knowledge of his prey.

"How's your buddy, Everett Kane? You and him have a little disagreement the other day? I was there, fuck! I saw it. How about the boys in Providence? They fix you up with any under-age whores lately? What do you owe them anyway? Better still, what the fuck do they owe you? You didn't count on Calderon though, did you? He's gonna come in and bury you. He's gonna rat you the fuck out. How you tried to set up this kid to cover up your fuckin' shit. It's all gonna come down upstairs, man. Get ready!"

Hayes' face was filled with shock and defiance. He wiped the puke and blood from the sides of his mouth with the back of his hand and stared at his accuser. His words wounded Michael.

"Calderon's fuckin' dead, or maybe you didn't hear it. Another junkie overdosed. My heart was fuckin' broken when I heard about it. Who the fuck are you anyway?"

Michael was riveted upon the evil before him. There was no reason to let this vermin survive. He wanted to splatter him across the floor and be done with it. As his fingers began to squeeze the triggers, Hayes smiled at him in a contorted, twisted way. He wanted to die!

Slowly, despite his rage, Michael began to lower the weapons. Something had come over him that drew him away from the abyss of that righteous bloodletting. Something that made him feel deep, unremitting pain in the depths of his soul.

"You wanna know who I am? I'm your last fuckin' hope, man, your last chance to make things right! You and I are from the same tribe. You still got a chance to change. You still do. Come clean up there. Tell the truth. Don't have this kid's blood on your hands. Save yourself, before it's too late."

Hayes sat transfixed on the floor. Michael couldn't decipher whether his plea had been accepted or rejected. Hayes said nothing. His eyes were without light, without emotion. They were the eyes of a man who had traveled too far along the dark path.

Michael watched as the detective slowly struggled to his feet, standing like a wounded jackal, oozing hatred and defiance toward his accuser. Deliberately, Michael laid Hayes' revolver on the bench, still training the Beretta on him. Cautiously, he reached behind himself and turned the lock. As he backed out the door of the Detective's Room, he left Hayes standing, staring into space.

CHAPTER 55

The jury had been selected. Eight woman and six men were chosen to decide whether Booker Webb was guilty of murder and then whether he should be executed. Each of the fourteen knew that it was a case of life and death from the beginning to the end. Sorett had delivered a masterful opening statement. It was tempered and reasoned, sufficiently detailed to convince, but never shrill, never emotional. Like a medical examiner, he had dissected the vitals of the case and laid them before the jury.

It was Christopher's responsibility to bring the cadaver to life. Booker Webb had to live and to breathe in order to have a chance at redemption. He had to be resurrected, transformed into a human with a heart and a soul, not a cardboard villain to be despised and disposed of. He was required to speak to their minds, but appeal to their hearts.

As Judge Aubregon nodded to him to commence his opening statement, his parched throat demanded relief. He knew that his opening statement would last just under fifteen minutes. He must take the water now and avoid a break in the rhythm of his introduction. From the black, plastic pitcher located in front of him, he poured the precious refreshment into a tiny paper cup. The tremble of his hands caused him to spill some of the water onto the counsel table.

He apologized for the delay and obtained a paper towel from the court officer to wipe up the errant liquid. Momentarily, he glanced into the audience awaiting his remarks. Lorna was there. Her expression and location had not changed. She still looked desperate. Suddenly, his attention was drawn to Michael, who was signaling him to have a conversation from a seat in the rear of the courtroom. Christopher asked the Court's indulgence and conferred over the railing that separated the arena from the spectators.

"What is it?" Chris asked nervously, attempting to conceal his concern from the jury.

"Hayes knows that Calderon is dead," Michael whispered.

Christopher's disappointment was evident. He knew that the last avenue of escape had been closed. He knew that he had to regroup and restructure the opening he had rehearsed repeatedly during his sleepless nights before the trial. From the doorway to Christopher's left, Hayes appeared. He paused and watched as Michael retreated from their conference back to his seat. Christopher watched as Hayes took his seat directly behind Lorna.

"Are you prepared to proceed, Mr. Conley?" Judge Aubregon inquired in a tone that was bordering on impatience.

"I apologize, your Honor, ladies and gentlemen. Yes, I am ready to proceed," Christopher replied. It was then that he closed his eyes momentarily and thought to himself, please God, help me to do it. He walked toward the waiting faces of those who had been chosen. He passed the anxious face of the one that had been charged. He stood in the middle of the courtroom, directly in front of the jury. It was too soon to get too close. They needed to trust him first. He began slowly, deliberately. His hands were held together as if he were praying. In a way he was.

"As you know, ladies and gentlemen, my name is Christopher Conley and I represent the accused, Booker Webb. Mr. Webb is twenty two years old and he stands before you pleading his innocence to the charge of murder in the first degree, a charge that the prosecution must prove beyond any reasonable doubt to each and every one of you."

Christopher paused. He didn't know exactly where to go next. He thought and again prayed that the words would come, that they would flow, that they would somehow find their way into the hearts of each of the jurors sitting attentively before him.

"A horrible crime has been committed, ladies and gentlemen. A young, loving father and husband has been taken from our midst, a protector, a man who swore that he would be honorable, that he would sacrifice even his own life for the safety and well-being of our society. Tragically, his life has been lost and the life of another protector has been irrevocably destroyed. Truly, the dimensions of this tragedy are enormous. What are you called upon to do, ladies and gentlemen? You have been called upon to examine this tragedy with all its emotion and all its yearning for retribution and decide whether the accused is responsible for it."

The Spirit had arrived. The thoughts and words were one. Christopher was one now, one with Booker, one with the jury, one with the audience that detested his client. He was there, in that wondrous sphere of inspired intuition. The golden horse had arrived and Chris had been spirited upon its back, about to soar.

"The truth is that Booker Webb is innocent. That he is a victim of circumstance, condemned by his addiction to narcotics to be in the vicinity of Martindale Street in the Grove Hall section of Roxbury on the night of November 2nd, 1991, a night when tragically, coincidentally, Detective Jack Panton and Detective Ron Domenico would be shot by a young, black man. A black man, ladies and gentlemen, who was not Booker Webb, a black man, ladies and gentlemen, who has never been apprehended.

All of us pray for the day when that man will be brought to justice. Justice! Justice! This entire case is about justice and injustice. You must listen to the evidence presented with justice as your reason, justice as your sword, justice as your shield. Your oath demands it and nothing less. With justice you will hear about a young, black man, snatched from the street by the police, a boy really.

His photograph is shown to the witnesses who caught a fleeting glimpse of the man who fired the fatal shots. Shown to the witnesses by a police officer bent on an evil course. A man who took an oath to protect and to serve, a man who has betrayed that oath by suggesting, by fabricating and by protecting those that are ultimately responsible for the tragedy that brings us here, Detective Kenneth Hayes."

Christopher crossed the courtroom toward the rail that separated the arena from the audience and pointed directly at Hayes who was seated behind Lorna. Christopher could see that the jury was staring as well. Twenty-eight eyes focused on the face of the veteran detective. He looked back. Slowly he lowered his head. He took a massive breath and removed a small cassette tape from the pocket of his overcoat and placed it on the bench beside him. A small piece of yellow paper with his handwriting surrounded it.

Christopher returned to his position in front of the jury. He had made the dramatic gesture. He didn't care that Calderon was dead. He didn't care that the odds against Booker Webb were insurmountable. Something in Hayes' face told him not to worry. Featherstone was right. Never underestimate the power of truth. The golden horse was soaring now, as Christopher made his plea to the humanity before him.

"I ask you ladies and gentlemen; don't be swayed by prejudice, by bigotry or even indifference. Be swayed by truth, by the love of justice. Listen to the evidence. Observe the witnesses as they testify. Hear what they have to say and weigh it in the hot white light of your reason and experience. Most of all, observe Kenneth Hayes. See whether he can hide from the truth that pursues him. See whether he can avoid the justice that must ..."

The thunder of the gunshot resounded throughout the entire ninth floor. Shrieks of terror followed almost immediately. The torso of Kenneth Hayes lay twisted and perched on the edge of the blood-drenched wooden bench where he had been sitting. His jury had returned with the verdict. His execution had been carried out. He had bent over, placed his lips around the cold steel of the barrel of his revolver, and blew his brain through the back of his skull, splattering it on the ceiling of courtroom 906.

EPILOGUE

O n the bench beside the dead detective, a court officer discovered the cassette tape encased within a note written and signed by Hayes. The note was delivered to Lloyd Sorett who read it to himself and then to Judge Aubregon in his chambers, with Chris in attendance.

The note implicated Everett Kane in Jack Panton's death and identified one of Kane's lieutenants as the man who killed Jack Panton and crippled Ronald Domenico. The note also stated that Booker Webb had been framed and was completely innocent of any wrongdoing in the case. The note ended with the following line: I deeply regret what I have done. I can't bear to live anymore with my guilt. I hope my death will stop the pain. Detective Kenneth Hayes, Badge #19041.

In the months that followed the suicide of Hayes, Lloyd Sorett dismissed all charges against Booker Webb. Chris was pleasantly surprised by the honesty of his adversary and the sincerity of his regret in seeking reparation for the months Booker spent awaiting trial in the Charles Street Jail.

He also convened a grand jury to investigate Everett Kane's involvement with narcotics trafficking in the city and persuaded them to return an indictment for murder in the first degree against one Clarence Gray, who was positively identified by Ron Domenico and Dan Sheehan, the Edison worker, as the murderer of Jack Panton.

As for Booker Webb, his sojourn in jail and the assistance he received from Michael caused him to overcome his addiction and eventually obtain his high school equivalency certificate. He had promised Lorna that he would attend college the following year, expressing an earnest desire to become a paramedic and maybe even a doctor.

Lorna Shaw continued in her position as the Director of the Dorchester Counseling Center, devoting her time to the assistance of the community's poor and homeless. Michael McLean became more and more involved with the Center, becoming one of its most effective counselors to young people from the inner city who were attempting to cope with drug addiction and the criminal behavior it created.

On a Monday morning, approximately nine months after Booker Webb's trial, Michael appeared at Christopher's office asking to speak with him. Chris had known that Michael's days as his investigator were numbered and accepted it. He was not prepared for the announcement that Michael delivered in the conference room where he and Christopher had planned Booker's defense. Michael and Lorna had made plans to marry each other the following September and they wanted Christopher to be the best man. He accepted the honor, and embraced his boyhood friend until the tears welled in his eyes.

Chris had rejected numerous overtures to write a book and appear on television following the notorious case of *Commonwealth v. Booker Webb*. He was content instead to devote himself to his family, to represent the injured and to never underestimate the power of truth. Such was the path he was meant to follow.